A THOUSAND MILES
—FROM—
SPOKANE

A THOUSAND MILES
—— FROM ——
SPOKANE

S.D. GOLDMAN

Published by S.D. Goldman 2020

Cover art courtesy of Emily's_World_Of_Design
Twitter @EmilyDesigner
Instagram @Emilys_world_of_design

ISBN: 978-0-578-67206-9 (PPB)

Follow the author:

Twitter @sdgoldwrites
Instagram @s.d.goldman

For my parents

"[The Story] lusts for a feel-good ending the material doesn't comfortably provide. One can't help wondering how dismal Jerry and Dorothy's life will be after the credits roll."

- Michael Atkinson, movie critic, on *Jerry Maguire*

Although "Jammin'" pulsed from the speakers, the pawnshop on the west side of Sioux Falls was far from the Caribbean. Outside, clouds covered the cool May sky, and the spring greenery had yet to emerge after the undeniably cold winter. Inside, however, Tom Wilson hummed along to steel drums as he read the *Gazette* from two days before.

Every so often, the entrance doors rang with the sound of another customer entering, and the shopkeeper casually adjusted his thick-rimmed glasses as he took notice of the incoming guest. Most times, the customer was only a teenager looking over something in the front case, and he was not going to waste energy trying to find a sale there. The *Gazette* was far more interesting.

The store had been in his family since Sioux Falls began, although he had tried his best not to continue the trend. Still, when the time came, he took on the ownership from his dying father and soon after was bartering all that South Dakota had to offer. It was a futile job, and he was happy his sons were not keen on following in the family business. He had the For-Sale sign ready for the day he turned sixty-five. From there, it was off to drink away his days wherever his RV took him.

Somewhere between his dreams of the islands and Yellowstone, the bells hanging over the door rang once again.

The man who strode to the counter was in his late twenties, though he looked much more chiseled and gnarled. Sporting an unkempt beard and a ball cap with a team Tom did not recognize, the newcomer looked tired.

"'Morning, sir," Tom said curtly, setting his paper to the side.

"Hey," the man replied. His blue jeans were faded, and his T-shirt distressed, though the clerk tried not to notice. "Wondering if you buy firearms?"

Although he had none in stock, Tom was immediately interested. Guns usually garnered the most attention.

"What kind of gun are we talking about?" he asked, layering his question with just the right amount of skepticism and intrigue.

The man reached into his back pocket, pulled out a cloth-wrapped bundle, and laid it on the counter. Tom used a pen to unbundle the fabric. A worn Smith and Wesson Model 36 was revealed.

"Thirty-eight Special."

"Yeah," the man said, unsure. His hand shook slightly.

"How much do you want for it?"

"I don't know…fifty?"

"Dollars?"

The man nodded.

Tom picked up the gun and noticed the soot around the muzzle. "Was it used in any crimes?"

The young man sighed. "I can take it somewhere else…"

"No," the clerk replied. "I'm sorry. None of my business. It's just…the cylinder's empty." He paused. "I'll give you fifty dollars."

The young man did not respond.

Tom counted out five tens and set them on the counter. "You don't know much about guns, do you?"

The young man shrugged.

"The gun's worth a lot more than fifty," Tom replied, counting out an additional hundred dollars. "One-fifty is a bit fairer."

The young man sized up the money before scooping it into his hands. He made for the door as the clerk watched.

"Did you get 'em, at least?" Tom asked.

The young man stopped in the doorway.

"The bad guys," Tom clarified. "Did you get them?"

The young man stood in the doorway only a moment more. "No," he said, "some bad guys need more than that."

"Are you sure?"

It was such a simple question. Yet as Ryan Collins stared across the electronics desk, he could scarcely believe his ears.

"Am I sure?"

The customer, a short brunette woman, stared back at him incredulously, as if he were the one with the issue.

Between employee and customer sat a perfectly crisp, unopened Nikon box. Carefully, Ryan turned the box toward the customer and pointed to the wording in the right corner.

"It says waterproof up to thirty-three feet."

"I know what it says," the woman said with a huff. "I can read. I want to know if that's accurate."

Ryan stared at the woman wordlessly. He had been through every camera until she had finally chosen this one, noting that it was not only the correct zoom length but also that it was orange. Yet she had continued questioning him even after putting it on the counter, and he was growing agitated.

"I'm assuming it's accurate…"

"Well, if I don't like it, can I return it?"

Ryan signed in to the computer, hoping that scanning the product would hurry her along.

"You can return it up to fifty days after purchase."

Ryan's radio went off at his side, startling him.

"Guest needs assistance in electronics."

Ryan turned and saw a bald man standing at the assistance button, not five feet away.

"I need a video game," the man said.

Ryan glared at the man. "I'm standing right here; no need to press the assistance button."

The man nodded. "I need a game, though."

"Okay," Ryan said. "Let me finish up this sale and I'll be right with you." He turned back to the woman in front of him, who had opened the Nikon box and was examining the camera.

"Miss, you need to pay for that before you can open the box…"

The woman shook him off. "That's dumb. I was just looking at it."

Ryan sighed as he scanned the product. He gently plucked it from her hands and placed it in a bag.

"That'll be $215.29," Ryan said. He took a deep breath and recited the company lines robotically. "Did you know you can open up a Gibson's credit card and get five percent off all purchases going forward? Even tonight's purchase can be put on it—"

The woman glared at him. She swiped her own card and completed the transaction. Ryan handed the bag over the counter. There would be no more selling to her.

"Guest needs assistance in electronics."

Ryan turned immediately to the bald man.

"Seriously, dude. I'm right here."

The man stood in the same spot, his hand on the button. "You said you'd help me after her."

Ryan shook his head. "And I planned on it. What game did you need?"

"Extended cut for *Mass Effect.*"

Ryan stared at the man. "Not available in stores."

"Really?"

"Yep."

"It's not here?"

Ryan sighed. "No."

The bald man did not seem to enjoy this answer. "You're not even going to check?"

Ryan's patience had worn thin. It had already been a long day.

As he was contemplating his response, a coworker approached the desk. His name tag read Scott, but Ryan knew his real name was Jake.

"Boss wants to speak with you, Ryan. I'll take care of these guests," he said as the assistance call box went off one more time.

Ryan signed out of the computer. "Okay. Those ladies need a TV." He pointed to two women down an aisle and then to another guy staring at cell phone chargers. "That guy needs a charger." He half-turned and pointed to the lady to whom he had just finished selling the camera. She was approaching the desk again. "This lady needs to learn how to read a camera box, and that guy—" he pointed to the bald man as he picked up the assistance box and removed the batteries— "needs to stop pressing that goddamn button."

With that, he left Jake alone and moved toward the front of the store, wondering if the day would ever get any better.

The annoyances and angst had started that morning. As he awoke from the evening's sleep, he found himself staring at an unmerciful alarm clock that continued to chime. He sighed as he spiked the snooze button, knowing that he was already late.

As he wiped the sleep from his eyes and rose from his bed, he shook himself awake, trying to forget the hours before. He shut off the alarm and stared at the clock.

9:25.

That left exactly thirty-five minutes to get ready and make the twenty-minute drive to work. Ryan sighed again.

Things were not looking up.

Ryan threw on his work shirt and slipped into his bathroom, examining himself in the mirror before opening the medicine cabinet and grabbing his toothbrush.

At twenty-four, he looked a bit young for his age. Perhaps it was the shaggy light brown hair that draped across his forehead or even the boyish dimples his mother claimed made him cute. He had tried to cover his youthful appearance by not shaving, but even his uneven facial hair was insufficient. Like his father, he needed several days of not shaving to see any difference. As a result, he was forced to accept being carded at movie theaters and liquor stores and to face mirrors as a green-eyed, slightly pale college graduate still living at home with his parents.

He slipped on the same khaki pants he had thrown in a corner the night before, generously spritzed on some body spray, splashed water on his face, and returned to his room.

Picking up his work bag, he threw it over his shoulder and headed down the stairs to the kitchen.

"Finally up, I see." His father's unmistakable voice resounded from across the kitchen. He was seated rather robustly at the island with the newspaper in hand.

"'Morning, sir," Ryan replied as he grabbed a box of cereal from the pantry and milk from the refrigerator. He gave his mother, a small but confident woman, a kiss on the cheek as she prepared the morning coffee.

"Funny thing," Ryan's father said over the paper. "I came downstairs this morning and looked in the key bowl." He indicated a small bowl to his left on the island. "And there was no rent check there."

With his back to his father, Ryan took a deep breath and poured his cereal into a bowl. It was going to be another long day.

"I get paid today; I'll cash the check and get you your money tonight."

His father chuckled. "Is that what you're going to tell your other creditors?"

Ryan shook his head. Same question as always.

"Don't shake your head at me," his father said. "I want to know. Do you think I can just tell my mortgage company that I'll pay them at my convenience?"

"I said I'd pay it yesterday," Ryan said.

"—And you're late by a day."

His mother, who had been silent for some time, finally spoke.

"All right, now, David, he said he'd pay—"

"Nancy, please," his father interrupted. "Stop defending that boy. It's bad enough that he has no ambition to make something of himself, but having his mommy defend him helps none."

Ryan leaned against the kitchen counter and put a spoonful of milk and cereal into his mouth, crunching it loudly.

"You think you're a smart-ass, don't you, boy?" his father said, raising himself from the table. "Who paid for that cereal? Who paid for the water to brush your damn teeth? It wasn't you! That's for damn sure."

"I said I'd pay you when I get home," Ryan replied, tone rising to meet his father's.

"Don't you raise your voice to me!"

"Well, it's the same thing every day!"

"Then leave if you don't like it! I'll pack your bags for you. For Christ's sake, you're out of college for a while now, and you can't even afford to pay your rent."

"I can afford rent," Ryan insisted. "I just can't afford it right now."

"I'm glad we spent almost eighty grand to get you that useless degree."

"It's not useless, David," came his mother's reply as she tried to control the situation. "He's working on using it."

"I'm sure." Her husband smirked. "Asking people if they need help finding anything is really college graduate stuff. How about your cousins? They helping people find something?"

Ryan did not answer, seemingly content in letting his father rant.

"How about Calvin in the Californian army? Or Brandon in St. Louis? What's he? In grad school? Are they screwing around at the bottom of the labor force?"

Ryan exhaled. "He's not in the Californian army."

"What?"

"He's in the army. In California."

"You know what I mean, smart-ass."

Ryan swallowed his bite of cereal. "You think I like working for minimum wage?"

"Well, you don't seem to have sense enough to do anything else!"

Ryan shook his head and attempted to move out of the room.

"How much money are you going to have after you pay us? Have you even planned that far?"

Almost to the doorway, Ryan stopped before deciding on his answer.

"I don't know. I haven't figured it out. Why do you care?"

Behind him, his father had already reached his hand into the key bowl and pulled out his son's wallet as well as his own.

"You see these wallets?" his father asked, completely ignoring Ryan's question. "You see the difference?"

Ryan turned around, cereal bowl in hand, and shook his head. He was not in the mood for games.

"Let me help you. You see," he said, gloating over the wallets in his hand, "I know exactly how much money is in mine. To the dollar. Why? Because I'm an adult, and being an adult means knowing your worth."

Ryan ground his teeth as he listened to his father's belittling.

His father threw his own wallet at him. "Look inside that wallet. Do you see your worth?"

"That's enough," his mother finally interjected. In one swoop, she grabbed her husband's wallet from his hand and her sons from the floor.

"Stop babying the boy!"

"Enough!" she snapped, glaring at him. She ushered Ryan toward the front door and followed him out.

"Ignore your father," she whispered with a smile, adjusting his collar. "Today's a bad day."

"They're all bad days," Ryan muttered.

"I know it's tough," she replied. "But you will be fine."

Ryan smiled weakly as she kissed his forehead.

"Do you need money for gas?" she finally asked.

Ryan looked back toward his Jeep. He knew he probably did.

"Take this," she replied, pulling one of the many credit cards from her husband's wallet. "Just make sure you bring it back."

"—And the rent money," Ryan replied coldly.

She looked up into his eyes and held his face in her hands. "Don't worry about all that. It'll be fine."

Ryan sighed. He finally nodded and stepped toward the door.

"Have a good day." She smiled sweetly. "I love you."

"Love you, too," Ryan replied. He glanced back again, still thinking of his father's words.

Had the conversation not been a daily occurrence in the Collins household, Ryan would have felt worse about it. Such instances, however, were far from uncommon.

He threw his bag into his car and jammed the key in the ignition. The engine struggled before finally turning over and firing. After only a few seconds idling in the driveway, he put the car in drive and was soon heading away from the house, wondering how the day could get any worse.

Less than six hours later, he found out.

Ryan had been in Steve Coltrip's office a handful of times, though never with the urgency of this meeting. Most of the time, Steve, a man every bit as amicable as he was fat, sat in his office and communicated to the floor via the paging system. Ryan knew he could count the number of times he had seen Steve on the sales floor, and it was not high.

"Sit down, Ryan," Steve said softly as Ryan peered in the doorway of his office. The voice held warm comfort, but it was nowhere near happy.

"What's up?" Ryan asked as he took a seat in a chair he knew he would not escape. Casually, he peered around the room, looking for evidence of what was about to happen. On the nearest wall was a poster board full of team member photos. Ryan had looked at the collage many times, and each time, he had failed to find himself.

Ryan scanned the wall behind Steve's desk but found nothing but Redskins gear and photos of a family he had barely met. Nothing seemed out of place in the office except him.

Steve had his chin in his hands as he stared pensively at Ryan. He looked neither happy nor sad, and from what Ryan knew, that was never a good thing.

After what seemed an eternity, Steve finally spoke. "What's wrong?"

Ryan cautiously looked at his boss, wondering about the hidden agenda in the words. "Nothing," he finally said. "Should there be?"

"Don't be a smart-ass," Steve retorted in a tone that was friendly rather than managerial. "What's wrong with you lately?"

Ryan struggled to comprehend. "What do you mean?"

Steve sat back in his chair and rested his hands behind his head. "Listen, when you came here, I knew it was going to be tough for you. College graduate wet behind the ears, eager to make the big bucks. I get it. Working for Gibson's Department Store wasn't in your plans. But your dad told me about your struggles, and I offered you the job anyway—not as a boss but as your neighbor." He paused. "Instead of acting like a big shot, you accepted the role and have been a great asset to us." He paused once more and let the information sink in. "Now, I know that electronics worker is far from public relations or journalism, but lately you've really fallen apart, and people are starting to complain." He took a deep breath. "I want to know what's up."

Ryan laughed softly. "Nothing's up. Just a rough week, I guess."

Steve shook his head. "It's been a month. And the complaints are growing." He moved closer to the table and lowered his voice. "Is it the pay? Dissatisfaction? What?"

"The pay has always bothered me, Steve," Ryan answered.

"You got to give me something," Steve said, his friendly tone quickly turning sterner. "I'm struggling here."

Ryan felt the obligatory phrase leave his lips before he had a chance to stop it. "Why does it matter?"

Steve's jaw tightened as he reached for a stack of papers.

"It matters," he said, "because I have a stack—a *stack*—of damn complaints against you. Fourteen, to be exact. *Fourteen!*"

Ryan tried to play it off as he stood. "You know how customers are…"

"Ryan," Steve cut him off, "ten are from fellow team members. And—"

The comment made Ryan sit down again.

"Apparently, you verbally assaulted a pregnant worker last night?"

Ryan felt his face tense up. "Assaulted a pregnant worker? What the hell?"

"She filed a report saying you became aggressive to her and caused her and her baby unnatural stress…" He picked up another set of papers from his desk.

"Bullshit! I called her an idiot for being an idiot."

"The report also claims you said she was too busy, quote, 'trying to find the father for her next child,' end-quote, to do her job properly."

Ryan shook his head in semi-agreement. "In my defense," he began, "Stacy is always pregnant. Now, I'm pretty sure a human pregnancy lasts nine months. But she gets pregnant, has a kid, and two weeks later is pregnant again. I don't get it. She has the fertility of the goddamn Nile delta."

"You cannot verbally assault a fellow coworker."

"I told the truth!" Ryan said. "If she spent as much time actually working as she does on her back, she'd be more productive than all of us."

"Ryan, you cannot say those things…"

"Why does this company even keep her?" Ryan continued, voice rising in intensity. "Giving her maternity leaves only gives her another six weeks to get pregnant again."

"You can't fire someone for being pregnant, Ryan."

"How about for being a shitty worker?" Ryan replied. "Can you fire her for that?"

Steve looked down to the report in his hands. "The report also says that you threw something at her."

Ryan stared incredulously at his boss. "That bitch."

Steve looked away. "I'm going to act like I didn't hear that…"

"I threw the baby lotion *past* her." Ryan got up from his chair. "And into the go-back cart for the baby section." He paused, and then said sarcastically, "The go-back cart? You know, the cart of crap people return that is *supposed to* be sorted for each area, and that I have to put back?"

"I know the go-back system, Ryan," Steve said as he turned to a television that was new to the room.

"The go-back cart that our guest service team is *supposed to* sort," Ryan continued. "The team that comprises people named Stacy Florez."

"We have the incident from last night on videotape, Ryan," Steve interjected, turning on the television and popping a disk into the DVD player. "Why don't you describe what happened."

Ryan took a deep breath as his mind replayed the previous night's events. There was no getting out of this.

It was a night that started out rough. As he hung up his phone and walked inside Gibson's for another full day and night of work, sweat poured off his body and clung to the green polo that he hated. He had never liked the color green.

As he made his way to the office to clock in, he could feel the number of people around him. He did not even have to look up at the many happy decorations to know they were in the middle of December, only the busiest of times for Gibson's Department Store.

What day it was exactly, Ryan did not know. The previous days and weeks were weighing too heavily on his mind. It was somewhere in the middle or end of the week, he thought. He reasoned that was close enough.

"Late again," came the voice of the human resources secretary at the desk. She was never a pleasant woman, though Ryan tried hard not to notice. He ignored her comment and clocked in at one of the computers before putting his things in a nearby locker. Exhaling, he looked at himself in the nearby mirror once more. He was far from work ready, but that mattered little now. Taking a deep breath, he pushed open the door and entered the sales floor.

For the floor team, work at Gibson's Department Store consisted of a night of arranging shelves and restocking what was missing. It was not challenging work, but it was tedious, especially when the fellow floor stockers cared about their work about as much as Ryan cared about the politics of Paraguay. It did not matter, though. He had his section to work on.

The store was not so much busy as it was steady, which allowed Ryan to take care of his section, pharmaceuticals and toothpaste, in a decent amount of time. Yet, as he moved through his aisles, his mind drifted. Before long, he was more aware of the thoughts inside his head than the medicine aisle he stood in.

He was not supposed to be here, at Gibson's Department Store. A year ago, he had stood on the stage at his graduation from Tampa State, journalism degree in hand. *What a difference time makes*, he thought. A year ago, he had had a degree, a girl, a promise for something better.

He had had a future.

It had all seemed so different then. Now here he was, standing between the incontinence aids and the Advil, wondering what had happened in the past year.

"Team, it's nine o'clock. Please return your foreign go-backs to Guest Services," Ryan's radio chimed. He checked his watch to confirm the time before returning to his own cart full of things customers had left that did not belong in his section.

The store was beginning to thin out, and Ryan enjoyed the quiet time. He looked at the few guests checking out as he pushed his own cart toward the front corner of the store, where Stacy Florez sat reading a magazine. As calmly as possible, he left the cart next to the register and set certain items outside the cart, namely foods and broken items.

"Hey, Stacy, this baby lotion belongs in the baby cart, not the pharmaceutical cart."

"Okay," Stacy said, not looking up from her magazine.

"It's the lotion that says, 'Baby Lotion.'"

She nodded, not caring to look up from her reading.

Ryan shook his head. Typical. Silently, he turned away from the counter and walked into the office to see his scheduled location for tomorrow.

Electronics.

Ryan sighed. It was better than anything else that had happened in the past few days.

He returned to his section to continue his work.

"Team, it's ten o'clock and the store is now closed. Please head to Guest Services to pick up your items and finish your aisles," came the voice on the radio. Ryan exited the office and returned to the main sales floor to watch as the last customer left the store before he returned to a rather vacant Guest Services. As he grabbed a cart to stockpile his aisle's belongings, he noticed the baby lotion at the top of the pile.

Ryan grabbed the lotion and set it on the counter again. "Stacy, did you hear when I said this goes in the baby section?" He motioned to the fifth cart, under a small heading that said "BABY," to clearly delineate his point.

"Yeah," Stacy replied, eyes still focused on the magazine. "Leave it there, and I'll take care of it."

Ryan could feel his muscles tensing. Now, above all, was not the time to play games. Relaxing his shoulders, he grabbed his cart and moved away from the Guest Services desk.

From the corner of his eye, he saw Stacy briefly set down the magazine, pick up the lotion, and throw it back in the pharmaceuticals cart.

Ryan stopped the cart and clenched his fists and teeth. Hastily, he returned to the Guest Services desk. Instead of gaining Stacy's attention through words, he walked up to her, ripped the magazine from her hands, and stared her in the eyes.

"What the—?" she yelped.

"What the hell did I just say?" Ryan snapped back. "What did I say about that lotion, not fifteen seconds ago?"

Stacy stammered, eyes wide.

"I said, it belongs in the *baby* section," Ryan said. "The *baby* section. Because it is *baby* lotion!"

He reached into the pharmaceuticals cart and pulled out the lotion before shoving it in her face. "You see here? It says *baby* lotion! Not *adult* lotion! Where does *baby* lotion go, Stacy?"

Stacy cringed.

"The *baby section*, Stacy! That's where the *baby lotion* goes! Do you get it?" Ryan mocked. "It has that keyword in it. You know. *Baby*. Are you really that goddamn stupid? Or can you only focus on magazines and finding your next kid's father?" He threw the lotion past her and into the baby cart. "Speaking of that, you have enough kids to start a daycare. You should know where the *baby* lotion goes!"

"I—I'm sorry…" Stacy stammered.

"You have one goddamn job here," Ryan retorted, motioning to the computer behind them. "You use that computer to scan items, and that screen tells you which cart to put the crap in. So, even if you can't read, you'd know that baby lotion goes in Cart 5. Let's test this!" He grabbed the lotion from the cart and quickly scanned it. In a matter of moments, "Cart 5" flashed onto the screen. "Jesus Christ, Stacy, look! It says that the *baby* lotion belongs in the *baby* cart! Do you believe that?"

Stacy said nothing.

"*Baby*, Stacy!" Ryan yelled. "*Baby!*" He threw the lotion back into the cart and turned around. As he began walking away, he exhaled deeply and kicked his own cart in frustration, causing a box of Band-Aids fell to the ground. He quickly picked them up and turned around to Stacy.

"Band-Aids go in *this* cart, Stacy. Not *baby* lotion!"

He returned to his aisles without another word. All the while, the security camera shone down on them like a witness to the crime.

Steve Coltrip stared at Ryan, who, in turn, watched the television screen, though he had already relived the scene over and over. Part of him felt bad for his actions, but deep down, he knew that a culmination of things had led to his lashing out. Unfortunately for Stacy, she had happened to catch the brunt of it.

"My hands are tied, Ryan," Steve began dejectedly. "You know I want to help you, but I can't allow these complaints to go unnoticed."

Ryan shook his head, finally accepting his fate. "I know, I know, I'll apologize and clean up-"

"Ryan," Steve interjected, "I have to let you go."

Instantly, the energy in the room deflated like a balloon. For a moment, Ryan stared at his boss and neighbor as though he had spoken another language. Shuffling his feet, Steve stared sheepishly at his Redskins gear.

"I'll help you in any way I can outside of Gibson's. I really feel that, in your current state, that's the proper—"

"Screw you," Ryan finally said.

"Or we can go that route..."

"M—my current state?" Ryan stammered. "What? Am I a little"—he stood up very suddenly— "*unstable?*" He gestured and drew closer to Steve, who attempted to stand but merely looked feeble.

"I'm sorry, Steve, if I can't have my shit together every goddamn day, but it's been pretty hard lately. But—" he stammered, "but instead of helping me out, you decide to take a dump on me. I appreciate that, Steve." He showed restraint as he approached toward the door, but then he turned to scold his ex-manager once more.

"And for your information, you're a pretty shitty manager, too. Maybe if you spent more time on the floor instead of popping donuts back here, you'd see that people don't give a damn when we put bagels on sale. Why not try some water? Or maybe some cereal, for Christ's sake? Secondly, the credit card promotion is crap. You want me to up-sell people into debt by telling them they can get their card faster? That's not a perk. A perk is something we give up to get customers, like no annual fee. Not the fact that the Gibson's owner is banging the FedEx heir. And finally, this office smells like crap. Clean it up. And choose a better football team."

Steve sighed as he spoke. "I don't choose when the bagels go on sale."

"Go screw yourself."

Steve sighed again. "Anything else?"

The tone fanned the flames even more. "Oh, yeah, your dog always pisses on our yard, your kids listen to their stupid music too loud, and how about parking in your driveway instead of the street?"

With that, Ryan strode out of the office, but not before returning to the doorway. "One more thing, Steve, in case you didn't hear—go screw yourself."

He kicked a nearby chair and raged off down the hall. Only a moment later, he was outside the store and storming to his Jeep. As he opened the car door, he threw his phone to the opposite seat, where it bounced off the cushion and landed on the floorboards. Next, he unpinned his name tag and tossed it out the window. In a matter of seconds, a year's work was gone.

Shifting the car into drive, he flew out of the parking lot. He did not look back, knowing that a moment of reflection would hurt even more. He was done with the job. He was done with it all. There was no use in trying.

He was already gone.

Chapter 2
Two Weeks to Spokane

Just past four in the morning, a new voicemail popped onto Ryan's phone. As he lay in his bed, somewhere between angry and sad, the tape icon blazed across the screen. He knew who it was from, and he knew he would not be answering it.

This was never how he had expected it to go.

In the corner of the room, his pants lay slung across the floor. Next to them, his old ball cap. Next to that, a sweater. It was his, technically, though he had given it away long ago, never preparing for when it would be his once more. Now it lay silent, illuminated only by the phone that occasionally displayed a new voicemail. The rest of the room lay in darkness.

He tried to recall the evening's events, but his mind was a haze. He attempted to process it all, yet he knew he never would. Everything was changing.

Everything had changed.

Ryan stared at his phone the entire night. As the morning came, he could feel his feet dragging him to the closet to begin preparations for work. He slipped the green polo over his head and down his chest before moving back to the corner of the room and grabbing his discarded jeans from the night before. He stopped as he saw the sweatshirt, and for a moment, his heart almost caved. He knew he could not keep it.

Without a second thought, he picked it up off the floor and moved down the stairs. There was a donation box outside Gibson's. It would take only a second to throw it on the pile.

"Rent's due tomorrow," came his father's voice from the kitchen as he reached the bottom step.

Ryan hung his head as he stepped into the kitchen to acknowledge the man.

"It will be in the key bowl tomorrow," he said halfheartedly. He was not even thinking, but he knew he had to give some sort of answer.

"You're right," his father replied. "It will be."

"You don't have to be so mean," his mother said from the other side of the kitchen.

His father faced her. "Stop babying him, Nancy. The boy will learn some discipline."

"He looks like he barely slept!" Nancy replied, walking over to her son. "What's wrong?"

Ryan shook her off. "Nothing, Mom; just a long night."

He could tell that she was not buying it, but nothing more was said.

"Maybe less time screwing around and more time sleeping for work," his father interjected. "Remember your priorities, son." The last word was tinged with kindness, but it did little to obscure the cold truth.

Knowing this, Ryan nodded. It just was not his day. Without another word, he turned and left the kitchen.

Stepping out the front door, he was greeted with a mild Florida December. He walked to his Jeep, threw the sweatshirt and his bag into the backseat, and climbed inside.

He tried hard not to look at his phone, but as he entered the Gibson's parking lot, he felt himself pick up and press the button for voicemails. As he raised the device to his ear, he could hear the hurt in her voice as she called out to him.

"I know we have our issues, but I really do think we can get back on track. Give me that chance, like

I gave you. Don't end it now. I love you. Call me back."

Tears welled up in his eyes, yet he pulled the phone away and deleted the message. She had almost won him over. She had almost forced him to hit the callback button. But he did not. One thing stood in his way.

"Like I gave you…"

The words bit. It was another frame of guilt. Guilt for his mistakes, both for the ones she knew about and the ones she did not. He could handle no more guilt. Their relationship came riddled with it. The time had come.

He knew she would leave more voicemails, but there would be no other chances. There would be no more guilt and no more pain for her or him. It was over.

He pulled the phone away from his ear as he walked into the store, leaving the relationship's last piece of evidence sitting in the back of his Jeep in the form of a discarded sweatshirt.

Several hours later, he would be throwing baby lotion. And the following morning, there would not be a rent check in the key bowl. Soon enough, none of it would matter. In only a day, Ryan would be leaving that same store without a job and with no direction of where to go.

***

2,860 Miles to Spokane

The sun beat down on the dark green Jeep as the early afternoon hours passed. Ryan sat in the driver's seat, staring at an ATM screen and gripping a steering wheel cover that was slightly tattered, much like the Cherokee itself.

With fading paint on the roof and hood, and a slow leak in the air-powered back window that sometimes rolled down on its own, the vehicle had certainly seen better days. Underneath, there was a small break in the transmission line and a bigger leak in the left rear tire that Ryan had just filled. In the interior, the headliner was gone—a victim of the hot Florida sun. Regardless of its condition, however, it was the one thing Ryan owned outright, and it was the one thing he was most proud of. It had suffered through trips back and forth to both high school and college, and it had been around longer than any of his relationships. It broke down and needed tuning, but it was the one constant in his ever-changing life—a life even more turbulent after the past hour.

Ryan stared at the ATM screen for what seemed an eternity. Around him, life continued.

Across the frontage road from the bank was a large box store, not entirely unlike the one that had fired him, though it was blue to distinguish itself from the green of Gibson's. Next to that, a perpendicular road distanced the box store from a Home Depot. This road intersected not only the frontage road but also Highway 19A, which stood like a six-lane beacon in front of the Taco Bell, the box store, and the Third National Bank, where Ryan now sat.

Ryan waited for the account to update before he gazed at the screen. It was not a good look. Even with the check he had just deposited, his account read one hundred and thirty-six dollars. The sixteen cents that followed were a mere formality.

He exhaled as he attempted to clear his mind from the previous hours. He thought about returning home, but he knew he was in no mood to talk about why someone who usually closed was home at four in the afternoon. It would only lead to more arguments and more distress.

It would only lead to more disappointment.

Twenty-four hours ago, life had looked so much different. Five years ago had looked more different still. Eight years ago...

He'd had a plan. He would graduate high school with high honors and go to an Ivy League school. He would advance with his journalism degree and get a six-figure job to pay for his needs. Then he would get a job doing what he was most passionate about.

But a passion had never developed. Soon, "undecided" turned into half-hearted "journalism," and Cornell turned into Tampa State. And after four years and countless résumé changes, potential six-figure jobs turned into nothing at all.

He was not supposed to be here.

Where had he gone wrong? Was it from the start?

Questions fired in his mind as he stared at the machine's screen, yet no answers came. Somewhere in the eight years since he had formed his plan, he had come upon a Jeep and one hundred and thirty-six dollars, and that was all that remained.

A loud horn snapped him back to reality. Glancing in his rearview, he saw a line of cars waiting for him to finish. Quickly, he retrieved his card from the machine and put the car into drive, inching it slowly from the lane.

The rearview mirror revealed that he looked like hell. His five o'clock shadow was now sitting at seven, and his polo was clearly wrinkled. He needed a shower, yet the only place he could get that was the one place he could not go.

From the bank's driveway, he turned onto the frontage road and merged with cars leaving the Taco Bell and the box store. It was the usual four o'clock traffic, though traffic was the furthest thing from Ryan's mind. He gazed out at the backed-up traffic as the cars waited to turn onto the intersecting road and then again onto the highway. Then he stared at the box store on his right. Maybe he could get a job there. Maybe that would be a new start.

His eyes then turned back toward the vehicles ahead of him, all waiting, just as he was, on the two-lane frontage road.

It was then that he saw him.

He was a little off to the right of the car in front of him, but Ryan saw him clearly. He was dressed a little too nicely for someone holding a cardboard sign, but it was not his clothing that caught Ryan's eye. Nor was it the bag that lay at the man's loafered feet. It was the sign. As he pulled closer, he could read the faded ink more easily. Before long, he had pulled even to the man on the side of the road and read his sign internally.

Heading home for Christmas. Anything will help. God Bless.

It was simple, almost elementary. There was no pining, no emotional pandering. No mention of anything more. It captivated Ryan.

Anything.

It was simple and discreet, yet boastful and resonant. It was all, and it was nothing. And it was exactly what Ryan needed.

Ryan looked away from the sign to the car ahead of him, but something lured his gaze back. In his mind, reason and logic were lost, and impulse was all that remained. As though unbidden, his hands moved to the control panel on the door. He felt the warm December breeze as his passenger window crept slowly down. The next thing he knew, he was looking back toward the man.

"Hey!"

The man with the sign, however, was not focused on the Jeep in front of him, for he, too, was   in a different state of mind. The warm breeze and bright sun had forced him into a sort of dream state as he stood alongside the road. Reality seemed to come crashing back, though, as he heard the loud voice right in front of him.

"Hey, man!"

The man looked at Ryan with what appeared to be trepidation.

"Hey, man, you there?"

"Yes?" the man finally spoke what seemed to be his first word in a while.

Not fully aware of the traffic around him, Ryan leaned over his center console as he addressed the man. "Where's home?"

The man looked at him quizzically, as if he were speaking another language.

"Your sign." Ryan pointed. "Where's home?"

The man looked down at the sign in his hand. Then he looked back to the vehicle in front of him, words forming on his lips.

"Spokane," he finally said.

"Where?" Ryan asked, louder this time. He suddenly became aware of the cars around him, waiting on him to move forward.

The man paused again before answering. "Spokane, Washington."

Ryan began moving his car forward to keep up with the traffic, but he kept his body positioned half on the wheel and half on the center console. "That sounds far from here."

The man began moving parallel to the Cherokee, finally engaging with the young man in the driver's seat.

"It is."

Ryan peered back at the cars before turning again to the man outside his passenger window. It took only seconds, but the man's sign and his own tangle of emotions made up his mind for him. He could barely hear the words he said over his own disbelief as he said them.

"Hop in."

The man looked as incredulous as Ryan felt.

"Excuse me?"

"Hop in," Ryan repeated, more confident this time. The confidence came from somewhere within him, but Ryan did not know where.

The man paused beside the door. Ryan looked over once again, and it seemed to be all the man needed. Quickly picking up his sign and his backpack, he moved over to the Jeep and opened the passenger door.

As he did so, Ryan grabbed his GPS from the dash.

"Spokane? Washington, you said?" Ryan asked as the man set his bag on the floorboard and grabbed his seatbelt.

"Yeah," the man responded.

Ryan finished typing and then set the device back on the dashboard, looking at it only briefly. The next thing he knew, the traffic began moving and he was back on Highway 19A heading north, following the GPS with a new companion alongside.

Chapter 3
Six Months to Spokane

He was unraveling.

One minute, he was standing in front of the balloon game. The next, he was walking down the alleyway between the games behind the girl who caused him so much grief and struggle.

"Wait!" Ryan bellowed, willing to do anything to stop her. "Rebecca, wait!"

"Why?" she retorted, spinning around, oblivious to all other patrons. "So I can hear about how I'm not good enough for you?"

"I never said that," Ryan replied, covering the ground between them in a step. "I never said anything like that."

"Then why do you act like everything I suggest is beneath you? I bet if Breanne suggested moving in together, you'd be fine with it."

"Really? You bring her up again?"

"Yeah! She's on your level."

"Why are you pressuring me about moving in now?"

"It's been four years." She exhaled, pausing "Plus, I didn't say now, Ryan. I said soon."

The carnival lights flashed, and the bells tolled on.

"And I said maybe."

"Why don't you face it?" Rebecca stormed. "You're never going to be comfortable with it, but you won't come out and say it. It's like you have more to hide. First, Bree; now, whatever this is. You'll always have something to hide!" Her voice rose as she spoke.

Ryan gritted his teeth. "I have nothing to hide, babe." In those three years, only a few of their fights had reached this level. As they argued back and forth, it became evident that the road had become nearly impassable. He finally hung his head. "So, what do we do from here? Break up?"

Rebecca folded her hands. "Is that what you want?"

"No. I don't want to let go that easy."

She shook her head and stared at him. "Then don't let me go," she finally said. "Prove to me that you don't want to let me go."

"How do I prove it?"

She sighed. "Figure it out."

Ryan finally seemed to notice they were standing in an alley of carnival games. Looking to his right, he noticed the Skee-Ball game. The sign read, "160 Wins Big Prize." He turned back to Rebecca.

"One quarter. One game. I win, you keep the prize and promise that we will work this out. I lose, and I'll take you home, and that will be the end. As a bonus, you can call me every name under the sun."

Rebecca rolled her eyes. "That's your proof? A game?"

"If I want you as much as I think I do," Ryan reasoned, "then I should will myself to win this game."

"It's probably rigged."

"Then I'll lose."

"And you suck at these games."

"Probably," he said. Probably. But he was not going to let her go without a bit of a fight. He looked up at the giant teddy bears hanging from the rafters.

"You know, even if you win, I'll still be mad at you."

"I'm sure," he responded. "But you'll find it harder to be mad holding a giant bear."

She only shook her head as Ryan inserted a quarter and waited for the nine balls to roll out. It took only two minutes. Nine rolls and a bell-ring later, Rebecca had a boyfriend and a bear to hold onto for the rest of the night.

***

2,837 Miles to Spokane

The sun was beginning to set in the west as the men drove past the stores and gas stations lining that portion of Clearwater's highway. Neither man spoke as the sunlight streamed through the Jeep's windshield.

Ryan kept his eyes focused on the road ahead of him, not caring enough to look over at his new companion. His mind returned to the past days and the guilt and ignorance of his actions. He was still angry, and he was still far from over it all. Finally, after an eternity of thought, he glanced at the man seated next to him.

The man was older than Ryan, though he could not tell by how much. He had a grizzled and weathered face that sat atop his long, lanky body and on this face his piercing deep brown eyes radiated, though they indicated more compassion than darkness. In fact, the more Ryan stared, the more they stood out like beacons in the mat of facial hair that stretched from a scraggly beard to a tuft of unkempt hair sprouting unevenly from his head. His clothing was worn as well: a faded orange Tommy Bahama shirt, ripped cargo jeans, and bare ankles above brown loafers that told the story of countless walks. He was a remarkable sight. Still, he was far from feeble and, as far as Ryan could see from his darting eyes, far from comfortable.

"You know," the man began, speaking in an uncertain tone, "usually when I get into other people's cars …" He trailed off, then began again. "Usually, when I get into other people's cars, I'm not the nervous one."

Ryan briefly turned his head toward the passenger, realizing that his silence and glances were unnerving.

"Oh," he responded with a half-chuckle. "Sorry."

The man returned the smile and nodded as he returned his gaze toward the road. "First time for everything, I guess."

Ryan took a deep breath and returned his eyes to the road. The seconds ticked by as rapidly as the businesses the car passed.

"Sorry," he said after some time. "It's been a long day."

The man acted as though he had been waiting for the conversation to take off, and he leaped at the opportunity to talk.

"Yeah?" he asked. "You woke up under an overpass, too?"

Ryan was unsure if he was meant to be offended or amused.

"Sorry," the man said. "It was just a joke. When you don't talk to a lot of people, your sense of humor gets pretty depraved."

Ryan looked at the man once more before returning to the road.

His passenger remained silent for a bit until clearly the urge to speak became too much.

"You don't talk a whole lot, do you, man?"

Ryan thought for a moment. His mind was in such a disheveled state he could hardly focus on the road ahead.

"Do you? I don't know," the man said, "want to start with a name?"

Ryan considered this. "Ryan. My name's Ryan."

His passenger seemed content with this. "Good a start as any, Mr. Ryan. Name's Bo." He extended his hand across the console. Ryan reciprocated while keeping his left hand on the wheel.

"Bo?" Ryan repeated.

The man nodded as he looked out the passenger window, seemingly content that he had learned his driver's name. "Yep, Bo spelled B-O, not B-E-A-U or B-E-A or anything else. Though I knew a B-E-A-U once. Good kid; wanted to fly planes and all that."

Ryan nodded along.

"Or," Bo continued, "if it helps, just remember Mister Bojangles. You know Mister Bojangles?"

Ryan nodded. "From the song."

"Exactly! Bob Dylan. Great guy. Barely understand a word he says, though."

Ryan smiled and felt himself warm a little to the man seated next to him. He could not tell if he was crazy or just personable, but either way, it was something to listen to outside of his own thoughts.

"So, where you taking me?" Bo asked. "Soup kitchen? Church? Whorehouse? You know, sometimes, you can find all three in one place."

Ryan looked at him incredulously.

"Sorry," Bo said. "My humor again."

"No, it's fine." Ryan returned his attention to the road with a smile. "It's just been a while since I've interacted with someone, I guess."

"I hear you," Bo said. "Before you rolled down your window, I swore the flies buzzing around me were debating politics, and I was thinking to myself, man, I need to talk to more people."

Ryan nodded. "Coincidence, I guess."

"For sure…But seriously, where are you taking me?"

Ryan looked over at Bo. "What do you mean?"

Bo stared back as if confused by how his question could fuel another. "I mean, where…are you…taking me?"

Ryan looked at his GPS before looking back to Bo. "Spokane. Isn't that what you said?"

Bo's jaw dropped. "Yes…but that's in Washington."

Ryan was just as confused. "And?"

"And it's in Washington…"

Ryan shook his head. "I heard that."

"But—"

"That's your home, isn't it?"

"Well …," Bo paused. "Yeah."

"And your sign said you wanted help going home for Christmas, right?"

"Yes…"

"All right, I'm helping you out."

"By driving me there?"

Ryan felt like they were going in circles. "You said you wanted help."

Bo seemed to consider this before replying, "Well, by 'help,' I'm usually referring to some money or a bus ticket or something. I don't know."

Ryan shrugged. "Well, I don't have any cash on me, so I figured I'd just drive you there."

Bo's eyes narrowed incredulously. "How the hell did you go from, 'Hey, I don't have any cash to help this poor bastard' to 'Hey, let's drive him to Washington'? Seems like a jump to me."

Ryan considered the brashness of his actions and instantly wondered if he was making a mistake. "Do you not want me to?"

"N—no," Bo stammered. "I mean…don't you have school? Or work? Or something?"

Ryan answered much too quickly. "Nope."

"Do you pick up people like me often?"

Ryan took a little longer to answer this question. "No. You're the first."

"Why?"

"I don't know," he said softly.

Silence.

"You do know that Washington is, like, several days away, right?"

Ryan considered this for a moment. They were already leaving the familiar landscapes of Clearwater and heading toward US 19. A glance at the GPS revealed forty-two hours left in the journey.

"I'm aware."

In the silence that followed, the hum of the tires and the soft clicks of the GPS counting down miles provided the only noise. Ryan sat stone-faced in the driver's seat.

"Can I ask you a question?" Bo asked.

Ryan did not reply automatically, mind still focused on the solid line ahead of him. Then, after a second or two, he stirred, aware that Bo had asked a question. "Sure…" his voice trailed.

"Well," Bo turned toward Ryan, "I don't know you at all, but you seem a bit…distant."

"Distant? How so?"

"Like, oh, I don't know, Neptune distant."

Ryan looked at Bo, confused.

Bo shook his head. "What I mean is, and I'm just going to come right on out and say it, are you on something?"

"On something?"

"Yeah, like weed? Coke? Booze?"

"No!" Ryan exclaimed, incensed.

"I was just wondering; I mean, I see it a lot—"

"You always ask questions like that?"

Bo seemed confused. "Questions like what?"

"Questions like that. Personal questions."

"I was just wondering. You seem really out of it over there."

"I told you," Ryan repeated. "It's been a long day." He paused. "And secondly, even if I was on something, who the hell are you to ask?"

"Well, you do hold my safety in your hands…"

Ryan realized this, but that did little to quell his temper, "Okay, that's true. But it still isn't something you ask someone you just met."

"Then you've got a lot to learn about me." Bo chuckled.

Ryan shook his head. "That may be true, but it's best if we save the personal and insensitive questions for a later time."

"How late?"

"I don't know," Ryan responded with an edge. "But not now."

"So, no personal questions?"

"No. Not now."

"How about non-personal questions?"

Ryan considered this. "Okay, I guess."

Bo seemed content. "Fine. So, what's wrong?"

Ryan shook his head in contempt. "What's wrong? That's the definition of a personal question."

"No, it isn't."

"Yes, it is," Ryan said, annoyed. "When you ask someone what's wrong, you're asking their personal self what ails or upsets them, and in turn, they respond with that personal detail. How do you not see that?"

Bo pondered this and then seemed content with Ryan's logic. "Okay, then. What good movies are out now?"

"What? You go from that to movies?" Ryan asked in disbelief.

"You said no personal questions. So, I asked a movie question."

Ryan shook his head. "You have no filter. You know that?"

Bo shrugged.

"How about I ask you a question," Ryan began.

Bo looked over. "Okay, shoot."

Ryan kept his eyes on the road. "How did you come to be in your, well, you know, predicament?"

"Predicament?"

"Yeah, your difficult current state."

Bo looked confused. "You mean homeless? Or riding with you?"

Ryan squinted his eyes at the jab. "I mean homeless."

"Thought we weren't doing personal questions."

"I said I wasn't," Ryan said. "You can answer, though."

"Well, that's not fair. I'm not answering personal questions if you don't."

"Fine."

"Fine."

There was another long pause as the vehicle continued on its path. Ryan took a deep breath after a long while.

"*Moneyball.*"

Ryan felt Bo turn to face him.

"What?"

He was almost as shocked as Bo to hear the word, yet deep down, he knew that his passenger did not deserve the brashness with which he had spoken previously. While it had been a terrible day, and perhaps his tone was justified, he knew that Bo had done nothing wrong and did not deserve to be treated unkindly. It was a difficult task, Ryan knew, but little by little, he forced himself into a calmer tone.

"*Moneyball*," Ryan repeated as if it made perfect sense.

Bo looked at him as though he was speaking a foreign language.

"You asked what good movies were out. *Moneyball* is a good movie."

Bo nodded, an unsure picture on his face.

Ryan mirrored the gaze. Although his tone had changed, he knew that he had little to say. He was tired of talking and tired of thinking. The silence would do him good. Deep down, he thought it was all he wanted.

As the miles ticked onward, Ryan continued up Interstate 75, leaving behind his sanctuary and the only home he had ever known.

If the first hundred plus miles had shown him anything, it was the longing for home. The silence that surrounded the car lunged at Ryan, and while his thoughts had been clear and fearless at first, they had since become murky and disoriented. This task was ridiculous. He understood that. Yet, he knew he was only a phone call away from that home: a phone call to his parents, his mother, who would assure him everything would be okay. All he needed was to be told it was okay. It was okay to come home, to give in.

To give up.

He did not know where he was, but the exit lights were intoxicating in the dark, and he felt the car leave the highway and merge onto a smaller road. Soon after, he felt himself turn into a roadside gas station and café, though he was only remotely aware of either.

"Hungry?" Ryan asked as he unbuckled his seatbelt.

Bo looked over and nodded. "Yeah, I could eat."

Ryan's thoughts had cleared to the point that he felt his hunger pains. As he exited the car to pump gas, he turned to Bo.

"Go grab a table in there. I'll be in in a minute."

Bo nodded again before removing his seatbelt and grabbing his bag.

Ryan watched as the man in the Tommy Bahama shirt walked into the truck stop café and took up a table near the window.

"What are we doing, Ryan?" he asked aloud, knowing that he looked and felt a mess both outside and in.

The gas pump clicked dollars away as he leaned against the car, once again deep in thought and wrestling with the task. Finally, the pump stopped, and Ryan returned it to its holster, knowing that his insecurities and longing for home had gotten the best of him.

For the first time, he contemplated getting back in the Jeep and driving south.

He opened the driver-side door but did not get in. Instead, he closed his eyes and leaned his head against the door frame, thinking everything over for the hundredth time.

When he opened his eyes, the first thing he saw was his cell phone lying on the passenger-side floorboard, just barely out from under the seat. This was his chance. He could call home. He would be told exactly what he needed to hear.

He walked to the other side of the Jeep, wrenched open the door, and grabbed the phone with his left hand. He sighed deeply as he pushed the power button, only to find that nothing illuminated. He tried again. Nothing.

Sighing, he threw the phone back onto the floorboard, knowing the battery was dead. As he shut the door, he looked back to the restaurant and saw Bo sitting at the table looking at a menu. Between himself and the café, positioned directly on the curb to the truck stop, was a payphone.

Ryan closed his eyes, knowing it to be a sign. He opened them as he walked back to the driver's side and scraped up a couple quarters from his ashtray before shutting the door and walking over to the phone, unnoticed by the patrons in the restaurant.

He inserted the quarters and waited for the dial tone to click over before he thought about dialing. Then he looked back to the restaurant.

The waitress had returned to Bo, who smiled in a friendly manner as he indicated something on the menu. Ryan watched as Bo motioned to the vacant seat opposite his own and then pointed back to the menu. Instantly, he knew Bo was ordering him some food.

Ryan felt the emotion wash over him like a tidal wave. He almost dropped the payphone that waited for his dial. Here he was, planning on running back home, while his counterpart was unaware and, more unbelievably, treating him with a kind gesture.

Everything that he had said, all the harsh tones and emotions, had not deterred Bo from being a friend—maybe the only friend he had left.

Sighing, he hung up the payphone without dialing a number. A few seconds later, he was composing his thoughts as he entered the truck stop diner and took his seat across from Bo.

The truck stop restaurant had seen its heyday in the early '80s, as evidenced by the décor that adorned the walls. Above the stainless-steel tables and wood paneling sat collectibles, signage, and items ranging from Casio's to *Gilligan's Island*. None of this, however, seemed to matter as Ryan sat down and looked at Bo, who seemed enthralled with the décor. Finally, Bo's gaze turned back to the table.

"I, um," Bo began slowly, "I ordered you a burger."

Ryan looked up, already aware.

"Cheese and bacon. Hope you like that."

Ryan smiled. "Yeah, sounds good."

Bo nodded with a laugh. "The waitress is nice. I think she thinks I can actually afford the food."

Ryan smirked, warming to the man slightly. "I'll get it."

"You sure? We can always do the 'left the wallet in the car' stunt."

Ryan laughed softly. "I'd like to avoid breaking any laws on this trip."

"Eh, some laws are worth breaking, especially if the food sucks."

"You sound like an avid dine-and-dasher."

Bo laughed. "Never done it, actually. I just couldn't think up a non-awkward way to get you to pay."

Ryan smiled again at the man across the table. "Your honesty is—"

"Refreshing?"

"I was going to go with callous. But refreshing works."

Bo smirked again. "Same thing, sometimes."

The waitress returned with a smile and delivered their Cokes and burgers, which Bo set to with intensity. Realizing just how hungry he was, Ryan began at a more deliberate pace, but it quickly increased to quell the stomach pains.

For the first few minutes, neither spoke, but finally, Bo opened his mouth through a mix of burger and fries.

"So, you like baseball?"

Ryan considered the question for a moment before replying. "Baseball?"

"Yeah," Bo continued, wiping his mouth. "Earlier, you brought up *Moneyball*. That's a baseball movie, isn't it?"

Ryan nodded at the logic. "Yeah, it is. About Oakland."

"You a fan?"

"Of Oakland? No. Just the movie."

"How about of baseball?" Bo asked again.

"Oh, yeah. I am. Probably my favorite sport to watch."

"Why's that?"

"It's just a fun game," Ryan began. "I mean, it can be boring too, but every game is a chess match. It's just about strategy. Something I like."

"You go to a lot of games?"

Ryan sipped his Coke. "Me and my dad used to. We used to go to a lot of games, actually. He had Rays season tickets along the first base sidelines, so we'd go after school sometimes. My mother hated it because we wouldn't get home until after ten, but it was fun."

Bo took the last bite of his burger and wiped his mouth. "What do they do for a living?"

"Dad works for a technology company doing finances, and Mom stays at home and watches *The View*."

"Sounds like a good life."

"Yeah, no kidding."

"What about you?" Bo set his napkin on his plate and leaned back. "Surely on a Tuesday night, you should be getting ready for work tomorrow instead of driving a grizzled man across the country."

Ryan laughed as he put his own napkin on his plate. "Well, I would, except I got fired today."

Bo stared at Ryan without quite knowing if it was a joke or not.

"It's okay," Ryan said after a moment. "I hated the job anyway."

"Where did you work?"

"Gibson's," Ryan replied. "You know Gibson's?"

"The box store with the green ugly polos?"

Ryan looked down at his shirt. "Like this one?"

"Sorry," Bo replied. "Christ. That had to be a terrible job. What did you do?"

"At work? Or to get fired?"

Bo considered the question. "Both."

"I worked mostly in the electronics section selling crap. I also worked on the sales floor, also selling crap."

"Ouch."

"Yeah. Pretty much a crap-selling job."

"Sounds painful."

"It was. And these polos are itchy as hell."

"Looks like it."

Ryan eyed Bo for a moment and then realized that he was being more supportive than actually understanding what Ryan was venting about. He laughed openly about his realization that he was indeed venting, and Bo laughed along with him.

"Sorry, man," Ryan said after calming down. "I guess I have some pent-up rage about that place."

Bo's laughter died down. He took another drink and looked back at Ryan. "So, this might be a dumb question considering your aforementioned rant, but what'd you get fired for?"

Ryan grabbed his drink and leaned back in his chair, knowing there was little reason not to tell the truth.

"I threw some baby lotion at a pregnant lady."

"Was it for her baby?"

Ryan chuckled again. "No. I was upset at her inability to do her job, and I lashed out. I didn't hit her or anything. I was aiming for the cart behind her. But the video made it look like I was trying to kill her."

"They got it on video?"

"Sure did."

"That sucks."

"No kidding. Plus, she claimed I verbally assaulted her. It just wasn't a good day."

"Anyone defend you?"

"Apparently, me pissing off people was a regular occurrence, so no."

"That sucks."

Ryan shrugged. "I deserved it. I shouldn't have treated her—or anyone—like that."

"How long did you work there?"

"Just under a year. I didn't like the job. Or the people. To be honest, I don't really like much of anything at the moment."

"Why's that?"

"Just a lot of reasons," Ryan replied, realizing he was doing a lot of talking about himself.

"Women?"

Ryan took a deep breath. He looked away and then back at Bo. "Seems like a random connection. What makes you think that?"

Bo examined the check that the waitress had just dropped off at the table before looking back to Ryan. "Usually, when a man gives a generic reason for something, it's because of a woman."

Ryan laughed again. "Still seems a leap."

"Is it incorrect?"

"I think our personal question session is over for now." Ryan smiled, getting up from the table and grabbing the bill.

"Aww, cutting me off after I've made some progress! That doesn't seem fair," Bo pleaded as he rose from his chair.

Ryan shook his head. "I'm sure we have plenty of time for you to learn all about my personal life." He gave the bill and his card to the cashier.

As they walked through the gas station store, Ryan paused near the main exit door, noticing a wall of sweatshirts and jackets.

"Everything all right?" Bo asked.

"I was waitlisted to USF," Ryan heard himself say as he gazed at the college apparel. He turned to see Bo staring at him wide-eyed. "There's something personal for you. They didn't think I was good enough to get in."

Bo shrugged. "Anyone can buy a jacket."

Ryan smiled. In his mind, truer words had never been spoken.

Five minutes later, the Jeep pulled out of the parking lot and onto the highway once more. Inside, the driver kept both hands on the wheel as he tried not to look down at the USF logo on his jacket. Behind him, the gas station lights grew dimmer. Before long, they faded out of sight altogether.

He no longer needed gas. He was no longer hungry. And best of all, he no longer needed the itchy polo that lay in the trash between pumps four and five.

Somewhere before midnight, Ryan felt his eyes begin to droop. He could not tell if Bo was awake or asleep, but he remained quiet. Occasionally, he would shift his body and exhale loudly, or even make a comment about the billboards or roadways, but as the night pressed on, the comments were fewer and fewer. Realizing he could not drive any farther, Ryan pulled into a rest area.

From the looks of the surrounding darkness, it appeared the rest stop was in a densely forested area. Ryan could not be sure though, as the plaza's low lights provided few hints. He found a parking spot in the semi-deserted lot and shifted the car into park before cracking a window quietly so as not to awake his companion, who was surely asleep by now.

"I've been thinking," Bo said loudly, making Ryan jump almost fully out of his seat.

"Jesus Christ! I thought you were asleep."

"You know, I thought you were, too. Which, given your role as driver, made for quite a predicament."

"Don't ever scare me like that. I about had a damn heart attack."

"Okay. Good to note. As an aside," Bo said, "I've been thinking about something."

Ryan reclined his seat and lay back, shifting his body to get comfortable.

"Can it wait until tomorrow?" he asked, realizing just how tired he was.

"I'd rather it not," Bo said. "It'll be quick. Just hear me out."

Ryan exhaled and turned, facing the man he had picked up not eight hours ago.

"It's about personal questions," Bo began. "You know, the kind you don't want to answer."

"What about them?"

"What if we have a game?" Bo offered.

Ryan rolled his eyes.

"Stay with me," Bo continued. "How about we each get to ask the other person *one* personal question for every state line we pass?"

"How many," he asked slowly, "state lines do we actually pass?"

Bo scratched his head. "I'd say seven or eight."

Ryan turned to lay on his back. He stared at the ceiling. "You won't give up if I say no, will you?"

Bo laughed. "If you say yes, you can go to sleep."

Ryan shook his head. "Fine. We'll start tomorrow."

Bo nodded. "Fine, and we also can ask whatever follow-up questions we want."

Ryan turned back to object, but Bo was already turning to sleep in his own seat.

"'Night, Ry," Bo said loudly, quelling any further talk on the subject.

The nickname was not lost on Ryan. As he sat in his seat, a smile crept across his face as he considered the quirky nature of the man in his passenger seat. Then, shaking his head, he turned to face his own door. As he finally got comfortable, he heard Bo's voice again.

"You aren't going to murder me in my sleep, are you?"

Ryan shook his head as he closed his eyes. "I'd pick a more deserted place than this."

Bo seemed to like this answer, and he closed his eyes as well.

Ryan opened his eyes once more, but it was only briefly. Then, with an expression of exhaustion and contentment on his face, he closed them once more.

"Goodnight, Bo," he said softly.

Chapter 4
Two and a Half Years to Spokane

"What are you doing here, Ryan?"

The words came from across the room and Ryan stood to attention, not allowing the editor to throw him off balance.

"What do you mean?" he asked.

John Colquitt adjusted his wire-rimmed glasses as he peered at the whiteboard with the giant words *Tampa Tribune* across the top.

"I mean," he repeated without taking his eyes from the board, "what are you doing here? Today. In this office. At this newspaper."

Unsure how to answer, Ryan watched his supervisor intently. His internship was in its second month, and while he felt as though he had a good grasp of the newspaper world, he was suddenly weary of everything.

"I'm here…to learn," Ryan finally said. "My professors said this would be a good way to add to my writing portfolio…by understanding the stories and—"

"And you get college credit," John interrupted.

Ryan nodded, though John's back was to him. "Yes, but with all due respect, journalism is all I've ever wanted to do."

"Why?"

"Because," Ryan replied, "writing is what I'm good at. I like figuring out stories and how to cover them. I like what you all do."

John finally turned around and smiled as he sat down at the large table that separated him from Ryan. He motioned for Ryan to sit as well.

"You know, people don't really read the paper anymore," John finally said, sipping from his coffee cup. "Most everything is online these days."

Ryan smiled in return. "Well, stories are stories. It doesn't matter if they're online or in print, as long as people read them. You told me that."

John laughed. "Yes. Yes, I did. I also told you that I'd have a job for you because you've impressed me."

Ryan nodded, though he was beginning to sense something was wrong.

John stared down at his coffee cup. Although Ryan had only known him for a few months, he knew he had served the man well, from simply sitting in on meetings to coming up with catchy headlines. In return, Ryan had truly gained an appreciation for the editor-in-chief. It was a tiresome job, but John did it with resolve.

After a long pause, John turned back to the whiteboard that listed the different sections of the paper, from sports to local.

"Do you agree with our choice for the local headline?" he finally said.

Ryan stared at the phrase "SWAT BUSTS PINELLAS DRUG RING – 6 DEAD" with the accompanying "HL" alongside.

Ryan chuckled. "If it bleeds, it leads."

"Do you agree with it?" John replied without a hint of humor.

Ryan immediately became serious as he stared at the other stories in the LOCAL section. "I mean, that's going to get the most attention."

"It's Section B, though," John countered.

"Still," Ryan said, recalling the previous two-hour meeting wherein all the editors had sat in these same seats and debated this, "Jenkins made a compelling argument."

"Screw Jenkins," John said. "I don't give a damn what Jenkins said. What would you do?"

Ryan searched the board, though he already knew the answer.

"I would have put the park modifications announcement first."

John stopped staring at the board and turned to Ryan. "The park?"

Ryan looked sheepishly to his notepad. "Yeah, the park."

"Defend it."

"Our main headline is about the number of deaths in the war. Page two, about the bombings in Egypt. Section C's headline is about football concussions, and even *Dear Abby* is about coping with the loss of a grandmother. It's a depressing issue."

"It's news," John replied. "It's always depressing."

"Yeah," Ryan countered, "but don't we determine what the people see?"

"And their eyeballs determine what we print. It's a cycle; you know this."

"I know, but—"

"Why are you here?" John asked again, silencing Ryan.

"I'm not…" Ryan stammered. "I don't know what you want me to say."

"I want you to tell me why you are here. Why did you sign up for this job?"

"I did!"

"No, you gave me the bullshit reason. You gave me the reason you give everyone when they ask you, 'Why do you want to go into journalism?' That's the reason you gave me."

Ryan stared wide-eyed at his editor.

John turned back toward the board and took another sip of coffee. "When I graduated and interned at the *Post*, I had an editor who was a real hard ass. He would push his staff to twelve-hour days, all to print on time. I learned a lot, but what I learned most was that I was too smart to be a beat writer. I wanted to put it all together. I wanted to sit at the head of the table and figure out what we were going to do. I wanted to be the hard ass. I wanted his job." He paused for another sip of coffee.

"So, I worked and worked and worked. I moved up to Sports Editor and finally his assistant before applying for and getting this job here in Tampa. I accepted it right away and started packing my desk. And as I packed, my now old editor-in-chief came into my office and sat at my old desk. Know what he said?"

Ryan shook his head.

"As he sat there at my desk," said John, seemingly recalling the memory, "he said, 'You've wanted my job for a long time, haven't you?' And I, standing there ready to go to Florida, nodded with this stupid grin on my face. My old editor looked me dead in the eye and said something I would never forget. He said, 'Why the hell would you want that?'"

John turned back to Ryan and slammed his coffee cup on the table. "He said I could have been anything, anything in the world, and for some dumb reason, I wanted to be him. He said he hated the job, but no one ever had the audacity to ask him his feelings. Everyone just assumed that the top was where they needed to go." John paused again, looking Ryan directly in the eye. "I spent fifteen years trying to be a man who didn't even want to be himself."

Ryan felt a lump grow in his throat. "Why are you telling me this?"

John turned back to the board. "Because, Ryan, you can be anything in this world. You truly can. You are smart, witty, gifted. You can do anything you want, and you shouldn't waste time on things you aren't passionate about."

Ryan stared at his editor with a mix of shock and discomfort. "You don't think I'm passionate about this?"

"Are you?"

Ryan did not know how to answer.

"You're good at it," John said. "Hell, you may be great. You might revolutionize the entire newspaper industry. You're already thinking about changing readers' perceptions and what they view as news, but it's all worthless if you don't care about it. And while I would love to have you on my staff, I decided long ago not to be like my old boss. So, instead of letting you walk the path like I did, I'm kicking you onto another."

Ryan could feel himself breathing, but he knew not what to say. In the blink of an eye, his entire world was altered.

"I'll let you finish your internship, so you get credit," John said after a minute. "But I won't be hiring you. I do hope you understand."

Ryan stood motionless as John made his way to the door. "I-I don't understand." He wondered how the conversation had changed so drastically. "Why did you ask me about the headline?"

"What?" John said as he reached the doorway.

"You started this with the question about the headline. Why?"

"It made my decision easier," John replied.

"I don't understand."

John put his hand on the doorway. "You'd still put the park first. It's the wrong answer." He paused once more. "But it also means it's not too late for you."

With that, he walked out the door, leaving a stunned student standing idly behind.

***

2,648 Miles to Spokane

The sunlight cascaded through the window and onto the right side of Ryan's face. It was warm, almost like home, welcoming him to face the morning as it always did. For a moment, he felt like he was back at home, lying in his bed next to his window. Sometimes he would lie there for an hour, just soaking in the morning rays of the sun before he threw the covers off and began the day. It was quiet at home, almost serene. There were few responsibilities in those mornings and very few concerns. He almost smiled as he pictured that restfulness, and he lost himself in the feeling, forgetting all notions of time and space.

Suddenly, the air brakes on a nearby truck released, and Ryan's eyes flew open. No longer was he at home.

He lay still and surveyed the scene. The rest area was busier than the evening before, though he had little idea what time it was. There were several trucks in the lot, and each seemed louder than the last. Ryan wondered how he had slept at all. He took a deep breath, quietly raised his head from the driver's seat, and cast a bleary eye at the passenger seat to find it empty. In his weariness, he wondered where Bo had gone.

Stretching his arms, Ryan opened the Jeep door and almost fell onto the pavement. Catching his breath, he shook his legs, knowing that he should have stretched further.

He ran his fingers through his hair, noticing just how messy and unkempt it felt.

Walking into the rest area, he moved to the sink and splashed water onto his face and into his hair in an attempt to look presentable.

In the mirror, he could see how the previous days had taken their toll. The USF logo on his body was the only thing that appeared even slightly clean, and he stared at it for several seconds before returning to his own face. It was hard to recognize his own reflection, especially in the jacket.

The December air was cool on his body as he exited the bathroom. Patting his damp hair, he returned to the car and opened the backseat passenger door. He rummaged through his work bag until he found what he needed: a baseball cap and a phone charger.

As he grabbed the items, his eyes strayed to the sweatshirt he had tossed there the day before. He thought of the memories it held and considered throwing it away, but another draft of colder air made him think better of it. He needed all the clothes he could get, especially the farther north they went.

He donned the Rays cap as he shut the door and looked around. Before long, he spotted Bo sitting on a picnic table some distance off, facing the highway.

Ryan stuffed the charger into his pocket as he walked toward the man, wondering just how long he had been awake and out of the car.

In any other scene, Bo would have looked out of place sitting by himself in such comical attire, but Ryan already had grown accustomed to the man's behavior and wardrobe.

"You don't sleep a lot, do you?"

Bo half-turned but kept his gaze toward the highway as Ryan approached. "Eh, I don't need a lot of sleep. Plus, your cushions hurt my back."

Ryan gripped his neck, knowing just how rough the old Jeep's seats were. "Yeah, they aren't the most comfortable things in the world."

Bo nodded in all seriousness. "Way too soft."

Ryan could not tell if the comment was a joke, but he thought it best to let it go. "You ready to go?" he finally asked, breaking the silence.

Bo stood and turned away from the table.

"Yes, sir. I was born ready."

The day was bright, and Ryan could already feel the rays of sun on his skin as he merged back onto the interstate heading north.

Casually, he leaned on the driver's door while keeping one hand on the steering wheel. The silence stretched as Bo fidgeted through the unseen contents of his bag. Meanwhile, Ryan slipped into his own consciousness as he reminisced about the past.

"Question time!" Bo's voice rang out next to him.

Ryan snapped back to reality to find that Bo was gazing at him. Clearly, he had been in his own mind for longer than he thought.

"By the way, you should always honk twice when you enter a new state."

"What?" Ryan asked, completely lost as to what he had missed.

"You should honk your horn twice. When you cross a state line?" Bo stared at him. "You know, honk honk?"

"W-Why?"

Bo looked back out the front window. "I don't know. I guess it wakes up the people who passed out in the previous state."

"Uh, okay," Ryan said. Nervously, he honked his horn twice.

Bo shot a forlorn glance across the Jeep. "*When* you cross the state line, not ten miles in."

"Sorry," Ryan replied sheepishly.

"Don't worry about it," Bo said. "But, it's question time."

Ryan was not quite sure what made it question time, but he sensed that somewhere in his millings and thoughts, they had crossed over into Georgia.

"I want to know," Bo paused as he thought. "Hmm...I want to know...what happened with the girl?"

"What girl?"

"You tell me. I suppose it's the girl who didn't make work easier for you."

"There is no *the girl*," Ryan lied.

"Bullshit," Bo said. "She's either someone you worked with or someone you know from work because you never denied a girl being one of the reasons you disliked your job."

Ryan admired Bo's memory, even if he was wrong.

"I said," Ryan began, "that there were a lot of reasons I didn't like my job. You assumed a girl was involved."

"Which you didn't deny."

"Well, I'm denying it now. A girl had no relevance to me hating my job. That just came naturally after a few months."

"Fair enough," Bo reasoned. "So, no girl issues?"

"Jesus Christ, you don't give up, do you?"

"Technically," Bo countered, "I asked, 'Who is the girl?' and you haven't answered. She could be job related or non-job related; I just asked who she was. I've now deduced that she is a non-job-related girl."

Ryan admired Bo's inquisitive nature, even if he was not in the mood to discuss his personal life.

"What's her name?"

Ryan took a deep breath. "Her name is Rebecca. Or was. Whatever."

"She die?"

"We broke up."

"Then she died?"

Ryan massaged his brow. "No. She's still alive."

"Fair enough," Bo said. "I'm just trying to...I don't know...understand."

"Well," Ryan countered, "understand that it's mostly my fault. I'm a pretty terrible person, allegedly."

"I take it...*Rebecca*...alleged that."

"Night before last. When we broke up."

Bo considered this for a minute. "So, let me get this straight: you broke up with your girlfriend and got fired the next day?"

Ryan nodded.

"Damn, that sucks. No wonder you're in a shitty mood."

Ryan smiled a fake smile. "Thanks, man."

"No, I mean that in understanding. Hell, a breakup alone makes some people do stupid things. Not to mention a job loss on top of that. Case in point, this..." he added, gesturing at himself and their current situation.

"I didn't pick you up because I wanted to be reckless," Ryan assured him.

"I don't deny that," Bo said. "I'm just saying it makes sense. Sort of."

Ryan considered this, wondering if perhaps there was some truth to Bo's assertions.

"Better than shooting up the store, I guess," Bo added, snapping Ryan back to reality.

"It isn't reckless, though," Ryan said. "I mean, yeah, it was a breakup, and yeah, it was a firing and a long list of issues before that…"

"I feel like you're proving my point."

Ryan sighed. "You ever just have one of those never-ending bad days that lasts for a long time?"

"Almost rhetorical asking that to a homeless guy, you know."

Ryan shook his head. "You know what I mean. Well, the past two days have just been the climax to that. It wasn't the breakup or the firing or the lack of money. It was—it's been everything."

"I assume women before her?"

"I've screwed up everything with all of them." He exhaled deeply. "Sad part is, I actually really liked some of them."

"That doesn't sound as romantic as you'd think."

"And if I am reckless, then oh, well. I deserve something, and I guess I'll take the ability to be reckless."

Bo chuckled softly. "Listen, Ry, you're upset and pissed, and you have the right to be."

Ryan nodded. "Thanks. I'm glad I have your approval."

"And all those things you're dealing with, they'll sort themselves out in time."

Ryan adjusted his hands on the steering wheel. "I'd rather they be done sorting themselves out now."

"In time," Bo replied.

Though Ryan feared dealing with his own issues, he reasoned that what Bo said was true. There was more to the man in the Tommy Bahama shirt than he let on. Yet little of that mattered now as they continued the drive north into the winter air ahead.

"Your turn," Bo said after a while.

"My turn?" Ryan kept his eyes on the road.

"Yep." Bo adjusted himself in his seat. "It's your turn to ask me a deep, personal question."

Ryan considered this for a moment but knew he had no questions to ask. He knew, however, that Bo was expecting a question, so he thought of one as quickly as possible.

"You, um," Ryan began, "you spoke a lot about baseball yesterday. How'd you know so much?"

Bo scrunched his brow as he considered the question. "When did I talk about baseball?"

"With *Moneyball*," Ryan answered. "You knew it was about baseball. How'd—how'd you know that?"

"I'm homeless, man. I'm not an idiot."

"I never said you were an idiot," Ryan stammered. "I just assumed that—"

"I'm kidding, Ry." Bo laughed, "I know what you mean."

Ryan exhaled in relief. "I just didn't know if a man in your state kept up with entertainment stuff."

"You make being homeless sound like so much fun." Bo laughed again. "Don't worry about being PC with me. As you can tell, I'm not big on formalities or sensitivities."

"Good to know."

"But," Bo began, "to answer your question, I will say that I'm actually a big baseball fan. Mets, mostly."

Ryan's curiosity was piqued. "Mets? New York?"

"Yep, the Metropolitans themselves," Bo responded, looking out the passenger window as though he cared little about the talk.

"You from New York?"

"Somewhat. I lived there for several years."

Ryan thought about this. "When you say lived there—"

Bo finished Ryan's thought. "In a house, yes. With a job; all that. We lived in a townhouse on the Upper West Side. I commuted to work every day and hated all the Yankee fans in Manhattan because they drove like assholes. Mets fans were more hospitable. Friendlier."

"When you say 'we' lived?"

"Well, don't you pick up on the words quickly," Bo said admiringly. "Me and my wife."

"How long ago was that?"

"That isn't really a follow-up to the baseball question, is it?"

Suddenly, it was Ryan's turn to be left hanging, and it was a feeling he did not enjoy. "It's only a question!"

"Yes, and when we cross another state line, you can ask it."

Ryan gave in without further pleading.

"But to answer your first question," Bo finally said after a moment's silence. "I read the Sunday newspaper every week."

Ryan thought about this as Bo continued to explain.

"The *Sunday Edition* has weekly sports wrap-ups so I can keep track of what happened," he added. "Plus, they play five or six games, so usually I just compare records to see what each team did for the week. The hard part is actually finding a hotel that provides the paper for free."

"Wait," Ryan interjected. "A hotel?"

Bo nodded, still looking out the window. "Yep. Every Saturday night, I stay in one. Now, mind you, it isn't a Four Seasons or anything like that, but a Days Inn or Super 8 off the highway usually doesn't mind as long as I pay cash."

"How—if I may ask—do you get the cash?"

Bo shrugged. "Doing exactly what you found me doing."

Ryan thought about their previous day's meeting, with Bo standing on the side of the road.

"Usually," Bo continued, "you can get fifteen to twenty bucks a day. Five of that goes to food and five toward anything I desperately need, like water or something like that. But the other ten I keep, and at the end of the week, I take that sixty bucks and get myself a nice motel room with a shower and a newspaper."

Ryan admired the ingenuity. "That's actually pretty smart."

"Even smarter when you realize that they give you exactly a week's supply of soap and shampoo. So, I just tuck that in my bag here and keep it for the following week." Bo tugged on his bag as if to show it off. "The best part is telling them that you left your toothbrush and toothpaste. Do you know that most hotels will give you that crap free of charge? I mean, it isn't free; I paid sixty bucks for the room, but still."

"That is pretty clever."

"TV sucks on Saturday nights, though," Bo continued. "And if they ask where your car is, always say that you parked it around the corner. Telling them you walked doesn't necessarily bode well for a room with a good view."

Ryan laughed at the comment. "You're one of a kind, Bo."

Bo nodded. "I'm a survivor." Then he added, "Plus, I hate the homeless people who smell. They give us a bad name."

Ryan laughed at this but said no more. Remarkably, the brief question session made him want to know more about his companion, but he knew no more questions would be answered. Until their next state line, however far away that was, they were relegated to small talk and general comments. Perhaps it was better this way. Ryan was not too keen on divulging his own secrets. Yet for the first time, the man at his side interested him. The feeling both surprised and confused him, as it had been a while since he had actually gotten to know someone.

"This thing got a radio?" Bo asked, motioning to the dashboard.

The comment interrupted Ryan's thoughts, and he fumbled to turn on the stereo system.

Bo turned the tuner dial until the static gave way to garbled music.

"What do you prefer?" he asked, flipping through the stations.

"Anything, but rock or classic preferably," Ryan replied.

"Nice. A classic rock fan. You like KISS?"

"I enjoy some of their stuff."

"I love KISS," Bo said, flipping through the stations continually. "Saw them at the Nassau Coliseum when I was just old enough to drive. When they played 'Love Gun,' the entire crowd went crazy.

"That's some good KISS."

"Hell, yes. Though I'd still take their older stuff over the newer. Songs like 'Firehouse' and all that still hit."

"They do, indeed," Ryan replied.

Bo turned his attention to the radio dial as he attempted to find a station. "They were rock gods. Still are. Them and Zeppelin and," the station turned, and familiar chords sounded, "Styx."

"Whoa," Ryan corrected him, "I'm thinking that 'rock god' and 'Styx' aren't said very often together."

"Really? 'Come Sail Away'? Or this one?" Bo responded, indicating the song on the radio.

"I'll give you 'Come Sail Away,' but 'Renegade' is a terrible song," Ryan retorted, shaking his head as 'Renegade' continued to play.

"Bullshit. This is a great song!"

Ryan shook his head. "There is nothing great about this song other than the fact that it paved the way for Bon Jovi doing a western song."

"Don't you dare compare 'Renegade' to 'Wanted Dead or Alive.'"

"And besides," Ryan continued, "if I'm going to call out the rock gods, I'd give it to Aerosmith or Pink Floyd."

"And Styx." Bo smiled, indicating the radio once more as the song played on. He turned away from Ryan.

"Christ." Ryan shook his head. "I'm not listening to this crap all the way up."

Bo, however, was not listening. Instead, he was seemingly focused on singing along to the melody without any care to his outward appearance.

"I remember exactly where I first heard this song," Bo said after a moment.

"Was it in hell?"

Bo laughed. "It was a seedy bar during my college years. My buddies were plastered, and for some reason I wasn't quite there yet." He took a deep breath. "Someone requested this song, and at first, I was confused."

"Accurate…"

"Eventually," he continued, "I began nodding along while all my buddies tried to sing the words they clearly didn't know." He smiled, tone changing. "Then Steve fell on the floor and spilled his beer all over this guy who was clearly annoyed with us from the start."

Ryan listened, knowing he did not want to interrupt such a reflective story.

Bo laughed. "Before the third chorus, that guy had Steve in a headlock, and we're all trying to pull him out. Beer was flying; people were screaming. It was great."

Bo paused once more, obviously pensive. He opened his mouth as though to continue the story, but then closed it. The memory clearly held deep meaning. After a moment, he blinked rapidly as if waking from a trance.

"Crazy how a song can do that," he finally said, shaking his head. His tone had shifted back to its usual cheerfulness.

Ryan noticed the quick change from deep thought to normalcy but said nothing of it.

"Well," he finally said, "your music taste still sucks."

Bo laughed loudly. "Whatever."

***

Just past one in the afternoon, the Jeep made its first stop of the day—a much-needed respite at a gas station north of Macon. The past hours had found the two men discussing music and then retreating into long periods of silence before returning to the conversation. Before long, it became much easier to communicate, and Ryan felt his residual uneasiness slide slowly away.

Lunch at the gas station was a hurried affair, but it did allow for Bo to use the bathroom and grab some snacks, which he paid for using money from his bag. Returning to the car, he threw a bag of pretzels at Ryan.

"Just spent my last money on two Slim Jim's and that bag of pretzels. Looks like I won't be eating until Washington."

Ryan laughed as he returned the nozzle to the pump. He was hungry, but he figured the pretzels would be enough. Moreover, he was suddenly worried as he climbed back into his car. The nozzle stopped at $41. Ryan did the math in his head and quickly realized what he should have known all along; he was about to run out of money. A quick tally of two tanks of gas and dinner meant he had only eight dollars left. He did not have enough money to get to Washington or to get back home.

"Dumb ass," Ryan swore under his breath as he thought of the money spent on the jacket he wore. His lack of planning was catching up with him. He knew, however, that he could not tell Bo the truth, especially not after having promised to complete the task. His pride was worth more than anything at this point. After all his failings, both in jobs and in love, and after losing both his confidence and his self-esteem, he was not about to fail in another task. There was already too much at stake for him.

In truth, he knew that there was little he could do but drive on. He took a deep breath and felt a bead of sweat on his brow.

He had no other choice.

Chapter 5
Three Years and Ten Months to Spokane

"She isn't for you," his mother said as soon as Ryan walked through the door.

"You just met her," he responded, not sure whether to laugh at the absurdity or growl at the insinuation.

"And I can tell she isn't for you."

"How?"

His mother sat in her chair and faced the television. His father was not yet home, but he knew this conversation was better between him and her. He had just dropped Rebecca at her house, and he knew this discussion would be awaiting him once he returned home.

"It's a mother's intuition. They always know what's right for their sons. And since I'm your mother, I know what's right for you."

Ryan shook his head, unsure if she was more interested in the conversation or the television. "What makes you so sure?"

His mother paused in contemplation. "She doesn't challenge you enough."

"What do you mean, 'challenge'?"

Her program gave way to a commercial, and she turned to face him.

"I mean," she said, "that she doesn't challenge you. She doesn't spur your intellect. She won't provide you with any obstacles in life. She's a nice girl, don't get me wrong, but she won't challenge you."

"Relationships have to have obstacles?"

His mother smiled. "Are you perfect?"

Ryan did not answer.

"Challenges and obstacles are meant to better you, my son. If you're perfect, then you don't need them, but no one is perfect. You need a girl who doesn't agree to everything— one who provides the obstacles that make you challenge your faults. That's what I mean."

Ryan shook his head. "And how can you tell that she doesn't meet those standards?"

"I just can," she answered. "It's part of being a mother."

Ryan felt his jaw tighten. Her answer was infuriating. "Maybe you'll be proven wrong."

She smiled as her television show resumed. "Maybe, but probably not."

Ryan shook his head.

"I know you don't like my answer, but you asked for my opinion."

"Actually, I never did…"

"Oh." She considered this. "Well, then I gave it freely."

"Thank you for that."

She laughed. "Listen, Ryan." She turned away from the television again. "I will always support your decisions. Always. Even if they seem ridiculous or if I don't understand them. If she ends up making you happy, I'll support it. If you decide to move on to someone else, I'll support that." She paused. "Hell, if you decide to run off and join a circus troupe, I'll question it, but I'll support it."

"I think circus troupes stopped being a thing…"

"You know what I mean," she replied as she stood up. "It's your life. Your job is to find your purpose and find your love. And I'll be here to give you my advice if you need it, but regardless, I'll still support you all the way—as long as you're safe. Always."

"You'll also always be biased."

"Biased?"

It was Ryan's turn to laugh. "Yeah. You think I can get supermodels and all that."

"Of course, you can. You're a handsome man!" She grabbed his shoulders as though this somehow signaled his attractiveness. "You can get anything you want. You can be anything you want." She let go and moved into the kitchen.

Ryan considered this. 'Anything' seemed far too big a concept. "What if I just want her?"

She answered from the next room. "Then I'll support you being wrong."

"You think you know everything, don't you?" Ryan laughed.

"Damn straight," his mother replied as she glanced out to him. "That's what moms are for."

***

2,319 Miles to Spokane

"I want to ask my next personal question," Bo said after a long while.

Ryan considered this for a moment and then laughed it off. "We still have at least a hundred miles in Georgia."

"I know, I know," Bo replied as he looked out the window. "I just underestimated how godforsaken long this state is."

"You made the rules…"

"I know I made the rules, but this is a one-time deal. A pay-it-forward kind of thing."

Ryan shook his head. "That isn't even close to what 'pay it forward' means."

"Are you going to argue semantics?" Bo asked as he turned toward Ryan. "Or do I get my question?"

Ryan pursed his lips. "If we're technical here, I should get my question first."

Bo scrunched up his brow. "Why's that?"

"You asked first the last time."

"Again, never a stipulation on taking turns going first."

"Well, that's my deal. I'll move the question up to now, but I get to go first."

The previous hours had consisted of sitting in Atlanta traffic and staring at billboards, and for the moment, Ryan was happy to be in conversation, even if he sensed he was agitating his companion with addendums. The conversation allowed him to forget the Christmas wreaths and décor he saw in the city, and it especially allowed him to forget the colder air that was now surrounding them.

"Deal," Bo finally said.

Ryan smiled and nodded. "Okay then," he said, changing lanes in the heavy afternoon traffic. "I want to know more about your wife."

Bo turned away, almost as though he had not heard the question. Ryan found the behavior perplexing.

"What about her?" Bo asked after a lengthy pause.

"Where is she?"

When Bo spoke, his voice was hoarser than usual. "She will be in Washington. In Spokane."

"How long have you been…separated?"

Bo was slow to answer. "A few years. To be honest, I've kind of lost track."

Ryan hesitated to push further. Whatever the situation was, feelings about it clearly still affected Bo.

"I think that's enough on that topic," Bo said rather abruptly.

Ryan continued staring ahead. "I'm sorry."

Bo remained unmoved. "No," he replied. "I'm sorry. I make a game and then break my own rules." He paused once more as if gaining courage. "Truth is, we just aren't together now. Fault or reasoning isn't something I think about, or else I'd never think about anything else."

Ryan nodded and glanced at his companion. "Well, I appreciate the honesty."

Bo looked out the window for a long while before finally turning back.

"I guess it's my turn for a question."

Ryan admired Bo's mood-changing abilities, but he said nothing. Instead, he continued driving toward his own fate.

"I want to know what's in your bag."

Ryan heard the question but did not fully comprehend it. "My bag?"

Bo nodded. "Yep. Your bag. The one in the backseat."

Ryan half-turned to look at the bag, incredulous at the ease of the question, before realizing he was, in fact, still driving.

"My bag?" Ryan repeated. "You spent the entire state of Georgia thinking of a question, and 'What's in your bag?' is what you came up with?"

Bo nodded. "Yep. That's it."

Ryan scrunched his brow as he looked at Bo. "What the hell does my bag have to do with anything?"

"You don't want to answer?"

"No, it's just a dumb question."

"I don't think so."

"Of course it is." Ryan replied, "You can ask anything about my personal life, and instead, you focus on that?"

Bo nodded but followed with something even more profound. "You can tell a lot about someone by the things they carry."

Ryan shrugged off this comment. "Even so, for only being the second question, it seems like you're fishing."

"Fishing?"

"Yeah, out of ideas."

Bo laughed a bit. "Well, it's my question, so you need to answer it."

Ryan thought about the answer, wondering just what was inside his old drawstring bag. He knew it was not much—just things he needed for work—but he struggled to recollect its contents.

"I have some Advil," he said, "and my phone charger and this hat were in there." He motioned to the Rays cap on his head. "A sweatshirt," he hovered on the word a bit, "and a book, and a pen."

"What book?" Bo asked, stopping Ryan short.

"What book?" Ryan repeated, "What does that have to do—"

Bo sighed. "Ry, are we going to do this for the rest of the trip? You should know by now that the game is question and answer. Not question and question."

Ryan shook his head, again trying to find meaning in these questions. "Dostoevsky."

"*Brothers?*" Bo asked.

"No. *Crime and Punishment.*"

Bo nodded. "Ah, Raskolnikov."

"Yeah," Ryan said. "Though I didn't how to pronounce his name until now."

Bo laughed. "Russian literature was always my favorite. Tolstoy, Dostoevsky, all of them. I do, however, like some Dumas sometimes, but the French can be quite wordy."

"So, you've read *Crime* before?"

Bo nodded. "Many times. It's quite an inspirational novel."

"Not very often I hear of a double homicide being labeled 'inspirational.'"

Bo peered at him. "Ah, you've read it too, then?"

"Once. I'm trying to get through it again, though. I've been reading it for several months now."

"Well, then I'm sure you understand my take on it being inspirational."

Ryan nodded, recalling the book's messages. "Perhaps, though I find it more cautionary than inspirational."

"A cautionary tale? How so?"

Ryan paused. "I mean, the book is about his internal struggle to come clean with his actions. He wanders the city streets driving himself crazy, and it is only after he meets the hooker that his suffering is eased."

"Exactly, because of her love."

"Yeah, but after coming clean, then his physical punishment begins with the jail time. He had to suffer twice over his actions. You don't find that a bit cautionary? That he's a living embodiment of punishment based on actions and thoughts?"

"I'm not following," Bo reasoned.

"I think that Dostoevsky is showing us that punishments await our actions, no matter if we are right or wrong."

"But Raskolnikov was wrong."

"True. In a legal sense, he was wrong to commit murder, but letting her live would have been a negative action as well, just because she was a terrible person."

"So, what does that say about us, then?" Bo asked. "That we're screwed to punishments no matter our actions?"

Ryan thought about this. "No, because even R had some positive moments."

"R?"

"That's what I called him. I couldn't pronounce Rask-lon-i-vick."

"Raskolnikov?"

"Yeah, that. I couldn't pronounce that," Ryan replied sheepishly.

"Well, isn't that inspirational as well? That no matter how bad their actions, people can overcome and be redeemed?"

"How so?"

"Well, you said he had positive moments," Bo began. "Notably after he met Sofia, who provided his only remorse. And in the end, she even says she'll wait for him, and that gives him strength, showing that a person can be redeemed from even the most heinous acts. That's love to me, and that's inspirational!"

"I guess," Ryan replied. "But I still like my answer."

"The best part of that novel was the part where they sit down, and she pulls out the Bible and reads. I'll never forget it, but the line reads something like 'and the murderer and the harlot read the Gospel.'"

Ryan smiled, remembering the line.

"That's some deep shit," Bo said.

"Profoundly deep shit," Ryan added with a laugh.

Their laughter lingered on the air before silence reigned once more. For a long while, neither spoke. Instead, the interstate crept onward as the mile markers flew by one after another. Before long, Tennessee was upon them.

"Don't forget to honk your horn," Bo said as the welcome sign became visible.

Ryan smiled as the car crossed into the Volunteer State. He rattled off two honks, despite several cars being around him.

"Thanks." Bo nodded, leaning forward to look out the window. "Tennessee seems lovely." He paused and continued his visual tour. "It's pretty and dark." He laughed as he said this last part, knowing that the sun was already close to setting, and the landscape had already become darker.

"And cold," Ryan acknowledged, realizing that his car thermometer read a chilly 46 degrees, a far cry from the 80s of Florida.

"We are going north, my friend," Bo replied. "It's only going to get colder."

Ryan felt the car pull as he rounded the curves of the Tennessee hills. Before long, they were out of the urban lights and into the full darkness of the night ahead.

The Jeep kept on its way with little effort from Ryan, who felt his eyes grow heavy as they moved up and down the Tennessee mountains. Bo kept silent, but Ryan almost would have preferred him to speak. The journey was growing quite tiresome, though it was only six in the evening. It had been a long day, and Ryan knew it was not quite over yet. He looked down at his gas gauge once the land leveled out and saw he was nearing the empty mark.

Looking up, he noticed a sign that indicated Nashville was about an hour away. He knew he would not make it that far.

"So," Bo finally said, startling Ryan. "Two more questions."

Ryan arched his brow. "What do you mean two more questions?"

"Two more personal questions…"

Ryan looked around as if expecting to prove a point in the December night. "We're still in Tennessee."

"Yeah, but I screwed you out of your last question, so I'm giving you a mulligan."

Ryan laughed. "How decent of you." He contemplated the statement. "I assume that means you want a second one, too?"

Bo just smiled. "I wouldn't be opposed to it…"

Ryan rolled his eyes and adjusted his hands on the wheel.

"Let's see…Let's see…Let us see…" Bo scratched his chin as he looked out into the cold darkness. "I want to know…hmm…what do I want to know?"

"How long did you live in Spokane?"

Bo turned to Ryan with a shocked expression.

"I go first," Ryan said, keeping his eyes on the road.

Bo thought about this before responding. "Okay, I guess you can go first." He paused as if thinking of an answer to his question. When he finally spoke, it was short and to the point, as if he himself had just become satisfied with the answer. "I lived in Spokane until I was twenty-three. I moved to New York on my own after that and lived there for years."

"Why'd you move?"

"Job, honestly. I went hoping to work for a firm, and I finally got set up in this ratty-ass first-floor cubicle as an intern. I put every dime I had into that move."

"What'd your parents think?"

"They were all for it. Hell, my dad wanted me out. He knew I was better than a small-time town. They always prepared me for the difficulty, though, and for that, I was grateful."

"So, you worked two years before meeting your wife?"

"Something like that," Bo replied. "But they were quite eventful years of traveling for the company before it became quite legitimate."

"Sounds like an American dream."

"That's me." Bo's reply was tinged with sarcasm. "The American dream."

"Any good memories of Spokane?" Ryan countered after a moment's pause.

"Is this your second question?" Bo asked with a smile on his face.

"No, it's more of a follow-up to the first."

Bo wanted to challenge this, but he saw little use in it. Finally, he just gave in. "My favorite memory…hmm, that's a tough one."

The miles flew by as Bo pondered his answer.

"I'd have to say," he finally replied, "boating with my dad on Chesdin Lake."

"Chesdin Lake?" Ryan asked, unsure of the place.

"Yeah, it's a huge lake about a half hour out of Spokane. All freshwater, too." Bo smiled as he recalled the image. "There's at least seven or eight different kinds of trout, as well as some perch. We'd take the boat out there in the early morning and fish until noon or so. Dad would pop a Coors from the cooler, and I'd sit and stare at the water, just waiting for a bite. Then, after we had enough to eat, we'd head on back to the house and do some grilling." He paused as he thought about the words coming from his mouth. "You ever had fresh rainbow trout?"

Ryan shook his head.

"Delicious. Best dish ever. Sprinkle some lemon juice and some salt on there, and it's quite a treat."

"Sounds good," Ryan responded, realizing just how hungry he was.

"How long did you live in Florida?" Bo countered.

Ryan looked toward the passenger seat, indicating what Bo already knew.

"Yeah, fine, I'll take it as a question."

Ryan smiled. "All my life. I was born and raised in Clearwater. Even stayed for college."

"What'd you major in?" Bo asked nonchalantly.

Ryan took a deep breath. "Journalism, with a minor in communications."

"Hm," Bo retorted as he thought about this. "You don't strike me as a journalistic type."

"Well, apparently, neither did the *Tampa Tribune*."

"What happened?"

Now more awake than before, Ryan adjusted himself in the seat while keeping one hand on the wheel. "I had an internship there for my senior year, and over winter break, they promised me that if I kept up my grades, I'd have a permanent position. Even promised me a daily beat. Granted, the pay sucked, but it was a good starter gig."

"You didn't keep up your grades?"

Ryan shook his head. "Oh, I kept up my grades, but halfway through, the editor said he had reconsidered my role and there'd be no job for me come June."

"I'd be pissed if that happened to me."

"Oh, I was. But what could I say? At the time, it was all a blur."

Bo looked over as Ryan kept going.

"The editor said that he felt I wasn't 'passionate' enough in my work to warrant a position. He said he felt as though I didn't care about the job, and that I could do 'anything I wanted,' that I shouldn't 'waste time doing things I wasn't passionate about.' Seems I wanted to do more reinventing than reporting."

"Wow," Bo finally said. "That sucks."

"Yeah, and you know the worst part?"

Bo shook his head.

"He was absolutely right," Ryan answered. "I didn't care about the job."

Bo seemed confused.

"Stupid, right?" Ryan continued. "Go to school for four years and lose your interest after spending so much money to get a degree."

"You didn't enjoy journalism?"

Ryan considered this for a minute. "I liked writing the stories, but after studying it for so long, I just didn't have the same passion. I knew it, but I tried hiding it every day." He took a deep breath. "Unfortunately, my passion wasn't measured in my tests, so my professors and everyone thought I was good at it and that I cared when deep down, I didn't. I got lucky on tests. That's about it. It wasn't until that internship that someone finally called me out on it."

Bo was silent.

"The most ironic part? I won that internship based on my interview alone. I beat several people who were much stronger candidates than me on paper. I have no idea how that happened."

"You must have some endearing qualities they saw," Bo reasoned.

"I speak well, I guess," Ryan countered. "I'm…articulate."

"That should count for something…"

"You'd think. But instead, I spent four years in school so I could work retail, and now I can't even do that." He barked out a laugh. "If that isn't wasting a degree, then I don't know what is."

"Not necessarily," Bo said with a straight face. "Life is all about finding passions, and you spent four years earning a piece of paper that told you one thing you aren't passionate about." He shrugged his shoulders. "That's something."

Ryan chuckled. "Great, so four years to eliminate one thing. I guess that means when I hit 167 and am indebted to student loans for billions of dollars, I might figure out what I want to do."

"Ha!" Bo laughed. "I doubt it'll take that long. You have to have things you want to want to do!"

"Yeah," Ryan said. "But last time I checked, reading books and traveling the country aren't really feasible sources of income."

"Good benefits, though," Bo replied with a sly grin.

Ryan shook his head, knowing that it was indeed true. He pondered this for a moment longer before noticing that his low gas light was illuminated.

"We need to stop," he said, noting that the next exit was only a mile ahead. His thoughts were no longer on the discussion. Instead, they reverted to something he had tried to forget: he was out of money.

The Jeep coasted to a stop next to a gas station just outside Murfreesboro.

"I'm going to go pee," Bo said as Ryan got out as well. Once Bo was out of sight, Ryan felt his body tense as he leaned against the Jeep, knowing he was seemingly at his endgame.

He felt in his pocket for the coins he considered using back in Florida and knew he had little choice but to call his parents and explain his situation.

Ryan kept trying to make himself buy into it. He kept thinking over and over how it was the right thing to give up—how Bo would understand. He walked to the payphone and inserted the coins. He felt himself dial the numbers. And he felt himself listen as the phone began to ring. He also felt himself reach into his back pocket and pull out his wallet, as if a final check of its lack of money would confirm that he was making the right decision.

But the lack of money was not what grabbed his attention. As the ringing continued, he stared deep into his wallet as if seeing it for the first time. His eyes were captivated by the only photo present: one of him and his parents. Yet it was not the photo itself that held his gaze. Instead, just behind the photo, with indentations that showed through the family portrait, was a thick card—a credit card. It did not, however, belong to Ryan.

With a look of horrified amazement, he pulled his father's credit card from his wallet. As the realization sank in, Bo emerged from the bathroom and joined him with a similar look of realization on his face.

Over the ringing, Ryan heard Bo exclaim, "Isn't that coincidental?" as he pointed toward the sky.

"Hello?" Ryan's mother answered the phone, but it was too late. Ryan was too absorbed in the moment to respond. He followed Bo's finger to discover the source of the coincidence, and everything became clear.

"Hello?" Ryan heard his mother repeat the word, but he could not speak. Like a moth to a flame, he gazed up at the dark green letters that read "Gibson's Gas." Only a moment later, he saw the main anchor store just behind the station itself. He quickly scanned the front of the Gibson's store to find the smaller sign he had desperately hoped to see.

"Is anyone there?" Ryan's mother said. "Hello?"

Ryan dropped the phone back onto the hook, slowly realizing what fate had lain before him.

Holding his father's credit card in his hands, he looked over to Bo and back to the store. He nodded slowly as the plan formed in his mind.

With a long, nervous stare, Ryan turned away from the payphone and began walking to the main store, Bo following behind. There was still time, he knew. There was still time to make it to Washington. Despite all the odds, he had made it this far, and he was not about to give up. He was not ready to give up.

Entering the store, he looked up again to ensure the sign he had hoped to see was still there. Swallowing the lump in his throat, he took a deep breath as he read the words: *ATM inside.*

Ryan had been inside a Gibson's Department Store less than twenty-four hours before, yet it felt like a millennium as he and Bo walked through the automatic doors and into the green-plastered retailer. Ryan breathed deeply, inhaling the familiar smell of a job gone by that even here, states away, permeated his senses. In front of him, the familiar Gibson's greeter stood and acknowledged them, though Ryan wanted little to do with the conversation.

"Why did we come in here?" Bo asked.

Ryan looked around once more, realizing that he was taking longer than a usual customer would to exam the store.

"Is that a question?" Ryan smirked, trying to downplay the situation at hand as he moved to the left and into the clothing section.

"More rhetoric, I suppose." Bo trailed off, noticing that Ryan was on the move. "I just find it odd," he continued, "that you'd be so eager to enter the establishment that fired you yesterday…"

Ryan considered this as he surveyed the store. "This establishment never fired me." He found the ATM near the first cash register. "The one in Clearwater did."

"Still…" Bo countered. He looked around the store. "Why are we here?"

"We're here," Ryan finally said, "to pick out clothes for you." He stepped toward the men's section on his left while eyeing the ATM across the main walkway.

Bo looked at him quizzically. "Clothes?"

Ryan nodded, though he was not sure how well the ruse was working. "Yep. Clothes."

"Why now?"

"What do you mean, why now? It's like 30 degrees out there, and you're dressed like you just got off the goddamn Tommy Bahama plane."

"I like my wardrobe." Bo indicated his Hawaiian-style shirt and pants.

"Yeah, well, you'll need a jacket or something. It's December, for Christ's sake. Pick out a jacket or a scarf or something."

"What about you?" Bo asked as Ryan turned away.

Ryan could feel the sweat on his brow as he kept up his lie. "What about me?"

"Don't you need a jacket? That college one is pretty thin."

Ryan considered this for a moment. "Yeah, pick out one. I'll meet you at the register. Hurry up."

Ryan moved away, hoping he was leaving enough time for Bo not to question anything anymore. He approached the ATM, turning so he was just out of Bo's line of sight.

He pulled the credit card from his wallet. Hands shaking, he inserted the card.

He looked around nervously and then focused on the screen.

Enter PIN.

Ryan stood still for a second, perplexed.

You know this, he thought. *Breathe.*

He punched in four numbers.

The main screen popped up. He touched the Withdrawal button slowly.

How much?

Ryan could feel his breaths. He looked over the screen.

Daily limit on cash advances is $2,000.

Two thousand dollars…

He nervously typed in a five followed by two zeros.

Are you sure?

The machine was judging, Ryan knew. Was he sure? Was he really?

Ryan hit Yes.

The machine made a series of processing noises, each of which made him quiver with fear. In seconds, however, the bottom door opened, and five hundred-dollar bills appeared.

Ryan blinked in disbelief.

He quickly reached down and pulled the money from the slot. He knew he could not spend too much time staring at it. He ejected the card and was stepping away from the machine in seconds. He stared at it in surprise for just a moment more before returning to the men's section.

"Checking out, sir?" a cashier asked as Ryan and Bo approached. She had a thick drawl that Ryan may have found as attractive at any other time, but now he was focused on other things.

Ryan glanced at the ATM and was instantly curious if she had been watching him the entire time. He could feel the sweat on his brow.

"I need to pee again," Bo said rather loudly, bringing Ryan back into the present. He stepped away from the counter, and the cashier watched him go. Her gaze returned to Ryan as though questioning the situation.

Ryan nervously set the jackets on the belt. "He…he just came back from overseas."

The cashier turned her head. "Overseas?"

"Yep."

"How long was he out of the country?" she asked as she scanned the first jacket.

"Two years," Ryan replied, perhaps too quickly. "Missionary work in Sudan."

She smiled and turned to the register. "We respect that kind of work 'round here."

Ryan knew he had dodged a bullet. "Amen."

"That'll be $85.65," she said.

Ryan pulled one of the bills from his wallet and handed it over.

"He probably isn't used to the cold," she said as she opened the drawer.

"Nope," Ryan replied. "That's why we're here."

She glanced back over her shoulder as if looking for Bo. Her voice dropped to a whisper. "I can only imagine how that amount of time would change a person…"

He could not tell if she was concerned or saddened, but he chose the latter.

Gulping down the lump in his throat, he nodded. "Yeah, his, uh, social skills are coming back to him slowly. It takes time." He grabbed his bags.

She nodded in understanding. "Well, you make sure you get him back and running, okay? He looks rough."

Ryan smiled in return. "Will do, miss."

"Have a good night, sir," she added as she handed him his receipt.

"You as well," Ryan replied as he turned away. He found Bo near the exit soon after. Together they made their way toward the door, and as they passed the ATM, he exhaled and closed his eyes. Clutching the receipt paper in a death grip, he stuffed it into his pocket. He opened his eyes and moved out of the store without ever looking back.

***

All thoughts of exhaustion left Ryan as soon as he got back into the Jeep. After filling up the tank with Gibson's gas and grabbing some snacks from the convenience store, they were back on the road without so much as a single question from Bo. Ryan tried to reason that perhaps the plan had worked so well that Bo had not noticed anything was amiss.

But the farther they went down the road, the more apprehensive Ryan became. The memory of his actions tumbled in his mind like a pair of dice, and he could not stop thinking about it. Surely, he set off some alarm. Surely, he was seen on one of the hundreds of cameras. Surely, he was moments away from being caught.

He kept glancing in the rearview, half-expecting flashing red and blue lights. Every headlight made him more nervous. The farther he went, the more it was becoming too much to bear.

Nashville came and went before Ryan had a chance to realize it, and before long, the darkness that began to plague his eyes once more. He glanced at the thermometer and saw that it had already dropped to 18 degrees. He turned the heat up. His hands shook as they turned the dial, and he could not tell if it was from nerves or the weather.

"This old Jeep isn't used to the cold…" Bo said next to him as he pushed his seat back. "Neither am I."

"What? Being from up north should have prepared you for this," Ryan replied.

"Ha! I haven't been up north in years."

"Why'd you move?"

Bo leaned back as if to sleep, though he kept on talking. "That your question for this state?"

Ryan shook his head. He might have agreed to this game, but now it was growing tiresome. "Sure," he finally said.

"I needed to get out of the city. I needed a change."

"So, let me get this straight…your wife leaves and moves to Spokane, and after that, you decide to leave?"

"Are you asking or telling me?"

Ryan shrugged. "Well, I don't know; it just seems strange. Why not just leave and move back with her? If you were going to leave the city and all…"

"It took me a little while to get to that point."

"Does she know you left?"

"No," Bo replied. He turned to look out the window, and Ryan could sense agitation. "Maybe?"

"Which is it?"

"I don't know."

"How do you not know?"

"Because I don't!" Bo snapped.

Silence.

Ryan stared at the road ahead. He had never seen Bo upset. Nevertheless, it did not make him nervous or scared, but rather curious as to what the man was hiding. Regardless, knew he had once again struck a nerve, and he decided it best to remain quiet. Soon enough, though, he noticed the Kentucky state line fast approaching, and he could not let the awkward silence hold strong.

BEEP BEEP

Bo looked over at Ryan, whose hand still rested on the horn.

"Ken—" Ryan said, though he could tell Bo was still upset. "Kentucky…"

Bo shook his head. "I'm sorry. I shouldn't have yelled like that."

Ryan remained silent.

"It's just … there isn't a whole lot to tell when it comes to my life, strange as that sounds."

"It's cool," Ryan replied. "But if it helps any, I still feel like I know nothing about you."

Bo chuckled. "There's plenty of time left, don't worry."

Bo laid back in his seat again. "Aren't you tired?" he finally asked as he looked over to Ryan.

"I am."

"Why don't you pull over to get some sleep?"

Ryan had already considered it. Finding sleep out on the open road, with any number of patrolling police? There was no way. He needed shelter more than anything else.

"I'm fine."

"Do you know where you're trying to make it to?"

Ryan exhaled. There was only one answer, and he had been thinking about it for the past few hours. As much as he had never planned to be here, he knew there was only one logical safe place ahead.

"St. Louis."

"What?"

"St. Louis," Ryan replied. "I'll sleep when we get to St. Louis." The words left his mouth, but he was not sure if he even believed it.

Bo seemed confused. "What's in St. Louis?"

"A bed. Or couch. Or something."

Ryan knew that Bo did not like that answer, but he said no more.

"Fine," Bo caved. "Make it my Tennessee question. Who's in St. Louis?"

Ryan sighed, not even remotely wanting to answer the question. "My cousin Brandon. He has an apartment west of the city. Hopefully, he'll let us crash there."

"You going to call him or anything?"

Ryan thought about it. "No, we're just going to show up and see what happens."

"I see," Bo responded without emotion. "You and him close?"

Ryan thought about this. "We used to be. We've kind of grown apart since high school. He went to FSU and then came up here for med school, and I stayed behind in Tampa, so yeah…we're kind of different people."

"Med school?"

"Yeah, he's, uh, pretty successful. At least that's what my parents say. Plans on graduating next year and already has his first job lined up."

"I'm assuming it's not Gibson's Department Store."

Ryan shook off the comment. "Not that I'm aware of."

"Does it bother you?"

"What? That he's not working in a department store? Or that he's actually working a job he likes? Or that he's a thousand times more successful than me? No, not at all."

Bo laughed. "Success is relative. Remember that."

"By relative," Ryan continued, "you mean it's my relatives who are always telling me how awesome and amazing he is? Right?"

"Clever," Bo chuckled, "But no."

Ryan shook his head. "His mom even sends us Christmas cards, highlighting the work he's been doing. Every year she makes it sound like he's the poster child for fixing spines. She even puts in medical terms, like 'Brandon realigned the C4 and C9 vertebrae during a February procedure, allowing the small child to walk again.' It's like he's Jesus or something."

"That is a pretty similar comparison…" Bo reasoned.

"Great," Ryan replied. "You can spend our visit worshiping him, then. Maybe he can walk across his in-ground pool that I'll never be able to afford."

Bo laughed. "Then why do you want to stay with him if you dislike him so much?"

Ryan already knew the answer. "It'll give us a break from the road." He was not sure if he even believed his rationale.

"I'm assuming it isn't pride…"

Ryan just shot him an icy glance. "He has a warm couch and a place to charge my phone."

"If you're going to lie," Bo laughed, "at least come up with a better one than electricity. You haven't cared about your phone since we left."

Ryan shrugged. "Because I'm trying to forget that it's under your seat."

Bo looked down at the floorboards and noticed for the first time that the phone was sticking out from under the seat. He reached down and picked it up before pushing the power button.

"Dead," he finally said.

"Hence, the need for a power cord," Ryan confirmed.

Bo studied the phone. "You didn't think you should charge it before picking up a homeless guy?" His voice dripped with sarcasm. "Don't you watch horror movies?"

Ryan thought about it for a minute. "No, not really."

Bo laughed, putting the phone into the center console.

Ryan laughed, too, but his smile faded after a minute. "Truth is," he began, "I know what's going to be on that phone once I turn it on, and I don't really want to deal with that."

"What's that?"

"Texts. Voicemails. Her voice."

"You seem pretty convinced that's what's going to be there."

Ryan shrugged. "It was the only thing on there two days ago."

"So, you haven't checked in two days?"

"Hard to check when its dead."

Bo considered this for a moment. "What if there aren't any voicemails or texts on there?"

"But there are."

"But what if there aren't?"

Ryan was slightly annoyed. "There are. I know it."

"Okay, but what if there weren't?" Bo repeated. "Follow me. What if there weren't any texts or voicemails or anything?"

Ryan thought about it, albeit with annoyance. "Then there wouldn't be any."

"And how would you feel?"

"I'd feel…I'd feel like I wouldn't be nervous about turning on my phone."

"Why?"

"What do you mean, why?" Ryan snapped.

"I mean…why? Why do her messages make you apprehensive?"

"Because they do!" Ryan snapped. He lowered his voice. "Nobody wants to hear messages from your ex *after* your breakup."

"You do."

Ryan shook his head. "What? No, I don't."

"Sure you do. You said so yourself. You said, 'I need to charge my phone,' meaning, 'I need to charge it so I can turn it on and look at it.'"

"Bullshit," Ryan interjected, "You just completely twisted my words—"

"I'd like to ask my question for Kentucky," Bo interrupted.

"Go to hell," Ryan replied. "You've already asked several questions."

"And you answered them willingly. So now I want to ask a question that you have to answer."

Ryan shook his head, knowing there was still no way out.

"Earlier," Bo began, "you told me that it was, quote, *your fault* the relationship ended. You said you were a terrible person. So, with all that said, why do you feel the need to punish yourself further by enduring these messages?"

Ryan stared at the road and contemplated Bo's words.

"You're going to have to say that all again."

"Listening to those messages," Bo said, "will bring you nothing but pain. So why do you have to listen to them? Why even bother? It seems like it's just compounding the pain you already feel. You're already days away from the situation."

Ryan felt the weight of the question in his stomach, but he could not begin to form a coherent thought or a semblance of an answer.

"I never said I had to listen…I mean, I just…" He paused, and Bo remained silent. "You think I want to punish myself?" he finally asked. "You think this,"—he motioned to the car— "all of this—the phone, the self-imposed exile—all of it is me punishing myself? That's what you think?"

"Not at all. I'm just listening to you talk." Bo adjusted himself in his seat as if readying for sleep. "I do, however, think that maybe you have a bit of Raskolnikov in you after all."

Ryan could not quite tell if Bo was serious in his assertions. The older man leaned back in his seat and turned toward the window, though Ryan was far from done on the topic.

"If I am aiming to punish myself," Ryan said, "why are you here?"

Bo rose in his seat and turned back to Ryan, contemplating the question. "What do you mean?"

"If this is me punishing myself, then what purpose do you serve in it?"

Bo considered it.

"Or maybe," Ryan continued, "maybe we are both punishing ourselves."

Bo chuckled at the notion.

"I'm serious," Ryan replied.

More silence.

"Maybe you're right," Bo replied.

Ryan considered this. "If I am…then what are you punishing yourself for?"

Bo turned back toward the window as he lay back in his seat. "I guess I'm still trying to understand that, too…"

Ryan laughed. "Well, when you figure it out, share it with me."

"Will do," Bo replied as he faced the window and closed his eyes. "Wake me when we get to Saint Louie."

Ryan yawned and nodded, keeping his foot on the gas. There was more there, he knew, but it was obvious that in his sleep-deprived state, none of it would make sense. Punishments and crimes, breakups, and voicemails—it was all too much to consider. Perhaps he did want to hurt himself. Perhaps there was more to his drive. Whatever the case, he would not solve the riddle tonight. Time was of the essence, and there were still many miles to go.

***

BANG. BANG. BANG.

Brandon Collins heard his door slam under the weight of the person pounding upon it. Waking from a sound sleep, he glanced at the clock on the bedside table that read just past two in the morning. He made his way to his closet door and threw on his robe.

BANG. BANG. BANG.

The pounding came again as Brandon hurried toward the front door, taking care to grab his glasses as he did.

"Who the hell—" Brandon breathed as he unbolted the door and threw it back. In surprise, he saw the familiar face on the other side of the screen door.

"Ryan?" he asked, though the tone was more suspicious than surprised. He opened the door and stepped onto the front stoop, glancing to the left to notice the man in the Tommy Bahama shirt as well.

Adjusting his glasses on his sharp nose, he cast Ryan a disappointed look.

"Shit," he sighed, looking his cousin up and down. "What'd you do now?"

***

The table Ryan found himself sitting at was more of an island than an actual table, yet it had the same level of hominess that he expected to find at his aunt's house, not in the house of his doctor cousin.

The fear that had gripped him on the drive seemed to wane. Although he dreaded the visit, he knew it would help him relax, and upon entering the house, he had felt just that. His Jeep was backed into a driveway where the plates were hidden. The street was quiet and calm. There would be no one looking for him here—if they were even looking for him at all.

Ryan's eyes wandered over walls mostly adorned with modern art, with a picture of the Parisian skyline over the only blank wall in the kitchen, as if it were a window and not merely a painting. He sat slumped over the table that separated the kitchen from the living room as his cousin stood in his robe over the stove, heating a pot of tea that he poured into two cups. He passed one to Ryan.

"Thanks for, you know, for letting us in," he said as he accepted the cup. His hands were now steady, a welcome change from the previous hours.

Brandon took off his glasses and wiped them onto his robe before leaning against the opposite wall.

Upon arriving at the house, Ryan was curious as Brandon asked little in the way of questions. He eyed Bo suspiciously but opened the door nonetheless. As Brandon had tried to maintain his hospitality in truly inhospitable times, Ryan was quick to assure his cousin that they would only be there for the night and that they would be gone come morning. Brandon did not respond directly to the comment, but instead showed Bo to the spare bedroom that included its own bathroom. As he did so, Ryan took his seat at the counter and waited for his cousin to return, though the weight of the day's travels lay heavy on him. Before long, Brandon had returned to the kitchen and started the pot of tea.

"I'm sure," Ryan began in earnest, "...I'm sure you have a lot of questions..."

"I hung up your jackets in the entryway," Brandon responded.

"I'm sure you have plenty of questions," Ryan repeated.

"I do," Brandon said abruptly, putting on his glasses.

Ryan sipped his tea. "Well, let me try to explain—"

"No," Brandon interjected. "That's okay. I don't want an explanation."

"What do you mean?"

Brandon raised his cup to his lips. "What do you mean, what do I mean? It's simple. I don't want an explanation."

"Why...why not?"

Brandon chuckled humorlessly. "My cousin, who I haven't seen in, what, two years? Anyway, my cousin, who should probably be over a thousand miles away, shows up on my doorstep with some stranger and says he needs a place to stay. That's a pretty big thing to have to explain."

Ryan set his cup down. "Well, I can. I promise."

"I don't want to hear it," Brandon replied defiantly. "Whatever reason you're here in St. Louis, or whatever reason you're with that guy, I don't want to know. I want to be ignorant of it."

"Why?"

Brandon's voice rose. "Because I don't want to know! The less I know, the better. That means the less I have to answer when someone asks me why you were here."

"No one knows I'm here." Ryan said it more to himself than to his cousin.

"And how long do you expect that to last? Wait." He paused, "Don't answer that. I don't want to know. Listen." He paused again, drawing breath. "I don't want anything to do with whatever you're doing, so I'll give you a bed and a shower, but that's it."

Ryan understood, but he did not like Brandon's accusatory tone.

"Just answer me one thing," Brandon finally said. "Are you okay?"

Ryan sipped his tea, knowing exactly what Brandon meant, though was not sure how to answer the question.

"I'm fine," he finally said.

"Good," Brandon replied.

Ryan looked at Brandon for a few moments, knowing that his cousin was conflicted inside. "I promise I'm fine. Don't worry. No one will ever know I was here."

Brandon closed his eyes and set down his cup. "Ryan, they might not know you're here, but they know you're gone."

Ryan eyed his cousin with worry.

Brandon continued, "Your mom called me yesterday morning. She hadn't heard from you after work, and your neighbor told her about you getting fired. Dude, she's worried."

Ryan stared at his cousin. "You talked to my mom?"

"We talk like once every other week."

"Since when?"

"Since always. I talk with your dad too."

Ryan became instantly annoyed. "What'd you say?"

Brandon sighed, "I told her you probably just hung out at a friend's house for the night and that she shouldn't worry. I honestly couldn't have cared less, but then you showed up here, and suddenly I'm involved now."

"A friend's house?"

"Yeah, she didn't believe me, either," Brandon replied. "But I guess she figured if anyone knew where you were, it'd be me for some reason."

Ryan shook his head and sipped his tea. "I guess she was right."

"Damn right, she was. And now I'll have to call her tomorrow and tell her you're okay."

"You don't have to do that."

Brandon crossed his arms, "What? You want your own mother to worry to death?"

"No...it isn't like that."

"Then you should call her tomorrow."

Ryan almost stood. "No..."

"No?"

"No. Listen, I didn't come here for your direction." His voice gained steam as he finally confronted his cousin. "I came here for your help and for a bed and for a shower that you said you'd provide. That's it. I don't need anything else, and I certainly don't need you to be my confidant. Now, if you don't want to help, I'll gladly leave, and you can forget I came." He semi-made for the door, but even he knew the threat was in vain.

Brandon shook his head. "I'm not going to let you leave at two in the morning when it's ten degrees out there."

Ryan paused before returning to his seat. "That's up to you."

Brandon sipped his tea in the ensuing silence. "Your confidant?" he asked finally, staring out over his mug.

Ryan shrugged. "I ran out of words."

"No, I liked it. It's classy."

Ryan sat back down. "Four years of college; I guess I got something."

Brandon smiled weakly before taking another sip. "I'll keep your visit secret," he said as Ryan nodded, "until she calls me again. But I'm not going to lie for you, Ryan." His voice was tense and strained, as if under a lot of stress. "I'll tell her you were here, but that you left, and I don't know where you were heading. And none of that will be a lie."

Ryan sighed. "Fine."

Brandon emptied his cup and set it in the sink. "We can continue this discussion in the morning, but for now, I need to get to bed. I have a lot going on tomorrow, which is why I might be a little more than stressed."

Ryan immediately felt bad, though he knew he could do little.

"You'll have to sleep on the couch since your buddy took the bed." Brandon moved to a cabinet in the living room and pulled out some bedding, "I have a pillow and a blanket here. You can use the bathroom beside the spare bedroom if needed. I'll put some more soap and everything in there for you tomorrow."

"Thanks, I appreciate it."

Brandon walked toward his own bedroom. "Make sure you turn the lights out."

Ryan nodded. "Will do."

Brandon paused at his door. "And Ry—" he began, and Ryan sensed his tone change. "It's good to see you."

Ryan smiled as he moved to the couch, not wanting to waste any of his night's rest. "Same."

"Goodnight," Brandon added. He closed the bedroom door, leaving Ryan alone.

Ryan sighed as he lay down on the couch and pulled the blanket over his shoulders. It had been quite a day, and it was seemingly only just beginning.

"What have I gotten myself into?" he whispered aloud. Before he could answer, his eyes drooped, and he was off into a deep and uneasy sleep.

Chapter 7
Four Years and Seven Months to Spokane

"How does it relate?" Mrs. Laurel asked as she stood in front of the class.

The group was silent as it struggled to answer. Air rattling through the vents provided the only noise in the room.

"I presented two ideas," she continued, "and I want you to tell me how they relate."

The students focused on the board, where the words "Rob" and "Gen Y" were written on opposite ends.

"You see," she finally said, "this is essentially Part Three of your AP test—receive a topic, pick a book, and make an argument. So, with that said, make this one for me."

In the back of the class, Ryan stared at *High Fidelity* on his desk, wondering if the record pieces in the picture would actually line up.

"Consider the overall question," she added as she held up a guidebook. "Psychologist Jean Twenge defined the Y generation, or millennials, as having traits of confidence and tolerance as well as narcissism and entitlement. A Pew Research Center examination called Gen Y 'detached from institutions.' Examine one particular character from the books listed below and explain how they fit the Pew, Twenge, or perhaps even your own idea of a millennial, even if they are not directly in the millennial generation."

Sensing that the class was still not grasping the concept, she moved to the side to show the board in full view.

"Let's start here. How is Rob Fleming a millennial?"

"He whines a lot…" a voice said near Ryan's right.

She laughed. "He's also been dumped five times. It's a good point, though. Tell me how whining fits into the question."

"Millennials are whiners?" another student said from the front. "My dad says that all the time."

She laughed again. "Let's start here. What does it mean to you then? Being a millennial?"

A student toward the front named Mindy considered it. "Technology savvy."

"That's a good one," Mrs. Laurel responded. "You all are more apt to use technology. What else?"

A boy in the back of the class spoke up. "We have more access to other cultures and people. We have the technology and the internet to learn from." He paused. "We know more about the world at seventeen than most generations knew at thirty or fifty."

"That's good, Deion," she replied. "Tell me more about the internet. How does that factor in?"

"We grew up with it."

"We also grew up without it," a student next to him said.

Mrs. Laurel nodded. "It's true. The beginning of your lives did not have computers or the internet. You're all coming up with a thesis right now. Keep going."

"We started in the dark ages, and now we're in a world so different from our youth," Deion said. "It can be overwhelming—2006 sometimes feels more like 2506."

"In what way, Deion?"

"We're no longer isolated. We can compare our lives to everyone else in the world. Myspace, AOL—we're no longer limited to people in our class. It's impossible not to become a little vain, knowing you're judged by so many people. We're the first generation exposed to that level of openness."

"So, you're saying," Mrs. Laurel interjected, "that your life, or life success, is no longer based on the siblings or classmates you see every day, but rather everyone in the world because you can see them online at any time."

"It's overwhelming."

Mrs. Laurel considered it. "Steven, you've been unusually quiet."

A boy toward the back of the class looked up from his textbook.

"What do you think?"

Steven considered it. "I feel...like maybe Rob just cares more about figuring out why he keeps getting dumped."

She laughed, and the class chuckled as well.

"How about on being a millennial?"

"I don't know; I kind of agree with Deion."

"In what way?"

Steven looked down at his book as he collected his thoughts. "It's like, we have nostalgia for the past, but not even a real past." He paused as he considered his wording. "It's a past where sports stars weren't tainted by steroids or politicians weren't tainted by affairs. Or even a past where people didn't divorce. We grew up on the pure stuff. Now, nothing in the past is pure. On the flip side," he continued, "we are disconnected from the future because it moved faster than we did. We evolved into Myspace and AOL, but now it's moved on to technology we can't grasp. We knew it would happen because everyone said it would, yet we were never able to prepare. That's how it feels. It feels like we missed a stop we spent all day waiting for. And we don't want to continue to sit on the train like our parents did and their parents before them, but we just can't quite make it off."

"So, what do you do?"

Steven considered this. "My sister joined the Peace Corps."

The class laughed.

A girl towards the left spoke up as the laughter died, "My brother just graduated and instead of college he moved to Seattle. Says he's taking time off."

"Time off Maggie?" Mrs. Laurel considered.

"Yeah," Maggie replied, "pissed my parents off to no end."

"Why do you think he did that? Or why did your sister join the Peace Corps Steven? How does that have to do with their generational status?"

Steven shrugged as his words formed. "I think they, or us..." He paused as he thought more. "We find purpose in experiences; in being fulfilled. In living in the moment. It's the only way we can feel like we are off the train, even if we aren't. So, we go on trips we can't afford. We move across the world, or to Seattle, to seek some form of enlightenment. We voice our opinions, and we live on whatever little money we have because it makes us feel *something*, and that makes us feel alive."

The class sat quietly as they pondered the words.

"That's some deep shit," Deion finally said, provoking more laughter among the class.

"I think that's a good thesis," Mrs. Laurel said with a smile. "Ryan, do you have anything to add?"

At the back of the class, Ryan pondered the words spoken by the boy seated directly in front of him, said, "No." He leaned back in his chair. "No, I think Steve summed it all up pretty good."

***

1,801 Miles to Spokane

It was quarter past seven when Ryan opened his eyes to a dawning sun. He raised his head, dogged by the pang of a tired headache. With a grunt, he raised himself from his makeshift bed, forgetting where he was for a minute.

The living room seemed much darker than it had last night. The shadows enveloped the room in shades of blue, and the artwork he had seen last night was indistinguishable in the darkness. If he squinted, it was almost like home. Even the air had a sweet hominess that he had forgotten he missed.

It had been three days since he had left.

Three days on the road, to a destination he had never been. Three days since he had packed his bag with his book and his charger and thrown it into the back of his Jeep. Three days since he had pulled out of his driveway for a job he would never go to again. Three days since he had naively thought everything was all right. Three days since a late-night breakup had started him on this path. Three days. Three long days.

Even his dreams would not give him peace. They were constant reminders of the troubles that had set him off and away from his home. Once he woke, though, the realization that home was a lifetime away sickened him more. There was no reprieve.

He sighed and shook his head as he put his feet on the floor. Standing wearily, he moved to the front door and peered out the side glass. To his relief, all looked normal and calm in the chilly December morning.

"Good morning." Ryan turned to see his cousin standing in the kitchen, sipping coffee, and reading a newspaper.

"Jesus Christ!" Ryan exclaimed, heart racing from the jolt.

Brandon smiled, though his mood had changed little.

"Looking for something?"

Ryan stepped away from the window and moved back to the couch. "Just checking the weather," he said after a moment.

"It's cold," Brandon replied, believing none of the statement. "December in Missouri." He rustled a bit in the kitchen. "Coffee?" he finally asked.

Ryan nodded. Although coffee was not his drink of choice, he would not turn down anything that could help him wake up.

Brandon filled a coffee cup while Ryan lay back on the couch and nursed his throbbing skull.

Moving into the living room, Brandon set the cup on the table nearest the couch as he examined his cousin. "How was the bed?"

Ryan sighed. "Bed's fine, just my head that's killing me."

"You could probably use more sleep."

Ryan picked up the coffee mug and took a sip. "I'd love to, but stupid dreams won't let me."

Brandon sat in a chair opposite the couch. "Rough week?"

"Rough year," Ryan replied.

Brandon got up and sauntered back into the kitchen. "This may cheer you up then," he said as he grabbed an item from the table and threw it to Ryan. "I believe this is yours."

Ryan looked down and saw a gray sweatshirt adorned with the Busch Gardens logo across the front.

"This is mine?"

"You let me borrow it the last time I was down there."

"Five years ago?"

"It probably still fits."

Ryan shrugged. "You could have kept it. I don't even remember this…"

"Well then," Brandon continued, "consider it a gift. A somewhat worn sweatshirt. I'm sure it's exactly what you've always wanted."

Ryan smiled. "All I've ever wanted…"

They both sat in silence before Ryan folded the sweatshirt and put it in his bag.

"You know," Brandon finally said as he leaned forward. "It can't all be that bad."

"Try me."

Brandon considered this. "Okay, how's the journalism thing going?"

"Considering your discussions with my mother, you should probably already know that I failed it."

"Okay, fair enough," Brandon said. "How's Rebecca?"

"Over, so I guess that's also a fail."

Brandon hung his head. "And your job I already know—"

"Failed it. As a matter of fact,"—Ryan sat up from the couch— "there isn't a whole lot I haven't failed at."

"I think you're exaggerating—"

"We just went 0 for 3," Ryan countered. "That'd be a bad ballgame, let alone life."

Brandon sighed. "Did you at least hit a few foul balls?"

"Out looking every time. It was as if the pitcher was throwing hundred-mile-per-hour heat from five feet away. I had no chance."

Brandon chuckled, though he took no pleasure in his cousin's misfortune. "What happened with Rebecca?"

Ryan lay back against the cushions and stared at the ceiling. "We mutually decided to end it."

"Mutually?"

He sighed. "I think that's what I'm supposed to say."

"It wasn't mutual?"

"It was yelling, and screaming, and a rough night." He looked at Brandon as if for the first time. "But you don't care."

"Of course I care! I'm your cousin."

Ryan leaned forward again as he downed his coffee. "Doesn't mean you have to care. You care because I'm here and sitting on your couch, and it's harder to ignore me when I seem this…messed up?"

"You don't seem messed up."

Ryan chuckled as he looked down at his three-day-old shirt. "I know how I look. I look like a mess."

"You look like you need help, and I'm here to help."

"You're giving me help," he said as he stood and handed his coffee cup to his cousin.

"And I appreciate it."

Brandon stood as he took the cup. "You need more help than I can give."

The comment hung in the air as Ryan stared at his cousin. Help. He needed more help. That's exactly what he thought. That's what they all felt.

A branch rattling against the window brought Ryan back to reality. He did not need help anymore. He was on his own. From the moment he had opened his car door, he was on his own, and he realized that he had never felt more alive. He was pissed and angry and resentful and full of spite, but he was here, and he was alive, and he had made it this far. He no longer needed any help. He had made his decisions. He no longer needed to hide.

He glanced up at his cousin.

"No," he said. "I need to get going."

"Going where?" Brandon followed Ryan as he walked into the bathroom and turned on the faucet.

"Last night, you said you didn't care." Ryan splashed water on his face and began to scrub with a bar of soap.

"I don't care," Brandon countered. "I just...dammit, Ryan, I want you to be safe."

Ryan laughed as he rinsed his face. "I am safe. Look at me. Safe and sound."

Brandon reached over and shut off the valve. "You know what I mean."

Ryan, slightly annoyed, grabbed a towel. "I'm fine."

"Do you even know this guy that you're traveling with? Ben? Bob?"

"Bo," Ryan replied as he moved quickly toward the front door. He peered outside once more, instinctively judging that his stay was growing less and less welcome.

"Bo," Brandon said. "Do you even know who he is?"

Ryan leaned down for his shoes and looked over his shoulder at his cousin. "Do I even know who you are?"

Brandon sighed.

"I haven't spoken to you in years; you know nothing about my life except what you hear from my mother." Ryan did not care how biting the words sounded.

"Same goes for you!" Brandon countered.

"Exactly—I know nothing about you." Ryan looked around. "Except that you seem to be doing quite well in life, so congrats." He began putting on his shoes.

"Why are you so bitter?"

Ryan snorted. "Because you don't understand anything about me. You think you do, but you don't."

"I'm just worried about your safety."

Ryan finished one shoe and began on the other. "And I appreciate that, but it isn't necessary. I'll be just fine." He finished and stood up. "And as for Bo, he's a nice guy from New York City, and...and he likes fishing for trout on Chesdin Lake in Washington."

"Trout?" Brandon replied, taken aback by the comment.

"Yeah, it's a fish," Ryan said before grabbing his bag and walking past his cousin toward the guest room.

Brandon followed him, pleading, "Ry, listen, don't leave like this."

"Brandon, please." Ryan made it to the door and pounded. "*Bo, wake up!*" He turned toward his cousin. "I appreciate your hospitality."

There was instant rustling in the guest room.

"Ryan, I don't know exactly what happened, but," Brandon began as the door opened.

Bo peeked out, still clad in his Tommy Bahama.

"What's going on?" he asked, still looking half-asleep.

"We're leaving," Ryan said with a fake smile, all while Brandon kept up his attempts at convincing.

"—You can fix the issues, get a new job, all that!"

"Oh, all right," Bo said, understanding the situation. He grabbed his bag. "Thanks for the room."

"Ryan!" Brandon pleaded, oblivious to the comment. "Don't act like it's all over! You still have so much ahead."

"Thanks for the couch," Ryan replied. He followed Bo out of the house with Brandon close behind.

"*Don't do this!*" Brandon shouted after them. "Ryan, stop it! Don't let this phase take control; you can still do anything!"

Ryan paused along the walkway to where his Jeep sat. He knew he had to choose his words wisely.

"This," he said as Bo got into the passenger side of the Jeep. "This is what I want to do."

He fired up the Jeep and squealed out onto the roadway. A second later, they were gone, leaving behind shelter, their jackets, and a cousin who stood bewildered on the doorstep.

The silence in the vehicle lay heavily as Ryan drove down the street a few blocks and pulled in at a gas station. He sighed as he put the car in park and rubbed his still-throbbing head. After a minute, he looked over and noticed that Bo was smiling faintly.

"Family, huh?"

Chapter 8
Four Years and Nine Months to Spokane

"I think she likes you," Michael said as he stuffed another fry into his mouth.

Ryan sat at the table across from him, somewhat incredulous. "No way."

Michael shrugged as he propped his feet on the booth. "I'm pretty sure, man. I can read these things."

"You can read these things?"

He stuffed in another fry. "Yeah, man."

Ryan looked up from his friend to see the girl look out from behind the counter.

"She's looking at us now," he replied, trying to look nonchalant.

"She's looking at you."

"She's worked here for maybe a month."

"I don't see how that matters," Michael said. "She's cute. Go for it."

"Go for it?"

"Yeah, man."

Ryan sat back and looked out the window to his left. In the sunlight, his name tag reflected off the glass, blinding him temporarily.

"She's got a nice butt…" Michael remarked.

"Why are you doing this?"

"Doing what?"

"This," Ryan replied. "Whatever the hell this is."

"Hooking you up with someone?" Michael sat back and wiped his mouth. "Because I'm a friend. And you can't keep hanging on to Lindsey like you are."

Ryan huffed. "I'm not hanging on to—"

"Dude, you've been in a six-month mourning period."

"I have not…"

"She doesn't like you."

"You don't—"

"She doesn't like you," Michael repeated. "This girl does."

"How do you—"

"Dude, she's always flirting. She's always looking at you while you're on the headset. Plus, I asked her."

"What?!"

"Keep your voice down," he said. "Listen, we're going to the movies tonight after work. Sit next to her. See what happens."

"And if I don't want to?"

Michael stood up and grabbed his tray. "You do."

"I do?"

"Dude, she's like the sweetest person here. She's funny, she's quirky, and"—he paused and sipped his drink— "I cannot stress this enough, she likes you."

"Then what? Start a relationship?"

Michael stared at him, wide-eyed. "Yes."

"And then what?" Ryan asked. "Get married? What about college? What about life after Chuck's Chicken?" He motioned around the restaurant.

"What about it?" Michael asked. "Jesus man, it's a movie. Go, sit, and see what happens. This mentality is why you're a virgin with one relationship under his belt."

"No," Ryan replied. "That's all because I'm awkward and not good looking."

"Whatever," Michael said. "I'm late from break."

"You really think I should?"

Michael turned around. "Yeah, man," he said, with his usual calm demeanor. "Like I said, you guys would be a perfect match. She's naïve. You're naïve. She's innocent. You're innocent. Every other guy here would just screw her over and break her heart, but you won't."

"I won't?"

"Really? You?" He paused once more. "That girl will break your heart before you break hers. Look at Lindsey. Look at anyone. You're not going to do that. You don't have that in you."

Ryan laughed.

"You're perfect for each other if you ask me," Michael said. "Just give it a shot and see what happens."

He walked away without another word, leaving Ryan staring into the distance. *Just give a shot*, he thought. His heart raced. *Just give it a shot. Take a risk. See what happens.* He sighed as he looked down at his watch. He was late from break. He looked up and saw Rebecca peering out from around the corner awkwardly. Smiling, he picked up his tray. She liked him, and he liked that. It felt good. It felt nice.

Give it a shot, he thought once more. *What's the worst that could happen?*

***

1,800 Miles to Spokane

Ryan sat still in the driver's seat. He stared out the window at the gas pumps ahead of him. At his right, Bo was still. All was silent except for the cars that passed on the roadway.

"Did you see his house?" Ryan said after a long moment, head propped on his arm next to the driver's window.

Bo did not respond. He knew the question was rhetorical.

"It was awesome, wasn't it? Full house, full kitchen. Artwork." Ryan barked a faint sarcastic chuckle. "Artwork. Christ, he had artwork."

He looked out the window, head still resting on his arm, but he did not care about what he saw outside.

"He offered me coffee…his own coffee. In his mug, on his couch."

"I think," Bo began carefully, "I think it's best not to focus on him."

"Why?" Ryan turned. "Weren't you impressed? Wasn't it a nice place?"

Bo swallowed. "It was a nice spare bedroom."

"Nice bed?"

Bo nodded.

"Dresser? Nightstand? The whole nine yards?"

Bo nodded again. Ryan's teeth clenched.

"Of course, he had it all. I bet he even had Egyptian cotton sheets or some bullshit."

Bo sighed. "It did have memory foam…"

Ryan threw his hands in the air and slammed his fists over and over on the steering wheel, cursing with a fury no man could stop. He threw open the driver's door and ripped himself from his seat, slamming the door behind him as he did. The fear from the night before was light years away.

"Ryan!" Bo yelled as he got out and followed. "Ryan, come back here!"

Ryan stopped dead in his tracks. He wheeled around with anger in his eyes.

"You're gonna tell me what to do now, too?"

Bo sighed. "No, I'm just…"

"Just what?" Ryan dared, "Just looking out for me? Just trying to help me?"

Bo raised his hands. "I'm just saying, I know what it feels like."

"Know what 'what' feels like?" Ryan retorted. "Failure? Complete and utter uselessness? The fact that everyone tells you 'you can do anything' except for, you know, anything?"

Bo remained silent.

"The fact that everyone says, 'it'll be all right' when you know damn well it won't?"

Bo nodded. "Yes. I know what that all feels like."

"With all due respect," Ryan challenged, "we are completely different."

He turned and walked away, but Bo was quick to follow. "And yet," Bo countered, "we both spent last night staring at a ceiling we don't own and lying on memory foam that wasn't ours."

Ryan stopped with his back to Bo, choosing his next words carefully. "You slept on memory foam. I had a couch."

Bo sighed heavily. "Yeah, well, it's all the same."

A moment stretched to eternity. Ryan finally turned toward Bo.

Bo stared at him for a long moment. "It sucks," he finally said. "It sucks when people try to fix problems they know nothing about. And if there is anyone who gets that, it's me."

Ryan considered the words. "It's like people finally try to take an interest in my life right at the moment I don't want them to."

Bo chuckled. "Well, in Brandon's defense, you did show up in the middle of the night with a random homeless guy, so that might be a bit perplexing."

"Still," Ryan countered. "I told him multiple times that I was fine."

"Come on, Ryan. No one believes it when someone says they're fine, and no one is ever fine when they say they are."

Ryan snorted. "Well, the way to help isn't saying I can do anything I want." He walked back to the Jeep and leaned on it.

"Yeah, that comment did seem to get you."

"I've been told that four times in the past few days."

Bo considered this. "What's wrong with that?"

"What's wrong is"—Ryan looked skyward, as if focusing on something miles above him— "that it's one hundred percent bullshit."

Bo did not know what to say.

"Astronaut, physicist, hell, even a doctor. I can't be those. I went to school for journalism, and I can't be that. Hell, I can't even work at a goddamn box store selling CD players."

"I think," Bo countered, "you're losing the context of the comment."

"No, I get the context of the comment. I can be *anything*. It means I can dream it and do it, and all this horse crap mumbo jumbo." He stared at the sky again. "Here's a great question, though. What if, hypothetically, I have no frickin' clue what I want to do?" He waited for Bo to say something, but nothing came. "I don't want to be an astronaut or a physicist. I sure as hell don't want to be a doctor. I spent four years on a degree in a field I don't care about, yet I have skills that are supposed to set me above other people because I finished school and have a piece of paper."

"Brandon, on the other hand, had his life set from the beginning, follows it to a tee, and now has coffee and artwork and a couch. I've spent two *more* years on this earth and have *less* than him. That makes sense. Oh, and in addition, I'm jobless, girlfriendless, and altogether the very definition of a mess, yet…yet he has a job and happiness."

Ryan sat on the ground by the driver's door and put his head in his hands.

"I—" Bo finally said, "I didn't see that."

"His job?" Ryan asked softly. "He's getting one when he graduates."

"No," Bo corrected. "The happiness. I never saw that."

Ryan scoffed.

"I'm serious. I didn't see happiness. I saw the coffee and the couch and all that stuff, but I didn't see him happy. I mean, he could have been, but I didn't see it. And if I recall, you never asked him…"

"That's your counter-argument? 'I didn't see it?'" Ryan laughed. "Let me guess, just because he has all that stuff, it doesn't make him happy."

"No, on the contrary, it probably does make him happy. I'm just saying that *we* don't know," Bo said. "What if he hates being a doctor and only does it because it was forced on him? What if he hates living alone?"

"Trust me, if he isn't happy, he's an idiot. He's got all that *and* money."

"And you have a car. And a family who takes you in when you need it."

"Quit it with that crap," Ryan snapped.

Bo looked around. "Hey, last I checked, I don't have a car. I did have a jacket you bought me, but it appears we left that…"

"You've made your point. It's always worse for you. I get it," Ryan countered. He shivered in the wind. "Damn, it's cold out here!" He got back in the car and slammed the door. Bo followed suit.

"I don't think I did," Bo replied, adjusting himself in his seat.

"Yes, you're saying that I shouldn't covet my neighbor or some other commandment."

Bo laughed. "No, not at all. I'm saying that you're too smart to be spiteful."

Ryan turned to him. "How do you figure?"

"Listen." Bo took a deep breath. "I may not 'know' you, but I know you. You aren't spiteful. You don't care what someone else has compared to what you don't have."

"Don't assume, because obviously, you don't know me," Ryan snarled.

"I'm serious," Bo replied with a fatherly tone. "That's not you. You are, on the other hand, at a very distressing point in your life, and with the distress come anger and rage and confusion."

"Distressing? What's distressing? Getting fired? Or the general lack of knowledge about where I am in life?"

"And you're sarcastic," Bo countered. "But most importantly, you are a terrible liar, and the real reason you're distressed and angry and confused is something much deeper than this surface-level bullshit."

Ryan scoffed. "Oh? And what's that?"

"I don't know. That's the million-dollar question, I think. So, why don't you tell me what the answer is?"

"The answer." Ryan leaned back in his seat. "Hell, I don't know."

Bo kept his gaze on his counterpart silently.

"How did we end up here?" Ryan said with uncertainty and confusion. "Hell, how did I end up here?" He paused. "You know...I graduated salutatorian."

"Really?" Bo replied. "That's like second in your class, right?"

Ryan laughed. "In my high school class, we had five valedictorians, so I was technically sixth, but you know."

"That's still impressive."

"I know. And I didn't earn it."

Bo chuckled. "You can't luck through four years of high school, Ry."

"I didn't luck through it either. I just didn't earn it." Ryan ran his fingers through his hair. "I didn't work hard. I barely studied. I would rather watch sports or something."

"Being naturally smart is still earning it, though," Bo countered.

"No, it isn't." Ryan took a deep breath. "The kids who weren't naturally smart, or smart enough to study—they're the ones that earned it. The five people in front of me, they earned it."

Bo shrugged. "I'm not following."

"I didn't study," Ryan replied. "I didn't apply myself. I listened in class and thought I was good enough to get by. And I was, except that instead of actually learning, I just...fluttered by. And you can't just flutter by in college." Cars rolled past the gas station, yet Ryan only gave them an occasional glance. "All those people," he continued. "All those people ahead of me, who actually *did* work, they soared. They had life figured out. They were the gifted ones. The ones getting grants and papers. I was just, you know...there."

"The sad part is, I thought I was the one who knew it all. I had it all figured out. I *could* be *anything*. I spent so much time waiting to *be* something that I never actually became anything." He gripped the steering wheel. "I wasn't smart. I was cocky. Arrogant. I didn't earn anything. I got away with everything. The medal they gave me was a fake. But they didn't know that. My parents didn't know that. When my college accepted me, they didn't know that, either. Even my internship. No one knew. No one figured it out."

"Until her." Bo finally said.

In an instant, tears welled up in Ryan's eyes. "She was pure," he began. "She was caring. She loved to impress me and show me how much she loved me. She was enthralled."

He took a deep breath.

"And I cheated on her."

Bo swallowed audibly. "Why?"

"Because...because...I don't know." He paused. "I was angry." Just the words brought back the emotion of the time. "Not on the surface, but underneath." He stared at the floor as he spoke his revelations aloud for the first time. "I was confused and upset, and the only way I could feel better was by tearing more things apart." He did not even know if that made sense. "And it was fine and good, and it made me feel better until it got to her."

"I still don't know what made me answer that text, but I did," he continued. "And the next day, all I could do was lie and lie and lie and lie."

"When did she finally figure you out?" Bo finally asked.

Ryan stared ahead. "Figure me out? That I was...*am* messed up? That I was destroying her? I don't know. Probably the first time she read my phone and saw my messages. Something inside her made her look, so she probably had an idea long before that. But she stayed with me, thinking I'd change. And...I didn't." He paused once more. "I haven't."

"What about the last night?" Bo asked. "Where did it happen?"

"Outside her house in front of my car," Ryan recalled. "She caught me again, and again I tried to plead with her. She fought more this time. Yelled. Called me names."

"Then what?"

"I didn't want to hear it. I wanted her to shut up." Ryan closed his eyes. "I needed her to shut up. I yelled at her, reeled at her. Then I told her...I told her I never loved her."

Ryan opened his eyes. "The look on her face was ..." He trailed off as he remembered it all. "She slid to the ground. One minute she was arguing with me, tearing me apart, and the next she was lying there next to her car, looking at me like I had just done something unspeakable."

"Then what happened?" Bo asked.

Ryan stared ahead. "Then, she cried. Not because I cheated, or yelled at her, or anything like that. She cried because I broke her heart."

"That was when I realized that we were too far gone. I told her I couldn't do it anymore. I couldn't be the person that kept disappointing her and lying to her. We just weren't going to make it. I told her that, and then I left.

"Worst of all...I broke her innocence, her heart. I made her someone she never was. The loving, caring girl I knew turned angry and spiteful because of me. When I pushed her far enough, I finally saw it."

After a long moment, Bo finally spoke. "How do you feel now, realizing it all?"

Ryan exhaled as he looked around. "Honestly, pretty shitty."

"I could see that."

"Maybe that's it. Maybe that's how I should feel." He sat up a little in his seat and ran his fingers through his hair. "Maybe I should feel that way because that's who I am. A shitty person."

Bo sat up as well. "You aren't a shitty person..."

"I'm not? Really? I cheated on someone who loved me, then told her I didn't love her at all."

"Okay, one example."

"Not to mention that I play with emotions and lead women on—"

"I think that's a bit much,"

"I verbally assaulted a pregnant woman."

"All right—"

"I have no respect for authority, be it my parents or any bosses," Ryan continued. "I gave up in school. I lie habitually. I have no regard for anyone's personal feelings, apparently. And what's worse? I blame all these things on everyone *but* myself. That's a pretty shitty person."

Bo stared at Ryan intently. "You're flawed."

Ryan gasped, "I'm flawed? That's like saying a Ferrari is a bit pricey. I'm a goddamn mess."

"Fine, you're a mess. Feel better?"

Ryan ignored the comment. "What's wrong with me?"

"You're a good guy, Ryan," Bo finally said.

Ryan laughed. "Wish I could believe you, but good guys don't cheat. They don't hurt people, and they sure as hell don't destroy hearts, lie, and run from their problems."

"Good guys have flaws, too." Bo retorted, "You just have some big ones that need working out."

Ryan scoffed.

"Most importantly, you need to realize your issues and let go of ones you can't change."

Ryan turned. "What do you mean?"

"I mean," Bo reasoned, "you broke her heart. You destroyed her. As bad as it is, you have to live with that and move on." He paused once more. "Did you love her?"

Ryan shrugged. "I loved who she was. I loved how we were. I just…knew we weren't meant to be."

"Well, you probably won't ever get to apologize."

"No," Ryan replied. "No, I've done too much damage to ever talk to her again. I don't deserve her forgiveness. She'll see that soon enough."

"Maybe she already has," Bo countered. "You haven't seen your phone. Maybe she's already moved on and accepted it."

Ryan exhaled. "Hopefully she has. She deserves better than me."

"Shitty people don't say things like that," Bo reasoned.

There was a pause.

"I'm not saying you're a hero, either," Bo added. "I'm just saying that you're flawed, and all flaws can be worked out." He looked around again. "I think the first thing we need, though, is to get you back to Brandon and let him help."

"Yeah, that's not going to happen."

"Listen, Ry, in all honesty—"

"In all honesty," Ryan interrupted, "I'm not going to talk to him. That will help nothing."

"He cares about you."

"And I'm glad, but you said yourself that I need to work on my flaws—"

"—Which include stubbornness—"

"Which include," Ryan corrected, "keeping my promises. And I promised to get you to Spokane."

"And I appreciate your courage, but—"

"But nothing, Bo. You need to get to Spokane, and I'm going to get you there." Ryan leaned forward and pulled his wallet from his pocket. Opening it, he noted the remaining two hundred dollars and change left in his pocket. Behind the bills, he pulled out the credit card in his father's name.

"What's that?" Bo asked, almost afraid of the answer.

"This? A credit card." He found his breath catching in his throat. His eyes darted around the car, as though pulling out the card would attract attention.

"For what?"

Ryan saw no one around and sighed with relief. They had made it this far. For all he knew, they had fallen off the grid. No one knew where they were or where they were going. They would not be caught.

Ryan put the card away and started the car. "For expenses," he said as shifted into drive. "Traveling expenses."

Chapter 9
1533 Miles to Spokane

"Ready for the next question?" Bo asked nonchalantly, somewhere between Kansas City and Iowa.

"Dear God," Ryan huffed. "We still playing this damn game?"

Bo stared at him incredulously. "Are we still playing—? Of course we are!" He shook his head in disbelief. "I can't believe you asked that."

"It's been like six hours in the car, and you haven't asked anything," Ryan countered. In truth, even he was surprised it had been that long. Nevertheless, he had kept quiet, allowing Bo to center the discussion on the passing cars and the Missouri scenery. The conversations of the morning had been intense enough.

"I never forget my questions," Bo said matter-of-factly. "And never assume the game is done."

"Suit yourself," Ryan said, changing lanes. "By all means, ask away."

"Hmm, okay...I believe we are up to Illinois for me and Kentucky for you."

"Sounds good."

"Good. Now, my Illinois question. Let me see...What's a good question...?"

"Come on, ask what you want," Ryan said, annoyed.

"I have to think, Ry."

"Don't act like you haven't known this question since we got into the car," Ryan countered. "Out with it."

"Fine, fine." Bo adjusted himself in the seat. "I want to know...did you get your phone charged at Brandon's house?"

"What?"

"Did you get your phone charged at—"

"I heard you," Ryan interrupted. "I just—What?"

"What, what?"

"You can ask anything, and you ask if I got my phone charged?"

Bo stared intently. "I feel like you never like my questions..."

"They're dumb questions."

"Not to me."

"I mean, come on." Ryan laughed. "Did I get my phone charged? What kind of question is that? You can ask anything you want, and you choose that one?"

"I think it's important."

"It's not."

Bo paused. "So, you didn't get it charged?"

"No, I didn't get it charged." Ryan sighed. "But what does that have to do with anything?"

"Is that your question?"

"No, it isn't my question," Ryan seethed. "And that wasn't your question. In fact, I'm going to punish you for asking that question by removing your next question. That's it. Done."

"You can't do that."

"I most certainly can. I helped make the rules."

"That's not fair!"

"Too bad. Don't ask dumb questions."

"It isn't a dumb question."

Ryan nodded. "Yes, it is."

"It isn't."

"How can you say that?"

Bo shrugged. "Because you specified that we needed to go to Brandon's to get your phone charged."

"And?"

"And you didn't get it charged."

Ryan shook his head. "I'm not following."

"Last night, you were concerned with your phone because of your ex. But the circumstances surrounding the night either made you forget or made you not care about the phone," Bo reasoned. "Now, if you did get your phone charged, it meant that you still cared enough to want to check. But if you didn't, that means you allowed other thoughts to cloud your intentions, meaning you were either letting go or devaluing the importance. Subconsciously, this proves you are beginning to move on, and that, hidden in my basic question, is what I was looking for."

Silence.

"And," Bo added, "I do *not* lose my question, but rather keep my question, and for questioning my use of questions, *you* lose a question."

Ryan stared ahead.

Bo smiled. "Don't ever question my questions again."

"Will do," a defeated Ryan said with a smile.

"Good, now it's your turn for your Illinois question."

Ryan leaned back in his seat. "For the record, I was a bit preoccupied with my cousin."

"Too late, ask your question."

Ryan glared at Bo before turning back to the road. "Let's see…" he said. "What's it like being…"

Bo leaned forward, clearly anticipating the question.

Ryan struggled. "You know…"

"Sexy?"

Ryan smiled. "Sans home."

"Homeless?"

"On the street," Ryan quickly added. "If you prefer." He paused. "What do you prefer? I think homeless sounds a bit…"

"Sad?"

"Yeah."

Bo shrugged. "Honestly, I don't really think most homeless people are concerned about what they're referred to. They just want the help." He paused. "Titles matter more to people with homes."

Ryan considered the weight of the statement.

Bo continued, "I assume you've never been…sans home, as you say."

Ryan nodded and shifted to place both hands on the wheel.

"Honestly," Bo began, "I don't know how to answer that."

"It's fine. It was a dumb question."

"It's madness," Bo said. "It's madness."

"Madness?"

"Yeah, that seems right."

"Madness?"

"Yeah. Insanity. Crazy. That's what it's like." He spoke evenly, though Ryan could tell he was deep in thought. "It's hard to prioritize what keeps you alive. You think of all these random things like bills and insurance and medicines. You've been trained to think of all that, but you forget about the basics—keeping warm, a rain cover, clean water." He paused. "I swear I would wake up in the morning thinking about something so trivial I'd almost forget where I was."

"Then there's the sicknesses," Bo continued. "Each time, you think you're going to die because you got nothing to help, and you remember how you used to have Tylenol or Advil or something for it. That's when it's the worst." His voice trailed off. "But you don't die. You never seem to get better, but you aren't sure if it's in your mind or not." He looked out the window. "Then you wonder about your life and about everyone else's. Pretty soon, you stop doing that because you realize you need things like warmth and rain cover and clean water. It's madness."

Ryan said nothing.

"I've never been asked that," Bo added. "I've been asked, 'How'd you get that way?' or something else. But no one has ever asked how it feels."

Ryan shrugged. "No wonder, with that depressing-ass answer…"

Bo chuckled, and Ryan was glad to hear it.

Outside, the cold December air chilled everything within its grasp as the Jeep rolled north along I-29. The trees were bare, and although there was little actual snow on the ground, the world outside seemed forever frozen. Occasionally, Ryan glanced at the temperature gauge on his dashboard, but it was either burned out or too cold outside to even register.

Sometimes, Bo would make another comment or statement and Ryan would continue a point, but most of the talk was superficial, consisting of passing cars or a witty billboard. Yet silence never reigned. Once participants of a struggling conversation, they were now companions enjoying each other's company.

"What do you keep in your bag?" Ryan finally asked, somewhere near the Iowa line.

Bo looked out the passenger window. The sun had started falling in the sky, and the days had undoubtedly grown shorter.

"That'll be my Missouri question," Ryan added, knowing Bo would soon critique him on the rules once more.

"Two questions…" Bo smirked. "In a row?"

"Yes." Ryan shook his head, regretting his decision.

"This game is growing on you…"

"I'm making conversation."

"Why do you want to know?" Bo finally asked, in a voice neither friendly nor argumentative.

"Well, you asked me yesterday, and…I don't know…it sounded like a good question."

Bo laughed, but he did not answer the question. Ryan adjusted the cap on his head as he looked over at Bo, wondering if he was stalling because he truly did not want to tell or because he was coming up with another answer.

"I have a shirt," Bo said. "Another one like this." He indicated his Tommy Bahama shirt.

"Two for one?" Ryan chided.

"Something like that," Bo replied with a smile. "And, let's see…a bar of soap, car keys…"

Ryan gaped at him.

"Kidding on that last one." Bo returned the gaze. "I have a newspaper from Jacksonville from about a week ago, and a book, like you."

"What book?"

"A Hemingway one. I can't remember the title."

"Fitting, given how you dress…"

Bo squinted his eyes. "Feel better making fun of a homeless guy?"

Ryan smiled. "I would have said it if you said *Of Mice and Men* or even *The Lord of the Rings*."

"Wow." Bo nodded. "Picking all the disheveled-looking dudes, huh?"

Ryan laughed.

"For your information, I didn't have a lot of options on the book front." Ryan shrugged, a feeling of guilt finally coming over him.

"—But I did love *The Two Towers*."

"So, you do know *The Lord of the Rings*?" Ryan asked.

"Of course. That was one of my favorites."

"Why that one?"

"It was much more adventurous," Bo replied. "First one was a bit tedious at times, and I never read the third one…"

"Wait…what?"

"Yeah. I never read the third one."

"How?"

"How what?"

"How is that possible?"

"I don't know."

Ryan's jaw dropped. "So, you have no idea how it ends?"

"Nope. Don't want to know."

"How can you say that? How can you read two-thirds of a trilogy and not want to know how it ends!?"

"How does it end, then?" Bo asked calmly.

Ryan was speechless. "How? What? How long ago did you read that book?"

Bo considered this. "A couple years?"

"You read it *years* ago, and now you just want me to *tell you* the ending?"

"Yes?"

"You're unbelievable! Don't you want to know if they make it? If they destroy the ring?"

"I do," Bo answered. "So, can you tell me?"

"No!" Ryan exclaimed. "Read the damn books."

"Fine, then." Bo returned to sitting in silence.

Ryan simply could not believe what he was hearing. "How could you go this long without knowing what happened?"

Bo laughed. "I *have* been a bit preoccupied," he replied. "It isn't like you panhandle for Tolkien."

Ryan considered the ignorance of his question.

"Plus," Bo added, "maybe I didn't want the story to finish."

"That's horse crap," Ryan retorted. "You have to want to know."

"I do," Bo repeated. "But I also like where I left off, so I stopped."

"Like where you left off?" Ryan raised his voice. "You don't know what happened! They could have died in Mount Doom! Sauron could be running the world!"

"Well, that's a depressing-ass story," Bo mocked Ryan's voice. "Glad I didn't read it."

"That's not the point!"

"I know." Bo adjusted himself in his seat. "They could have lived happily ever after or they could have died. Point is, I don't care. There's something…worthwhile in not knowing the answer, in leaving the story on your own terms."

"You're one screwed-up person."

Bo laughed. "Put it like this. Let's say that Merry and Pippin and Frodo and Sam all lived happily ever after. Roll credits. End book. What if they died the next day? Or what if, in the next year, another war tore across Middle Earth?"

"Well, that isn't in the story."

"Exactly. The story is only what the author gives you. I wanted to make that my own and leave them on their adventure. That's why I stopped."

Ryan sighed, knowing he was not winning this battle.

"Let's face it; most books only capture fleeting moments in a character's life. A beginning, middle, and an end. There's much more to their life than the story the novel focuses on. I mean, how often does a writer come out with a sequel book that completely changes the events of the first? Like what if Frankenstein was actually a dream? Or Atticus Finch was a racist?"

"I doubt that will happen," Ryan said.

"Writers do it all the time. I don't like it. So, I liked *The Two Towers*, and I stopped reading after that."

"Because you were afraid of the next book," Ryan deduced.

"Because I liked how my story ended. To me, it doesn't matter what happens next. They were all fighting toward a common goal. They were all still alive, mostly. They still had hope."

Ryan laughed softly. Somewhere during their talk, Missouri had given way to Iowa.

"Imagine Raskolnikov dying in that Siberian prison," Bo finished.

Ryan considered this. "That'd suck."

"Exactly."

They were silent for a moment before Bo resumed the discussion.

"Your question reminded me of a good one, so whenever you're ready, I'm ready to ask."

Ryan exhaled. "All right, go ahead."

"What's it like, being you?"

"Being me?"

"Yeah, being you."

"You'll have to elaborate. Do you mean me as in the guy driving you to Spokane?"

"That and being a twenty-something now."

"A millennial?"

"Sure, if that's what they call you."

"That's two questions…"

"So be it."

"I like that you relate a Siberian prison to being a millennial…"

"Seemed relevant to me." Bo smiled.

Ryan took care to keep one hand on the wheel as he brushed his hair back from his forehead and leaned slightly on the driver's door.

"That hard of a question?" Bo asked after a while.

"I don't know how to answer," Ryan replied. "I remember in school some kid came up with a good answer."

"What was that?"

"He said"—Ryan reached back into his memory— "he said that my generation feels like they're on a train awaiting a stop that doesn't come."

"Interesting…"

"It's the same train all the previous generations were on, but we realize that we can get off it, unlike the past ones. We aren't bound to the train. We know it, yet we still don't get off. Instead, we watched the next generation take what we learned and get off, and we find ourselves left behind."

"Do you believe that?"

"I don't know. It sounds good."

"It does."

"Personally, I think we're just tired of conforming."

"We? Or you?"

Ryan considered this. "I got $35,000 in student loans before I ever learned what a student loan was. That's pretty messed up, right?"

"Certainly."

"No one ever taught us taxes in school, or how credit works. It was 'go to high school to get into college'. 'Get into college to get a job'. 'Get a job to support a family.' Eventually, you'd become your own parents, just with college degrees."

"Is that a bad thing?"

"It feels like it's predetermined. It feels like we're reliving the same cycles, just with the goalposts moved. Now a college degree is almost as useless as a high school degree. I have friends in fast food with a four-year degree. Hell, look at me; I wasn't much better."

"So, what's it like?"

"It's frustrating," Ryan replied. "It's overwhelming. Sometimes you just want to do something that makes no sense whatsoever because it's the first thing you get to actually do—" As heard the words as they left his mouth. Silence filled the car.

Bo smiled and sat back in his chair. "I don't think your generation is alone in some of those thoughts."

Ryan stared ahead as they passed another car. He adjusted his feet and looked over to his companion.

"How on Earth did we ever find each other?"

Bo laughed and looked out his passenger window. "I don't know…But if I ever answer it,"—he turned to Ryan with a smile— "I'm charging that as your question."

Ryan finally pulled into a hotel in Sioux City. Approaching the front desk, he noticed an ATM outside the door, and he pulled out his wallet under the cover of December darkness.

He quickly hit the withdrawal button and hit $200, the max on the machine. He knew the buttons well, as he had gone through the same routine at each of the day's stops. As the cash dispensed, he took the receipt and threw it in the trash, just as he had done before. Quietly, he added the $200 to the other bills in his wallet.

Eight ATMs down—$2,200 total.

Ryan exhaled audibly as he entered the hotel. Surely, one day, he would ask for forgiveness. Surely, one day, he would need that reprieve.

But that day was not today.

***

It was near eleven when Ryan checked the nightstand clock on his right. He had tried sleeping, but to no avail. The conversations and actions of the past few days weighed on his mind. It had truly been exhausting, but sleep would not come.

Next to him, Bo snored softly. Though his breathing was barely audible, it was enough to keep Ryan awake. The day's events did not seem to bother him much.

Ryan got up and retrieved his pants from the bedside chair. He pulled them on, grabbed the USF jacket, and slipped silently out the hotel door.

It was surprisingly light for a December night as the streetlights bathed the area around the hotel in a faint orange. Ryan could see his breath as he shook off the cold. He heard a truck roar by on the highway behind him, but he paid it no attention. He walked past the lobby toward the next establishment on the road, a restaurant that nearly connected to the hotel.

Sensing from the cars outside that the place was still open, he stepped inside. The interior was small and dank, with a few purple-lit booths and a pool table in the corner.

He moved toward the bar and ignored the few people seated there as he undid his jacket and sat down at the bar.

The bartender, an older man with thinning hair and a towel on his shoulder, was quick to approach.

"What are you drinking?"

Ryan sighed. "Rum and Coke."

The bartender laid down a coaster and moved toward his stock of liquors.

Ryan adjusted himself on the uncomfortable barstool. Sitting upward, he reached into his pocket and found his cell phone and charging cord. He had not even remembered putting them there.

He sighed as he laid them on the bar top.

The bartender came back around and set the drink on the coaster.

"You want me to charge that?" The bartender's voice snapped Ryan out of his reverie. He looked up to see the man pointing to the phone.

Ryan swallowed the lump in his throat. "Yeah, sure."

The bartender grabbed the cord and reached behind the bar top. He plugged in the cord and then attached the other end to the phone. The light on the phone illuminated red for the first time in days. The bartender set the phone on his side of the counter before moving on down the line.

He reached for his glass and realized his fear for the first time. Panic consumed him. All his talk about his phone, and now it was suddenly charging. His mind raced as he sipped his drink. How many missed calls? From his parents? From her? From anyone?

How many missed texts? How many regrets would come flooding back? He had done his best to put his thoughts on the back burner, no matter how often they came up, but here, in this dark and dank bar, he would finally see them all.

He took another drink, staring at the phone as if it were his own death. He did not want to turn it on. He tried hard to reason against it. Yet after only a moment he felt his arm reach out. It grabbed the phone and pressed the power button.

The screen glowed brightly for an eternity before turning black and giving way to the home screen for the first time in days. Ryan set the device on the bar and waited, sipping his drink once more.

The bar hummed around him. Someone broke a game of pool in the corner while conversations at two separate booths faded into one another. To Ryan's right, a man sat watching SportsCenter while sipping his gin, and to his left, a couple was arguing— whether in jest or in reality, he could not tell. He did not care. All that mattered was the phone in front of him.

Ryan took another sip. As he did, he watched intently as the phone began vibrating. First, it was a sole vibration—a text, maybe a voicemail. Then another. Then another. Two more. Ryan swallowed the lump in his throat. He lost track of the vibrations. Each induced more panic.

Then, suddenly, it stopped. The phone lay silently, as if it were off once more.

Ryan considered that maybe it had died once more, yet the red charging light indicated otherwise.

The drama was too much. Ryan set down his drink and grabbed the phone. He opened the home screen to discover all that he had missed.

Seventeen texts. Nine voicemails.

"Another?" came the bartender's voice as though from another world.

Ryan looked up. "Yeah."

As the bartender made the second drink, Ryan pushed the first empty glass across the counter and unlocked the phone.

He had no idea what to expect. Demoralizing texts from his ex? Perhaps more yelling, screaming, begging, and pleading. Maybe even messages from his old boss. Maybe there were more harassment charges, more repercussions from his past life. Whatever it was, it was not going to be pleasant.

He checked his messages first. One text from Stacy, two texts from Melissa, three texts from dad. Six from mom. Five from Rebecca.

Five from Rebecca.

Ryan hung his head as the bartender replaced his drink.

"Call me…let's talk about this."

"Please…"

"Don't throw this away…"

"It's been a day now, talk to me."

Ryan swallowed again.

"Listen to my voicemails…" Dated December 17. Two days ago.

Ryan took a drink. He did not know what to feel, but he knew he had to finish what he'd started.

"Voicemail one, received three days ago from...Steve Coltrip."

Ryan jumped at the voice. It seemed like an eternity ago.

"Ryan. Just wanted to let you know that I'm sorry for how things went down. I hope you understand. I'll mail your last check."

Ryan shut his eyes and took another drink.

Delete.

"Voicemail two, received three days ago from...Rebecca Millsap."

He felt as though his heart would stop.

"It's been two days now. And I guess you aren't talking to me anymore. Maybe...maybe you think this is better, but I don't. I think it sucks—"

Delete.

"Voicemail three, received two days ago from...Rebecca Millsap."

"I don't know why I keep trying to talk. You obviously don't want to. And you know what? That's fine. I don't owe you an apology. I owe you nothing—"

Delete.

Another sip.

"Voicemail four, received two days ago from...Sallie Mae..."

"Hello, we are looking for...Ryan Collins. Ryan...your Department of Education loan is past due. You have a past-due balance of...one hundred...sixty-seven dollars and—"

Delete.

"Voicemail five, received two days ago from...Mom..."

"Ryan, just talked to Steve...he said you were fired? Where are you?"

Delete.

Only four more, Ryan thought.

"Voicemail six, received yesterday from...Mom..."

"Ryan, it's been two days now...I'm starting to get worried, where—"

Delete.

"Voicemail seven, received yesterday from...Mom..."

"Ryan, call me ba—"

Delete.

"Voicemail eight, received today at 10:05 AM...from...Mom..."

"BRANDON JUST CALLED US—"

Delete.

He took a deep breath. One more.

"Voicemail nine, received today at 8:06 PM...from..."

Ryan held his breath.

"Rebecca Millsap."

"I stopped by your parents' house today." Her voice was soft, flat. It was as though she had endured a lot. His finger hovered on the delete button. *"Your mom says she hasn't seen you. I gave her back your stuff, though. Probably better this way."* She paused. *"I, uh, I got to thinking about everything and, well, I don't know what happened to you. I'm not just talking about us, but you. You said I deserve better, and I now realize you're right."*

Ryan could not hit the delete button this time. He deserved this.

"I do deserve better. Someone who doesn't cheat. Someone who loves me. It isn't you. You need help,

or...or something." She paused, as if sensing she was being harsh. *"I'm going to delete your number now. I suggest you do as well. Goodbye and I...I hope you figure yourself out. It's the least you can do for those that still care about you."*

"Message end...to replay...press four..."

Ryan kept the phone at his ear for a moment before hitting the "end call" button and setting it on the counter.

"Another?" The bartender asked.

Ryan stared at the man. His thoughts were flowing.

She, along with everyone, finally saw him for who he was.

"No," he replied, downing his drink.

The bartender nodded and moved toward the cash register.

Ryan picked up the phone again, opened the messages, and glanced over the texts from his mom and dad, and then Rebecca's...and then Melissa's, and Stephanie's. He went on to look at the list of old messages. Other names like Michelle popped up, along with Katie and Maddie. The list went on and on. Some of the names he knew well. Others, he barely remembered.

The bartender came back and set the check next to the phone.

"Waiting on a call?"

Ryan took the check and threw down a twenty-dollar bill.

"Not anymore," he said with a sigh.

That phone, those lists of names, they seemed a lifetime ago. That was not him. It could not be. How could he play all those girls? How could he be so careless?

No more. He was no longer careless. He cared now. The weight of a thousand transgressions, from past women to his career to his life—they all followed him out of the bar. He wanted to cry out, but he knew it would do no good.

He shivered as he walked across the parking lot. Light snow fell on him, but he could not have cared less. His mind was much too preoccupied.

He began to feel dizzy as the alcohol caught up to him. Reaching the hotel, he found a wall and slid to a seated position. He sat there for a few moments, head in hand, until his pocket began to vibrate.

Taking a deep breath, he contemplated not pulling the phone out, but he knew he had to. Extracting it from his pocket, he saw that it was only a text message and he was instantly relieved. It was better than another voicemail.

He swiped the screen. To his surprise, it was not from Rebecca. It was not from his parents. It was not from a girl.

It was from Brandon.

Ryan cocked his head as he saw the picture attached to the message. It was a screenshot of a Google search that clearly read, "No matches. Please try again." In the subject, Ryan saw, was a distantly familiar place.

"Chesdin Lake, Washington."

Beneath this picture, Brandon had typed a clear and unmistakable message...

"There is no Chesdin Lake..."

Ryan sat unmoving, staring at the screen as the snow continued to fall. Somewhere to his left, he heard the soft hooting of an owl. The simple text captivated him.

His immediate thought was curiousness. For the past three days, he'd thought little of his companion's motives, other than what he had discerned from his questioning. Yet it seemed there was now something more to his partner.

Bo...had *lied?*

Ryan quickly opened his internet browser and typed the words *Chesdin, Lake, Washington.* No matches.

He went back to the search. *Chesdin Lake.* There were a few matches this time, but nothing remotely close to Washington.

His curiosity turned to unease. Ryan tried a new search.

Bo. New York. Lawyer.

No matches.

He racked his brain, but for the life of him, he could not think of Bo's last name. Had he even told him?

Bo. Lawyer.

Nothing.

Ryan gritted his teeth.

Bo. Spokane.

He hit enter, but as he did, the phone powered down. He tried again, but to no avail. The battery was dead once more.

Ryan felt the rage building in him. One more thing to go wrong. Shaking, he stood upright and threw the phone before he knew what he was doing. As though in slow motion, he watched as it sailed through the air until it crashed near the restaurant's dumpsters some distance away.

Gasping for breath, he stared at the broken device. He knew he should pick it up, but something inside would not let him. Instead, he turned and walked back toward his motel room.

The snow had increased in intensity as he reached the motel door and pulled the key card from his pocket. Yet as he put the key card to the slot, he half-turned, noticing his own Jeep in the parking lot. Sitting upright in the passenger seat was Bo's orange bag.

Why had he left it there? Had he forgotten about it? The more he stared at it, the more the bag seemed to be mocking him. What else was Bo lying about?

Ryan turned from the door and moved to the passenger side of the Jeep, taking great care to be as quiet as possible. Unlocking the door, he slipped inside and sat with the bag perched on his lap.

A war raged in his head. He knew he could not open the bag and snoop on his companion, yet somehow, he felt as though he had to.

In truth, he knew so little about his partner. What if Brandon was right? What if Bo was something more sinister—even dangerous?

The questions came even heavier. Who was Bo?

He grabbed the sides of the bag and pulled it open to reveal the contents. *There's no going back now*, he thought as he peered inside.

Lying on top was a dated copy of the *Ocala Free Press*, which Ryan pulled out and set aside. Underneath was, as expected, an unwrapped bar of soap and another colorful shirt that matched Bo's omnipresent apparel.

Ryan exhaled. It was as expected, right down to the bottom of the bag, which was, as he discovered upon removing the shirt and soap, a book.

His breath caught in his throat.

Perfectly placed, with its cover facing up, was *A Farewell to Arms.*

Ryan gazed at the cover before turning to the newspaper that lay at his side.

He froze.

A page was coming out of the *Ocala Free Press*. He carefully pulled it from its hiding spot.

It was a single article, cut specifically to avoid anything else. It looked much older than the other newspaper, but without a date, Ryan could not be sure. The story itself was devoid of any pictures. The title, however, was bold and sharp: *Beloved Spokane Doctor Loses Loved One in Vehicle Wreck*

Under this, in smaller font, read part of the story:

Dr. C, as he is called by most of his patients, only ran a practice in Spokane for a little over two years, yet in that time, he was known for both humanitarian and community contributions across the area. Winner of several prestigious awards, Dr. C is a household name in the community, which makes it especially difficult to understand the most recent events surrounding the doctor, culminating in the vehicular death of a woman, 23, on an icy road, minutes from the doctor's home. Details are still emerging…

The paper was ripped as if the rest of the story was unimportant.

Ryan's breath stuck in his chest. Why had Bo kept this? What did it mean? It was as though the man's life had suddenly become a puzzle devoid of pieces. Clearly, there was more to Bo than he had let on.

Ryan turned his eyes back to the bag and the book that lay inside. He reached inside, hoping to find more clues. As his hands met the border of the book and lifted, however, he noticed a distinctly different feel than expected. At first, he thought it was only in his mind, yet as he pulled the Hemingway novel out, he knew his thoughts were correct.

The book was heavy.

He looked around to be sure no one was watching. Seeing that he was alone, he set the book carefully on his lap.

As the snow fell around him, he opened the book as slowly as possible, fearing what he would find.

Peering downward, his dread became realized.

Hidden among the pages of the book, which had been cut to conceal it, was a Smith and Wesson revolver.

Shannon, South Dakota, lay a few miles east of the Missouri on Interstate 90. It was a quaint respite for summer vacationers heading to the Black Hills, but it was hardly a place where Ryan could have envisioned having breakfast, especially in winter. But after the previous night's discoveries, as well as a headache from either the alcohol or a lack of sleep, a full breakfast, even from a truck stop diner, was both hardy and worthwhile.

 Bo was typically chatty, but he was especially so on this morning. As Ryan stretched out his legs on his booth seat, Bo talked on about the prospects of farming and what he saw himself doing with the money he did not have. Ryan occasionally dropped an "mm-hmm" or a "sounds good," but he mainly concerned himself with the sausage and eggs on his plate. He no longer felt as comfortable as he once had.

It was not that he feared for his safety; he was simply more uncertain than ever before. He'd spent a long time in the passenger seat of his car, staring at the weapon in the bag and unable to comprehend its presence. Why was it there? Was it Bo's? Had he used it before?

One thing was certain. For whatever reason, Bo neither spoke of it nor seemed to intend to use it. If he wanted to harm Ryan, why go through all this? If he wanted the car or money, he would have just done it. Moreover, if he were set on bad intentions, wouldn't he have done the most damage at Brandon's house? There, he could have had much more than just a car and a wallet of money. It made no sense.

Maybe Bo kept it for safety. Ryan did not know anything about the life of a homeless man, but maybe it was for personal security.

He seemed to like this answer most of all—until he considered that a man who struggled to own shoes somehow owned a gun. Surely food, water, and shelter would be more easily acquired and necessary than a firearm. There must be a reason, Ryan thought, although he himself had no ideas that seemed probable.

He had slipped everything back into the bag as he'd found it and returned to the room sometime around one in the morning. Mind still reeling, he'd opened the door softly and crept to his bed, taking care not to wake Bo. Sleep, however, had never come. His mind had been much too preoccupied.

Between Brandon's texts and his own discoveries, major questions came to the surface. How much did he really know about Bo? How much had the man divulged? How much was true? This led Ryan down a rabbit hole of questions he could never answer. He tried to suppress them, but one simple thing stood out: if he were going "home" to Spokane, why keep the gun?

When the sun finally rose, Ryan reasoned that he'd had maybe thirty minutes of rest. It was of little matter, however, as he was more interested in getting to Washington than ever before.

"I was thinking," Bo said through a mouthful of bacon. The comment snapped Ryan out of his thoughts. "I was thinking about our timing out west." He grabbed his water glass.

Ryan pushed his remaining eggs around with his fork. "Timing?"

"Yeah, timing," Bo replied with an air of nonchalance. "It's what? December 20th?"

Ryan nodded before picking up a forkful of eggs and eating them.

"Well, figure two more days of driving, and that'd be all day, so figure three to be safe…" He paused and gulped his orange juice. "That puts us there the twenty-third. Even if you kick me out of the car as quick as possible, you aren't getting back to Florida until after Christmas."

Ryan considered this. "And?"

"And what about your family? I mean, I'm sure they're worried now, but I can't expect you to miss Christmas!"

"I know." Ryan downed another forkful of eggs. "I've thought about that." He had actually thought little of the subject, but given the current circumstances, he was not about to start thinking of it now.

"Ry," Bo said, "I can't have that."

Ryan wiped his mouth. "So what? You going to fly me back from Spokane?"

Bo laughed. "No, but I thought of something else." He looked thoughtful. "What if instead of going all the way to Washington, we drive to Wyoming today, and you drop me off in Gillette?"

Ryan spread out in the booth again. "Gillette?"

Bo took another drink. "Yeah, Gillette. From there, I can hitch a ride with a trucker coming up the 25, or one continuing on 90 toward Montana."

Ryan stared as Bo spoke, his thoughts from the night before creeping up again. "And you think," he finally said, "you'll be able to hitch enough rides to get home by Christmas?"

Bo shrugged. "I think so." He wiped his mouth again. "Plus, that means you can start back tonight, maybe make it to Rapid City, and be home in three days, easy. You may even get a nice Christmas Eve dinner."

Ryan gazed out the window. "I thought the point of all this was for me to get you home."

"It was!" Bo countered. "And you've done more than I could ever thank you for. I'm closer to Spokane now than I've been in a long time." His voice dropped. "I never thought you'd actually get me this far."

The comment hung on the air. Ryan looked at Bo, who seemed engaged in his empty plate.

Just then, their waitress, a young woman in her early twenties, came by. She wiped her hands on her blue apron.

"Sorry to interrupt." She smiled, first at Bo, and then Ryan. "But can I get you two anything else?"

Bo looked over to Ryan, and his happy disposition returned. "I'm good, what about you?"

"Same," Ryan added. "Food was great."

The waitress pulled the check from her apron. "Awesome; glad you enjoyed it." She set the check on the table. "They will take you up at the counter. Have a good morning." She smiled again and moved on to the next table, but not before taking another look at them.

Ryan grabbed the check and moved out of the booth, followed shortly by Bo. He knew he was leaving the man hanging by not responding, but he wanted to figure out a way to word a response. At the counter, an older man with a tough face accepted the check and the bills Ryan handed him. Bo sidled up beside Ryan as the cashier calculated the change.

"How about this?" Ryan lied, accepting his coins with thanks from the cashier. "Let's get to Wyoming first, and then we can continue this discussion."

Bo seemed open to this suggestion. "That could work."

Ryan pushed open the door to the diner. "Good. Now let's get going."

Ryan adjusted his seatbelt and signaled to get back onto Interstate 90. He felt more awkward than usual without his phone or charger, but he tried to keep his mind on the task at hand. He found himself constantly glancing at Bo and, more specifically, the bag. His breath caught in his throat every time Bo moved toward it, but each time Bo simply adjusted it on the floorboard or moved it to one side. He acted no differently than before, save for his constant reminder that Gillette would be good enough now.

"Must have snowed a lot overnight," Bo said after a mile or so down the road.

Ryan nodded. He scratched his scalp and glanced at his passenger once more.

"Winter gets rough here," he continued. "Every day is a new adventure, as they say."

Ryan smiled along with him. After a second, he turned to his companion.

"I'd like to ask my next question."

Bo's eyes froze as he looked to the north. He cleared his throat and looked straight ahead. "Well then," he said, "go ahead, I guess." There was a distinct change in his tone.

Ryan changed lanes and looked back at his passenger. "I want to know," he said slowly, deliberately. "I want to know what your last name is."

Bo nodded. "My last name?"

"And middle, if you have one."

"May I ask why?"

Ryan laughed. "You can, but it'll be your question."

Bo looked back to the north as if deep in thought about the question that was easiest of all. "Well, in that case…"

It was then that chaos erupted.

The car lurched. Ryan gripped the steering wheel tightly, instantly forgetting the conversation at hand. Smoke began to pour from under the hood as the warning lights on the dash illuminated: "temp," "oil pressure," "check engine." He quickly threw the gearshift into neutral and eased onto the shoulder of the interstate. Luckily, no cars were around him.

The smoke billowed as he coasted, applied the brakes, and finally brought the car to a stop. Shutting it off, he fervently looked over to Bo, whose expression registered a similar shock.

"Something's wrong with the car," Bo said after a moment.

Ryan rolled his eyes. "You think?" Hurriedly, he opened his car door. A truck blew past, causing him to jump.

Bo nodded as he, too, undid his seatbelt and stepped outside, where Ryan already had the hood up.

Underneath the car, a mixture of liquids flowed from all parts of the engine, from the block to the radiator itself. Even the tailpipe was dripping.

"Perfect," Ryan sighed, leaning on the upright hood, unaware of how cold he was becoming.

"What do you think?" Bo asked, looking around and noticing just how isolated they were.

"I think," Ryan muttered as he jiggled wires and hoses, "…I think we're screwed."

Seconds turned to minutes as they stared at the car. After some time had passed, a Chevy pickup pulled up behind the lifeless Jeep, and the driver, an older man with a Pioneer hat and paint-stained khaki pants, walked up along the passenger side.

"Car problem, boys?" the man asked in a gnarled voice.

Ryan had heard the man pull up but knew he could do little to prevent the conversation. He stared at the engine with a blank expression.

"I believe so," Bo answered, shaking the man's hand. "I'm Bo; he's Ryan."

"Curtis," the man answered, taking a quick glance at the Jeep. "Need some help?"

Ryan finally gave up looking at the engine and turned to the new arrival.

"A phone or something would be great."

Curtis grabbed a cigarette from his pocket and lit it. "Can't do that. Got a CB, though. I can call my brother. He runs a shop in Shannon."

"Great," Ryan said. "Anything would be great."

Curtis walked back to his truck while Ryan went to his own backseat and grabbed his sweatshirt and ball cap. As he shut the door, he heard Curtis hailing on the radio behind him.

"Ran-dell, got a copy?"

Ryan leaned against his car door as a truck blew past, throwing salt remnants and leftover snow into the air.

"Go ahead, Curt," came a voice that sounded even older than Curt's.

"Mile 279, westbound, Jeep requestin' service."

There was a pause, as if the old man on the other line was trying to figure out the radio. "Copy, 279. Be there in ten."

Curt exited the truck and approached Bo on the passenger side.

"He'll be here in ten or so. He'll help you out."

"Thank you so much," Bo said, extending his hand once more.

"Thanks," Ryan added from the other side, though his reply was far less enthusiastic.

"You all are lucky I was heading this way," Curtis said, tapping the ash off his cigarette. "Gets lonely out here in winter. Where were you all heading? Rushmore?"

"Gillette, actually," Bo answered quickly. "Visiting family."

Noting just how quickly the lie had formed, Ryan turned from the conversation. There was something almost gleeful in Bo's manner, as if the car problems were a reprieve from a sentence.

After a twenty-minute conversation that he largely ignored, Ryan saw a crude tow truck pull in front of the Jeep.

"That'll be Randall," Curtis said as if there were any question about it. He extinguished a second cigarette in the snow.

Ryan turned toward the truck as Randall emerged slowly. His voice matched his look, as he was clearly near eighty years old with thick-rimmed spectacles that fogged up in the cold air. He was bundled in cover-all denim with a hat and earmuff combination that left only the lower part of his face uncovered. He was taller than Ryan had expected.

"What happened?" Randall asked in greeting, obviously not wanting to spend time in the cold.

"Steam poured out with fluid; no warning," Ryan replied, doing his best scientific explanation.

Randall nodded as he pulled chains and a winch from a toolbox. "I'll have to bring it to the shop. That okay?"

Ryan watched him hook chains to his Jeep's bumper. "Not many options now, are there?"

"What the hell are you doing up here this time of year?" Randall asked as he crawled under the car.

Ryan found it hard to lie, though he honestly did not know if he was lying or not. "Visiting family for Christmas."

Curtis and Bo continued to talk on the passenger side.

"They make planes, you know," Randall said with a laugh. Ryan tried to chuckle, but he was in no mood for mirth. "All right, stand clear."

In just a moment, Randall had the Jeep up onto the tow truck. He exited the truck once more to give it a good look.

"Lots of fluid," he said. "Nothing we haven't seen before."

"Good," Ryan replied, trying to find something decent in the situation.

"You ride with me; your friend can ride with Curt."

Ryan nodded as he walked to the side of the tow truck. "Thanks again for this."

"Don't thank me yet." Randall replied with a laugh as he got into the truck. "You ain't seen the bill."

***

"You're joking." Ryan leaned on the counter inside Randall's shop.

Behind the counter, Randall washed his hands. He took off his hat and set it on the counter beside the sink.

"'Fraid not," Randall replied. "I can't get a water pump in here until at least Monday, and that's with me driving to Sioux Falls to get it. It'd be at least Wednesday if I tried mailing it here."

Ryan sighed as he looked at the calendar near the sink where Randall stood. That was a whole weekend without a car.

"Unfortunately, that's the best I got," Randall concluded. "Usually, I got some spare parts here, but when a water pump and a fuel pump blow, especially on a rarer Jeep like yours, we are at a struggle."

"How much will it be?"

"Debatable, but if everything goes right, it should be under $500."

Ryan closed his eyes as he turned from the counter. When he opened them, he noticed Bo standing outside the glass doors of the service shop with his head held back, eyes closed. Around him, snow flurries fluttered to the ground. Some broke upon his face like soft bits of cotton. He seemed as content as ever.

Taking a deep breath, Ryan turned back to the counter. "You said at least Monday. Does that mean Monday or Tuesday, or what?"

Randall wiped his nose on his sleeve. "It means I call today, get the pump delivered by Monday morning, pick it up, and bring it back. Drive time, installation, and all that means probably Monday night. Maybe Tuesday."

Ryan calculated in his head. Monday would be the twenty-third. Tuesday, Christmas Eve. Barring any other issue, they would be close to making Christmas in Spokane.

"Do what you have to do," Ryan countered, pulling his wallet from his pocket. He opened it and counted out a stack of twenties on the counter.

"No need to pay until it's done," Randall said.

"It's fine," Ryan answered. "Here's $700. Consider it an incentive to get it done Monday."

Randall glanced at the man and then down to the stack of twenty-dollar bills on the counter. "I can't accept…"

"I wasn't negotiating." Ryan smiled. "You also got us off the highway and all that."

Randall walked up to the counter and adjusted his glasses on his nose. "That's awful generous."

"Just get the work done. Sooner the better."

"Of course." Randall hesitated and then brushed the money into his register.

"Thanks." Ryan turned and made for the door.

"You know," the old man's voice rang out as Ryan's hand touched the doorknob, "Miss Barbara has an inn two blocks from downtown near the highway. I'll phone her and give you a ride if you need a place to stay."

Ryan considered this, knowing he had no options.

"She makes a mean sausage gravy…" Randall added.

Ryan turned from the door with a smile. "That'd be fine."

The Shannon Inn was not so much a B&B as an actual one-story hotel that seemed to extend from an old brick manor. While most of the town was stately, tree lined, and plain, the inn seemed almost out of place, with a large open lot and vegetable field behind it. The main house, however, was well maintained, with a beautiful wraparound porch and snow-covered rocking chairs on the deck. The place exuded warmth, though as Ryan and Bo stepped out of Randall's truck, the cold forced them inside quickly.

Closing the door behind them, they found a spacious main room. Several sets of tables and chairs were set up around the lobby, which was covered in ornate décor that harked back some fifty years.

"You must be the Collins family," a mousy voice said to the right.

Ryan and Bo turned to a small, fragile woman carrying a bag of laundry down the stairs from the main house's second floor.

"Indeed, we are, miss," Bo responded, setting his bag on the floor.

"Welcome to our inn," the woman said, walking behind a makeshift reception area and pulling out a well-worn binder. "Randall told me of your problems. I'm sorry about that."

"No worries," Ryan countered, speaking for the first time. "We'll be fine, I'm sure."

"You certainly will," she agreed, donning a pair of glasses. "He's a smart man, that Randall." She squinted as she read her own writing in her book. "Now he says you'll be here three nights?"

"Most likely." Ryan answered.

"Good, I'll give you room 104 then." She closed the book and removed her glasses. "All of our rooms were remodeled two years ago, so you should find the heat and water to be plenty good. My Willard did it all by hand with our sons."

Ryan did not press about Willard or the sons, but he did wonder why she seemed alone on a Friday afternoon.

"That said," she continued, pulling a key on a nice flowered keychain from a drawer, "this place is still an old farmhouse." She made herself chuckle. "We added on guestrooms some forty years ago, back when the interstate was being built. Added bathrooms to most rooms a few years later. I guess it's what you'd call a work in progress."

"I'm sure it'll be fine," Ryan replied, pulling money from his wallet. Although she had not mentioned a price, he was safe to assume his estimate would be enough.

"How generous," the innkeeper said when handed the folded bills. "You boys can stay as long as you like."

She grabbed her coat as she led both outside and toward the room. "I'll have breakfast ready at eight. Try to make it because it'll spoil if you sleep in. If you need towels, just bring the dirty ones to breakfast, and I'll replace them." She reached the door after much effort and inserted the key. "Keep your room clean, and don't waste the hot water."

As the door opened, Ryan was surprised to see what appeared to be a room not unlike most hotels, with two twin beds, a bathroom with sink in the back, and a large chest that dominated the room next to a smaller desk that sat near the door.

"Alarm clock works pretty well," she continued in an instructive tone. "Just wind it up. And if the heat goes out, come knock on the main house."

"Thank you for the hospitality," Bo said, turning to the woman.

Ryan stepped inside and set his bag on the bed nearest the door.

"You boys have plans tonight?" Barbara asked. At first, Ryan thought she was joking.

"If not," she continued, "the town's having their Christmas celebration. Lots of free food. And tomorrow," she continued, "the school is doing their annual Christmas musical. That's a good time. My grandson is playing two parts, both Harry and John."

Ryan smiled, having no clue who she was talking about.

"You won me with free food." Bo laughed as he set his bag onto his bed while still examining the room.

"Well, you boys enjoy your stay. Let me know if you need anything." She turned as she set the key on the desk near the door. "I'll see you tonight or in the morning."

With that, she pulled the door closed, leaving Bo and Ryan alone once more. The silence filled the room as Bo stepped into the bathroom and inspected it. Near the door, Ryan fell onto the bed. He lay face up, thinking about the past four hours and how their eventful trip had turned even more so.

He tried to be angry at the situation, but upon lying on the bed, his tiredness was more pressing. He could not control the issues, he knew, so he did the only thing he could think of: he closed his eyes.

Bo stepped out of the bathroom. He looked toward where Ryan was sleeping deeply and took a deep breath, gritting his teeth as he exhaled.

Quietly, he opened his bag and looked down at the contents. He moved the shirt to one side and saw the newspaper clipping and, finally, the book at the bottom.

He ran his hands over the Hemingway cover.

Spokane was calling him. He could feel it in his bones. The weight of a thousand memories was drawing closer and closer. As much as he adored the town they were stranded in, and as much as he adored the room, the farmhouse, and the essence of wintertime, he knew it was no match for what was calling him ahead.

He exhaled as he closed his eyes. Not even a town as idyllic as this could hold his thoughts at bay. There was nowhere he could hide. There was nothing he could do.

Spokane was calling, he knew, and soon enough, he would have to answer.

Chapter 11
1,083 Miles to Spokane

It was a dreamless nap for Ryan, but he awoke with such a start that he began to sweat. For a moment, he knew neither the time nor where he was. He turned over to the nightstand and found that the alarm clock read 6:40. Whether a.m. or p.m., he did not know. As awareness of his surroundings returned, the first thing he noticed was the most obvious: Bo was not there.

Taking a deep breath, Ryan rose from the bed and stretched his arms. He noticed the occasional drone of a car engine passing outside. In the bathroom, he turned on the faucet and splashed water on his face. Wiping it with a towel, he moved back into the room and noticed a pad of paper near the alarm clock. Approaching it, he read the scribbled letters.

Went to the town celebration thing. Meet me there. Bo.

Ryan yawned. He looked at his bed once more, debating the merits of following the letter or getting more sleep. He felt his stomach rumble and knew the former was his only choice. Donning his shoes and sweatshirt, he found himself slipping out the door.

The outside air was surprisingly warmer than Ryan expected, though it was still cold to his Floridian body. Closing the hotel door, he found that he had no idea of his location within the town, but he saw a distinctly brighter sky toward his right.

He followed the lights. In minutes, he was deep in the town, passing rows and rows of old brick country houses adorned with Christmas lights. Some were decorated with wreaths and classic icicle trims. Others channeled a mini-Las Vegas, with inflatable décor and larger-than-life nativity scenes. Overall, there was a distinct calm, and Ryan found it peaceful. It was a pristine slice of Americana adorned with a blissful layer of new-fallen snow.

Ryan could hear the drumming of voices. Turning toward the sound, he soon found himself in downtown Shannon, which more than perfectly fit the hometown feel of the surrounding homes.

Streetlights glowing with images of candles and reindeer, the entire picture was bustling with activity. Families moved around brightly lit storefronts, sipping cocoa and eating undefined treats and snacks. In the foreground was a square park with carolers singing and children playing in the snow. It was truly a postcard-perfect scene.

A faint smile on his face, Ryan walked into the setting and down the nearest street, where a hardware store blasted Bing Crosby and a bank handed out gingerbread cookies. Nodding, he accepted a cookie as he walked, passing families who were oblivious to the stranger in their midst. Moving down the next street, he passed a throwback barbershop and a city café that smelled deliciously of pie and tarts.

"Pot pies here!" a voice to his right called out. Turning, Ryan saw the city hall, where a larger balding man was setting the food onto plates and handing them out one by one. He found himself moving toward the man and accepting the warm dinner.

"Have a Merry Christmas," the man said to Ryan as he moved onto the next plate.

Looking at the plate, Ryan smiled in return and offered a quaint "You too."

Moving past the next set of businesses, he devoured the pot pie quickly before accepting two cookies from another café and a cup of hot chocolate from the post office. Hands full, he made his way across the street to a vacant park bench and sat in awe of his surroundings.

He realized that he had yet to see Bo anywhere among the festivities, though he was far from worried as he watched several families enter an antique store with glee. Sipping his cocoa, he sat back on the bench.

"I didn't expect you to be here," a voice said from close by.

At first, Ryan did not react to the sound, but as he heard the footsteps nearby, he found himself turning to the source of the words.

"Honestly, I thought you'd be long gone."

With a look of surprise, Ryan found himself looking at a woman about his age with hair tucked up under a black cap. Her hands were tucked into a long black wool coat.

"Excuse me?" he asked, briefly looking around to make sure she was speaking to him.

The woman laughed as she moved closer and sat next to him. "It's you, right? The guy with the Jeep?"

Incredulously, Ryan looked around again. "H-how," he finally stammered, "do you know I have a Jeep?"

"I saw it parked outside the restaurant." She spoke as if her words explained everything, but Ryan was still lost.

"This morning," she added. "I was your waitress…At the diner this morning?"

"The diner!" he recalled. "I'm sorry, yes, yes, that was me." He paused, vaguely recollecting the morning's activities. "It's been a long day."

"Tell me about it," the girl said, taking off her hat and revealing light blonde hair that could have fallen past her shoulders had she not kept it up in a tight bun. Readjusting the hair tie, she put the cap back on. "Fridays are always busy at the diner."

Still perplexed, he finally spoke. "You'll have to forgive me, but I don't remember your name." He was not sure if he ever actually knew it.

"Melanie," she said quickly. "But Mel works, too."

"Mel," Ryan repeated. "Mine's Ryan."

She nodded, not repeating the name but simply letting it settle on the air for the moment.

"Pretty lively party," Ryan said after a moment, not wanting the conversation to spoil.

Melanie's gaze was fixed on the festivities. She watched the crowd intently. Ryan knew little about the woman seated next to him, but he could tell that her attention to detail was second to none. She seemed wise for her years, and although she was quite personable, he could sense distance as well.

"It's cohesive," she finally replied. She turned her gaze back to Ryan.

"Cohesive?"

"Yeah," she replied. "All the people come out of their winter hibernations for this weekend, then return for Christmas." She sighed as she looked around. "Happens every year, like a well-oiled machine."

"Cohesive," Ryan repeated.

"But it's a good time," Melanie replied, breaking his gaze as she settled onto the park bench.

Ryan nodded, wondering if it would have been easier for her to start with that. "I've been having fun. Good food." He paused and looked around as the silence between them grew.

"Looking for someone?" she asked after a moment.

Ryan let the question linger a moment. "Actually, yeah…" He thought about his next words carefully. "I can't seem to find my dad."

"Your dad?"

"Yeah," he said, constructing the lie slowly. "I mean, he's a grown man, but I just thought I'd meet him here." He knew he was talking himself into a bind, but he did not know what else to say. "Surprised he isn't more tired, honestly. All the travel to visit family and all that…"

"Ryan." Melanie's smile silenced him. "You don't have to lie to me. I honestly don't care."

His jaw tensed as he stared out into the crowd. He tried not to let it show. "What makes you think I'm lying?"

Melanie laughed as she adjusted her coat. "Well, you're a guy."

Ryan nodded. "Seems a bit rude…"

"A guy," she countered, "who is giving me way more information than I asked for."

He could only chuckle a bit and look sheepishly down at the snow. "All right, I guess that's true."

"Don't be upset," she replied. "I just don't need to know details."

He nodded. "Well, I'm sorry then. If it helps, I felt dumb saying it."

Melanie laughed. "I take it most people don't believe the father-son thing?"

"Everyone who's asked actually has."

She laughed again, this time with a little more sarcasm. "You're kidding," she finally said. "You look nothing alike."

Ryan dragged his foot across the ground, "Well, most people don't look past his beard or my"—he rubbed his jawline "—whatever this stubble is."

"I mean, I could see that happening," she countered. "I don't know. I guess it was just how you interacted."

"Watching us eat now? You've gone from rude to stalkerish…"

"You know what I mean," she said. "You talked like, I don't know, like equals."

"Equals?"

"That probably isn't the word I'm looking for, but you didn't act like you were vacationing with daddy."

"All right, Miss Enlightened." Ryan laughed. "What are we doing, then?"

"I mean, your car is at Randall's…"

"Back to stalkerish."

She smirked at him. "I walked past his lot on my way here. I recognized the car."

"Your nosiness is astonishing."

"Or my attention to detail is astonishing."

"Same thing," Ryan replied.

"But to answer your question, *we* are sitting on a bench in the middle of BFE watching the cohesive machine that is the 'Shannon Christmas Celebration.'"

"You know what I meant," Ryan countered.

"I do, and it isn't something I care about, so I have no guesses."

"Isn't something you care about?"

"Nope." She paused. "The truth is, I saw you at breakfast, and I saw your car at Randall's some twelve hours later, so I deduced that you were either sleeping at the inn or here. What happened before this morning, or in those twelve hours, or anything more, really doesn't matter to what's here and now."

"And no," she continued, "I wasn't stalking you or anything like that. I simply saw the car, recognized it, and went 'Hmm, wonder what those two non-related people are doing,' much the same as you would wonder what anyone you recently interacted with was doing if you felt inclined enough to wonder what they were doing."

"That was a lot of words," Ryan finally said.

"Sorry," she said. "I tend to ramble sometimes."

"Plus, you pay attention to things."

She smirked. "I live in a small town. What else am I going to do?"

They watched as the carolers on the other side of the park moved toward the center.

"So," Ryan replied, "you've lived here a while, I'm assuming?"

Melanie shot him a look full of snide. "You want to learn about me, now?"

Ryan returned the look, still trying to figure her out. "That isn't acceptable?"

She laughed. "You could ask a thousand questions—why on Earth do you want to know how long I've lived here?"

He shook his head. "I don't know; just thought it was a good question."

"A better question would be what song those inept carolers are trying to sing. Or why we choose to do this festival in twenty-degree December instead of a logical time like September or April."

"I could ask those, but I'm more concerned about you, I guess."

"About me?" She was obviously taken aback. "Well, aren't you a charmer."

Ryan smiled, wondering if he had finally rendered her speechless.

"Keep that up, and all these country girls won't be able to resist."

His jaw dropped and he felt his tongue push against his teeth.

"Am I frustrating you?" she asked with a smile.

"I don't know if 'frustrating' is the right word. You're intriguing, though."

"Why's that?"

He sighed. "I don't know. Maybe because in the ten minutes you've known me, you've both ridiculed me and challenged me more than most."

She laughed. "Your friends don't challenge you?"

"You have to have friends for them to challenge you."

"Ah, a lone wolf," she replied with a nod. "Friends are overrated, anyway."

"I never said that."

"I did." She adjusted her coat again and turned to face him. "I always preferred solitude. Most people just want to know things about you; they don't actually care about you."

"I'm surprised to see you're cynical, too," Ryan replied stoically.

"Sarcasm?"

"Indeed."

"I don't find myself cynical, per se…"

"Now you're cynical about being cynical."

She turned away with a huff. "Fine, suffice it to say that I prefer being a closed book."

"I'm shocked…"

Melanie smiled again. "All right fine, Mr. Sarcasm. To answer your question, I have lived here in Shannon, South Dakota, my entire life, save for four years of college at SD State. Happy?"

Ryan's expression turned to pure amazement. "My God, I feel like I've known you forever."

"Shut up," she countered. "Believe it or not, you know more about me than most people in this town."

"Well, you know I drive a Jeep, so I guess it's likewise for me."

"The difference is," she said, finally standing up from the bench. "I didn't prod to get that info."

"Prod?!"

"Yep. Prod."

Ryan laughed in disbelief.

"Are you coming?" she finally asked after standing awkwardly for a moment.

"Coming?"

"Yeah, I'm hungry."

He looked around, unsure of what to do.

"Don't read into it," she said. "It's just food."

Ryan chuckled awkwardly and stood up. "Sure," he replied finally, joining her as she began walking back toward the main section of the festival.

If the air had grown cooler in the darkness, Ryan did not notice, for his attention was focused on the girl beside him. Although the top of her head barely reached his neck, she commanded much more stature and exuded more confidence than he had never seen before. Even in such an informal setting, she seemed to both speak to him and examine her surroundings with a thoughtful air, focusing on two things when most people would only attempt one. Most importantly, however, was her treatment of him, though he could not discern whether she was interested in him personally or merely making conversation with someone who listened. This feeling would not leave him anytime soon.

"Since you seem nosey, I'll just go ahead and ask it," she said after they'd passed a restaurant handing out cocoa. "What's Florida like?"

He turned his head in surprise.

"Your license plate, it was Florida," she answered with seeming annoyance.

Ryan walked briskly to catch up to her. "For someone not interested in people's past, you sure have a keen sense of detail."

"That summarizes it well."

He shook his head.

"So, Florida?"

"It's hot."

"Hot?"

"Yes, as in, it has an elevated temperature."

"I get that—"

"Okay…"

"I'm just wondering why you led with it." She walked over to a cookie stand and snatched a few. She offered one to Ryan.

"Is hot not a good description?" he asked, accepting one.

"I mean, sure, but there's more to a place than temperature."

"Fine, it's humid, too."

"Better."

"And people suck at driving."

"I've heard that."

"And it's a lot of people from a lot of different places all within very confined spaces."

"What about Disney World?"

"What about it?"

"Is it a fun place?"

"I guess. If you like happy people."

"Then no," she replied, finishing her cookie before grabbing another sample from a stand.

"Me either," he replied.

"Beaches nice?"

"I guess."

"I feel like I would like the beaches."

Ryan considered this as they strolled the perimeter of the town square.

"They're nice, but it's a lot of sand and salt."

"You seem to find the negative in things."

"I like to start there," he countered. "That way, you aren't set up for disappointment."

"Way to give a guy answer."

"Thanks?"

"I'm just saying, a beach seems so…"

"Sunny?"

"Constant."

"Constant?"

"Yeah, constant. Like in the movies where the characters are at the beach, it's always either introspective or releasing. The characters are either relaxing, or they discover something about themselves or something like that. Great movies always end at a beach."

"What movies have you seen that you classify as great?"

"*The Shawshank Redemption.*"

"All right, there's one."

"*Forever Young.*"

"That was technically a lighthouse."

"Okay fine, seashore, beach whatever!" she exclaimed. She picked up a cup of cocoa from a table and sipped it. "What about *Pirates?*"

"*—of the Caribbean?*"

"Yeah, it ends at a beach," she reasoned.

"Yeah, it's also not a great movie."

"The first one is."

Ryan laughed. "You're right. *The Godfather, Citizen Kane*, and *Pirates of the Caribbean.*"

"Okay, smart-ass, maybe that isn't the best movie to include."

"What you should admire, from a movie sense," he interjected, "is airports. A lot of good movies end at airports."

"Examples?"

"*Casablanca?*"

"Too cliché."

Ryan stood with his mouth agape as she looked at a local vendor's sidewalk display of artwork. "You can't just discredit it because it's overused."

"Sure I can."

"What about *The Graduate?* Hell, even *Up in the Air.*"

"*Love Actually?*"

"Once again, a crap movie."

Now it was her turn to gaze at him as though he had just cursed wildly. "*Love Actually* is a good movie."

"No, it isn't. And technically, it doesn't end at the airport."

"Bullshit, it does too."

"No, it ends with Hugh Grant at that podium about to tell everyone he's into that girl or something."

"That fades into images of people meeting at airports." She chose a piece from the selection of artwork and proceeded inside the store to the vendor.

Ryan followed and wracked his brain, "Okay, that's a technicality."

"It's also not a crap movie."

"It's a crap movie. It is a terrible Christmas movie and an even worse chick flick."

"And why do you think that?" she asked as she waited for the vendor to place her item in a bag.

"Because! Liam Neeson is way too emotional, that guy who tries to steal Kiera Knightly is a total tool, and, most importantly, it glamorizes Alan Rickman's cheating."

"And? It's real."

"Plus, there's no way anyone would vote for Hugh-freaking-Grant."

"All right, I'll give you that." She laid out a twenty-dollar bill and took the change and the bag from the cashier. "Thanks," she added. "But chick flicks aren't always supposed to be bubbly and girl-ends-up-with-guy-roll-credits."

"All right, then," Ryan continued, walking out the door with her. "What are they supposed to be?"

"They're supposed to show that love is a many-faceted thing."

"By showing Hans Gruber's infidelity?"

"No." She considered it. "Well, yes…Look at the movie from the secretary's position."

"The freak?"

She laughed at this. "Yes, the freak. For her, it was a simple falling-in-love story."

"Yes, but if that was the story, why show the wife and kids and all that crying?"

"What if I said that Alan and the secretary got married and celebrated a fifty-year wedding anniversary?"

"I'd ask how Alan Rickman lived to be 110 years old."

"Follow me here." She moved into a store that was crowded with patrons. "What if that happened? What if that's who he ended up with, but it took many years and a lot of heartbreak to get there?"

"If that's the story," Ryan reasoned, "why not tell it?"

"Because you have to infer it if that's the answer you want."

"Come again?"

"That's why chick flicks are so good. They show love. And, most importantly, they show how we become better humans through love."

"You lost me."

"What I'm saying is—" She looked over another item. "What I'm saying is that in a movie, you are shown a piece of an overall story. It's the piece the screenwriter wants you to see, but not necessarily the piece that defines the overall story."

"All right."

"In a chick flick, that piece is somehow tied to love. The idea, the falling into, or the falling out of."

"And *Love Actually* pertains to this how?"

"It shows that love piece so perfectly. Sometimes, love is pretty shitty. Sometimes it's pretty good. Sometimes someone's love ends so someone else's begins. Regardless, in a chick flick, characters become better humans through love: either great love or really shitty love. And no movie hits that so well."

"Plus," she added, "that scene with Liam's boy running through the airport to catch his classmate to tell her he loves her...so good."

"That'd never happen today."

"What do you mean? Kids can't show love?"

"That and tighter security."

"True. You can't just distract the TSA agent today..."

"Such a shame..."

"There hasn't been a good chick flick that shows love since." She thought for a moment. "Except maybe *The Notebook*."

Ryan scoffed as everyone around him turned to look. He quickly grew silent.

"What?" she asked softly, sensing his sudden embarrassment. "You don't like *The Notebook*, either?"

"No. But I've never met a girl that hasn't liked it."

"So, by that calculation, you're assuming you're right." She led him out of the store. "Instead of the millions of women in the world? You, one sole person, versus all of them?"

"You've made your point."

"It's an excellent movie that depicts hardship through love."

"It's predictable and tiring," Ryan replied.

"Predictable, yes, but tiring? Never. Every girl wants that kind of love."

"What? The one where she bitches and moans and has to break the heart of a veteran who got blown the hell up, all so she can run back to a guy who has no regard for amusement park safety, solely based on his ability to build a wraparound porch?"

She laughed. "Talk about animosity."

"I'm just saying, Ryan Gosling was a total dick."

"And?"

"And? I don't see it. Because he wrote to her?"

She laughed again. "Yes, because he wrote to her, and because he was a total dick."

"Once again, your reasoning fails me."

She took two cups of cocoa and offered one to Ryan as they continued walking. "Girls like total dicks; it's pretty simple."

"Why? Why is that?"

"Why do you like sports?"

"Who said I like sports?"

"Play along. Why do men like sports?"

"Because they're fun. Is that the connection? Bad guys are fun."

"No," she countered. "Why do grown men follow sports, specifically their teams, even when they suck?"

Ryan began to understand her logic. "Because you hope they change into something good?"

"Ding-ding!"

"But people, not just guys, watch sports for other reasons too, you know."

"Sure, but that's why girls like bad guys like Ryan Gosling. We know they're bad, and mistreat us, and are completely indefensible, but we continue hoping that one day we'll see them change and become good guys because of us."

They found their way back into the park and sat on another bench, this one farther from the carolers.

"There's nothing more romantic than the person you love changing because they love you."

"And then," Ryan added, "they build you a porch."

"Exactly."

They sat in silence for a bit.

Ryan sighed. "I guess Gosling wasn't a total dick…"

She turned to him.

"I mean, I'd be pretty pissed if I spent a long time pining for someone that gave up on me…"

"I don't think she gave up."

"You know what I mean."

She laughed. "In one way or another, I guess."

Ryan felt satisfied with this answer. "So, that's your favorite chick flick?"

"Oh, no. It's up there, but not the favorite."

"Enlighten me."

"My favorite?"

"No," he mocked. "I want to hear about the weather…Yes, your favorite."

"I don't want to say."

"Oh, come on."

"No, you'll make fun of it."

"I will not."

"You will, too. Trust me; it's a pretty bad favorite."

"Don't worry, my expectations are low," he countered. "You did call *Pirates of the Caribbean* a great movie."

"I don't want to tell if you're going to mock."

"I'm kidding." He laughed. "Go ahead."

She sheepishly lowered her voice and mumbled.

"What was that?"

"*Jerry Maguire.*"

"What?"

"*JERRY MAGUIRE,*" she yelled mockingly.

"Dear God," Ryan muttered.

"What? What's wrong with *Jerry Maguire?*"

"Nothing's wrong," he said. "It's just…"

"Just what?"

"Just…I don't know…" He paused, searching for the words. "Probably the most cynical chick flick ever."

"Way to quote the lines."

"I'm just saying."

"And?"

"And nothing. It just says a lot about you."

"That I'm cynical?"

Ryan shrugged. "Sure."

"Why sure!?"

"Why do you like that movie?"

"What do you mean?"

"Why that movie?" He turned to face her. "*The Notebook* seems logical, and to a depressing love-hater, I could even see *Love Actually*. Hell, even *Pretty Woman* or *You've Got Mail*…"

"Both decent movies."

"Why *Jerry Maguire*? I'm not even sure Tom Cruise likes that one."

"You really want to know?"

"I'm on the edge of my seat."

"Fine, smart-ass. I like it…I like it because it is the most real love story I've ever seen."

"In what way?"

"Think about it, especially in the context of movies living past the credits."

"Think about what? Them living happily ever after?"

"You can't be serious."

"What?"

"You can't be serious," she repeated.

"What? They didn't?"

"Do you actually believe they lived happily ever after?" She paused once more. "Do you believe that today, twenty years later, Dorothy and Jerry are sitting on some porch somewhere waiting for their twenty-six-year-old son to come home on winter break from the college of medicine where he is pursuing his second doctorate?"

"Doctor?"

"He knew how much the head weighed. I just figured…"

"Oh."

"But do you actually believe that?"

"I think you don't believe that."

"*Of course not!*"

"Why?"

"There's no way in hell that Jerry freakin' Maguire is getting that marriage to last past a year. Hell, he barely made it through two hours!"

"But he did make it—"

"By running through the airport…"

"Ah," Ryan smiled. "Airport…"

She ignored him. "…to get back to his woman to tell her that he's essentially an asshole, but it's okay because we are all assholes, and that somehow makes it okay."

"His was a bit more poetic…"

"Seriously, he made *one* good decision—to leave that game and run through the airport to get to her. That was it. Everything else was just a precursor or reaction to that one— and, most likely first—good decision he made in his life."

"And?"

"And! And that's it! Nothing changed. He was still an agent. He still hadn't, to our knowledge, stopped being an asshole. All he did was realize who he was. All the issues that he had, that they had—they're going to come up soon down the road. And you know what happens then?"

"What's that?" Ryan smiled, living in the sound of her voice.

"Divorce. And child support. And arguments and all that. Pretty soon, that doctor in training will be slinging coke down off 42nd, and Dorothy will be living with her sister from *Jumanji* wondering why she gave Jerry freakin' Maguire another chance."

"Was that the same woman that was in *Jumanji?*"

"I don't know, but whatever, you get my point."

"All right." Ryan adjusted himself in his seat. "Then why, after all, that, is that your favorite chick flick?"

"Doesn't that answer it?"

"Not at all."

"It's simple, really." She leaned back, looking up at the stars. "It's a movie that's not about a happy ending. It's about understanding what it takes to get there."

"Come again?"

"The movie isn't about Jerry and Dorothy living happily ever after. It's about Jerry realizing that he's a total dick *because* of his love for Dorothy. He's too far gone to ever make it work, but in that shining moment when he finally decides to do something good, you see the real, honest, and powerful strength of love. It can change someone, or at least put them on a course to be changed. No other movie tackles that side of love." She paused as if truly looking at one of the many stars with intent. "Every movie wants to show you how the results of 'love' feel, but no one wants to show you what it takes to get there. *Jerry Maguire* does that."

Ryan let her proclamation hang on the air. "So, in your world, they're divorced? Or they divorced soon after the movie ended? And the kid is a drug dealer?"

She laughed as she thought about it. "That might be too harsh," she said finally. "Honestly? I'd like to say separated. They'd try to make it work, but eventually, Dorothy would realize that although he shows potential to change, he changes much too slowly for her. Then she'd cut ties with him, probably wouldn't ask for child support because she's just too humble for that, and she'd let him go. Then, in return, that ending would truly force Jerry to change, and he'd become a good guy with a new family."

"That's still super depressing."

"Not really. Not if the point of love is to make us better human beings so that we can be better for others."

"No. It is."

"Well, I don't think so."

"Well," Ryan sighed. "Maybe one day I'll see it that way. Either way, that'd be a terrible sequel."

"You kidding? It'd be a perfect sequel!" she exclaimed. "All sequels these days are depressing in some way!"

"Not like that!"

"Maybe not that hardcore, but they do tend to kill characters that were spared in the first, and they do tend to mess up perfectly wrapped-up stories."

Ryan did not say anything, knowing she was partly true.

"Consider all part twos in movies—*The Empire Strikes Back. Aliens.* All of those are much more emotionally taxing."

"You named two…"

"And the theory holds true. Sequels are meant to be depressing. They are meant to make you nostalgic for the peace of the first one."

"You have quite the theory."

She sighed. "I think my story would make a perfect Jerry sequel."

"Whatever you say." Ryan laughed.

There was a long pause as she continued looking at the stars. Around them, the festivities were slowly dying down. Even the carolers had ceased their singing. Before long, only the buzzing sound of streetlights and the drone of vendors closing lingered on the air.

"It's been a while since I've talked about movies like that," Mel finally said, turning to Ryan for a moment. "It's nice to banter, even if we're wrong."

Ryan laughed. "What could we possibly be wrong about?"

"I don't know, just saying." She looked back to the town ahead of her. "People nowadays want to correct everything. No one can just be wrong."

Ryan looked at his feet in the snow and smiled. "Good thing we aren't wrong, then."

She looked back at him with a smile. "Good thing."

Footsteps crackled in the snow behind them, causing Ryan to jump from his seat. Mel barely turned.

"Awful late for you kids to be out here," the voice said, sounding as though the trek to the bench had been a lot to handle.

Ryan turned to see a police officer approaching the bench.

Mel, however, turned back around upon hearing the voice. "A crime to be out on a Friday night?" Her voice was biting, almost pugnacious in its tone.

The officer huffed sarcastically. "You know what they say. Nothing good happens to people after ten, especially when those people aren't good to begin with."

Mel sniffed. "I'm fairly sure those people have never had fun, period. Too busy saying long, convoluted things."

Ryan was taken aback at her brashness, but he said nothing.

"Who's your new boy, Mel?" the officer replied, turning to Ryan for the first time.

He was younger than his gruff voice made him sound, which Ryan concluded was caused by the cigarettes that gleamed in the breast pocket of his jacket. Ryan estimated the officer to be in his early thirties, though he could not be sure. The man's dark, piercing eyes and chiseled, strong-jawed face clearly gave him the look of classic masculinity. In addition, the man's facial hair was impressive: a full beard and mustache that covered most of the visible skin. He wore only a thin black jacket and Ryan deduced that the man had to be cold, but somehow, he did not shiver.

"Well, Garrett, I believe he is more man than boy—" she quipped.

"That's Sheriff Ransom to you."

"And it's Ms. Willis to you."

The officer seemed annoyed at this response and turned back to Ryan.

"What's your name, boy?"

"His name is Jerry," Mel replied as if Ryan were mute.

"Jerry?" Ransom repeated.

Ryan nodded.

"Last name?"

"Jesus." Mel turned. "Is it a crime to sit on a bench?"

"I'm talking to the boy," the officer replied, turning back to Ryan. "Where you from?"

Ryan swallowed the lump in his throat. He did not like where this conversation was going.

"He's from Mitchell," Mel answered, "and he's here trying to enjoy our nice hospitality."

The officer dismissed her with a glance before turning back to Ryan, who looked at Mel before nodding in agreement.

"She always speak for you?" he said in an ominous tone.

Ryan attempted to talk, but once again, she answered the question.

"I don't think our business is of any concern to you."

The officer turned with a biting glance toward her.

"You should watch your tone, miss," he hissed, emphasizing the last word a bit too much. Then he turned back to Ryan. "And you should watch who you hang out with around here, bud." He pulled out a cigarette and lit it, blowing smoke as if deciding his next move. After an eternity, he flicked the ash and took a deep breath.

"Enjoy your stay," he said to Ryan, though it was laced with contempt. "I'm sure we'll meet up again."

He turned and walked back into the shadows of the park, the smoke that hung on the air the only remainder of his presence.

"Friend of yours?" Ryan asked as sarcastically as he could muster.

"Can't you tell?"

"He seemed—"

"—To hate me?"

Ryan nodded. "Slightly, yes."

"Well..." She rolled her tongue against her upper lip. "Guess that's what happens when you break hearts..."

Ryan turned as if not understanding.

"He and I used to be a thing," she replied to the unasked question.

"Oh," Ryan replied, somewhat surprised she was divulging the information.

"Yeah."

"So, you broke up with him?"

"Yep."

"And he hates you?"

"Yep."

"Makes sense."

"His whole family hates me."

"Logical."

"Maybe. But I genuinely believe his father hates me more."

"Why?"

"Garrett was a star quarterback," she replied calmly.

Ryan waited for her to continue. "And?"

"His father blames me for ruining his career."

"Did you?"

"Did I what?"

"Ruin his career?"

She thought about it. "Maybe."

"Maybe?"

"We dated off and on through high school and into college. Who knows what would have happened if we hadn't stayed together."

"Off and on?" he asked, picking apart the first of her statements.

"Yeah," she said. "On when he wanted to be; off when he was off cheating."

"Oh," Ryan sighed. "That sucks."

She turned to him for the first time in a while. "Why? He's a jock boy. Of course, he's going to cheat."

The statement confused him. As if sensing this, she continued, "I'm not naïve. I understood who he was. That wasn't the problem. The problem was everyone else found out, and when that happens, there are social protocols to follow, so every month, we'd be off, and then we'd come back around."

Ryan shook his head. "I'm sorry, but I feel like you're setting women back at least fifty years here…"

"Trust me…He wasn't the only one out and about. But I always came back to him. He was hot. It was fun."

"So, what happened?"

"I don't know. I just got tired of that. He wanted to play football forever. He liked game-day celebrations and getting trophies. I ended up deciding I didn't want that life. So, I ended it."

"Huh," Ryan replied.

"South Dakota State lost their next two games," she continued, "and he got some shoulder issue that made him go from top recruit to the police academy in Fargo. If you ask me, it's all coincidental. His father, however, pegs a bit more blame on me." She paused. "Not sure why, he made sheriff pretty quick…"

"That's…a…pretty messed-up story."

"Yeah, well." She got up from the bench. "I'm not proud of everything, but that's life. One of the many reasons I dislike this town."

"Everyone here hates you because of that?"

She laughed. "All the State fans, yes, but I do have a few allies."

"Seems like you need them."

She motioned for him to get up as she turned to walk. "Yeah, well, you should probably keep that alias going while you're here."

"I didn't do anything!" Ryan squeaked, causing her to laugh some more.

"Association, Jerry from Mitchell," she replied.

Ryan shook his head.

She laughed as she spoke. "He's probably Googling Jerry from Mitchell in his car."

"I don't need any more enemies," Ryan retorted.

"Sure, you do," she replied. "They're easier to make. And let's face it…they're much more reliable than friends."

The air had turned cooler. Together, he and Mel walked back past the town square and into an adjoining neighborhood; he following her without trepidation. The celebrations had wrapped up, and now the air was filled with the buzz of streetlights while a thin layer of snow settled on the ground. The world seemed at peace as they continued their walk.

"You must think I'm quite a bitch, huh?" Mel asked without provocation.

Ryan walked at her side, not caring about their destination. "What makes you say that?"

"I don't know, just what you've learned tonight. The ex and all that stuff."

Ryan shrugged. "No, I don't think that."

"Well, you should, because I can be one."

"I think anyone can be if pushed there."

"I mean just in general. I do stupid stuff."

Ryan laughed. "I haven't met anyone who hasn't."

"Well, still. I understand if you think that."

"Well, I don't," he answered. "I think you're human."

"A bitchy human."

"Listen. Anyone examined close enough looks bad for something. It's just the nature of being human, I guess."

They continued walking, changing streets every so often.

"You already know more about me than I wanted to tell," she said. Ryan could sense that she was telling the truth.

"I won't tell," he replied with a smile.

She glared at him.

"What are you doing tomorrow?" she asked as they reached the edge of a tree-lined street.

Ryan was curious. "What do you mean?"

"I mean," she continued, "what are your plans for tomorrow? Do you have any? Or are you going to sit and watch Randall not work on your truck? Maybe sleep all day?"

"I get the question," he replied. "I'm just wondering why you're asking."

"I can't ask? Is your business that private?"

"Fine. Nothing that I know of."

"Good. My brother is doing that Christmas concert thing, and I'm supposed to pick him up from his morning practice."

"Oh."

"And you're welcome to join if you want."

He instantly became perplexed by her invitation.

"You don't have to. No pressure."

"It's not that," he countered. "I guess I'm just a little confused—"

"Don't be. If you want to go, then go. If not, then don't. Not everything has to be something."

Ryan shrugged. "I'm sorry. I guess my mind is running in a thousand places."

Her pace slowed as the Shannon Inn appeared in the darkness. "It's fine. Do you want to go?"

"Sure," Ryan answered. "I'll try to make it."

"Cool." She stopped near the front of the hotel. "You are staying here, right?"

Ryan laughed. "Yeah, I am."

"Good. Well, get some sleep." She started to turn away. "I'll see you tomorrow."

"Wait," Ryan said. "Wait a minute."

She stopped. Ryan could tell she had taken a deep breath.

He stared at the ground before meeting her gaze. "Thanks for joining me tonight."

She smiled, clearly not wanting the moment to linger. "No problem. Now get some rest." She turned and made for the sidewalk.

Ryan walked to his door and watched her only a moment before shaking his head and inserting his key.

Countless thoughts ran through his mind, but before he could digest any of them, he was greeted by a beam of light as he pushed the door open. Bo sat on his own bed, clad in a towel and his normal shorts. He was propped on pillows and reading a magazine Ryan did not recognize.

"Hey," Bo smiled. "There he is."

"Hey," Ryan replied, slipping inside and setting his key on the counter.

"What have you been up to? I haven't seen you all night."

Ryan blew out his breath as he saw the orange shirt hanging in the bathroom. The rest of the room remained as sterile as when he had left.

"Well," he began, not knowing what to say. "I guess I woke up and made my way to that festival thing."

"Wasn't it amazing?" Bo exclaimed. "Seriously! All the cookies and cocoa. Plus, they had that meat on a stick and those sausages."

"Food was good," Ryan replied, smiling before moving to the bathroom.

"Everyone was so friendly," Bo continued. "I felt right at home, which for me doesn't say much considering where my home is…"

Ryan chuckled, though felt bad doing so.

"Then what?"

Ryan wiped his face on a towel. "Then I sat on a bench, and our waitress from this morning sat down by me."

"Melanie?" Bo asked, causing Ryan to step out and look at him.

"How'd you know her name?"

Bo looked up from his magazine. "You said she was our waitress…"

"I know that," Ryan countered. "How'd you remember her name?"

"It was this morning." Bo continued looking at his magazine. "I just remembered it, I guess."

"Do you remember all our waitresses' names?"

"Ry, I'm sorry if that scared you," Bo replied. "I promise I won't remember anyone's names from here on out…"

Ryan returned to the bathroom. "It's not that," he called out. "I just didn't remember her. That's all. I'm surprised you did."

"She was a nice girl."

"Yeah, she is," he replied, moving into the room, and pulling back the covers on his bed.

"What'd you all talk about?" Bo asked.

Ryan sighed as he took off his shoes. "Movies, mostly. A little bit about life, I guess. But then she asked me to hang out tomorrow."

"And?" Bo asked, still reading his magazine.

"And I don't know. It's been a while since someone asked me out."

Bo laughed. "You think it was like a *date* ask out?"

"Yeah, I do. What's funny about that?"

"Seems bold after one outing."

"I agree."

"What'd she ask you to? Like, dinner or something?"

"No," Ryan replied, pushing his shoes away from the bed. "She asked me to go to some Christmas concert practice."

"Oh, the elementary school thing? Yeah, that wasn't a date then."

"What?"

"It's not a date."

"What do you mean?"

"I mean, she didn't ask you out on a date. She asked you to hang out."

"How do you know?" Ryan replied. "You weren't there."

"She asked you to a practice," Bo replied. "I don't think that's a date."

Ryan sighed as he slipped under his covers. "You're probably right."

"Did she hug you or anything tonight?"

"No. She actually moved away pretty quick."

"Then, there's your answer."

Ryan did not reply.

"Did you want it to be a date?"

Ryan turned back to Bo. "No, I just...I don't know...maybe?"

"So, you like her?"

"It was a couple of hours."

"And?"

"Isn't a couple of hours a bit soon to like someone?"

"I don't know," Bo considered. "You already seem to be debating it..."

"Listen," Ryan replied, turning away. "Not everything is something."

"What the hell does that mean?"

"I don't know." Ryan sighed as he turned away. "It's something she said."

"Quoting her, too?"

"I'm tired. I'm going to sleep."

Bo laughed from behind him. "Seems like a predicament you've gotten yourself into."

"Yeah. Goodnight."

Bo continued chuckling. "Keep me posted."

Ryan listened as Bo rustled in his own bed. Before long, he had put the magazine down and slipped under his own covers before turning the light off and casting the room into darkness. There was silence once more.

Ryan's eyes stayed open. Turning onto his back, he gazed at the ceiling for a long time.

His mind raced with questions he felt he could never answer. What did it mean? Not just her invitation, but the entire situation. Clearly, they had a connection, but what was there to make of it? Or was it a real case of falling for someone? There was too much to discern, and it had come much too soon. He felt small and unsure, and that feeling was foreign to him. He figured this was how all small things felt, like a leaf in an ocean or a mouse on the savannah. None of those fit, however. She was much too passionate and intense for those comparisons.

A wildfire, he thought. She was a wildfire. Burning with the radiance of a thousand suns, she had blazed into his path without care or warning. He, on the other hand, was a withered branch in the grips of her fervor, and there was nothing he could do. The time for precaution was gone, and there were no provisions to be made. It was much too late for all that. All he could do now was hold on tight, embrace the heat, and clasp her light.

She was a wildfire, he knew, and as dangerous as she was, he could not help but fall for the flames.

Chapter 12
1,083 Miles to Spokane

Ryan awoke unceremoniously to a tap at the hotel door. Eyes blinking open, he stared at the door for a moment to gauge not only the hour but his locale as well. His sleep had been deep, and now he was left treating his location and time as though they were quantum mechanics—problems he could never solve in his current state.

There was another light tap at the door. Ryan threw the blankets off and moved to the door, checking briefly to see if Bo was awakened by the noise. Seeing as he was not, Ryan cracked the door open.

"Morning," Mel said, leaning in the doorway with an orange in her hand.

"Mel?" Ryan breathed, shielding his eyes from the morning rays.

"Yeah, time to go."

"Time to go?"

"Practice," she replied, eating a piece of orange. "My brother? For the concert?"

"Oh." Ryan shook his head. "Right."

"Go get some pants on," Mel said. "I'll wait."

Ryan looked down, saw that he was in an undershirt and boxers, and immediately felt embarrassed. He retreated to the room and shut the door as he searched wildly for his pants. Finding them, he dressed quickly but quietly, taking care to put on his shoes after. He grabbed his jacket from the chair and pulled it over his head as he reached for the door and proceeded outside.

"USF?" Mel uttered, still leaning on the doorway with her orange.

Ryan ignored her comment about the jacket and glanced at her. "What time is it?"

"7:45. Here, breakfast," she replied as she threw him another orange. "Figured you'd feel at home."

"Thanks," Ryan said, looking down at the fruit.

"Let's go." She turned and walked toward the sidewalk.

Ryan followed closely behind as he began to peel his orange. He was still in a daze.

"Miss Barbara said her grandson was going to be in this concert, too," Mel began as they walked. "Maybe we'll see him."

Ryan recalled the innkeeper talking briefly about the concert, though the details escaped him.

"You don't do mornings well, do you?" she asked as Ryan lagged behind.

"Sorry." He breathed in the cold air.

"It's fine, we'll be on time."

"Do you"—Ryan sucked down a piece of orange— "you know, walk everywhere?"

She laughed. "If you're asking if I have a car, the answer is no. I don't."

"You don't?"

"No," she replied, changing streets. "I did have one. But when I moved home, I decided to give it to my father. It's his car now."

"And you…walk?"

"Mostly, yes. It's a small town. He takes me to work, mostly. But I enjoy walking."

"What if you want to leave town?"

"I don't. But if I do, then he'll usually drive me. Or I guess I could take it, but I haven't in a long time."

"And your mom?"

"Died eight years ago."

"Oh." Ryan stopped mid-peel. "I'm sorry."

"It's fine. Cancer sucks."

"Yeah, it does." He upped his pace to meet hers. "How old is your brother?"

"Nine."

"Quite a difference, then."

"Him to me? Yeah, fourteen years."

Ryan nodded.

"Siblings?" she asked, changing streets again.

"No," he replied, eating another piece.

"Ah, an only child. I understand."

"Understand what?"

"Just nothing." She laughed. "Your parents coddle you?"

Ryan shrugged. "I guess. I don't know." He paused. "Sometimes, more attention isn't always good."

"Harder to get away with shit, I'm sure," she said.

He nodded, though he could not tell if she saw or not.

They rounded another corner and a school appeared. As they approached, Ryan saw little in the way of commotion outside, though some cars were in the lot. The sign outside read "Shannon Elementary."

Mel led him past the cars and toward a side entrance. Once inside, they were hit with a blast of heat. Ryan quickly saw that they were in a lobby of sorts, complete with accolades covering the wall and bright blue and gold shining on the walls.

"Bobcats?" Ryan asked, looking at the awards.

"Yep," Mel replied, leading him through another door. "Shannon Bobcats."

She grew quiet as they entered a small auditorium, complete with a basic stage and some thirty rows of seats. She moved past two rows before sliding into the third, moving down slightly so that Ryan had a seat as well.

Sitting down, Ryan saw the stage full of kids of all ages, eagerly following what appeared to be the conductor. They appeared mid-set. About a dozen parents watched the practice from the audience. Some smiled wildly while others were more reserved.

On the stage, two boys and two girls were dressed in tuxedos reminiscent of a bygone London era. One boy sat behind drums, while the other three stood to attention as the conductor gave orders.

"This is always a big draw," Mel whispered, "because it's really the only time our chorus and band play together for the elementary school."

Ryan nodded, wondering more about the eclectic group of kids on the stage. As the tuxedo group took orders, another group stood to the right of the stage. These five children all wore wigs that made them resemble teenage boys, although three were girls. Behind them, another four kids were dressed as normal adults, although one girl wore dark sunglasses and a black wig.

"I'm not following…" Ryan finally said.

"Following what?"

"Whatever the hell this is," he whispered.

"It's a Christmas concert. They'll play music."

"I get that," he replied. "I just don't understand what they are doing."

"Oh," Mel whispered back. "United Kingdom Christmas."

"You say that as if it makes sense."

"The kids all dress up as bands from the UK. Those kids are U2," she said, pointing to the group in the back. "Those up front are the Beatles."

Ryan was even more confused. "U2 are Irish…"

"You act like these farmers are going to know the difference."

"All right then," he said. "What does any of this have to do with Christmas?"

"It doesn't," Mel laughed. "But our instructor likes to always do something out of the box. Last year, he did a concert based on famous Broadway plays. It's just his thing."

Ryan considered this as he watched the kids begin singing. "All right, who are those kids?" He motioned to the group of five on the far right.

"One Direction," she replied.

"Who?"

"A new band. The instructor likes to be hip."

"Oh."

"Yeah, it's a bit weird, and most people here don't get it, but whatever."

"What is your brother playing?"

"He's playing Posh Spice."

"What?"

"Posh—"

"No, I heard you. I just…what?"

"What? A boy can't play Posh? You do realize that a girl is playing Paul McCartney…"

"I get it, I'm just…surprised."

"Why?"

Ryan thought for a moment. "I don't know, this just seems like a pretty conservative place…"

"It is, but each year the instructor pushes the envelope. Plus, it isn't like he'll be singing Spice Girls. They all sing the same song while some play instruments. It's just more for show."

"Oh…"

"Yeah. Last year he had three students sing 'Rent,' and since none of these country folks knew it was about everyone dying of AIDS, they were none the wiser."

"What they don't know…"

"Exactly."

As they spoke, the Spice Girls took the stage, and more students filled in behind. Together, they all joined into some sort of hymn while the Beatles, Coldplay, and the Who all played instruments around them. The conductor kept everyone level, and Ryan was surprised by how good the group sounded.

Before he knew it, the singing had ended, and all the kids had returned their costumes to a rousing procession of applause from the parents watching.

"Concert is tonight at six," the director said into a microphone before collecting his notes and moving from the stage. Ryan reasoned that he was a better instructor than a speaker.

"Good job, bud," Mel said to a young boy who joined them. He was dressed in the white coat portion of his costume with blue jeans underneath.

"Thanks," he said with a small smile. He looked at Ryan, who got up and followed Mel to the end of the aisle. "Who's he?"

"This is Ryan," Mel said as she bent down and wiped some glopped hair gel from his face. "He's a friend of mine."

"Oh, where's he from?"

"Florida," Mel said. "He's spending the weekend here."

"Oh," he replied, peering at Ryan once more.

Ryan stood there awkwardly, not quite knowing what to say. "I enjoyed your practice," he finally said.

"Thanks," the boy responded.

"You were good, Max," Mel continued. "Plus, you looked good, too. I love this jacket."

"It's hot," Max replied. "I wish I could have gotten Tyler's part." He looked over to another boy dressed in a tank top and athletic pants.

"Yeah." Mel stood. "But Posh is so much better than Sporty Spice. Isn't that right, Ryan?"

Ryan stared at her. "I have no idea."

She laughed as she turned back to Max. "Let's go get something to eat."

"Diner?" Max asked, holding her hand as they walked toward the door.

"Diner." She smiled and turned back to Ryan. "That okay with you?"

Ryan returned the smile. "Sounds good to me."

"Did you really like the practice?" Max asked after a moment.

"I did," Ryan responded, knowing the question was aimed at him.

As they walked to the diner where Ryan had first seen Mel a little over twenty-four hours before, Max and Mel talked endlessly about the upcoming concert and what the instructor wanted from each group of performers. Ryan tried to piece it together, but with each child dressed as someone, yet singing and playing together as a group, he found it hard. For the most part, he kept quiet until they reached the diner and took a seat.

"Was it weird?" Max asked. He sat up on his legs and leaned over the table.

"It was…different." Ryan laughed.

"I told Ryan," Mel interjected, "about the musical piece last year."

"Oh, yeah," Max said. "That was a weird one."

"I liked it!" Mel laughed.

"Well." Max looked at her dubiously. "You're weird."

"Hey, now." Mel continued laughing as a stranger approached the table.

"How was practice?" the stranger asked, rubbing his hands onto an apron at his side.

"Awesome," Max replied, clearly knowing the man.

"Good," the man replied, then eyed Ryan. "Who's your friend?"

Ryan was confused and did not know whether to stand or sit as he looked to Mel and then back to the man.

"Dad, this is Ryan. Ryan, my dad."

Ryan's eyes went wide as he stood up to shake the man's hand. He was a taller man with a balding head and dark circles under his eyes. His gruff disposition was magnified by his even gruffer face, yet there was kindness in his eyes.

"You know Mel, I take it?" the man said to Ryan.

"I waited on him yesterday," Mel interrupted, "and we met up at the festival last night."

"Oh," the man responded, turning back to Ryan. "In town for the festival?"

"Not really," Ryan replied slowly, debating the logic of lying. "I actually had some car problems, so I'm stranded here for the weekend."

The man either did not care or believed it for a lie. He turned to his daughter and son. "Well," he said, "there are worst places to be stranded."

Thankfully, Max changed the subject. "Can I get bacon and eggs?"

His father looked back to Ryan and then to his son. "Of course. You want anything, Mel?"

"Coffee, I guess. Ryan?"

Ryan's stomach ached, but he could not bring himself to ask for anything. Instead, he just shook his head. "I'm good," he responded, more to himself than anything.

The man nodded and walked back to the kitchen. As he left, Mel started laughing.

"What?" Ryan asked softly, leaning over the table.

"You look terrified." She giggled. Max also found humor in the situation.

"I'm sorry." Ryan chuckled as well. "I just wasn't expecting your father to walk out here…"

"Dad frightens a lot of people." Max laughed, not quite getting the true reason for Ryan's unease.

"I can see why!"

Mel's laughter died down. "Yeah," she said, "he's owned this diner for about ten years. Fixed it up and did a good job."

"Kept his mind off our mom," Max continued. It was a comment that made both Mel and Ryan turn their heads. "What?" he asked innocently. "That's what he said."

Mel smirked. "He does say that a lot. It's probably true."

Ryan looked around. The diner was close to full. "And you decided to help him out?"

"More or less," Mel replied. "He did a good job at first, but it's gotten harder in the last few years. He's getting older, and there just wasn't much help to be found. So last year, I decided to help him out."

"I help out, too," Max added as a waitress delivered water to the table.

"Yes, you do," Mel acknowledged. "You come clean the place during summers."

Not long after, the same waitress brought a plate full of bacon and eggs to the table, and when Max offered some to the other two, Ryan leapt at the chance.

"Are you coming to my concert tonight?" Max asked after he and Ryan had put down some bacon.

Mid-bite, Ryan looked at Mel to find her smiling at him.

"I think so," he said. "If you want me to."

Max crunched loudly. "Yeah, I'd like that."

"Good."

The young boy continued eating his bacon at a record rate before throwing another question Ryan's way.

"What are you doing here, anyway?"

"That's a rude question," Mel laughed.

"Not like that," Max clarified. "I just, wondered why you were in Shannon. Is your car really broke down?"

Ryan wiped his mouth. "Yeah, it really is."

"Huh," the boy said, downing a bite of eggs. "Where were you going?"

"Where was I going?" Ryan repeated, although he'd heard it the first time.

"Yeah," Max continued innocently. "Where were you going? Was it like a trip or something?"

Ryan took a deep breath, feeling Mel's eyes on him as he spoke. "It was something like that."

"Where to?"

Ryan paused again. "Well." He looked toward Mel and then returned his gaze to her brother. "We were actually heading to Washington."

"Why?"

Ryan shrugged with a smile, debating the answer in his head. "Well," he began, "I'm helping out a friend of mine."

"Helping him do what?"

"He's—" Ryan looked to Mel once more. "He's actually trying to see his family for Christmas."

"Oh." Max continued eating. "Doesn't he live with them?"

Ryan sniffed. "Not...exactly. He's from Florida, like me." He could sense that his answer did not quite meet Max's expectations. "And you see, he wasn't doing so good, money-wise, so I decided to help him out."

"What about your family?" Max asked.

"My family?" Ryan repeated, vacillating between lies and truth. "Well, I thought his situation was more important. Plus, I'm sure my family understands."

"Hmm," Max replied. "Are you guys, like, best friends?"

Ryan laughed. "I wouldn't say that. I really haven't known him long, but he's a good guy. He deserves to see his family."

He could tell that his answers had finally appeased the boy. After a minute of contemplation, Max finally spoke. "That's nice of you."

Ryan nodded with a smile, sitting back in the booth as if he had just survived a harsh interrogation. Casually, his glance left Max and fell upon Mel. It was then that he noticed her staring into him, and he wondered if she had been doing so the entire time.

The trio left the restaurant around noon. Much to Ryan's delight, he did not have to say anything more to their father, save for a thank you. Instead, the older man focused on his children, thanking Mel for picking up her brother on her day off, and making sure she knew what time he had to be to the school. Ryan tried not to listen to the conversation, but he could not help but feel for the man who ran not only a diner but also a family. They were a close-knit group with ample love between them.

"My concert's at six," Max called back to Ryan, who followed the siblings as they walked down a street lined with frozen fields.

"Okay," Ryan replied, "I look forward to it."

Mel leaned down to her brother as they approached an intersection. "Run ahead," she whispered.

Before Ryan knew what happened, she turned back toward him.

"I need to get him home and get his costume ready and all that."

Ryan nodded. "Oh, okay. That's fine."

She smiled. "You know your way back to the hotel?"

Ryan looked around, noticing that Max was turning right at the intersection. "I assume," he said, "it's that way?" He pointed in the opposite direction.

"Down that road, take a right. You'll see it." She paused for a second. "I'll be at the school at five, by the way, so come sometime between then and six. Bring your friend, too. I'll save you a seat if you want."

Ryan smiled at her kindness in inviting Bo. "That'd be good."

He figured their conversation was finished, yet she did not turn back around. Instead, she stared at him for what felt like an eternity.

"What?" Ryan asked, feeling as though he was missing something.

"You didn't lie to him," she said.

"What?"

"To Max. When he asked where you were heading. You didn't lie."

"Oh." Ryan responded, not sure what else to say.

"You could have said anything," she reasoned. "He's a kid; he'd believe it. But you didn't. You told him the truth."

Ryan half-turned his head with a smile. "You sure I didn't lie?"

She did not smile in return. Instead, she stared at him with some sort of amazement, which Ryan found both comforting and uncomfortable. "Yeah, I am."

He shrugged, still not knowing what to say.

"Why?" she asked. "Why not lie?"

Ryan swallowed before looking back at her. "I don't know." He broke the gaze as he looked around. "I guess I just didn't want to…"

Her face broke into a smile.

"What?" Ryan asked accusingly.

She turned from him, still smiling. "Nothing, you're just…different."

"What does that mean?" he asked, increasing his pace to keep up with her.

"Nothing," she laughed, moving farther away. "I'll see you tonight." She turned, leaving him alone once more.

He watched her walk away without glancing back. Shaking his head, he turned down the opposite street, more confused than ever before.

***

"I have nothing to wear," Ryan lamented. He looked over his belongings, which consisted of a jacket on the hotel chair and little more. The time since meeting Mel had passed rapidly, and now he was rushing for the occasion.

In the opposite bed, Bo sat upright, watching a television program Ryan did not know. He was dressed in his usual clothing, which looked more peculiar than normal given he was simply watching TV.

Bo was honored to be invited to the play by someone he barely knew, but Ryan could sense that his usual chipper demeanor was more reserved than usual. He pondered this briefly, but a quick look at the clock forced his attention to a more pressing matter: his lack of clothing.

"I can't wear the same jacket," Ryan continued, more to himself.

"You've worn the same thing with me every day," Bo said as he changed the channel.

Ryan glared at him. "I'm aware."

"I mean, granted," Bo countered, "small sample size. But five days and one outfit lead me to think you don't shop much."

"How about you?" Ryan replied. "Last I checked, you had one bright-as-hell shirt."

"Two. One's in the bag."

"Whatever. You aren't a Tommy Hilfiger, either."

"No, I'm Tommy Bahama." Bo laughed.

Ryan found little amusement in this.

"I'm not seeing the big deal," Bo replied. "You don't smell. Your clothes, while worn, are still pretty clean…"

"The deal is," Ryan turned, "it's a semiformal event. And I have a jacket and blue jeans and two sweatshirts in the back of my Jeep."

"Wear those, then."

"No."

"Why?"

"It's a somewhat nice event…"

"And?"

"One's a Busch Gardens sweatshirt."

Bo sighed. "*And?*"

"Jesus…"

"Wear the other…"

"No."

"Why?"

"It's…ratty."

"Ratty?"

"Yes."

"You sure?"

Ryan gritted his teeth. "Yes. It's ratty. Too ratty for this."

"Yet you keep it instead of throwing it away like you did your work polo?"

Ryan took a deep breath. "I'll look like…"

Bo stared at him. "A homeless guy?"

"You know what I mean…"

"Yeah I do, and it's pretty much what you are."

"Okay," Ryan seethed. "Maybe I don't want her to know that."

"*Her.*" Bo smiled. "She is now a *she.*"

"Don't turn this into—"

"It's okay if you like her!"

"Jesus, here we go."

"I'm just saying…"

Ryan began dusting his USF jacket as if needing something to do. "Why do you psychoanalyze everything?"

"I don't know what that means."

"You always want to know what's going on in my mind. What I'm thinking or feeling." He scrutinized the jacket before turning back. "Maybe I just want to look nice for an outing."

Bo sighed and shook his head. He turned back to the TV. "Take my shirt, then."

"What?"

"My extra shirt. Take it." He motioned to his bag on the table near the television.

Ryan looked at the bag and then back to Bo. "You're serious."

"I am."

"Why?"

"Why? It's a clean shirt. It's nice. And you need a shirt."

"Don't you need it?"

"Not tonight. I'll just wear this one."

Ryan thought about it. "So, we'll wear the same shirt?"

"At least it's clean. Or as clean as the rainwater from an interstate overpass can be."

Ryan cocked his head.

"I'm kidding," Bo laughed. "I washed it at a Super 8 last weekend. I wash my clothes at the hotels, too. Usually for free. Amazing how much change people leave lying around."

"You are a world wonder…"

"Seriously, though. Take the shirt. And if you're worried about walking into that place with a twin, we can even go separately."

At Bo's offer, Ryan turned away from the bag. "What do you mean?"

"You have a girl to impress!" Bo answered, "I understand not wanting to be seen with some guy in the same shirt."

"Bo, of course I want to go with you."

Bo laughed. "Ry, you don't have to. I do understand."

Ryan faced Bo as the latter sat up from the bed and looked at the clock on the nightstand.

"Bo, you're my friend," he finally said. "And friends stick together."

Bo froze. "What?"

Ryan smiled. "You're my friend." He turned back to the bag. He reached inside and found the shirt sitting atop the Hemingway book. He pulled the shirt out, leaving the book untouched.

Turning back around, he saw Bo dabbing at his eyes with a tissue.

"You okay?" Ryan asked, concerned.

"Fine, fine," Bo replied, turning away.

"What?"

Bo exhaled. "Nothing…it's just been…"

"Been what?"

Bo squinted as he wiped the last of his tears. "It's been a while since I've been a friend to someone."

Ryan felt his own emotions well up, but he turned toward the bathroom before letting them show. The comment had hit him deeply. Damming his emotions, he swapped his shirt for the orange Hawaiian attire and moved back into the main room.

"Well, you are a friend," he said, not wanting to continue the emotional discussion. "You ready?"

Bo nodded, not altogether recovered from his tears. He stood and walked to Ryan. He patted him on the back and then moved toward the front door.

Once again taken aback by the gesture, Ryan took a deep breath before following Bo out the door. As he did so, he thought about his counterpart and how this was perhaps the first speechless moment he had felt since their meeting. The silence, however, was short lived.

"I kind of feel like the Genie to your Aladdin," Bo said as the door shut behind Ryan. Ryan managed a chuckle.

"It's almost like we're heading to Agrabah to meet the princess, doesn't it?"

Ryan shook his head. "Whatever you say, Bo. Whatever you say."

As they walked into the cold afternoon air, Ryan let his thoughts move past his friend Bo and on to the apprehension of the night ahead. He thought of Mel and of her invitation to the play. He thought of his conversations with her, of the memories from earlier in the day. He thought of all these things, and only of them.

"You want me to change the subject?" Bo asked.

"I do," Ryan breathed. "I do."

"I can talk about how this town got its name…"

"How do you know that?"

"Learned it today."

Ryan shook his head, allowing his mind to clear as Bo continued talking.

He did not think of Spokane. He did not think of Florida. He did not think of past failures, or of his life before yesterday evening. He did not think of his mom, dad, or even Bo. He did not even think of the ridiculous shirt he was wearing or the fact that, up until five minutes ago, it had sat atop a gun in a book possessed by his friend. He thought of none of those things.

All that mattered was the present. All that mattered was tonight.

Not even Hemingway could counter that.

Chapter 13
1,084 Miles to Spokane

If it was colder than earlier in the day, Ryan did not feel it. In fact, he felt little as he walked beside Bo down some street he did not know the name of. As on the night before, he knew little of his destination, but he followed his senses, and the growing number of pedestrians finally led him back to the school he had visited earlier in the day.

"You came here this morning, right?" Bo asked sometime between leaving the hotel and arriving at the school.

"I did," Ryan replied, answers becoming ever curter as his nervousness grew.

"Was the play any good?" Bo asked. "What you saw of it, I mean?"

Ryan looked around. "It was…weird."

"Weird?"

"Yeah," Ryan countered. "Something about British bands and kids acting like them."

"Oh, well, that isn't that weird."

"Is to me."

"Grown women acting like cats climbing down the theater seats…That's weird."

Ryan tried to quell the discussion. "I guess."

"I do love *Cats*," Bo continued. "Not a *Phantom* fan, though. Too '80s."

They arrived at the edge of the school grounds amid what was now a large group of people. Ryan glanced around for even the slightest sign of Mel, but she was nowhere to be seen.

"She here yet?" Bo asked, having ended his Broadway talk altogether.

"Not that I see."

"Maybe she's inside."

"Probably."

They made their way unceremoniously toward the lobby doors, attempting to blend in as much as two Hawaiian shirt-clad men could. They were feet from the door when Ryan felt a hand on his shoulder. At first, he thought it was Mel. But soon enough he knew that this was not the grip of a friend.

"Jerry from Mitchell," the gruff voice said in a voice only Ryan could hear.

Sweat broke out on Ryan's brow, but he did not turn around. On his right side, Bo was oblivious to the newcomer as the crowd surrounded them.

"I'd like a word," Sheriff Ransom said, almost in a whisper.

He let go, and Ryan gritted his teeth, knowing there was little he could do.

"Go check inside," Ryan finally said aloud toward Bo.

Bo turned to see Ryan standing among the crowd. "What are you gonna do?"

"I'll wait out here for a minute. See if anyone turns up."

Bo smiled. "And by anyone, you mean h—"

"Yep," Ryan interjected, sweat beading in the cold air. He knew the sheriff was listening to every word. He quickly left Bo behind in the crowd, leaving no time for a reply.

"Mitchell-man has a friend, I see," the sheriff purred in a low, even voice.

Ryan watched Bo enter the building. "What can I help you with?" he retorted in a seething voice as he turned to face the man.

"What can you help me with?" the man responded with a chuckle. "Well, isn't that kind of you?"

Ryan thought about a sarcastic retort but decided not to press his luck.

The sheriff, out of uniform and wearing a gray coat and an even darker cowboy hat, calmly pulled out a cigarette. He took his time lighting it.

"I just," the man began. He took a long draw on the cigarette. "I just wanted to apologize if me and you got off on the wrong foot."

The silence that hung on the air was thick, but Ryan did not risk destroying it with words. Instead, he let Ransom break the tension.

"Usually, when someone apologizes, the other person accepts…"

Ryan shrugged his shoulders, not daring to reply.

"In this town," the sheriff continued, flicking the ash onto the snow, "I'm looked at as a protector, a fighter." He spoke with such candor that Ryan almost considered buying in. "And with that said, I feel a great responsibility to take notice of newcomers." He paused and looked thoughtfully at the growing crowd. "We've got a great town—a wonderful small town." He turned back to Ryan. "And in this town, hospitality is what we pride ourselves in, and we're damn good at it. But hospitality is a thing of karma; you get what you give." He took a step forward.

Ryan watched him, not bothering to interject.

"Now, if you come here to visit our stores or dine at our tables and socialize with our people and all that," the sheriff continued, "I'd see you as a decent man worthy of this town's great hospitality. I'd even say hello on the street, and I'm sure, being a man of decency, you'd reply with courtesy." He flicked the cigarette again. "But when my first interaction with a newcomer is as ours was, especially in the company that it was in, well, then I start asking questions and wondering about the decency of our visitors."

Ryan took a deep breath. "I'm sorry to give that impression."

The sheriff smiled. "Maybe you are." He breathed in again. "But two things are for certain. Your name's not Jerry, and you're as much from Mitchell as I'm from a horse's ass."

"Excuse me?"

"Don't 'excuse me,' boy," he replied, his voice low and mean. "You heard me. I didn't believe your story the moment that dumb bitch said it. You can't fool me, you hear?"

Ryan shook his head. "I don't know what you want from me."

The sheriff laughed gruffly. "Want from you? You got it all wrong." He drew again on the cigarette. "It isn't what I want from you; it's what you want from me."

"What I want from you?"

"Exactly."

"What do I want from you, then?"

The sheriff flicked the butt on the ground and stepped on it. "You want protection."

"Protection?"

"Yep. You want protection, and I want to protect you. Even though you're lying to my face, I feel obligated to protect you from the devils that accompany you."

"In what way?"

"In every way."

"I don't understand."

"How much do you know about your little friend?

"I don't—"

"She tell you about her previous life? About her and me?"

"I don't want to be involved in your—"

"So, she did?"

"I don't know."

"Don't bullshit me."

Ryan half-turned. "I don't have time for this." The sheriff gripped his arm roughly, preventing him from moving.

"She ruined my life."

His voice was no longer curt and cold. Instead, it was filled with anger—distressing, bitter anger that came from deep within.

"I gave up everything for her. I gave up football. I gave up my family."

"I have no interest in what happened between you and her," Ryan countered.

"She told me she'd be with me forever," Ransom continued, ignoring the comment. "And she walked out on me soon after I gave her the ring."

Ryan's eyes grew wide as he tried to quell his deepening curiosity.

"She always leaves that part out," Ransom added, voice returning to normal.

Ryan looked at the pain in the sheriff's eyes. "That's between you and her. Not me."

"But you're wrong," Ransom said gruffly. "It involved you the moment you stepped into her life."

Ryan swallowed the lump in his throat. "I'm not in her life."

"Oh, but you are," Ransom responded. "You are in her life. And if you stay in her life, she will destroy you, just like she destroyed me."

Ryan did not respond.

"She's a disaster, Jerry. She destroys everything."

"I need to go," Ryan replied. He turned again and this time, he was not held back. He managed only a few steps before the sheriff's voice hit him.

"Don't worry, though," he said to Ryan's back. "She won't destroy you before I do."

Ryan shook his head as he turned around. "What?"

He stood rigid. "She needs to feel pain." His voice was both simple and dangerous. "She deserves it, and so I will destroy everything she cares about to see that she gets it."

Ryan cocked his head as he heard the words, unable to process.

"That includes you."

Ransom's voice continued in its deadly tone. "Whatever lies you're telling me, whatever you're hiding from this town…I'll find them."

"What makes you think I'm lying?" Ryan replied in a curiously cautious tone.

The sheriff stared. "Everyone lies, Jerry. To me. To you. To her. No one goes unscathed."

Ryan turned back around, not caring to hear anymore. The crowd had already filed in, and regardless of what the sheriff said, he had someone waiting for him.

Perhaps it was confidence, or maybe cockiness. Regardless, Ryan was done listening to the words of a man he barely knew. He had too much at stake inside to ever walk away now.

"You made it," Mel whispered as Ryan and Bo clambered into the aisle seats in the fourth row. "These were the closest seats I could save."

She sat in the row ahead of them, and Ryan could sense it had been difficult for her to save the seats. "These are perfect," he said as he sat down.

"Nice shirt," she whispered.

Ryan laughed quietly as he noticed her father seated on her right. He did not attempt to turn to Ryan, and for that, he was grateful. On the other side of Ryan sat Bo. He did not attempt to join the conversation but instead sat staring at the stage, waiting for the performance.

Within seconds, the lights on the stage dimmed, and the curtain opened, revealing a crudely made set design comprising plants and the Who's logo.

The crowd roared with applause as the school choir group walked out, adorned in many different British costumes. The singing began in earnest, filling the hall with music and melody.

Mel turned around slowly, making eye contact once again.

"Thanks for coming," she mouthed as discreetly as possible.

"Anytime," Ryan mouthed back.

"Meet me outside after," she replied inaudibly.

Ryan felt his heart jump as he nodded with a smile. She returned the smile and turned back around.

Blinking wildly, he exhaled and swallowed the lump in his throat. Suddenly he felt more nervous than the kids on stage.

"Wonder what she wants…" Bo whispered so only Ryan could hear. "A carpet ride, perhaps?"

"Shut up."

"*A whole new world…*"

"Be quiet."

Bo laughed. "That shirt's looking pretty good now, ain't it?"

Chapter 14
1,084 Miles to Spokane

Snow was beginning to fall as Ryan exited the school. It was warmer than before, but the weather was the furthest thing from his mind as he scanned the crowd on the lawn before him.

He turned back toward the school and looked inside. Not seeing what he was looking for, he back to the lawn and walked down the stairs into the crowd.

"Looking for someone?"

He turned back to see her standing on the steps behind him. In seconds, she was beside him.

"Not anymore," he replied coolly.

"Okay, Romeo." She laughed, grabbing him by the arm and leading him through the crowd.

"Where are we going?" he asked, more focused on her than the surrounding people.

"You'll see."

Soon enough, they were through the crowd and out onto the open street, which shimmered with fresh snow. The streetlights reflected off the surface, bathing their route in an orange glow.

"Did you enjoy the play?" Mel asked after a moment.

Ryan took a second to answer. "Yeah, it was great."

"You had to think?"

He laughed. "I like to consider it all."

"As in?"

"As in what?"

"Consider all of what?"

"All of the play." He shrugged. "The ambiance, the crowd, the story." He looked around a bit more to play off the awkwardness of his words. "And it was all good."

She looked to him with a smile. "You're something else."

"Thank you?"

"Where'd your friend go?" She stopped mid-walk, and Ryan did the same.

"What?"

"Your friend," she repeated. "He left during the show."

Ryan remembered that Bo had said something before stepping out. "I think he needed to use the bathroom or something."

"You don't seem too concerned…"

Ryan smiled. "Bo's a big boy. He'll be fine. I'm sure he found something to occupy his time."

"You fine if we leave him?"

"Leave him?" Ryan asked. "To go where?"

She began walking. "You'll see…"

Ryan pondered this for a moment before following. "I guess he'll be fine."

The snow crunched under their feet as they walked through town. Though he tried to keep up with her, his focus on her instead of the path ahead caused him to lag. If she noticed his attention, she said nothing.

"Will your family be joining us?" Ryan asked as they reached the edge of town. There was no other soul around.

"Nope. Dad likes to take Max out for ice cream after his shows. It's their tradition."

Ryan felt a lump in his throat. "And you don't partake?"

"Sometimes. Usually I stay behind, though. It gives them time together."

He considered the absurdity of the statement.

"You're judging me," she finally said.

"A little…"

"For not going to get ice cream? Or for not spending time with family?"

"Both? But more that you'd rather spend time with me…"

"Don't go that far," she said quickly. "I just feel like we have good conversations. I'm interested in that."

"Interested?"

"Yeah, interested."

"In what way?"

"I don't know. What about you? You seem to have no problem spending time with me. In fact, you seem more than content staying in this shithole town."

"I don't think it's that bad…"

"It's a shithole."

"Well, then, why did you come back?"

"Come back?"

"After college."

There was a long pause.

"I don't know," she finally said. "Why are you on your trip?" Her tone was defensive.

"I told you," he said, "I'm helping a friend."

She smiled. "A friend who, ten minutes ago, you didn't even know was missing."

He laughed. "Touché."

"Let's do each other a favor, then," she said as they walked past snow-covered fields. "Let's not ask each other personal questions. Let's keep this to the now."

"The now?"

"Yeah, the present."

"Why didn't you just say present, then?"

"Jesus, fine; let's keep this to the present."

"What do you mean, *this*?"

"Oh, my God."

"I'm kidding!"

"This is why guys are difficult. They always need everything explained."

Ryan laughed. "Generalize much?"

"It's true. Everything has to be something."

"Well, fine," Ryan conceded. "I will stay in the now. Besides, it's not like I know much about you to begin with. South Dakota State, a brother and father, and some football star ex are about it."

"Well, that's too much," she replied, though Ryan could not tell if she was joking.

"I'll ask no more."

"Good."

"Same with you."

"Huh?"

"You can't ask about me."

"Wasn't going to."

"Well, fine then." He shrugged.

She smiled, still a step ahead of him.

Ryan trudged on behind her, the walk becoming more difficult with his lack of proper boots.

"I am curious," he finally said. "Since I interest you so much, how do you intend to figure out anything about me without me saying anything?"

"You are really making me regret this."

"I'm just saying—"

"Well, don't 'just say.' Forget I said anything about being interested."

"Ouch," he replied.

"Hey, I tried being nice."

"My apologies if I offended—"

She took a deep breath and faced him. "Don't apologize. Let's just stop having this conversation and enjoy this nice night." She turned back around and led him farther into the night.

Ryan nodded behind her back.

They were silent for a while. They trudged forward, moving neither quickly nor fluidly, but instead crisscrossing their steps and balancing between the banks as if partaking in an ungainly dance.

"Almost there," Mel called out.

Ryan looked up to see an old farmhouse, complete with a barn and silo, though little in the way of actual machinery or equipment.

Mel approached the front gate and silently pushed it open.

"Whose house is this?"

"It's mine," she responded, walking up the steps to the large white front door.

"Yours?"

"Well, my dad's. Ours, I should say." She opened the old door with a heave.

"What are we doing here?"

"Dinner." She walked inside and motioned for Ryan to follow.

As he looked around, he could tell that the house was indeed old, as though its walls held memories of many generations.

He entered a windowed porch that overlooked the front yard. To his left, a doorway led to a kitchen, where Mel began her work. Ahead, he saw a semiformal dining room and an additional room behind it.

The walls around him were hung with pictures. He recognized some of the people as Mel and her brother. Others he did not know. In addition to the family pictures, Ryan also noticed a fair amount of sculptures ranging from garden gnomes to Tiffany lamps. All seemed unique for a farmhouse setting.

"Chicken okay?" Mel's voice sounded from the kitchen.

"Sounds good," he replied, feeling more out of place with each passing second.

"Feel free to look around," Mel laughed. "Since you seem to be doing it already." The din of pots and pans eclipsed further conversation.

Ryan continued looking around the porch area, noticing more and more of the house's eclectic nature. For every fragile glass figurine, there was a Hot Wheels toy. For every modern amenity, such as a phone or television, there was a well-worn book.

He found himself moving into the dining room, which seemed more like a time capsule than anything else did. Gone were the toys and modern electronics. In their place was a large oak table with even larger chairs, all adorned with intricate carvings and designs. On the right side was a wall-length buffet that held silverware and glasses, though most looked untouched. The entire room was coated with a thin layer of dust.

He moved on to the third room and found a large nook and window seat along the back wall. He noted a couch and an ornate desk to the left. To the right was a series of built-in shelves near a large, curtained window. His attention turned to the shelves.

Each row was filled with books, and although he found familiar authors, from Dumas to Brontë to King, his gaze was pulled to the handwritten binders between the classics.

"An Evaluation of Marriage in 19th Century Literature," by Melanie Willis.

"Relating Chopin to Millennials: How The Awakening *Speaks Beyond Feminists," by Melanie Willis.*

He found more of the same as he moved to the next set of shelves.

"In the Piton Valley," by Melanie Willis.

"I hope Shake 'n Bake is fine."

He jumped at the sound of her voice and swiveled around as though caught in a compromising position.

"What?" he replied hurriedly.

"Shake 'n Bake. For the chicken."

"Oh," Ryan said. "Yeah. Sounds fine."

"Good," she said. "I can't really cook much else." She stepped in a bit closer. "I see you made it to our highly classy library."

"Better than anything at my house," Ryan said.

"My dad put it together for me. It gives me a place to turn to."

"Seems like you are quite a writer yourself."

She laughed. "At one time, yes. He used to put my finished papers or books on the shelves on purpose. He said they belonged there."

Ryan turned back to the shelves and saw more of her titles. "You don't do it anymore?"

"Not as much. Blue box macaroni fine, too?"

Ryan barely heard the question. When it registered, he nodded. He returned to the second shelf and perused the contents before choosing the Piton cover from the shelf.

Taking a seat on the bench, he opened the binder carefully, as though holding a fragile parchment. He glanced up to see that Mel had returned into the kitchen. Without wasting another second, he turned his attention to the binder in his hands.

The first page was unassuming—just the title and author in a small font in the center. The second, however, was much different.

To Ryan's surprise, it was mostly a book of poetry, with drawings filling most of the paper. Two solitary mountains, both of similar size and each as green as an emerald, bracketed a desolate jungle coastline that jutted up against the most idyllic blue ocean one could dream. At the base of the ocean was a small group of words Ryan read with wonder:

No highways I can find
To follow trade winds east of here
For life is as blue as the ocean

And my memory is always there

He flipped to the next page, where a rather crude drawing showed a waterfall and accompanying stream. Flipping once more, he saw a bird on a tree branch, and another from a high-up vantage point looking to another green peak in the distance. All were at different levels of completion, but each had its own lines of poetry, from full verses to a collection of one or two lines.

"I didn't think you'd actually read anything."

Ryan looked up from the book, aware of where he was for the first time in a while.

"Sorry," he replied, closing the book, and returning it to the shelf.

"Pitons?"

"Yeah." He nodded, not making direct eye contact. "It looked beautiful."

"Have you heard of them?"

"Pitons? No."

She entered the room, took the book off the shelf, and sat on the bench.

"They're two mountains—well, semi-volcanos. Non-erupting ones but, like…what's the word? Lava domes?" She opened the book to the first page and showed the image of the twin green mountains.

"Where are they?" he asked, taking a seat next to her.

"Saint Lucia, along the west coast," she replied, looking at her own artwork. "Two beautiful peaks. There's this bay between them where boats just make anchor and sit, and the beaches are exquisite."

"When did you go?"

"Go? Never."

"Never? You've never been?"

"Nope."

"How do you know so much, then?"

"I read. Watch Travel Channel."

"You drew this picture based on a place you've never seen?"

She looked over the picture. "I drew all of them based on places I've never seen."

Ryan considered the magnitude of her statement. "What does the poem mean?"

"It means that…" she contemplated her words. "It means memory doesn't need a roadmap or direction. You can have a memory about places, regardless of how you got there."

"Or if you've never even been there at all," Ryan added.

She smiled, though she did not look up.

"Visiting an island like this is a dream of mine," she sighed.

"Saint Lucia?"

She closed the book. "Doesn't have to be that one, but some tropical island."

"Like where?"

"I don't know. Any of them."

"You have to have some ideas."

"I really don't. Saint Lucia is good. Maybe Aruba. I live in South Dakota; I'll take anything."

"All right, well, you have to have a top place," he countered. "What is it?"

"My top place?"

"Yeah."

"Fine," she paused as if debating further elaboration. "Hawaii."

"Hawaii?!" He laughed sardonically.

"Yes," she said defensively. "Hawaii."

"Why the hell would you choose that?" He was still chuckling.

"Why the hell wouldn't I?"

"I mean…" he realized he was becoming offensive. "I just—it seems so cliché."

"What does?"

"Hawaii does!"

"Why?"

"Because you could choose anywhere. Tahiti, Bermuda, Crete. Shit, you could even go to the Galapagos. Hawaii just seems so…regular."

"Maybe that's what I want."

"Maybe. I didn't mean to offend. I just expected somewhere more…exotic."

"I think you have serious issues with Hawaii," she countered. "What is it? Bad memories?"

"No," he retorted. "Never been, actually."

"So, you're judging based on a place *you* haven't even been."

"I'm judging because it's Hawaii."

"And?"

"And it's so *typical*. It's a place someone would go to get away from life. Like those movies where the main character gets dumped or fired." He paused, considering his words. "It's like the writers are all like, 'Hmm, where can they go that's accessible…hmm, what about Hawaii?'"

"Outside of *Joe Versus the Volcano*, I can't think of anything that helps your point."

"Every sitcom goes to Hawaii."

"Every sitcom goes to Disney World, too."

"I'm just saying," Ryan offered, "Hawaii is cliché. It's where people go to vacation or to forget, but in reality, it's as American as anywhere on the mainland."

She laughed. "Well, I'll go to Hawaii, and I'll let you know if I'm able to forget my life here. Sound good?"

"I wish you the best of luck." Ryan laughed as well. "I'm sure you'll forget just fine up until you see the next Burger King or Starbucks."

There was a long pause.

"If you're that passionate about islands," she finally said, "I'd hate for you to actually read my controversial stuff. We could be here a while."

He looked around the room—from the books to the window that framed the snowfall outside in the night—and back to her. It was as though he saw her for the first time. In the dim glow of the lamp, he noticed that she wore little makeup and that her hair was pulled into a haphazard ponytail. She smelled like boiled water and Shake 'n Bake and her clothes were anything but tidy, but Ryan could not have cared less. She was beautiful as could be.

"I don't mind," he finally said, watching her examine the books on the shelves. "I don't have anywhere else to be."

***

"I don't understand," Ryan sputtered between bites of chicken.

"What don't you understand? It's all in the abstract," Mel reasoned, picking up the binder and sliding it his way.

They sat on the floor of the den with paper plates and bowls all around them. There was no formality to their dinner—metal utensils mixed with paper water cups and embroidered napkins.

"I don't understand how you can make a point on feminism using a Chopin book that has *already* been written."

"What do you mean?"

"*The Awakening* is already a feminist book. Done and done. The point has been made. It's like making Susan B. Anthony hold a book of Angelou poems. We get it. Nothing else needs to be said."

"I'm not making the point that it's a feminist book," Mel reasoned. "I'm saying that *today*, it is more than that. It is a book describing our generation. And, I'm making *that* point *as* a feminist *and* a millennial."

"All right, I'll bite," he said as he used his fork to pick up another piece of chicken. "Mind you, I haven't fully read your findings, but tell me: how does it describe our generation of women?"

"Not just women. Men, too."

"Excuse me?"

"Men, too. All of us. All of the millennials."

"A book about a woman who hates her husband, has an affair, and walks into the sea describes me?"

"Yep."

"All right, go on."

Mel took another bite of her dinner. "First, we need a few points of clarity."

"All right."

"The basis of my argument must consider three crucial points. Namely, A, she wasn't in love with her husband."

"I don't think that point is far off," Ryan said, mouth full. "She did kill herself to be rid of him."

"B," she continued, "she wasn't in love with Robert."

Ryan considered this. "Debatable…"

"Not to me."

"How?"

"That was feasibly the only real guy she had exposure to. If you compare him to her husband, then, of course he looked better. Doesn't mean she loved him. She just wanted him more than her husband."

"Pretty sure she said she loved him."

"Trust me, if you ate Spam all your life, a Quarter Pounder would feel like a ribeye." She took another bite. "Doesn't mean the Quarter Pounder is good."

Ryan laughed. "Fair enough."

"C, we have to assume she willingly went into her marriage."

"Why do we have to assume that?"

"We have to assume she did, because giving her the object of choice makes my argument."

"Isn't the meaning of her death, though, that it was the first *choice* she got to make?"

"Agreed. This is the hardest point. I do believe, however, that her death was her first true feminist choice. It was her TLC 'No Scrubs' moment."

"But not her first *choice* moment."

"Stop saying 'choice' like that. But yes, you're right, and it isn't too hard to imagine. Although women had little status, truly forced marriages were hard to find. Influenced marriages, yes. I'm sure her parents didn't help, but she could have run at any point."

Ryan exhaled. "All right, I will consider these three points in my analysis."

"Fine, moving on." She focused on her bowl of macaroni. "I'm going to ask you a question that you need to answer. Scholarly, not personal."

"And if I don't answer?"

"You don't get to figure out my logic."

He laughed. "All right."

She took another bite. "What did you want to be as a child, and why aren't you that now?"

Ryan stared at her. "Who says I'm not that?"

"You wanted to be a guy driving a hobo around?"

He gritted his teeth. "Fair enough."

"I'm serious."

"Fine. I wanted to be, I don't know, a baseball player."

"Really? You?"

"Scholarly…"

She laughed. "All right, fine. A baseball player. Why aren't you that?"

"Because I sucked at tee ball."

"All right. What did you want to be after realizing you sucked at hitting a ball off a tee?"

He gritted his teeth again. "I don't know. Some sort of scientist sounded cool."

"What about in college?"

"I went for journalism."

"And now?"

"Definitely not a journalist."

"Why not?"

"I lost passion, I guess?"

"Do you see where I'm going?"

"Not at all."

She laughed and then flipped to an appendix page of her binder. On the page were several photocopied pages of dated and worn documents.

"These are copies of my parents' report cards from elementary school." Mel pointed. "Look at the bottom."

Ryan saw space at the bottom for a multiple-choice question:

What do you want to be when you grow up?
a) Parent b) Farmer c) Doctor d) Lawyer e) Policeman f) Model g) Teacher h) Other

Ryan looked up and saw that Mel was eyeing the card as he read.

"I studied my parents for all twelve years." She finally said. "My dad put 'farmer' eleven out of twelve years. The only one he changed was a second-grade doctor ambition. My mother chose 'parent' for her first two years, and 'model' for the next ten." She paused. "I went to their school and asked for statistics on this question alone. In the ten years between the graduating classes of 1970 and 1980, the average student changed their answer to this question only twice in all twelve years. What's more surprising, only one student ever answered H. He did so in the tenth, eleventh, and twelfth grades. He wrote that he wanted to be an astronaut. Do you know what he went on to be?"

"An astronaut?"

"South Dakota's first."

Ryan sat back from his meal. "All right, so kids in our parents' generation didn't change career paths much."

"If ever!" Mel exclaimed. "But that isn't the point. The point is, *why* didn't they?"

"Why didn't they what?"

"Why didn't they change paths?"

"Because they were kids."

"And? You were, too."

"Huh?"

"You were a kid, too. Yet you changed career paths at least twice. Probably more, if you're honest. Hell, I went from wanting to be a dancer to a singer to a princess and a vet and a writer, all before I was in high school."

"Fine, fine," he conceded. "But what does this have to do with Chopin?"

"I'm getting there." She took a breath mid-thought. "But to get there, we have to answer that question: Why didn't the previous generation change career goals?"

Ryan pondered the question.

"Let me assist," Mel continued. "Who wrote this question on their report cards?"

Ryan shrugged. "Their teachers?"

"Who were?"

"Old?"

"Exactly."

"Huh?"

"They were old!" Mel exclaimed. "They were the World War II baby boomer generation." She seemed quite pleased with herself. "Now, considering your knowledge of American history, what did those baby boomers go on to be, profession-wise?"

Ryan thought for a moment. "Farmers, doctors, teachers…"

"Parents, policemen," she continued. "Factory workers, laborers, et cetera." She paused. "There were no baseball players. No journalists. No scientists."

"But there were baseball players and journalists out there…"

"Those careers were just unattainable to our parents, generally speaking, because of their class."

Though she did not know anything about his parents, her generalizations hit home.

He took another bite. The food had grown cold. "So, our parents went on to be farmers and parents?"

She laughed. "Not exactly." She sipped her water. "You see, somewhere around the '60s, this generation realized they didn't want to be farmers and teachers. So, they rebelled. Smoked pot. Went to Woodstock. Saw Elvis shake his ass on a Christian TV."

"Damn hippies."

"Right? The issue with this?" She paused. "They couldn't do anything about it. They were already grown. They were rebelling against what should have been, not what could be." She took another sip. "Unsuccessfully, they tried to fight the system but ended up right back there, with only a few ever rising above it."

"Depressing."

She laughed. "All wasn't lost, however, because these hippies soon had children of their own, and they made damned certain their kids wouldn't fall into the same trap they did. The trap of mediocrity."

As Mel spoke, Ryan flipped through the appendices and came upon a handwritten note from her mother that she had photocopied into the book. His eyes were drawn to a highlighted sentence halfway through the note.

"And you know what they would tell their kids to prevent this trap?" Mel asked.

Ryan's eyes widened upon seeing the words on the page. It was his whole life in front of him. It was everything he had ever heard.

"They would tell them," she said as he read along, "*you can be anything you want.*"

Ryan stared at the page. He read the words in front of him at least twice more, as though a new reading would change their meaning. Nothing changed. The handwritten note remained just as it had been.

"Something wrong?" Mel asked after a minute.

"No. Not really." Ryan finally looked away. "It's just…I've heard those words a lot."

"From parents?"

"And teachers, old bosses…neighbors. Everyone."

"You aren't alone." Mel flipped to yet another appendix. "I took testimony from more than fifty people at my school."

Ryan looked down and saw pages of typed conversations, each with key highlighted phrases, such as "anything you want," "confused," "lost."

"Turns out," Mel continued, "everyone our age is led to believe we can be 'anything,' and none of us knows what to make of it." She paused and wiped her mouth. "I concluded that we, as a generation, have unlimited possibilities put in place by our parents, yet none of us have the passion or disposition to actually achieve anything, and this is due"—she paused again—"to choice overload."

"Choice overload?"

"Yep. Too many places to eat; we can't decide. Too many dreams and occupations to achieve; we can't focus."

Ryan took a deep breath. "All right, all right. You have yet to explain how *The Awakening* is relevant."

"It's obvious, isn't it?"

"No."

She began picking up their dishes. "We are Edna."

"We are?"

"Yes."

"Both of us?"

"All of us."

Ryan paused. "I'm not following."

She sighed. "Instead of making decisions about our lives, we are choosing to kill ourselves in the lake, metaphorically speaking."

Ryan stared blankly at her.

"Ugh." She shook her head. "Edna didn't run into the lake because she hated her husband and loved another man. She did it because she knew she couldn't be happy knowing she turned down a potentially better path. She learned that she had choices. She was out of the Matrix, and she couldn't cope, so she ran out into the lake. That's what we millennials are doing now. We can't cope, so we're taking the other way out. We are quitting school. Or worse, working at Pizza Hut with college degrees. We're piling on debts in grad schools we couldn't care less about! We have no idea where we're going, and that scares the living shit out of us, but we can't change it and go back because we know we won't be happy. We're up to our necks in that sea, but we continue walking because either we know too much, or we just don't give a damn."

Ryan admired the beauty and passion in her logic.

"Look at you," she continued. "Out here, on the road. You have a barely working car and a companion you don't even know." She paused. "Look at me. Waitress at Dad's restaurant. One more college degree than anyone in my family ever has had. We are the paper definition of success, yet here we are."

She stood up. She almost seemed ashamed that she had gone on for so long, but she said nothing. Instead, she turned and walked back into the kitchen, leaving Ryan alone with the binder.

He had many questions but no courage to ask them. He flipped the book back to the report cards and stared at them.

"My mother," he finally said. "She had this exact same type of report card. I remember looking over them."

"Do you remember what she put for career choices?" Mel asked from the kitchen.

Ryan smiled at the recollection. "Model, I think." He thought more about it. "I think she put model almost every year…"

"Did she ever change it?"

Ryan laughed. "I barely remember…"

"Well, think!" she pleaded as she returned into the room.

He smiled. "I honestly think she left her twelfth-grade one blank."

"Blank?"

"Yeah."

Mel took a seat in front of him, and he saw that she had two beers in her hand. She offered him one, and he gladly accepted. "She sounds like a rebel!"

He laughed. "Or maybe she forgot to fill it in."

"Don't ruin this idea, man." She sipped from the bottle. "Your mom might have been a true pioneer among her generation."

"I doubt my mother has ever read Chopin…"

Mel shifted in her seat. "Speaking of that, you reminded me of another main point in my argument." She took a breath and gathered her thoughts. "Do you know how we stop walking?"

"What?"

"Referring to Edna walking into the sea." She took another drink. "Do you know how we stop walking?

"How's that?"

"I don't know." She laughed.

He laughed, too. "I guess," he said, taking a sip, "we'll just have to find something that makes us stop."

He had not meant for it to come out as it did. He was immediately embarrassed, but instead of scolding him, she took another sip and contemplated his words.

"Wonder what the hell that'll be," she finally said, apparently oblivious to his embarrassment.

Ryan sighed in relief. "Who knows?"

She looked off into the distance. "Maybe that's what happened to your mom." She returned her gaze to him. "Maybe she found a reason to stop…"

Ryan smiled, feeling a bit awkward discussing his mother so much. "Maybe."

There was another long pause as the two sipped their beers.

"For the record," he finally said, "My car is not even 'barely working' at the moment."

She smiled. "True," she responded as she sipped again. "God, it's been a while since I've had a good debate like that."

Ryan smirked. "Not me. I recently had some crazy lady try to tell me that *Love Actually* is a good movie."

She laughed along with him.

"Pretty soon, I'll hear how *Twilight* is an American classic."

The din of laughter grew as she attempted to speak. "*Twilight* and 'classic' are words I will never say together."

"And I should believe you?" Ryan retorted. "You also think Hawaii would make a great place to live."

Their laughter continued.

"I'll find you with Hugh Grant posters in your Hawaiian bungalow with *Breaking Dawn* in your hand."

She attempted a sip amid bursts of laughter. "The posters and bungalow, yes, but the book? Change it to Poe or Tolkien."

"You're a Tolkien fan, too? Seems to be a lot of them these days."

"Just *The Hobbit*. Never read the others," she said between sips. "But it's one of my favorites."

Ryan looked at her as he took a drink and saw her looking back.

"Does that surprise you?" she asked with a cheeky smile.

"No. Nothing about you surprises me anymore."

***

The snow had stopped by the time Ryan opened the big farmhouse door to leave. He had no idea what time it was, though Mel's brother and father had arrived home sometime before. He'd been nervous at first but had calmed when he'd heard them head to bed.

"Free meal and good conversation," Mel said as he stepped outside. "You'd be hard pressed to top the excitement of this night."

"Who knew South Dakota had so much life?" Ryan laughed.

"Indeed."

"Thank you for dinner," he said as sincerely as he could.

"No need." She brushed the comment aside. "Thank you for coming to the play."

He stood there for a moment, awkwardly deciding what to do next.

"You know how to get back to your hotel?" she asked after a precariously long period of silence.

Ryan smiled, knowing how idiotic he looked. "Yeah, I do."

She laughed. "Good. See ya later."

"Goodnight," he said sheepishly.

He walked to the edge of the yard and through the open gate before turning onto the country road. It was here that he finally heard himself breathe.

In the house, Mel watched him go, and she too finally sighed as she shut the large farm door. As she entered the den, she found herself staring down at the binders and books she and Ryan had debated for hours on end. She looked to the wall at a clock Ryan had not seen. It read 5 a.m.

She grimaced as she bent to retrieve the books. Exhaustion washed over her as she rose. This, however, was secondary. A much deeper feeling was first in her mind: one she felt in her very being. She shook her head and tried to remove the thoughts.

Perhaps it was the alcohol, she thought, or maybe even the sleep deprivation. She drank a glass of water in an effort to emerge from the stupor, but it was no use. Try as she might, there was nothing she could do. She sighed as the thought latched on. She felt full of passion and bliss. She had not felt this way in a long time.

Exhaling hard, she looked up from the sink to her reflection in the window. She blinked and stared at herself once more.

"Great," she said, shaking her head with disdain. "What the fuck are we going to do now?

Chapter 15
1,083 Miles to Spokane

It was surprisingly sunny for late December when Ryan woke the next morning. He blinked as he looked at the clock, not even bothering to think about how little sleep he was running on. He looked over to the other full-sized bed, only to find it empty. Bo was not around.

For a moment, he considered the absence strange, even more so considering that he had been missing since the middle of the play last night. Yet as Ryan dragged his body into the bathroom to wash his face, he heard the rattle of a key in the door and was worried no more.

"'Morning," he heard Bo say. "Got some donuts from the lobby if you want." His voice was tired and strained, but Ryan tried to not read into it.

"Thanks," Ryan said from the bathroom doorway.

Bo looked at him for a moment. "You look like you had a long night."

"I guess I did," Ryan replied.

Bo looked back toward his own bed. "That include losing your pants?"

Ryan looked down and realized that he was in his boxer shorts. Walking back to his own bed, he found his jeans from the night before. "My apologies. Forgot about them."

Bo managed a quick laugh. "So, Prince Ali, manage to get the princess?"

Ryan had to sit on the bed to don his jeans. "I don't know. Is that your South Dakota question?"

Bo looked at his own bag on his bed as he pondered the question. "I thought you forgot about our game."

"By 'our game,' you mean *my* torture. How could I forget?" Ryan walked back toward the bathroom sink.

"I don't know…" Bo finally said, seemingly at a loss of words. "A lot has happened."

"Nothing's happened," Ryan replied, splashing his face with water again. "I'm still here."

"You say that…but I know she means something to you."

"She lives here. I don't." Ryan dabbed his face with a towel, thinking about his words as he spoke them.

"So, you're good with just ending it when we leave?" Bo finally asked.

Ryan swallowed the lump in his throat. He thought about it for a few seconds before realizing that his delay was hurting his credibility. He stepped out into the main room.

"When we need to leave, of course." Ryan looked directly at Bo and noticed that he seemed suspiciously different and more hesitant. "You okay, Bo?"

"Why do you ask?"

"You seem … concerned."

Bo returned Ryan's gaze before returning to his bag. Again, Ryan found a lump in his throat.

"Concerned?" Bo replied, gazing deep into the bag.

"Yeah." Ryan was growing weary.

They sat in silence for a moment, then Bo reached for the bag. Ryan stepped back a bit, but instead of a book, Bo pulled out a folded-up piece of paper.

"Just tired, I guess," Bo responded. "Forgot to tell you"—he held out the piece of paper— "Miss Barbara said you had a message. She took the call and wrote it down for you."

Ryan stared at the piece of paper hesitantly, still trying to slow his heart rate.

"I didn't read it," Bo said. "Figured it best to just let you."

Ryan wavered a second more before finally stepping forward and grabbing the paper. He wondered if it was from Mel, or even from the hateful sheriff. As he unfolded it, however, he found that it was from neither.

Ryan,

I have repaired your Jeep, and the keys are in the ignition. I was able to steal a pump from a junker we found just east of Humboldt, and I made it work. I know you said, 'the earlier, the better.' I'll be out of town today, but you can pick it up at my shop anytime. If not today, I'll drop it by the hotel tomorrow.
Randall

Ryan looked up from the letter to see that Bo was closing his bag.

"What'd it say?" Bo asked, placing the bag on the dresser, and then sitting on his bed.

"It was from Randall," Ryan replied, choosing his words carefully. "It said he's still working on the car."

"Did he give a date?"

Ryan sighed. "No," he said through gritted teeth. "Just that he'd let us know."

"Ah," Bo said, staring into the distance.

"We still have a few days," Ryan reasoned. "Plenty of time before Christmas."

Bo gave no indication that he had heard.

"Three days is plenty of time," Ryan continued, looking at his watch as he put it on. Not even he believed what he said.

Bo sat motionless, as though deep in contemplation. Suddenly, he turned to Ryan and smiled as if he had flipped a switch. "I'm sure we will make it."

This gesture confused Ryan even more, but he said nothing about it. He was already focused on the complexity of his situation and the line he walked to balance his attraction and his obligation. He hoped the day ahead would give him clarity.

"Where are you off to?" Bo asked.

Ryan barely heard the question. "Breakfast."

"Oh," Bo replied, turning to the donuts that Ryan seemed to have forgotten.

"I'll be back later," Ryan replied, slipping on his shoes.

A moment later, he was gone.

***

There were three days, Ryan thought. Three. Monday. Tuesday. Wednesday. He checked his watch again. By his logic, the absolute latest he could leave was Tuesday afternoon. That gave him twenty-four hours to arrive in Spokane by Christmas dinner. Twenty-four hours for how many miles? Five hundred? A thousand? Fifteen hundred? That sounded right, he thought. Fifteen hundred over twenty-four hours.

He attempted the math in his head. Twenty-four into one-fifty…never mind. Twenty-four into a hundred. That's four. So, forty, with some remainder. Round up, so fifty miles each hour. *Factor in a couple hours of sleep time, and that's possible*, he thought. *Easy.*

And if they left Tuesday, that meant two more days in Shannon. Two days. A lot could happen in two days.

His mind raced but came to a screeching halt on an idea he could not get past.

I just have to finish helping my friend. Three days, tops. I'll be back before the weekend.

I'm not leaving, I just need to finish this up.

It's just a quick task. That's all.

He thought about his earlier discussion with Bo.

If he still says that I can drop him off in Gillette, then I'll be back before Christmas is over.

He took a deep breath. None of it sounded great, and he wondered if he even believed himself. Sadly, though, it was all true. He had every intention of returning. He did not care about Florida or Spokane. Those places were nothing but burdens. Right here was exactly where he wanted to be.

"Can't say I'm shocked to see you," came a familiar voice.

Ryan smiled as he shifted in his booth. Turning, he saw Mel approaching the table.

"I heard the service was more than friendly," he replied.

"Someone lied to you," she said. She looked tired but was otherwise expressionless.

He laughed.

"So what? I cook dinner and now have to wait on you?"

"At least convention says I have to tip you here."

"True, but something tells me you aren't a high tipper."

He found himself without words.

"Drink?"

"Orange juice is fine."

"Sure, Florida Boy," she replied before walking away.

He half-expected her to sit across from him for a few minutes, but her disposition this morning was matter-of-fact. While it concerned him slightly, he brushed it off as an effect of being on the clock.

"What time are you off?" he asked as she approached with his juice.

He heard her sigh as she set the juice on the table. "Probably around five," she said. "Dad wasn't too happy about my late arrival at work."

Ryan nodded. "Sorry about that."

"Fault is as much mine." She smiled.

"Well, I had a great time," he replied, knowing how corny he sounded.

"Good."

He had hoped she would return the sentiment.

"Food?" she asked.

Ryan stared confusedly for a moment, forgetting the setting. "Oh, toast is fine."

She nodded and walked off once again.

He turned to look out the window. The sun glinted off the snow covering the ground. He glanced toward the parking lot and saw a host of pickups with a scattering of rusty SUVs. Two police cars were parked in the front row.

His breath caught in his throat. He turned to see a trio of officers in the back corner of the diner. The sheriff was unmistakable. As he and the two younger officers rose, Ryan turned around in his booth.

Ryan swallowed hard as the officers passed. He barely made eye contact as the sheriff offered an icy smile.

"'Mornin' Jerry," Ransom said softly.

Ryan did not look up.

"He giving you trouble?" Mel asked after the officers had left.

Ryan found that he was instantly calmed by her voice.

"No more than usual."

She set down his toast. "Well, his 'usual' is a lot more than a sane person's 'usual,' so watch yourself."

"What are you doing tonight?" he asked quickly, knowing that catching her off guard would be more honest.

"T-tonight?" she stammered, looking around as though needing to escape.

"Yeah," Ryan replied, not lowering his voice.

"Um, I don't know."

"Good. Be ready at six."

"Ready for what?"

"Just be ready."

"Ryan, don't—"

"Hey," he countered, biting into his toast. "You got to surprise me yesterday. Today is my turn."

"It was just blue box and some books…"

He took another bite. "Don't worry. It isn't a four-star dinner."

"You don't have to…"

"I don't. But I want to."

She exhaled.

"Six," he repeated, downing his orange juice.

"Fine," she replied, walking off without another word.

He smiled as he took the last bite of his toast. He wiped his mouth and pulled a twenty from his wallet. Leaving it on the table, he finally stood.

"That went well," he said sarcastically.

***

After eating a late breakfast and walking the town, Ryan was contented as he walked back to the hotel that afternoon. The air was more manageable today. Despite his lack of winter wear, he did not find himself shivering.

He was deep in thought as he walked into the lobby, focused more on his plan for the evening than on any other endeavor. He knew that he was putting the cart before the horse in inviting Mel out, as he had no idea what to do or where to go. At least he had one thing he hadn't before—access to his vehicle.

"You seem quite happy," came Barbara's unmistakable voice.

Ryan turned to see her sitting at a lobby table. He noticed for the first time that he had a smile plastered across his face. He stopped in his tracks and managed a chuckle.

"For some reason, yes."

"Some reason?"

"Yeah, still figuring that part out."

She sipped from a coffee cup. "You're young. That's a good enough reason to be happy."

Ryan nodded. He noticed a large map of South Dakota on the wall behind her.

"Your friend's been visiting me a bit," she said after a moment of silence.

Ryan stared at her, wondering how much she knew about his situation.

"Has she?"

Barbara laughed into her coffee. "I was referring to your suitemate, Bo."

"Oh…"

"Says you two are heading west."

Ryan leaned against the wall. "Eventually, yes." He thought for a moment more. "He told you anything else?"

She laughed again, this time more quietly. "No, no. Just that you two are traveling."

"Well," he said, moving to the table and sitting next to her. "That is true. And we probably would've made it if it weren't for car troubles."

"You still can," she replied. "Though I think you may have some difficulty leaving now…"

It was his turn to laugh.

"Your happiness isn't from youth, my friend, but from love." She got up and poured a cup of coffee for Ryan. "Anyone knows that happiness."

Ryan did not want to argue with the nice old woman, but deep down, he did not know if he agreed with her assumptions.

"You going out with her tonight?"

"How'd you know?"

"I didn't. Just guessed."

Ryan shook his head. He did not like giving up so much information.

"Mel is a good girl," Barbara replied. "She's had a hard life, but she's always been a good kid."

Ryan nodded.

"I see a lot of myself in her," she continued. "Both of us always had the boys chasing after us."

His ears perked up at this, and Barbara knew it.

"A lot of boys?" he heard himself ask.

"Her or me?" She laughed. "Of course, she has. Look at her. None have tied her down, though." She looked over to Ryan. "At least not yet."

He felt his cheeks turn red as he tried to ignore the comment.

Barbara continued gazing out the window. "Yes, indeed. She is a rare breed of woman. Confident. Independent. Courageous. She's a hard one to tame."

"I don't know much about taming anything." Ryan laughed.

Barbara smiled but did not laugh in return. Instead, she stared out again, looking at something in the distance.

"I remember when my husband first talked to my daddy." She turned back to Ryan. "Now, my daddy, he knew I wasn't easy to win over. I hadn't brought that many men home, and Daddy knew that when I did, it meant something. My daddy was also a bit of a hard ass, so I knew I had to listen in when he spoke to my future husband." She paused. "You know what my daddy told him? He said some words I'd never forget." She paused again, and he could see her growing emotional. "He told him that there were a million ways to lose the love of a woman. A million ways. He then told him that there was only a handful of ways to make her stay." She dabbed at her eyes. "A million ways to lose her. A handful to make her stay. You know what Daddy said next?" She searched Ryan's face, but he did not attempt to answer. "Daddy looked him dead in the eyes and said, 'If you truly love her, you'd better not confuse those ways.'"

Ryan smiled at such a passionate memory. He knew it meant a lot to Barbara.

She wiped her eyes before straightening up. "I know I may be an old lonely stranger to you, but you seem like a good guy. I feel like those words could help you, too."

Ryan considered the statement and then wondered if the woman could be of some more help. He chose his words carefully. "Let's say we are going out tonight," he finally said with a smile. "And let's also say that I need a good place to go for some food. You know of any?" He turned around and looked at the map behind him.

Barbara pondered this for a moment. "Around here?"

Ryan peered at the map. "Not here," he said cautiously. "What about here?" He pointed to the map.

"There?"

"Yeah."

She took another sip of coffee. "I have some ideas."

***

Ryan had just one more major task to complete before picking up his companion for the evening, and he set out around five o'clock to accomplish it. He had spent the previous two hours talking to Barbara and then retiring to his room for a shower. He had not seen Bo anywhere around, and in all honesty, he preferred this, as their last encounter had made him more than uncomfortable.

Dressed in his USF jacket, he strolled a familiar path toward the town center, veering slightly to the west until Randall's shop came into view.

As he approached, he noticed the yard and shop were uncharacteristically quiet, and he welcomed the lack of noise. His Jeep was sitting peacefully in the corner of the lot near an Oldsmobile and a scrapped Pontiac.

Smiling, he walked over and found the driver's door unlocked. Nodding in approval, he stuck his head inside to find a freshly vacuumed interior. It even looked as though the seat rip in the passenger side had been sewn back together. The headliner was still amiss, but he knew that even Randall was not that much of a miracle worker.

Finally, he investigated the backseat, and after only a moment, he saw a relic from the past in the form of a sweatshirt. Unfolding it, he saw the familiar Busch Gardens logo.

"At least it's clean," he said to himself as he took off the USF jacket and threw it in the back. Donning the sweatshirt, he sat in the driver's seat and closed the door, taking a moment to soak in the comfort of a familiar place.

He turned the key, and the Jeep started immediately. Even though this was to be expected, it surprised him nonetheless, and he celebrated the victory with an ecstatic whoop. He shifted the car into drive and crept slowly toward the shop, knowing he had one more task to accomplish.

He parked the car, opened the driver's door, and quickly walked into the unlocked and empty shop. He stepped behind the counter and searched until he found exactly what he was looking for—a pencil and paper.

Scribbling a quick note, he signed it and set it near the cash register before walking briskly back out of the office. Looking back at the clock over the desk, he saw it was 5:30.

Plenty of time, he thought. There was plenty of time for him to drive it out and bring it back without a soul noticing. Nevertheless, the note he had written indicated that he had taken the Jeep and that it would be returned later. It was a simple note, he knew, but it was better safe than sorry. He did not need any stolen car notices on his head.

He turned up the only radio station he could find as he drove the Jeep away from the shop and onto the road. He began thinking of the night ahead, and soon the smile crept across his face again. It was not a smile of love or admiration, however. He knew it now: it was a smile of calm, of serenity. Of normalcy.

With all the issues troubling him, he was astonished that he was more concerned with what he had planned for the evening. It was not naïveté that found him thinking about such things, but the simplicity of having something "normal" to worry about.

With the money he had stolen using a credit card that was not his, and with an untrusted companion growing more impatient in a town neither of them knew, here he was: a boy wondering what to do with a girl.

Chapter 16
1,084 Miles to Spokane

The sun had long set on December 22 as the black Jeep made its way down the street toward the north part of Shannon. Without lights, it would have been nothing more than a shadow in the night, but with the headlights blazing, it looked like any other vehicle out on a cold night.

It was not just another vehicle, however. Blaring an old country song on the speakers, Ryan drove the unfamiliar route slowly, cautiously. This was one night he did not want to screw up.

He felt the weight of a thousand expectations on him, and most were self-placed. The more he considered the night ahead, the more nervous he became. He truly felt as though it was his one chance to impress.

He wanted her to like him as much as he liked her.

It was nearly six o'clock when he pulled up to her house, the fenced-in front yard and large farmhouse door now familiar to him. He pulled the Jeep up to the gate, shifted into park, and took a deep breath before shutting off the engine and opening his door.

Upon stepping outside, he realized that his Busch Gardens sweatshirt was not nearly as heavy as the USF jacket. He closed the door and walked to the gate, glancing up and noticing what seemed like a billion stars.

"Hey," he heard Mel say. He stopped dead in his tracks as he saw her sitting at the bottom of the steps. The gate still separated them.

"Hey," he replied, instantly nervous again.

She pulled out a cell phone and looked at the time. "Six on the dot."

He smiled. "I was told never to let someone wait on you…" He did not know who, exactly, had told him that, but it sounded good.

She ignored the comment. Silence hung between them as he waited on her to choose her words. Finally, she spoke. Her voice was not amicable or cordial, however. She sounded cold and quiet.

"What are we doing here?" she said, still sitting on the step.

He stared at her. "What?"

"What are we doing here?"

He leaned on the gate. "Well, you're sitting there, and I'm—"

"Don't be a smart-ass. Answer my question."

"I don't understand your—"

"Yes, you do." She stood up. "You understand it; you just don't want to answer it."

He rolled his tongue into his teeth as she stood there, waiting for an answer. "I don't know what you want me to say."

"I want you to say what we, what you and I, are doing here."

"I am here to take you to dinner—"

"On a date."

He chose his words carefully. "I never said that."

"But that's what this is. That's what you think it is."

"No."

"You like me, and this is a date."

"No…"

"Then tell me what this is. What are we doing here?"

"Why are you being like this?"

"Why are you lying to me?" Her words felt colder than the air.

"I'm not lying."

"Yes, you are."

"I don't know what you want."

"I want you to be honest with me." She stood with arms folded. "And stop fucking lying."

He gritted his teeth. "Fine," he said after a moment. "Honestly? Fine. I do like you. There. I said it. I like you. But this?" He opened the gate and stepped inside. "This is not a date. This is a guy taking a girl to dinner because he wants to. Because he…Because I…enjoy your company for some bullshit reason that I question every moment of the goddamn day. Is that what you want to hear?"

She said nothing.

"And honestly?" he continued, stepping forward. "Yesterday, you didn't want to know anything about me. Why the change now?" He stopped some ten feet from her. "Honestly? I think you like me, too, but are too afraid to say it."

She laughed slightly, almost maliciously. "A girl questions you, and suddenly she likes you?"

"No…a girl spent ten hours talking books and movies with me and made me dinner. That's why she likes me."

It was her turn to grit her teeth. "I don't want to date you."

"And why not?" he asked quickly, ignoring that he had just discredited his dating intentions.

"Why not? Why not? Three days ago, I didn't know who you were. Three days from now, I may never see you again!"

"And?"

"And I don't know you. You don't live here. Hell, I don't even know why you're here to begin with."

"That didn't stop you before. You approached me, remember."

"And it was a mistake."

He stared at her. "Don't say that."

"It was."

"Don't say that."

"Why not?"

"Because. You're just saying that because you're afraid."

"Afraid?"

"Yeah."

"Of what?"

"I don't know."

"Don't patronize me."

He gritted his teeth again. "Why don't you tell me what you're afraid of?"

She stared back at him. "I'm not afraid of anything." She paused. "I'm just rationalizing whatever this is, and it can't work."

"Because?"

"Because you are going to leave."

"I don't have to."

The silence that followed was profound. "Don't you say that," she whispered.

"What?"

"That's not fair."

"What's not?"

"You, saying that."

"It's true."

"No, it isn't."

He took a step forward. "Yes, it is."

She stared daggers back at him. "What? You're going to come back here? Get a job? Live here? Is that your big plan?"

"It can be."

"You're so stupid."

"Why?" he asked. "Why is that stupid?"

"Because. It is."

"You act like I have a life somewhere. I don't." He looked back at his Jeep. "My life, it's all there. I have no job. I have no attachments. Why can't I live here?"

"Why would you want to?"

"Because you're here."

"That's bullshit."

"What if it isn't?"

"Because, Ryan," she countered, "people don't change lives for people they've barely met, let alone people they barely know. That's stupid." She took a deep breath. "You can't alter your life just because you think you know me. It makes no sense."

Another long pause.

"Listen," he said, stepping forward again, "I'm not stupid. And I'm not crazy. And I know, I've known you for three days. But those three days have been the best three days I've had in a long time. That's no coincidence." He looked her directly in the eyes. "I'm not asking for anything from you but dinner tonight. It's not a date, it's not forever, and I'm not here to scare you. But …" he paused once more. "If you accept, I can promise that I won't go anywhere unless you want me to. All I want is dinner with a friend."

She looked around as she pondered the offer. "You can promise that? That you won't go anywhere?"

"Yes."

"How?"

He looked back at her. He almost needed her to repeat the question before his realization hit. He shook his head. "I just know. I'm not going anywhere."

She took a deep breath once again as if to consider the weight of the situation. "Where's dinner?"

He smiled. "So, that means you accept?"

She moved off the step and onto the sidewalk. "No. I'm just hungry. We can table this for another time."

He laughed as she walked past him. "You're something else."

"Shut up," she replied, opening the passenger door by herself. "Or you'll eat alone."

"I assume we're done with personal questions for tonight." Ryan chuckled nervously as he pulled the Jeep onto the main road.

She smiled, though he could tell she did so reluctantly. "Yeah, I think so." After a moment, she spoke again. "What about your friend?"

"What about him?"

"What's he going to do?"

"Tonight?"

She rolled her eyes. "If you stay here."

Ryan had not thought about this. "I don't know," he said after a moment, knowing that the answer was important. "He'll have to find a new ride. Hell, I'll give him my car if he can't find one."

"You're an idiot." She laughed.

"What?" He echoed her laugh. "I'm serious."

"How did you get this car back, anyway?"

Ryan smiled. "Randall was finished with it."

"And he dropped it off?"

"More or less."

"How is that more or less?"

"More or less meaning that he said I could come pick it up when I was ready to."

"And you were ready tonight?"

He laughed. "Of course; it's my car. Plus, I was tired of walking around this damn town."

She laughed along with him and then grew silent. She stared out the front window. "It's been a long time since I've been in the front seat of a car."

Ryan was happy to see the topic change, and he was eager to continue the new direction. "So, you never drive? Like never?"

"I haven't driven in months. Maybe even a year. Even then, it'd be for five minutes tops."

"And the passenger seat?"

"My brother always has it."

"I don't understand how you can go months without riding in the front of a car."

"I don't understand how you can want to give your car up to someone else."

Ryan laughed. "Actually, I think you do understand that."

She turned to him. "Mine was for family."

Ryan shrugged his shoulders. "Mine is too."

She stared at him for a long while, her astonishment turning into a slow smile. "That would have been an adorable comment had you not predicated it with 'He'll have to find another ride.'"

He laughed. "Yeah, all right, that was a bit harsh."

She went back to looking out the front window. "So, where are we going?"

"This little place I know about."

"And how do you know of this little place?"

"I have my ways," he countered. She looked at him incredulously. "And Barbara helped me."

"There it is."

"What? I can use my resources."

"Fine, at least tell me where this 'little place' is."

"Why?"

"So I can help you when you get lost."

"When I get lost?"

"Yes."

"I'm not getting lost."

"How do you know?"

He turned to her with a smile. "Because I know how to get to my home."

She turned to him with a confused look on her face as he looked back at the road. From the corner of his eye, he saw it dawn on her.

"Mitchell," she said with a smile. "You're taking me to Mitchell."

He shrugged. "Of course. Jerry has to show off his hometown."

***

Clouds had moved in to cover the stars, and the air had become damp as though snow was a given. The night was otherwise calm, with outside sounds limited to the buzz of streetlights and the droning of a passing car.

"You know there are at least twenty restaurants in this town?" Mel asked as she sat at the table across from Ryan.

"I know."

She stared at him before looking to her left. "Some that aren't Kentucky Fried Chicken."

"Have you had KFC before?"

She glared at him. "Everyone's eaten KFC."

"That's because it's delicious."

She shook her head. "I could have picked something a little different."

"So could I." He smiled. "But this isn't a date. And I wanted chicken."

She smirked and gritted her teeth.

"You always this stubborn?" he asked as an employee brought their tray of food.

"I'm not good just going along with things."

"I can tell."

"All right." She sat back. "Fine. You're in control. I won't offer any more input."

"Good," he said, biting into his drumstick.

"Good."

She stared at him a moment more before leaning over the table and unwrapping her spork. She picked up a chicken thigh and took a bite.

"Good, isn't it?" Ryan said, wiping his mouth.

She glared at him.

"Ah? Ah?" He laughed. "I think someone is enjoying her KFC."

She wiped her mouth. "I don't think delicious is an apt description, but it is good."

"Finally, a compliment!"

She opened her mouth in shock. "You make me sound like a horrible person."

"I didn't say that!"

"Sounds like it!"

"I'm just saying, compliments are not your strong suit. You're a tough nut to crack." He took a bite of his chicken. "It's nice to hear something nice."

She shook her head. "Same goes for you, you know." She took another bite. "You don't say nice things a lot."

"Um, did you forget your front step? I believe I said that you're the best thing that's happened to me these last three days…"

She sighed as she took another bite. "Oh yeah…"

"So there. Would you like another?"

"God, no…"

"You look nice tonight," he said.

She looked up from her food and caught his gaze. For a second, neither spoke. Finally, she burst out laughing.

"What?"

"You're good," she countered. "You are good."

"Good?"

"Charming."

"Charming?"

"Yeah." She dug out some potatoes. "You're charming. You ooze it. Even in that sweatshirt."

He looked down at the clothing. "That a bad thing?"

"I didn't say that."

"But you laughed."

"Because it's funny how charming you are."

"I don't see the joke."

"You aren't a girl…"

He considered this comment, unsure about its meaning.

"Your father this charming? Or did your mother teach you?"

He took another bite of his own food. "I don't know…"

"I bet it was your mother. I bet she taught you how to charm the ladies. Woo them, so to speak."

He wiped his mouth. "You clearly don't know my mother."

"Tell me, then." She moved closer to the table. "What's she like?"

"My mom?"

"Yeah."

Ryan opened his mashed potatoes and took a bite before moving back to his chicken. "Isn't that on the personal side?"

"It is," she responded, taking another bite. "And?"

"I thought we weren't doing that."

"Well." She looked around. "When you bring me out to such a fine establishment, I figure I should at least pretend to care about you…"

"Oh, pretend?"

"Yep."

"Well, in that case," he said, "I suppose I should warn you; I don't open up much…"

"Then we'll do well with each other," she countered. "Answering personal questions by trying not to answer them…"

He took another bite and washed it down with a drink.

"Your mother?" She paused. "Something more than her modeling career or report cards, please…"

He laughed. "She's a very strong woman."

"How so?"

"Just her personality. My family is full of strong women."

"She from Florida?"

"Illinois, originally." He took another bite. "Moved to Florida with my dad before I was born. Supposedly, it was a dream of hers to live there, and it just so happened that my dad's family owns a farm near Ocala, so they packed up and moved." He paused. "He was a salesman in Chicago, so it was an easy decision on his end. He says he just wanted to make her happy."

"So, your dad is the charmer?"

"I guess…"

"Did you live on the farm?"

"God, no." He took another bite. "Grandparents still live there, though."

"Your father just wanted to up and move to Chicago?"

"At one time, I guess. He got tired of the farm; I suppose. I don't know. He's very career driven. Motivated. Things I am not."

"Funny how it works." Mel paused. "The older you get, the more you realize how like and unlike your parents you are."

"Seems more the latter lately," Ryan replied.

"That why you're here? A million miles away from them?"

The question was so bold, so forthright, that Ryan did not have time to process it. He took another bite of his chicken and began picking the bones of meat, taking care to wash it down with his drink. He took a deep breath.

"Come on," she replied, almost prodding. "What are you running from, for real?"

Ryan exhaled and turned away. "I don't know…life? My life? The fact that I'm twenty-four years old and have absolutely no idea what the hell I'm doing or where I'm going in life? The fact that I spent four years getting an education and preparing for a job that I don't even want anymore? The fact that I'm more unsure of the future now than ever before, and all around me, everyone else seems to have it figured out?"

She smiled. "So, you did run away?"

He laughed. "I didn't run. I drove. And yeah, I guess I did."

She stared at him for a long time, and he wondered just how much she was judging him.

"That's awesome."

"What?"

"Seriously." She leaned across the table. "That's fucking cool. To just run away? To get into your car and peace out with the middle finger up?"

"It wasn't exactly like that."

"Doesn't matter. It's fantastic. What a millennial thing to do."

"Run away?"

"Yeah!" She laughed. "Listen, no generation in the history of the world would take a comfy bed, a prepped education, and tangible goals and piss them away like you did. That's bold. All because you wanted something different, and you were true to yourself."

"I'm pretty sure all the '60s flower kids did that…"

"No, they were about something different. They were about anti-establishment and understanding that you have to enjoy where you are. You, on the other hand, much like many of your peers, don't give a damn about establishment or anti-establishment or politics or anything. You, like I wrote about, are following personal beliefs and irrational thoughts to a higher level. You are that Chopin novel."

He smiled. "And here I thought I was giving a homeless guy a ride..."

"You know what I would give to just up and leave like you did? You know how much I dream about it?"

"Why don't you, then? Why aren't you off on your way to, where was it you wanted to go? Hawaii? For some reason?"

She laughed softly. "I don't know."

He leaned back toward the table. "Well, I guess it's too late to leave now..."

"And why's that?"

"Because I'm here..."

She seemed taken aback at first, but her shock gave way to a small grin. "There's that charm..."

"Sorry," he replied, leaning back once more as she got up from the table with her tray. He could tell she was still at a loss for words, and this pleased him for a moment.

"What about your parents?" he asked as he stood up.

"What about them?"

"What was your mom like?"

She moved toward the door with him close behind. "She was...wild."

"Wild?"

"Yeah, wild. Kind, but wild."

"You'll have to do more explaining that that."

"I figured I would..." They moved out the door and into the cold air. She kept a half-step in front of him as they ambled down the street. Ryan waited for her to speak.

"This town isn't that big," he finally said. "Eventually, we will run out of sidewalk."

She finally stopped and took a deep breath. "You know how many people I've talked to about my mom?"

"I assume not many."

"It's not something I do."

"Then you don't have to," he replied. "I won't make you. We can talk about anything."

She closed her eyes with a deep sigh. Opening them, she stared deeply at Ryan before moving to the edge of the sidewalk and sitting down with her feet in the street.

Ryan took a seat alongside her.

"My dad says she was a lot like me," Mel finally said, "when she was younger."

"Where'd they meet?"

"Take a guess..."

He thought for a moment before the realization dawned on him. "Hawaii?"

She laughed. "She was a student. He was on a bachelor trip with his brother, back when people could actually afford Hawaii."

"Suddenly, it all makes sense." He smiled wryly. Deep down, he felt bad about his earlier ridicule.

"Shut up."

He chuckled as he changed the subject. "So, was it love at first sight?"

She exhaled. "Not even close. My dad said that he lost her more times than he didn't, yet somehow they always came back together."

"I'm sure the distance was hard."

"Of course. She lived in Pennsylvania, originally, and after he left Hawaii, he had no clue how to find her. He had to find a roommate, who got him in touch with her parents, who said she was somewhere in Oregon, around Crater Lake. Without a second thought, he just drove there, not knowing if he'd find her or not."

"He knew what he wanted."

"Exactly. And he knew he had to pursue her. He couldn't make a single mistake."

"A smart man."

"Yeah…" she trailed off, looking at the empty downtown that stretched before them. "She was so different. So free. She taught me to be strong and fearless."

"Sounds like you listened to her."

"Damn right."

He smirked as he, too, looked down the street.

"She never could have been a housewife. At least not in the traditional sense. It never fit with her. She loved her kids, though. Does that make sense?"

"Sure, it does…it's just interesting that you write about millennials seeking some difference from their parents, and yet the author has such a maternal connection."

She considered this as she rested her hands on her knees. "I guess I'm a conundrum."

He smiled. "There are worse things to be."

She smirked at him, and he could almost hear the word "charm" though it was never said.

"Enough about me." She sighed. "You already know way too much."

"I don't mind."

"I'm sure you don't." She laughed. "But seriously, it's too much."

"Fine, then," Ryan replied, adjusting his legs. "What would you like to discuss?"

"Anything else."

"Anything?"

"Yes."

He pondered for a moment as he reveled in the feeling of sitting next to her. It was a moment he did not want to end. Finally, he spoke. "You see that hardware store down there?" He motioned to a façade somewhere neither of them could see.

"What hardware store?"

"That one, way down there," he said. "That's the one me and my dad used to frequent."

She smiled as she followed his pointing finger, realizing the joke. "Is it?"

"Yep. Billy's Hardware. Nails and duct tape for cheap."

"Is that the slogan?"

"More or less. His marketing department was a bit lacking."

"I can tell."

"And that coffee shop right there?" He pointed across the street to a shuttered door. "Best milkshakes around. Used to go there after school after every test I passed in science class."

"How are you not a thousand pounds?"

"I didn't pass that many…"

"Oh."

"And just on the next block is a library that I stole a book from."

"What book?"

"*Huckleberry Finn.*"

"What a rapscallion..."

"I actually did do that, but don't tell," he whispered as an aside.

"Charming and devilish," she whispered back.

"And at the very end of the street," he said in his normal voice, "was Sarah McAllister's house."

"An old flame?"

"First girl I ever liked. Broke my heart."

"You poor thing."

"It was traumatizing, to say the least. But when you're eight, everything is."

"How did you manage?" she asked, finally unable to control her laughter.

"I don't know," he answered, breaking character through his laughs.

"Th-this s-sounds," she managed to say between struggled breaths, "like a wonderful place."

He lay back and continued chuckling. "It was a hellhole."

"Then, I guess Mitchell and Shannon have a lot in common."

In her laughter, she had managed to put her hand on top of his and for a moment, he felt like it was intentional.

There was no awkward silence in that moment. Instead, a serene calm lingered longer than any memory could have. It was the calm of two people completely content in the moment, and neither wanted it to end.

The hum of the streetlight meshed with the drone of a semi on the highway some miles away. Those were the only audible traces of life as Ryan and Mel stared at the empty storefronts of downtown Mitchell.

"Can I ask you something?" Mel asked as they walked toward the Jeep in the KFC parking lot.

"Of course," he replied, pulling his keys from his pocket.

"It's more of a favor than a question..."

"Sure," he said as he moved to the driver's door. As he inserted his key, he noticed she was standing at the hood.

"Can I drive?"

He met her sheepish look.

"Can you what?"

She stood more upright, more assertive.

"Drive."

"This?" he asked, indicating his Jeep.

"Yeah."

"Now?"

"Yeah."

He removed the key and looked around.

"I just"—she moved toward him— "I just haven't driven in forever. It kills me. I feel so...useless in the backseat all the time."

He laughed, understanding more and more. "Of course. I mean, sure you can drive."

"Really?"

"Yeah."

"You're serious?"

He held out the key. "Of course."

"You're letting me drive your car."

"I am."

She walked to him briskly and took the key, as though he might soon change his mind.

"This is awesome!" she shrieked as she inserted the key and opened the door.

He smiled as he walked around the back and toward the passenger side. Looking inside, he could see she was already adjusting the seat and mirrors with a look of complete satisfaction on her face.

He knocked on the window, indicating that his door was locked. She popped the lock, and he climbed in.

"This is so cool," she said again. "Thank you so much."

Taken aback at her appreciation, he buckled his seatbelt. "You're driving me. I should be thanking you."

"You don't understand. No one lets me drive. Ever. It's been months, if not years."

"Well, don't hit anything…"

"I won't," she replied. He watched as she inserted the key and waited for the engine to crank before firing off.

"Brakes aren't great, and the tires are mostly bald, but she still runs."

"Reminds me of my old car," she said, hands on the wheel. She smiled ear to ear as she sat a moment longer. "Ready?"

He smiled over at her. "Ready."

She shifted into reverse and slowly, glacially, backed out of the parking spot. Her head was like an owl's, pivoting from side to side as she took great care to be aware of her surroundings.

Shifting into drive, she let the Jeep inch forward. She pulled toward the vacant main road with both hands on the wheel.

Sitting in the passenger seat of the only thing to his name would typically have made Ryan anxious, but to his surprise he was not nervous at all. He was content and peaceful, happy to watch the smile on her face as she used the turn signal and moved out onto the road.

"This is so cool," she breathed as she turned.

They only passed a few other cars as they crawled through the neighborhoods and out into the country, but Mel kept both hands on the wheel and her eyes alternating between the rearview and windshield.

"Do you know where you're going?"

"I don't care," she replied with a grin.

He smirked as he turned on the radio and began shuffling through static-filled stations.

"There," she indicated abruptly.

"What?"

"That song. Back a bit."

He realized she was referring to a station he had passed. Instantly, he moved it back.

"Yeah," she replied, "that one." It was a newer, bluesy, country song. While not Ryan's first choice, he gladly let it play.

"I love this song."

He sat back in his seat. "It's only fitting that the driver picks."

She kept her gaze on the road, but he could tell she was still smiling.

They barely exchanged words as she drove west along the empty country roads. Every so often, he could hear her singing along, and occasionally he found himself tapping his feet.

How weird it was—a passenger in his own car listening to music he had never liked before. Yet somehow, despite the inconceivable setting, he felt this was music he could definitely get used to.

Chapter 17
1,089 Miles to Spokane

She drove all the way.

Ryan had thought she would stop outside Mitchell, maybe on some dark stretch of pavement, and relinquish control to him. He'd thought she would get tired, that once the thrill of the drive was done, she would decide it was time for the night to end. He'd thought all these things, but never once did he think she would drive all the way.

She leaned against the driver door with one hand on the wheel the other lightly touching her blonde hair. He could tell she was not thinking about ice on the roads, the bald tires, or the worn brakes.

He did not know where they were, but that did not matter to him. He spent his time watching the road ahead and casually looking over to her, astonished ever more by her demeanor.

"This is so cool," he heard her say more than once, though each time she seemed more enamored than the last.

"Glad you like," he finally said. "Not everyone thinks this old car is as cool as you do."

"It's awesome. People just don't have good taste anymore."

He laughed, noticing that their conversation was much quieter in the darkened night.

"It has such character," she continued. "Plus, it's a Jeep."

"A fan of Jeeps?"

She looked over at him. "Every girl likes a Jeep."

"Good to know," he said.

"The owner isn't too bad, either," she replied.

Ryan kept his eyes forward, wondering if he had heard her correctly. Swallowing hard, he turned and looked at her. Their eyes met briefly before she chuckled and returned her attention to the road.

"You know your way around pretty good for not driving," he said after a few minutes of silence. She had turned several times, and he wondered if she was just driving in circles.

"Some things you don't forget," she responded with a sigh. "Back in high school, we'd drive to Mitchell to visit my mom."

Her words and his realization hit him deeply. "I'm sorry...I didn't mean..."

"It's fine," she replied. "It's nice to make the drive when you don't have to." She considered her words. "That sounds bad, doesn't it?"

He shrugged, knowing he could never understand the truth. "It sounds honest."

"I've never said those things to anyone. They're usually told to a mirror or an empty room or something."

"I think it's all right. When I say terrible things, it's usually to my parents, which typically ends up worse for me."

"I don't think they care," she replied. "Parents were us once, too."

He smirked as he looked out the passenger window. "I'd like to think so."

"You disagree?"

He chuckled. "I mean, obviously not. Clearly, they were kids once."

"Then what?"

"I don't know. Just seems like the gap is growing."

"Maybe it is," she replied. "And maybe one day it won't."

"Going back on your *Awakening* thoughts already?"

She laughed. "Not yet." She ran her fingers through her hair. "But I could see it happening."

The Jeep continued to hum along on the pavement.

"Thank you again," she replied, looking at him once more.

"Anytime," he replied, returning the glance.

The car began to slow along a barren stretch of road somewhere only she knew. Looking out, Ryan could not see any discernible landmarks, but given the time driving, he knew they had to be close to Shannon.

"I figured you'd want to be the gentleman on this date and drop me off…" she said after turning down the radio and putting the car in park. "My house is a mile up the road."

He smiled as he undid his seatbelt. The date comment was not lost on him. "Of course."

He opened his door and walked around the back of the Jeep to the driver's side, stopping to open her door and allow her to step out. She walked around the front of the vehicle, illuminated by the headlights, and he smiled as he climbed inside and followed her movement. It was then, halfway between the headlights, that he saw her do something peculiar.

She stopped.

Illuminated, she stood like a statue as snow fell around her.

The world hung on a string as he stared at her figure and wondered what, exactly, she was doing. In the background, he heard a faint country voice singing something he had never heard before. He tried to ignore it, but between her standing alone and the otherwise silent world that surrounded them, ignoring was an impossibility. After what seemed an eternity, she looked up at him through the windshield, wearing a vastly different expression than before.

Sensing that something was wrong, he opened his door and prepared himself to join her in the cold. But in the time it took him to open the door, she had walked briskly back to the driver's side. He had one foot on the ground as she rounded the door, and in less than a second, she leaned inside the car and grabbed his arms before pressing her lips to his.

It was unlike anything he had felt before—a rush of blood to the head that he could only hope to one day define. He could feel her skin against his, and her hands gripped his arms. He was rendered completely powerless.

After a few seconds, she pulled back and looked down at his foot.

"Move your foot," she commanded.

He swallowed his confusion and apprehension and found himself picking the foot up and moving it back inside the car.

She brushed back her hair and reached down between his legs, and for a moment, his body went numb. He quickly realized that she was in search of the seat adjuster, however, and before he knew it, she had found the lever and lifted it. He felt his seat inch all the way back.

She climbed inside and on top of him, facing him in the driver's seat. He looked up at her as he felt the driver's door close.

"What are we doing?" he finally asked, knowing full well what they were doing.

"Shut up," she replied, once again bringing her face to his and engaging in deep, lustful kisses.

"Okay," he heard himself say between touches.

She pressed her chest against his. He felt her hands reach out for his and place them on her back pockets as she delved deeper and deeper.

He felt her reach down once more, though this time it was his belt. His breath caught in his throat as they continued onward, past the point of no return.

She pulled back from him as he felt his pants unbuckle.

"Don't think," she whispered into his ear, as if sensing his trepidation. "Just go."

Leaning back in his seat, he looked into her eyes once more, believing what she said.

He ran his hands up her back to her neck and pulled her against him.

This, however, was never his lead.

As he ran his fingers across her chest, she caressed his back and continued kissing him madly. In minutes, she had his shirt off and pants on the floorboards. Only then did she allow him to do the same to her.

Time stood still as she placed her hands on his bare chest and pushed herself away from his lips, taking time to let the moment hinge on her next move. His breath caught in his lungs as her hands found him, and as he looked back up to her, he found her biting her bottom lip, a look of complete serenity mixed with deep lust on her face.

He thought about saying something, but nothing came out. There were no words for this.

Seconds later, she shifted her waist. At that moment, they finally found each other.

Breathing deeply, she continued kissing him, wordlessly engaging in passion he never saw coming. He could feel everything, and it was all he'd ever needed. On and on, moving with a rhythm only lovers could—bodies intertwined with heat and vigor.

It lasted only minutes more, and when it was over, she collapsed onto him and he held her close, never wanting to let go.

In the sound of their heaving breaths, he thought he had heard something about love. Maybe he had said it, or perhaps she had, or maybe he had only heard it in his head. His confusion was complete, and he knew he could not be certain.

After a minute, he smiled, knowing that vocalizations hardly mattered.

Who needed words when actions spoke so loudly?

***

"You asleep?" he heard her whisper as she lay on his chest, skin to skin. They had lain together in silence for what seemed an eternity as he'd wondered what she was thinking.

"Not anymore," he whispered back.

He could feel her smile against him.

"You really like Jeeps," he finally said, eyes still shut.

Another smile.

He continued, "I can only assume that was the culprit for all of…you know."

"You got it," she agreed. "I only get with guys for their Jeeps."

He nodded softly. "Glad I didn't choose the Camry."

"Jesus," she breathed. "No one gets laid in a Camry."

"The more you know," he whispered back.

Neither moved. In the silence, snow landed gently on the fogged windows.

"It's almost Christmas," she said softly. He could not tell if it was meant for him or not.

"Almost," he repeated.

"It's always nice when it snows on Christmas. It always feels,"—she let the words hang— "special."

"Sounds wonderful."

"It is. I think you'd like it."

For a moment, there was a stillness in her words, a sense of contentment that he had not heard before. She was so strong, so able, and yet her words were spoken timidly, like a child seeking confirmation.

"Did you really mean it?" she asked after a few minutes.

"Mean what?"

"What you said earlier, about not going anywhere…"

He exhaled, caressing her bare back with his right hand. "Of course."

"You're just telling me what I want to hear."

"I'm telling the truth."

There was another pause.

"God," she finally said, "I sound like a fuckin' teenager."

He laughed, sensing that her naïveté was gone. "Look around you." He continued caressing her. "I'm pretty sure this is the definition of being a teenager."

He felt her laugh in response. "I guess it isn't so bad."

They lay still in each other's arms.

"I'm not ready to go home yet," she finally said.

He smiled down at her blonde hair draped across his chest. "I'm not ready yet, either."

"Good," she replied. "Let's just stay here."

"Fine with me," he agreed. "I can't think of a better place to be."

She turned her head, looking up at him with her chin on his chest. "Shut up."

"It's true!"

"You're cuter when you don't talk."

"At least I have a Jeep."

He could feel her smile once more as she lay on him with closed eyes. "This is true."

Part 3
Chapter 18
2,648 Miles and Four Days to Spokane

He grimaced as he stared at the vending machine. His stomach ached with hunger. He had not slept at all, and around him, the silence of the rest area was palpable as he stood longingly looking at the snacks. Finally, he stepped back and walked into the restroom.

How did I end up here? he wondered, splashing water on his face, and staring at the grizzled face in the mirror. He wiped his hands on his pants, clutched his bag, and walked back outside toward the Jeep in the parking lot.

Sighing, he saw the boy asleep in the driver's seat. For a moment, he watched him lying silent and calm. He could leave him here. He knew that. He could hitch a ride back down to the coast where he wanted to be, and in mere seconds, he would be nothing but a faint memory. There were tens of trucks on the other side of the highway; it would take nothing more than a thumb and a few steps.

His mind pulled him that way, but he could not force his feet to take the step. He had been south. He had made it. Yet here he was. It did not make sense.

He thought about the last few days and everything that had led him here. It had to mean something. How could he deny that fate? And what of the boy? What had led him here? What force had brought them together, and why? This, too, made little sense.

Such were his thoughts as he stared at the Jeep in front of him. Finally, he moved to a picnic table some distance off and took a seat.

Taking a deep breath, he set his bag beside him and reached into his pocket, where he felt a familiar business card. Pulling it out, he studied it intently, as though it were a sacred text.

It had been a long day and night, and he did not know how much longer he could keep up the façade. It was already beginning to take a toll. But he knew that if he wanted answers, he had to persevere. Perhaps it would make sense in the end.

As the minutes ticked by, he sat listening to the early-morning highway traffic.

"You don't sleep a lot, do you?" Ryan's voice came from his right. He discreetly slipped the business card into the picnic table crack and turned toward the boy.

"Eh, I don't need a lot of sleep." He smiled. "Plus, your cushions hurt my back."

"Yeah, they aren't the most comfortable things in the world," Ryan replied.

He nodded in all seriousness, choosing his next words carefully. "Way too soft."

He watched Ryan's face screw up a bit.

"You ready to go?" Ryan finally said, breaking the silence.

He turned and stood from the table.

"Yes, sir. I was born ready."

Not long after they walked away, the wind dislodged the business card and blew it into the grass. Face up, it waited for someone else to come along and read its contents:

Bo Williams, Century 21, Clearwater, Florida

***

1,083 Miles to Spokane

The sunlight cascaded through the window as Ryan lay face-down on the hotel bed. His eyes fluttered briefly, and his open mouth stuck to the sheet as he tried to gauge the time of day. He lay there for a long time, allowing his tired eyes to adjust. He closed them once more and breathed deeply, instantly noticing a distinct scent. It was sweet, almost flower-like, and he knew it was the scent of her, etched into his mind as it was on his skin. It was her perfume, her shampoo, her conditioner. It was her breath. It was her.

For a few minutes more, he soaked in all that he felt before finally raising his head from the pillow and allowing himself to examine the day.

"Good to see you up," Bo said. Ryan turned and saw him standing in the bathroom door.

"Yeah," Ryan said, "long night."

Bo did not respond, and Ryan could tell something was amiss. Looking at the dresser, he saw Bo's bag sitting neatly upright.

"Everything all right, buddy?" Ryan asked, throwing off his covers.

"Yeah," Bo replied, still in the bathroom. "I'm just ready to move on."

Ryan swallowed the lump that rose in his throat. "Move on…to?"

Bo stepped out. "Spokane." He stared intently, and Ryan could tell this was not the same person as before.

"Spokane?" Ryan repeated.

"Yeah," Bo said curtly, returning to the bathroom.

Ryan tried to think of something else to say, but the tension grew. Finally, Bo emerged from the bathroom. He walked over to his bag and threw it over his shoulder.

"You ready?" Bo asked, turning to Ryan.

"Ready? For what?"

"To leave."

"Leave?" Ryan repeated. "Now?"

"Yeah. Now."

"Right now? Wh—what's the rush?"

Bo turned. "I just need to get there."

Ryan rose from his bed. "Did something happen? What's wrong."

Bo sighed. "Nothing's wrong. I just decided that we need to get going."

"Let's slow down a minute."

"I'd rather not."

"I'd rather we do, Bo." Ryan took a step forward. "Do you have any idea what happened last night?"

Bo closed his eyes. "No."

"Heavy shit, Bo." Ryan raised his arms. "I mean, some heavy shit."

"And?"

"And! And I can't just run away now." Ryan turned toward the window and then back. "I can't walk away. She…she really likes me."

Bo did not seem amused by this answer.

"And…I promised her I wouldn't run now."

"You promised you'd take me to Spokane."

"I know." Ryan gritted his teeth. "I just didn't think—"

"I need to go now."

"Okay," Ryan said, "but, but what about our car…it's still in the shop!"

"Then I'll hitchhike."

"You can't do that."

"Why? That's how I got here," Bo countered, making for the door.

"You can't…"

"Why? You'd feel guilty?"

They stared at each other in silence for a moment, and Ryan found himself in the unusual position of not knowing what to say.

Just then, there was a tap at the door. It was soft, yet clearly audible, and neither Bo nor Ryan knew whether to address the conversation or it.

Ryan exhaled as he made for the door and pulled it slightly ajar.

Standing in the doorway was Randall. Beyond him, Ryan saw his tow truck with Curt at the helm. The boom of the truck was lowering Ryan's Jeep into a parking spot.

"Hey, Randall," Ryan said, just as confused to the scene outside as he was the inside.

"Mr. Ryan, nice to see you," Randall replied rather sheepishly, as though saying the words out of discomfort.

"What's going on?" Ryan asked, motioning to the truck behind him.

Randall scratched his head. "Well…I decided to bring your truck back to you…" He held out the key.

"Okay…" Ryan replied, still confused. He could feel Bo's gaze on him.

Randall adjusted his ball cap on his balding head. "It was good doing business with you…"

"What's wrong?" Ryan asked.

Randall turned back to the truck and then shuffled his feet before meeting Ryan's gaze. "Listen," he began, "you seem like a nice guy. And your…"—he considered his words—"your partner, he seems like a good fellow, too."

Ryan leaned against the doorway.

"I got no problem with you. Two traveling guys paying cash…listen, I don't ask no questions. Your business is your business."

Ryan cocked his head.

"But," Randall continued, "not everyone, especially in this town, is as trusting as me. Some people see two strangers holed up in a hotel payin' cash as a potential issue." He shuffled his feet some more. "Our sheriff is one of those people…"

Ryan felt the breath catch in his lungs.

Randall saw the expression change on his face. "Now, don't get all sideways on me. Nobody knows nothing. Nothing. But…he's been askin' questions. Questions that people like me just don't ask. Now, normally those questions ain't a problem to ignore…"

"But?"

Randall exhaled. "But this morning, he gives me a call all dark and deep-like. Says that the rumor was I had the boy's car and was fixing it up. Now, Ryan, I ain't about to lie to an officer of the law, even if it's that scumbag sheriff."

"What'd you say?"

"I said that I do."

"And?"

"And he asked to see it. Said he'd be right over. Now before you ask, I told him no. Said that it was too early; that my old lady was still asleep. I could tell he was upset, but he finally obliged. Before I hung up, though, he said that he wanted me to bring him the VIN and plate numbers. Said he'd get them from me at breakfast."

Ryan stared at the old man, growing more panicked by the second.

"Ryan," Randall continued, "I don't know what you've got going on, and I don't care...but this sheriff, he does. And he doesn't usually lose when he sets his eyes on something. I know the moment I give these numbers; he'll find what he's looking for."

Ryan nodded, realization and dread etched in his face.

Randall made eye contact. "I wish I could help you, boy, but all I can do is give you back a running truck and hope you understand."

Ryan looked back into the room and saw that Bo was listening, face screwed up as though he was unsure of the situation's magnitude. Ryan turned back after a moment.

"How long do we have?" Ryan asked, voice almost cracking.

Randall sniffed and rubbed his nose. Turning back to his brother in the parking lot, he nodded his head. "I guess I need to go drop off the truck, and...well...I could take the long way to the diner."

Ryan smiled faintly. "Thank you, Randall."

"You take care, Ryan," Randall replied, turning from the young man.

Ryan shut the door. Turning around, he found himself caught in Bo's piercing gaze.

"What was that about?" he asked as Ryan moved toward the bed.

"It's time to go." Ryan grabbed his jacket off the floor near the bed and moved to the dresser, which he yanked open to remove the few items he had put inside.

Bo continued to stare at Ryan, obviously confused.

"Let's go," Ryan coldly said.

"What was that about?" Bo repeated.

Ryan moved to the bathroom and splashed water onto his face. He turned to Bo as he wiped it with a towel. "It doesn't matter."

"It sounds like it does."

"Two minutes ago," Ryan said, brushing past Bo toward the door, "you were hell-bent on leaving. I'm ready now. Let's leave."

He flung the door open and pulled the room key from his pocket as he moved hastily toward the hotel office. Seconds later, he was shoving the Jeep's key into the ignition. Bo wordlessly opened the passenger side and climbed in.

Blinking away tears, Ryan flipped the truck into gear. In a moment, they were gone, leaving not even a cloud of dust in their wake.

Chapter 19
1,801 Miles and Three Days to Spokane

"It's good to see you, too…" Ryan replied, staring at Brandon as he stood in the doorway of the large house.

"What are you doing here?" Brandon repeated. He looked both annoyed and tired.

"We need help."

"We?"

Ryan turned to him and then back to Brandon.

"This is Bo."

"Bo?"

"Yep. Name's Bo…" he began. He stretched out a hand that was not acknowledged.

Brandon stared at him intently, trying to gauge something that neither of the other two could delineate. Finally, he turned and opened the front door fully, unkindly beckoning them into the home.

"What exactly do you need from me?" he asked, moving into a living room off the entry.

"A place to crash," Ryan replied. "One night."

"Both of you?" Brandon asked. Bo knew this was directed more his way than Ryan's. Nevertheless, he tried to ignore the comment and instead concerned himself with examining the house.

"Yes," Ryan replied, "if that's all right."

He watched as Brandon walked out of view with Ryan in tow, presumably to exchange some words. He tried to eavesdrop, but the whispers were hushed enough that he could only make out a few words. Before long, Brandon returned into the room and motioned for him to follow. Ryan did not reappear.

"You're in the guest room tonight," Brandon said, motioning to a room down the hall. "Bathroom is through that door."

He hung at the door for a moment as he peered inside. He looked from the room to Brandon and back. Silence hung in the air.

"You…have a lovely house," he finally said.

Brandon stared at him as though confused by the compliment. "Thanks," he finally said.

He entered the room and allowed Brandon to pull the door closed.

Sighing, he studied the room, from the hardwood that creaked under his tattered shoes to the popcorn ceiling above. He moved to the bed and sat down, closing his eyes at the softness of the mattress. It had been a while since he had felt that feeling.

He could hear Ryan and Brandon murmuring, yet try as he might, he could not make out their words. He finally moved to the bathroom and flipped on the light with slight trepidation.

The bathroom was simple, with a sink, toilet, and tub shower, but the décor provided distinct character, from the perfectly folded towels to the tissue box turned slightly askew on the sink counter. It was clean and pristine, the very picture of hospitality.

He turned off the light and returned to the bedroom.

Exhaling again, he found his bag on the edge of the bed and opened it partway. He stared inside before closing it back up.

He pressed on the mattress and felt it give way under his hand. It was the definition of inviting. It was perfect comfort. For a moment, he could almost smell the fabric softener clinging to the quilt.

He laid his head on the pillow to his left and found it cool and pleasing. In his euphoria, he almost forgot he was sitting in a guest room in a house he had never been in, owned by a man he had never met.

He closed his eyes, but they did not stay closed for long. Lifting his head from the pillow, he grabbed his bag and slid onto the hardwood. He curled into himself on the floor and tucked the bag under his head for a pillow, though one hand remained entangled in the bag strings. He turned away from the bed that raised above him and finally closed his eyes.

It was there that Bo slept, on the floor and away from the furniture. Six hours later, he was already awake when Ryan came calling. Soon after, he'd be out of the room and back in the Jeep, leaving behind a room as clean as it had been when he'd entered; almost as though no one had been there at all.

***

1,014 Miles to Spokane

The speedometer hit 80, but Ryan kept his foot pressed hard on the gas. Several miles ago, he had turned the rearview mirror to the side, but he still found himself trying to look back. He had done all of this wordlessly, as he had yet to speak since leaving the hotel. The 70 miles since Shannon had gone by in a blur

Bo sat in the passenger seat, eyes occasionally darting to the driver, but he, too, was quiet. Strangely, it felt as though just a second had past, but the miles kept rolling by.

"You gonna tell me what's going on?" Bo finally asked.

Ryan seemed to ponder this for a full minute. "No," he finally said.

Bo shook his head and gave it another minute.

"You don't think I should know what that was all about?" he continued, rephrasing the question.

Ryan feigned ignorance. "What was what all about?"

Bo gritted his teeth. "Randall. Your Jeep. The sheriff."

Ryan nodded and faced the road ahead. "Oh," he finally said. "No."

Bo sighed. "Fine. Don't answer." He sat for a minute more, occasionally looking out the window, before he finally turned to Ryan. "I want to ask my South Dakota question." he said loudly.

"Screw you," Ryan said.

"What was the Randall thing all about?" Bo repeated, as though he had not heard Ryan's retort.

Ryan maintained his silence. His agitation rose.

"It's my question," Bo added.

"Fine," Ryan finally replied. He had reached his boiling point. "Fine, you want to ask your question? Fine. I want you to answer mine, too." The car jolted to the right as he hastily exited the highway and pulled onto a narrow gravel shoulder. Beyond it was an open gravel field intended for truckers or emergency stops.

"You want to ask questions? Then I'll ask my South Dakota question too," Ryan snapped, shifting the car into park as they stopped in the middle of the gravel field. "And as a matter of fact, I'll ask my Wyoming question, my-my Montana question, and any other state's question that we pass, so here we go."

Bo half-turned as Ryan continued his assault.

"One: why do you have a gun on you?"

Bo turned back toward the windshield, clearly annoyed.

"What's wrong? Didn't know that I knew?" Ryan taunted. "Quite a secret to keep if I do say so myself. Question two: how much did you enjoy Chesdin Lake, being as it doesn't fucking exist?"

Bo turned back to Ryan, surprised.

"Oh, that's the one that astonishes you? Jesus, man, has anything you've told me been true? Wait, I don't want that question. Here's a better one. Question three: even though I highly doubt your honesty regarding pretty much anything, answer me this: What the hell are you doing here? You going to rob me? Kill me? Why did you get in my car?"

Bo opened the door, undid his belt, and flung it to the side as he jumped out of the car. Ryan was quick to follow him.

"I'm not done! I have one more question!"

Bo stopped ten feet ahead of Ryan, but he did not turn.

"Between the gun, and the lie, and everything else, I have to ask—," his voice turned back to normal as he could clearly tell Bo was within hearing distance. "What's in Spokane?" Knowing he had already said too much, and knowing it was too late, he repeated the question, though slightly softer than before. "What are we going to find in Spokane?"

Bo exhaled once more and turned around. Looking Ryan directly in the eye, he gritted his teeth and spoke with true determination. "You first."

Ryan returned the gaze and scoffed before rolling his eyes.

"Fine. The truth is…" he began bitterly, standing awkwardly in the middle of the gravel. "Truth is, I had no money. I picked you up without a plan, and when it came time to get gas, I decided to steal money from my father…and…"

Bo was not looking at him. Instead, his eyes were focused on something far in the distance. Ryan stopped talking and followed his gaze.

The highway was empty save for an occasional truck, but even in the faint snowfall of the South Dakota morning, they could clearly make out the flashing blue and red lights of a cop car careening down the road as if undeniably possessed.

Lights still flashing, the car screeched to a halt behind the Jeep after only a few seconds.

"Shit…" Ryan said. He closed his eyes.

Time froze, and even Bo felt the magnitude of the situation. He stared at Ryan, but he just stood there, eyes closed, as if anticipating the worst.

The car turned off and the door opened. Bo could not make out the driver, but he knew that Ryan's attempt to outrun the situation had been in vain.

"Well, well, well…" Ransom's gruff voice drawled as he shut the door and strode toward them. "Christmas Eve eve, and you boys don't look like you're shopping…"

Bo saw Ryan swallow a lump in his throat and open his eyes.

"With six grand in cash off their daddy, not to mention some identity theft and, considering you boys got eighty miles in, oh, about forty-five minutes," he said, looking at his watch, "a heaping dose of breaking the speed limit. I'd say you all were in some kinda hurry to buy those presents.

"But it's funny," he continued as he examined the Jeep, "I don't see no wrapping paper or bows." He turned back to Ryan. "Hell, I don't even see a gift in that Jeep." His pace steadied until he was three feet from Ryan. "So…that leaves me to believe something different. Instead of being in the Christmas mood, it stands to reason that you boys,"—he sniffed as he got within a foot of Ryan and stopped, looking him directly in the face— "you boys must be on the run."

Ryan ran his tongue against his bottom teeth as he chose his next words carefully. "Fuck you."

A smile crept across Ransom's face. Ryan attempted to smile back. As he did, Ransom delivered an uppercut. The blow caught Ryan squarely in the stomach and sent him to the ground.

Bo took a step forward.

"You stay right there, homeboy," Ransom snarled. He moved dangerously to Ryan's side. "You take another step, and I'll put a bullet in you."

Ransom looked down at Ryan.

"I think," he began mockingly, "that your problem is a lack of respect."

Ryan coughed hard and squirmed on the ground.

Ransom eyed his prey unmercifully and walked around him in a circle. "I think that you don't respect your daddy…or the law." He aimed a swift kick into Ryan's gut.

Bo stepped forward again.

"What did I tell you, you son of a bitch!" Ransom roared, unholstering his gun and holding it at his side. Bo jumped back.

"You thought I was playing," Ransom continued, turning back to Ryan. "But I think you clearly know differently now…" He aimed another kick, which Ryan attempted to block with his knees. Ransom kicked his legs away and knelt onto his chest. He put the gun near Ryan's head and aimed the muzzle toward the gravel.

"I told you to leave, boy…" Ransom whispered as Ryan cowered under the weight of his knee. "I tried to be nice. I tried to be reasonable. But you wouldn't listen." He brought his face closer and balanced his hand on the gun. He smiled as he brought his grizzled chin within inches of Ryan's terrified face. "You'll listen now…"

He stood abruptly and grabbed Ryan by a handful of hair to pull him upward. Bo saw Ryan grab his stomach and wince, and he could hear the young man's anguish as the sheriff yanked on his scalp. Ryan had neither the strength nor the valor to lash out.

Ransom dragged him, stumbling, back to the squad car. In the gap between the rear of the Jeep and the front of the Taurus, he flung Ryan over the edge of the hood and onto the gravel next to the passenger door. He turned back to Bo and jabbed a finger at him.

"You get into that car, homeboy," he said, motioning to the Jeep. "And you drive on outta here. You hear me?"

Bo stood rigid for a moment. Ryan's anguished cries rang through the air.

"You ignore that boy." He flung an arm toward Ryan. "This is 'tween him and me. You move on outta here and forget about this."

Bo swallowed the lump in his throat and nodded.

Ransom stared at him. "Well, go on. Get your ass outta here."

Bo nodded again and moved to the driver's side of the Jeep as Ransom turned and walked between the vehicles. He could see that Ryan had attempted to crawl away from the car, but the escape attempt was futile.

"Come here, boy," Ransom scoffed, grabbing Ryan once more. "You ain't going nowhere." He cuffed Ryan and stood over him victoriously. He grabbed him by the hair again and flung him like a ragdoll into the passenger door.

Bo winced as he heard Ryan's body thump against the door. Sliding into the driver's side of the Jeep, he shut the door. Behind him, he heard every word that Ransom threw out.

"You should never try to escape," Ransom huffed. "It only makes this...harder."

Bo heard a punch land. He heard Ryan wheezing.

"When I get done, jail will look like paradise..."

Another punch. Another thud. In the Jeep, Bo flinched.

Opening his eyes, he looked in the rearview mirror and saw the gruesome scene behind. Ryan's face absorbed yet another punch. He slid to the gravel with his wrists cuffed behind him.

Tears welled in Bo's eyes. He closed them and heard another thud.

And another.

And another.

He reached for the keys with shaking hands. Somehow, he managed to start the Jeep. In the rearview, he saw Ransom open the Taurus's back door and drag Ryan to the door well. Ryan turned his glazed eyes toward his Jeep and the driver inside as Ransom hauled him up.

Blood oozed from his face in several places, and his cheeks and eyes were already bruising to a deep purple. His left eye was swollen shut, and his nose was wet with blood and mucus. For one brief moment, his eyes met Bo's in the mirror.

Their eyes locked for less than a second, and then the sheriff dealt Ryan yet another blow to the back of the head. He fell into the car, barely conscious. All the while, Ransom continued to mock and laugh as if his Christmas had come early.

Bo saw it all. He felt it all. Every kick, every punch. He winced in pain as he felt Ryan's body collapse under sheriff's fury.

His hand found the shifter. Tears streaming down his face, he let out a sob as he lurched the vehicle into drive. Taking his foot off the brake, he inched the truck forward.

Blinking through his tears, he stared ahead as the Jeep rolled on and away from the terror behind.

Chapter 20
1,083 Miles and Two Days to Spokane

He heard the hotel door close before he had fully woken. Turning onto his side, he saw Ryan's shadow hurry past the window.

He blinked and sat up half-heartedly. It was early. He ran his fingers through his long, matted hair and put his feet on the floor. He looked down at the bed he sat on.

It was hard to sleep well.

He lifted himself from the bed as the sunlight filtered in through the curtains. He shuffled to the bathroom and exhaled deeply as he stared in the mirror.

His beard had grown long. It was beyond unkempt and looked more like a tangle of brush than ever before. His eyebrows were unruly, and his blue eyes were sunken, as if a jolt had moved them back into their sockets. Perhaps they were retreating. He did not know. He almost did not recognize his image.

He took a drink from the faucet before moving back into the bedroom. He then grabbed his bag.

Stepping out of the room, he gave his eyes a moment to adjust before walking to the main building of the inn.

"'Morning," came Miss Barbara's unmistakable squeak. She stood at a dining table just inside the foyer.

"'Morning," he said with a brief smile.

"Breakfast?" she asked, wiping a seat.

"I'm actually looking for a laundry room..."

"For that shirt?" she asked, motioning to the one on his body.

He opened his bag. "Actually, this one." He pulled the matching shirt from his bag and unfolded it.

"And that one." She motioned again to the shirt he wore.

"And this one," he said awkwardly.

"Take a seat." She smiled. "And give me both."

She went off to another room. He stood still for a moment before moving toward the table.

He unbuttoned the first few buttons on his shirt as she returned with a towel.

"Wrap up in this while you eat," she said. She snatched one shirt from his hand and the other from his back.

He sat down in the chair and wrapped the towel around his shoulders as Miss Barbara stepped into a room to his left. He waited silently, unsure what to do next.

"Eat a biscuit," he heard her call. "I'll be back in a minute."

He saw the plate of biscuits on his right and reached out slowly to grab one. Putting it onto his plate, he deliberately broke it in half before starting his meal.

"Dough was a little tough, but I think they'll do," he heard her say from the kitchen. Looking up, he saw her near the stove with a pan in hand.

"They're very good," he finally said between mouthfuls.

She moved to his seat with a plate and a pan. Before long, he had a plate of gravy and eggs in front of him.

"What was your name again?" she asked as she moved back into the kitchen.

His mouth watered as he surveyed the food. "Bo," he said.

She placed the pan in the sink and rinsed it before retuning into the dining room.

"That your real name?" she asked. "Bo?"

He sat for a moment before picking up his fork and wordlessly taking a bite of eggs.

She sat in the chair opposite him. "Bo works," she finally said. "Eggs good?"

"Very," he replied, taking a sip of the orange juice she had poured him.

"Good," she replied matter-of-factly, as though already knowing the answer. "What's your friend out doing so early?"

He was becoming more and more ravenous as he ate. "Not sure…he left before I woke up."

"Yeah, I saw Mel around here," Barbara replied.

He looked up from his plate.

"He told you about her?"

"Briefly," he replied, taking another drink.

"She's a good girl, full of vigor," she replied. She poured herself a glass of juice. "Reminds me of me, honestly. She'd have made a fine southern girl."

He smiled as he wiped his mouth.

"She'll probably break his heart," she added. She sat for a few moments and stared out the window. "If he doesn't break hers first." She turned back and looked at him as though her words were unwarranted. "Sorry." She blushed. "Words get carried away sometimes."

He nodded and sat back silently in his chair.

"You had time to look around the town at all?"

He sniffed, savoring the tastes of the food, and welcoming the change of subject. "Somewhat," he said softly. "It's a nice town."

"It has its good parts," she replied. "Do you know how it got its name?"

"The town?"

"Yeah," she answered. "Shannon."

"How?"

She sat back and took a sip of her orange juice. "Supposedly, and that's all history is, but supposedly"—she set the glass down—"a young man left his home in Virginia to go mine in the Black Hills around 1874 or 5. Out there, he fell in love with the scenery but also realized the brutality of the Lakota lands. Upon returning home, he told stories of what he had seen, from the rugged landscapes to the death and destruction. Crazy as it was, he missed it."

With each word, he felt himself becoming more and more absorbed in the story.

"Anyway," she continued, "he decided that he wanted to return with his family, but the Indian Wars and the revolts made the Dakota Territory even more treacherous, so instead of settling back in the hills, he went as far west as he felt comfortable with and set up shop there."

"And Shannon?" he asked.

"He was a miner, not a scholar." She laughed. "And he gave up trying to spell Shenandoah."

He smiled. "Why'd he choose that?"

She took another sip. "Well, to my original point, back in the early 1800s, a lot of folks saw the Shenandoah Valley as the edge of America. They thought anyone who ventured past there was crazy and sure to die. Move to the late century, and that miner thought the same thing about the Dakota Territory. Hence the name."

"But he had already been farther west…"

"Exactly." She turned back to him. "And he still felt that way…he felt that anyone who went past this point was either insane or driven beyond reason. Now, in reality, he was already in the middle of the Lakota lands, but it didn't change anything for him."

"Did the Indians ever get him?"

She smiled. "Nope. He lived out his days here, and that was that. Plaque in front of the grocery store even commemorates his full life."

"Guess he made the right decision to stay here…"

"Yep." She stood and looked out the window. "But you have to wonder—if hadn't taken the risk earlier in life…would he ever have known when to stop?"

There was silence as he followed her gaze.

"More OJ?" she asked finally, stepping into the kitchen as though answering her own question.

He continued staring outward, deep in thought.

"I always like to think," she said, returning from the kitchen, "how do we know?"

He turned to her. "What do you mean?"

"How do we know that this is it?" She motioned around her. "How do we know that this is where we are meant to be? Did we stop exactly where and when we were supposed to?" She paused. "How do you know?"

"You don't until you do…" he replied paradoxically.

She smiled again. "You don't until you do. Until you figure it out, you'll never know."

There was another long pause.

"I guess," she finally said, "the only thing to decide is if you're the settler, or if you're still mining."

He turned back to her, a puzzled smile on his face. "Why are you telling me this?"

She sighed as she looked around the room and back out the window. Her face was old, her eyes sunken, yet she was full of life. As she sat unmoving, he tried to gain a better perspective of her. Perhaps she was leading him to a greater purpose, or perhaps she could sense his affliction, but if she were doing either of those things, she was not about to tell him now.

"I don't know," she finally replied. "Just making conversation."

***

The lights went down. The curtains were drawn. In front of him, the spotlight shimmered from left to right on the school stage as the tech struggled to keep it steady. A few seconds later, a young boy stepped onto the stage.

"This is cool," Ryan whispered.

Bo looked over to him and then back to the stage. He was trying to forget the surroundings—specifically, the memory of his morning talk with Miss Barbara. He had to remain steady, even if it was growing harder and harder. Looking around, he saw so many people, all eagerly taking in the play before them. For the first time in a long time, he did not feel like the spotlight was on him. He was an audience member in a place where he could fade in.

Perhaps Barbara was right; perhaps this was the perfect spot to glimpse the edge and stay. He knew Ryan felt that way. Maybe he should, too.

The program was lively— scenes intermixed with singing and dancing. It was all great fun, and the audience laughed and applauded throughout. It was so lighthearted that he almost forgot he was watching a play. Periodically, he found himself looking at Ryan on his right.

"Bathroom," he whispered sometime in the second act. He moved into the aisle as the song changed again. In seconds, he had slipped through the back doors and into the silent atrium.

It was cool in the entryway, and he shivered in the transition. In the bathroom, he realized that he could still hear the music in the gym. He smiled as he heard the audience laugh.

Outside the bathroom, he saw a large panel of glass cases housing class photos from the previous years. Marveling, he followed the images back to 1924.

Suddenly, he heard the tempo change in the gym behind him. The riff instantly caught his ear.

I hear you calling me, he heard a young voice sing.

You called me when the moon had veiled her light.

He turned from the photos and walked slowly, as though in a trance, toward the door.

Before I went from you into the night...

A lump was growing in his throat as he reached for the handle and pulled open the door. The same cast as before stood on the stage, but now they were in a starlit setting, all singing earnestly.

He stepped into the gym, tears welling in his eyes.

I came—do you remember? —back to you.

He closed his eyes as the tears fell across his cheeks. Wave upon wave of imagery entered his mind, conjuring emotions he had not felt in some time. The song played on.

He stood unnoticed by all, but once more, he felt front and center.

For one last kiss beneath the kind star light...

He wiped his eyes as the thoughts rolled like a mighty current, breaking down the dams he had put up so long ago.

I hear you calling me...

He was in a place he had never been before. He was in a state he had never felt. He was no longer Bo. He was no longer who he had been.

The song finished, and the crowd rose in applause. Yet in the back of the gym, near the central exit, the aisle was empty. The man who had stood there seconds before was no more. He had gone, leaving behind an empty space and a closing door.

***

1,000 Miles to Spokane

The Jeep stopped.

Fifty feet forward from where it previously sat, the wheels came to a stop.

Bo swallowed the lump in his throat as he wiped the tears from his eyes. Looking into the rearview once more, he saw the sheriff slam the rear door and move toward the driver's door. He had a smile on his face and paid no attention to the truck in front of him.

Bo looked to the man's hands and saw they were covered in blood. He saw his own face reflected in the corner of the mirror.

He knew what he had to do.

Taking a deep breath, he thought of Ryan lying in the back of the car. He knew he was the only person who could relate to his feelings. He knew he was the only person who understood. They had made it here for some reason, brought together by means he was only just beginning to understand. He could not leave him behind.

He knew what he had to do.

He grabbed his seatbelt and buckled it. Staring ahead, he slowly grabbed the shifter.

It was now or never.

Ryan groaned in agony as he lay face-up on the backseat of the squad car. His entire body radiated with pain. Ransom shut the passenger door and walked around to the front as Ryan coughed in anguish.

Ransom opened the driver's door and sat down inside, paying little heed to his prey in the seat behind him. Whistling softly, he pulled out a notebook and begin writing, clearly content with the situation.

Ryan turned onto his side and raised himself in an effort to ease the pain of his cuffed and swollen wrists. He moaned as he peered out the windshield in a daze.

"Shut up back there," Ransom growled as he continued writing.

Ryan cocked his head. His Jeep was stopped directly ahead. Biting his lip, he starred wide-eyed as the reverse lights illuminated.

For a moment, he sat there like a statue, frozen at the sight of his Jeep hurtling backward toward the cruiser. The moment passed in an instant, however, as he flung himself back onto the seat just in time.

The impact surged through his body. He felt the car lurch backward, and his head slammed the back of the driver's seat. He fell onto the floorboard and onto his right arm. For a moment, he could feel everything—a brief pause as the wreck ended, then the blast of cold outside air as his door opened. He even felt his arm radiate pain he had not felt before. He heard his name as he was lifted off the floorboard, and then his mind went blank.

Bo pushed the driver's door open. Stumbling out onto the gravel, he hurried to the battered cruiser.

Pulling open the driver's door, he saw the sheriff's bloody face. The airbag's impact had knocked him out. Reaching inward, he felt for a pulse. Finding one, he grabbed Ransom's gun and threw it over the car into the bushes. He grabbed the sheriff's second pair of handcuffs and attached one to his wrist and the other to the steering wheel. He then pulled the keys out of the ignition.

He backed away from the car to test the sheriff's alertness, but Ransom was out cold. He raced to the back of the car and opened the door to find Ryan lying on the floorboards.

"Ryan!" he shouted, grabbing the boy's waist, and pulling him out of the backseat. "Ryan!"

He could see him wavering on the edge of unconsciousness. As he grabbed his arms, he felt a mass protruding from under his right shirtsleeve.

"It'll be okay," Bo said softly. He picked Ryan up and carried him to the Jeep.

He opened the back door and gingerly laid Ryan onto the seat. Reaching underneath, he undid the handcuffs using the sheriff's keys. Swallowing his own anguish, he moved to his bag sitting in the passenger seat and grabbed his second shirt.

Bo quickly fashioned a makeshift bandage for the fractured arm and then tucked one of Ryan's sweatshirts between his arm and the seat. He shut the door before sprinting around the front of the Jeep. In seconds he was back into the driver's seat.

Shifting the car into gear, he threw the sheriff's keys out the window and then eased the Jeep's bumper away from the mangled and smoking grill of the cop car.

He looked in the rearview and found that the sheriff still sat unconscious. Looking downward in the mirror, he saw that Ryan did as well.

"I'm so sorry," he whispered, knowing there was nothing more he could say.

There was a loud crunch as the Jeep wrenched free from the cruiser.

"It'll be all right," he added, knowing the boy could not hear him. He pressed the gas pedal and pulled off the gravel and back onto the main highway. "It'll be all right."

The gray sky loomed overhead. There was not a car in sight in either direction.

Ryan did not stir, but Bo kept constant vigil in the mirror.

"I know you can hear me," he finally said between glances. "Somewhere in there, you can." He swallowed hard. "I want to answer your questions." He paused as if expecting an answer. "You deserve the truth."

A truck passed them going east, but he never noticed. His foot was on the gas pedal, and his eyes were focused straight ahead. A song played in the recesses of his mind, jogging his memory as it had done before. Though completely alert, he was in a trance. He was here, and he was there, reliving it all, telling the story for the first time.

"I've never lived in Spokane," he began, voice cracking into a low whisper. "And I never planned to visit family." He broke his gaze as he looked into the rearview to see that Ryan was still unconscious. He returned his attention to the road.

"Most of all," he said, "my name isn't Bo…"

Chapter 21
2,872 Miles and Seven Days to Spokane

As he stepped off the semi, he found himself holding the railing to maintain his balance. His foot tingled with the numbness of a quick wake up, and he slammed it onto the pavement. Shielding his eyes against the harsh sun, he peered out across the vast parking lot, unsure of his next move.

The air brake of the semi startled him. Before long, bag in hand, he was walking in an unknown direction toward an unknown destination.

"Over there..." he heard the driver say in his head. His mind's eye recalled a general forward motion, so that was what he followed. It was the only thing he had now.

It was at least 90 degrees, and he found himself sweating under his pants and the weight of his bag. It was mid-December, but winter never came to this part of the world.

He took a deep breath and crossed the street, paying little heed to the cars that whizzed by. Around him, folks in all manner of summer attire roamed restlessly. As he walked, some cast their gazes in his direction, and others continued without a glance, never sensing that he did not quite fit in.

A gull called out overhead, and he found himself crossing another street. This one was busier than the last, but again he walked out into the traffic, dodging cars with nary a care.

On the other side, a large outcropping of buildings lined the road like sentries on a wall. This forced him to switch direction, and he walked along the row with no mind for the people who passed.

Before long, a break in the fence led to a parking lot to his right, and that parking lot ran between the high rises that lined the road. Stepping across the hot pavement, he stopped abruptly as he reached the last row.

There, some hundred yards before him, lay the sight he had been walking to see—the bright blue calm of the Gulf.

He removed his tattered shoes from his swollen feet and held them as he walked onto the sandy dunes that separated him from the water. He did not notice the throngs of people around him. Even if he had, it would not have changed much. He had made it. That was all that mattered.

He dropped his shoes somewhere between the sand and the surf and, fully clothed and with his bag on his back, he threw himself into the Gulf, allowing it to crash over him and swallow him in its splendor. The saltwater tickled his nose as he submerged his head, but it was of little concern. As he resurfaced, he felt something different, something unique. Lifting his fingers to his face, he felt the burn of the salt on his cracked lips, but it was not the feeling on his lips that was unique; it was the shape they were in.

The edges were turned up. He closed his eyes as he felt the warmth of a smile upon his being. It had been a long while since he had felt such emotion.

He woke to a bright light shining in his face, and for a moment, he was blind. He heard the swell of the waves, though they seemed distant in the moment. Blinking, he lifted his head from the sand, though it took much effort.

"He's awake," said a voice above him. It did not sound pleased.

"Beach is closed," came another voice, this time from his left.

Still blinking, he allowed his head to drop back to the sand. He wondered why he was not in the ocean. He thought about his bag. He no longer felt it on his back.

"Hey, man," came the second voice, this time closer. "Beach is closed."

"Come on," spoke the first. The toe of a boot prodded him—not roughly, but not gently, either.

He lifted his head again and looked back to see a moonlit low tide.

"You speak English, man?" the first voice said, flashing the light again.

He nodded.

"Got a place to go?"

He nodded again, raising onto his backside, and shaking sand from his hair. He looked around for the bag he had lost.

"Well, you'd better get there, because you can't stay here."

Looking at the men, he realized they were police. Both were younger than him.

"Come on, get up."

He felt the second man grab his arm, and he was lifted to his feet. Once he was standing, he felt the man recoil and heard him exhale in disgust.

He could feel their exchanged glances as he faced the ocean.

"Where you headed?" one officer said.

No answer.

"You done any drinking today?" the other asked.

He shook his head.

"All right," the second officer said. "Time to go, though. Let's move." A hand on his shoulder turned him away from the ocean.

"I was going that way," he finally said, pointing back to the water.

The one officer stifled a laugh. The other looked from his partner back to him. "Not without a boat."

He looked down to avoid the bright flashlights.

"Out's that way," the first officer finally said, using his flashlight to indicate the parking lot to the right.

He looked back to the water and sighed.

"I'm not telling you again."

He began walking toward the parking lot, afraid of the thought of staying.

Behind him, he heard the second officer. "…kitchen just down the road…"

"You want to spend all night driving hobos to the shelter?"

"All right, point made…"

He reached the parking lot and was relieved to find the pavement had cooled. Looking up, he saw the stars in full glory and judged it to be well past midnight. Sighing, he walked to the edge of the main street and glanced back to see if the police were still there. Not seeing them, he turned to the left and back to the break in the fence. In a few minutes, he was back on the sand.

He saw no signs of the officers, but they were no longer his main concern. Running back to his spot, he looked around until he found what he was looking for.

Somehow, the bag was untouched near the edge of a small dune. He hoped the contents were still there. He approached and stared for a moment before he grabbed it and sat in the sand.

Holding his breath, he opened the bag and rummaged around, taking no care for the books or the shirt inside. His hands found the plastic he was hoping for, and tears filled his eyes. It was still there.

He knew it was time. His hands steadied as he held tight to the plastic bag and allowed the larger bag to fall to the sand. He turned and walked slowly to the water, allowing it to wash over his feet and then his legs and knees. Before long, he was up to his waist. He closed his eyes, opened the plastic bag, and turned it over, allowing its contents to fall onto the surf below. After a moment, he placed it in the Gulf and allowed the waters to wash over it.

Tears welled in his eyes as the contents scattered through the water. It was all he had hoped for. Serenity washed over him as he knew the task was done

The salt stung as he wiped his tears, yet he paid it no mind.

The night air was calm as he sloshed back to the shoreline. He lay back on the damp sand and bunched his bag under his head as a pillow. He then gazed at the stars as the sounds of the surf mingled with his heartbeat.

After a moment, he sat upright and watched the water flow in and out. He stared for a moment before he finally turned his body completely around and lay back on the sand closer to the surf, taking great care to move the bag back under his head as he did. He was finally ready to go. Soon, his tiredness would be gone. Soon, he would be no more. Soon, he would no longer be alone.

Arms folded once more, he nodded in approval before falling into a deep sleep.

The sun shone brightly on the beach—so bright that he wondered where he was. As he blinked himself into consciousness, he had a brief glimmer of hope, but the sound of the water brought him back.

"You almost drowned," came a voice to his left. He realized he was no longer headed down to the water. In fact, he was nowhere near the water. He sat up some fifteen yards from the edge of the Gulf and looking down, he saw the drag marks in the sand.

"Some runner saw you about to go under, and he dragged you up here."

He blinked again and squinted as his eyes adjusted to the sun. Around him, the sounds of beachgoers filled the air.

"You all right?" the voice continued. He turned and found a guy wearing a Beach Security shirt, though he could not tell if the shirt was real or a gag.

He nodded.

"Good, because drowning would be a terrible way to go."

He looked to his right and saw his bag sitting half-covered in the sand. "There are worse," he muttered.

"You ain't from around here, are you?" the man continued. He seemed eager to talk to someone. "Folks from around here aren't as pasty as you."

He got up and grabbed his bag, glancing up and down the coast as his frustration mounted.

"Listen, man…you want a sandwich or something? There's a shelter not too far from here."

He sighed, fully content to be left alone. "Thanks anyway."

"You sure?" The man was relentless. "I insist. It's kind of my thing?"

He began to walk but stopped in his tracks upon hearing the comment. Confused, he turned back to the man.

"I used to be on the street. Shelter helped me. I always said I'd help if I found anyone needing it. Plus, it's Christmastime."

He stood there, bag in hand, knowing the man would not leave until he agreed to the request.

Gritting his teeth, he finally nodded and allowed the man to help him toward the parking lot.

"You picked a much better place to be out in the air than I did," the man continued, almost as if he were not talking to a stranger. "Boston, January. Damn snowstorm had me up to my waist in the crap. Plus, it was cold as hell. No place for a man in that predicament. Where you from?"

They reached the car, and he instantly saw that it matched the man's disposition, from its worn exterior to its bold paint job that did not quite fit the minivan's style. He got inside as the man continued talking.

"Lots of folks need help 'round here. Never can quite get to them all. In Boston, it's no different."

He did not reply, though it mattered little. The man shifted the car into drive, backed out of the spot, and pulled out of the parking lot onto the main road. He was not sure if he had even checked the traffic before doing so.

"I always tell people, it's no wonder there aren't more people needing help in this economy. But it's the families that I can't believe—families kicked out of their homes, forced onto the streets. This housing crisis—and it is a crisis—it's screwing everyone. Hell, pretty soon, we'll all be homeless. Pretty soon, everywhere will be like Florida. Do you know that in Miami, whole developments are going under because people are getting evicted?" Between his speeding and his knack for hitting green lights, the driver was making exceptionally good timing, and for that, he was grateful.

"It's ridiculous," the man continued. "But I said it from the start. I said, banks can't expect poor people to pay when they got no money. What happens when no money really becomes…no…money? You can't get milk from a male goat, am I right?"

They drove for a few more minutes before the man abruptly stopped the car in front of a large brick building that would have been out of place even without the disheveled people around it.

"Here you are."

He smiled as he got out, thankful that the ride was over.

"Hey!" the man called out as he began walking away. Stopping mid-step, he half-turned back toward the driver, who leaned over the passenger seat with the window down. "Take my card in case you need anything."

Looking around, he walked back to the van and accepted the card without a sound. He then retreated to the sidewalk as the man leaned back to his seat.

He looked down at the card, reading the bolded words in his mind: *Bo Williams, Century 21.*

"Hey," he heard himself say toward the driver, his first words in a long while.

The driver shifted into gear and turned back to the passenger window.

"Why'd you get…" he said, gesturing at the shelter and the people around it, "you know…out?" In hindsight, he knew a better question was "how."

The driver smiled. "I told you," he said as he shifted into drive and began rolling, "winter in Boston."

He cocked his head, not quite understanding.

"I got tired of being cold."

A second later, he was gone.

"What's in the bag?" the old man asked as he lay back along the tree line.

He sat on the curb separating the asphalt from the grass and gazed at the orange glow of the parking lot at twilight. The old man sat behind him in the shadow of the trees, sprawled out with a tattered blanket.

"A book," he replied, "and a shirt."

He had spent the day walking aimlessly among the streets and buildings of a town he did not know, eventually arriving at this grove of trees that provided welcome respite from the hot sun. It was almost too good to be true.

"Books keep the mind sharp," the old man said rather breathlessly as he shuffled in his blanket.

He had spotted the old man sleeping on the mulch as soon as he'd arrived. Sensing it rude to disturb, he sat near a tree and soon fell into a nap himself. He'd woken to find his companion eating a stale bag of pretzels—food that he wordlessly offered and food that was wordlessly accepted.

"You look like hell," the old man said. His words seemed unfriendly for someone he had just met.

"I tried to kill myself last night," he said without emotion as he continued staring off into the lot.

The old man lay back on the mulch. "Tried?"

"Yeah."

"Must not be too good at it."

The pair sat in silence for a moment.

"Or maybe you ain't meant to."

He looked back to the old man, who made no eye contact.

"Or…maybe death ain't what you're looking for."

The old man turned away and said no more. Turning back to the parking lot, he exhaled deeply, holding his bag between his knees. He had come here to finally solve it all, not be left with more questions.

A breeze rolled through the parking lot. It was a cool breeze, but he barely noticed. If he had, he would have guessed that a change was coming—that perhaps somewhere, something was rolling through the fluid atmosphere and heading directly for him and his patch of trees and his parking lot.

He awoke the next day, sprawled on the grassy side of the curb. Looking behind him, he saw neither the old man nor his blanket, and for a moment, he wondered where he had gone.

Grabbing his bag, he waited for his eyes to adjust to the sun before he finally stood up. Glancing skyward, he guessed it was late morning or maybe even early afternoon.

He slung his bag on his shoulder as he walked into the large box store. He was barely noticed amid the throngs of shoppers. Once inside, he hung a right and walked directly to the restrooms, where he rinsed his face and washed the grime from his lips. Rubbing his neck, he emerged from the bathroom and immediately left the store, taking care to avoid anyone who would notice his appearance.

Back in the parking lot, he took a deep breath and walked down a long row of cars in what he judged to be a westward direction. Approaching a road, he stopped to let a few cars pass.

"Hey!" a familiar voice said loudly.

He turned and saw the old man to his right at the edge of a street corner, sign in hand.

He nodded in greeting.

"Come here. I need some help."

Adjusting the bag strap, he approached the man.

"I'm starving," the old man said, "but people are just handing out their cash. You mind taking my place so I can go get something?"

He hesitated as he pondered the situation.

"I'll bring you back something."

Sighing, he dropped his bag and held out his hand.

The old man handed over his sign and wordlessly walked back toward the box store.

Gritting his teeth, he turned toward the road and held the sign stomach high, taking care to alternate his stance so as not to hurt his already blistered feet.

He had no interest in sign holding. He had not come here for it. Yet the old man had been kind to him the night before, so in truth, he supposed it was payback.

The sun beat down as he stood on the corner, and the minutes dragged on for an eternity. He thought about the day before—about how the talkative man, peculiar as he was, had gone out of his way to help him out. Feeling the card in his pocket, he thought about his message upon departing and the absurdity of the statement. As if it were that easy. He thought about the old man last night and how his attitude had been sage but despondent. Truly, this place had some unique individuals.

Most of all, however, he thought about the beach. If his full night's rest had given him anything, it was clarity. He could not worry about the rhymes or reasons. He had come here for one thing. It was all he wanted, and he would not stop now.

Closing his eyes, he felt the warmth of acceptance on his face as he made peace with his decision. He could almost feel a smile on his lips as he thought about it.

"Hey, man!"

He snapped back to reality and saw a black Jeep in his direct line of vision, complete with a young man leaning across the console.

"Hey, man, you there?" the boy repeated.

He stood for another second or so, confused by the boy's sudden arrival.

"Yes?"

"Where's home?" the boy asked, leaning further over.

He looked to his left, still debating whether the boy was talking to him.

"Your sign." The boy pointed. "Where's home?"

He glanced down to the sign he held, and it all became clear.

Heading home for Christmas. Anything will help. God Bless.

Mind racing, he looked back at the boy. He almost did not hear his own words as he spoke them, and even after he said them, he wondered why he had.

"Spokane."

"Where?" the boy asked, louder.

The man swallowed the lump in his throat as he spoke again. It was not entirely the truth, but he'd said it, nonetheless. It was a place he'd never wanted to return, but a place he needed to go. He had not known it before, and he could not explain it now, but it was the truth more than anything else.

"Spokane," he replied. "Washington."

***

708 Miles to Spokane

The sky was beginning to darken as Bo wordlessly pulled a twenty from his pocket and walked briskly across the gas station parking lot and into the building.

"Pump two," he said curtly.

"All of it?" she asked emotionlessly.

"Yeah," he replied as he walked away.

A stop back, he had checked on Ryan in the backseat, noticing that his shirt was beginning to darken, and that the boy's breathing had become much softer. He still had not stirred. With a heavy soul, he reached into the young man's pocket and pulled out a few bills, cursing himself as he did so. He knew it was the only way forward.

As he began pumping, he opened the backseat door and saw Ryan in the same position, his breathing unchanged. Examining the fracture once more, he saw that it, too, was unchanged, except that the red stains had grown slightly.

"It'll be okay," he whispered as he put the pump up and closed the gas door. Minutes later, he was back on the interstate and back on course.

"Ten hours and fifty-one minutes." He recognized the GPS for the first time in a long time.

"Eleven hours," he said aloud as he looked in the rearview. "You can make it."

He pressed the accelerator harder as his mind faded into the past.

***

3,132 Miles and Eight Days to Spokane

The summer had been hot.

It was not the heat of the North, which usually lingered for a day or two and then moved on, like a guest visiting an old friend. The heat of the South was blistering and humid. Relentless in its cover, it wrapped itself around the magnolias and mangroves like a blanket.

The fall had seen several storms, and with each, the blue sky had disappeared from memory. The waters had roared, washing the sand into the raging sea.

This coast was no place to unwind.

He'd spent several weeks traipsing the South Georgia coastline, and while he'd found beauty in the ancient forests and swampy depths, it was not what he sought.

The sun had blistered his face some time ago, but his beard covered the scars that remained. If he had looked mangy before, now he was a full-blown stray. It had been some time since he'd spoken to another human.

He sat on a curb as the sun sank into the west. He opened his bag and extracted a plastic bottle of water with the label worn away. It had been the same bottle since Savannah.

Wiping his face even though he did not sweat, he exhaled as he stood, and he moved toward the truck stop door.

Taking care to follow a family of four in, he avoided all eye contact as he followed the signs to the bathroom. Entering the spacious, well-lit space, he moved to a sink and carefully pulled out the empty bottle, taking care to tilt it to fit the confined sink. Filling it to its max, he capped it and tucked it in his bag. He ducked his head as he left the bathroom and the building.

He stood in the parking lot for a few moments and gauged the activity around him. It was not entirely busy, so he began a well-worn practice of surveying the lot from corner to corner, stopping every so often to pick up the dime or penny that lay unclaimed.

By the time he finished, the sun was low in the sky. He collected one last nickel, returned to the store, and wordlessly plucked a pair of hot dogs off the rollers.

Moving to the clerk, he set the food on the counter and then carefully pulled the collection of coins from his left hand.

"That's $1.75," the clerk said, looking at him as though he would never have enough.

He laid his findings on the counter and then carefully reached into his bag to retrieve a quarter and a dime.

The clerk counted and then recounted the change. She swept the coins into her hand and deposited them in the register.

"You get a candy bar, too," she said as she turned back to him. "Special for the day."

He looked at her, clearly confused.

"Two hot dogs get a free candy." She motioned to the shelves beneath her.

He looked down at the candy and then around, realizing there was no signage to indicate such a deal.

"Take a candy bar," she finally said, almost in a whisper.

He did not hesitate another moment. He quickly grabbed a Snickers and his hot dogs and exited the truck stop.

The outside air was still humid, though it had cooled over the past few hours. He sat on a curb just outside the door of the truck stop and quickly ate his meal, washing it down with the water from the bathroom sink.

He had come to view truck stops as beacons in the past months, as the South had plenty of them along the roadways. He felt less judged among the patrons, perhaps because he was mirroring their usual quiet, workmanlike attitudes—or perhaps his appearance resonated with the drivers.

"Got a light, brother?"

He turned and saw an older man in a Marine hat standing to his right. Nodding his head in acknowledgment, he pulled a well-worn pack of matches from his bag and handed them over.

"Thanks," the man replied, lighting a cigarette. "Where you headin'?"

He took another bite of his hot dog. "Key West. Gulf side."

The man took a drag and exhaled the smoke. "Keys, huh? Not too many truckers down there. What are you hauling?"

He took another bite. "Nothing."

"Picking up?"

"Nope."

Clearly confused, the man took another drag. As he blew out the smoke, the situation dawned on him.

"I—uh, I'm sorry, man."

He looked up as he finished his hot dog. "It's fine," he said as he rolled up the foil.

"I appreciate the light, though." The man handed back the matches.

He nodded. He stood up and threw away the foil before picking up his bag and dropping the matches back inside.

"Listen," the man said as he began to walk away. "I ain't going to the Keys, but if the Gulf is what you're after..."

He stopped his movements as he listened.

"I gotta make a stop in Orlando by early morning, and then I'm headed over to the Gulf side."

"Where at?" he asked with his back still turned.

The man ashed his cigarette. "Clearwater. It's past Tampa. I think my stop is a couple blocks from the coast."

He finally turned, still hesitant. "You'd take me there?"

The man stepped on the embers. "You bring the rest of them matches, and I'll call it a deal."

He slipped his bag off his shoulder. In an instant, he had extracted the matches and handed them over.

The man slipped them into his pocket and smiled. "Well, then, let's get on with it."

As the semi rolled down I-95, the men were quiet in the darkness. On the driver's side, the trucker smoked and kept his focus on the road, every so often mouthing the words to an old Hank song on the radio. The man in the passenger seat found himself gazing out the window into the Florida night, bag clutched in his lap.

He had finally achieved the goal. It might not be the Keys, but he figured the Gulf itself would be good enough. It would not be long before he was sitting on the beach with his bag in hand, allowing the calm waters to overtake his body and send him into oblivion. It would not be long now.

He closed his eyes and rested his head on the window. The same peaceful thought rolled through his mind like the waves he so desired. It would not be long now.

It would not be long now.

***

318 Miles to Spokane

Bo stretched his hands on the steering wheel. Occasionally, he glanced at the speedometer to ensure he was still going as fast as he needed to go. Even more occasionally, he glanced into the backseat, telling himself that he had enough time to make it all the way.

Around him, the night and the Rockies surrounded him. He was an island in the dark, and he was never more aware of it than now. With each uphill climb and downhill sprint, he felt more and more pressure. Both the landscape and the darkness were suffocating.

He thought he had heard Ryan stir several times, but he wondered if he was just projecting his own wishes.

The seat under Ryan was becoming stained, and the shirt that Bo had wrapped around his arm was now crimson.

He took a deep breath, allowing the wave of anxiety to pass. He knew he could make it on one more tank of fuel. He knew he was closer now than ever before.

Deep down, though, it was not fuel, landscape, or darkness that worried him.

His mind raced as he looked in the rearview. He still had so far to go…

***

3,357 Miles and 254 Days to Spokane

"What are you doing here?" the voice said aloud. Looking around the room, the speaker sat at noon in the circle of chairs, carefully measuring up each participant to ensure his message was received.

"That's the question to answer," he continued, "—more than anything else. Why are you here?" His voice was soft but clear. He looked to the man seated at his left. "Ronnie, why are you here?"

Ronnie raised his gaze when he heard his name.

He shrugged. "Why are you picking on me first, Mr. Williams?"

"I'm not picking on you. I'm just trying to get a dialog started."

The leader of the group, Williams, was a young man of about thirty. Thick-rimmed glasses obscured his boyish face. He barely looked twenty, but he dressed in confidence, all the way down to his shined shoes.

"I'm here," Ronnie finally replied, "because my granny asked me to come."

"And?"

"And what?"

"And that's it? She asked so you came?"

Ronnie looked annoyed. "Yeah, that's about it."

"What about you? Did you not want to?"

Ronnie shrugged. "No, I wanted to drink…"

The crowd laughed, and Williams let them have their mirth.

"But…" Ronnie paused as the laughter died. "I think about when I hit her, and then I kinda lose the need to drink…" The room grew silent.

"And you don't want to relive that again," Williams concluded.

Ronnie sniffed. "No, not really."

"What about you?" Williams directed the question to a young man across the room.

The man sat upright. "Baby boy born a week ago." He nodded. "Felt like as good a time as any."

"What's your name?" Williams asked.

"Elliot," the man replied.

"Like E.T." A man next to Ronnie laughed.

"Yeah." Elliot smiled, "like E.T."

Williams smiled. "Thank you, Elliot."

The conversation continued among the group of nine men, some participating and others choosing to remain silent.

"Next question," Williams asked after some discussion. "What are you looking for?"

No one spoke.

"Well?" he asked, looking around.

"You mean here?" Elliot asked.

Williams smiled. "Anywhere."

More silence. Around the room, the men looked down and away. Williams let the question soak in for a moment more before judging it was time to further it. He opened his mouth, yet it was not his voice that was heard.

"A beach," came a low voice from the left.

Williams turned his head. "Excuse me?"

Silence.

"It's okay." Williams eyed the man to his left. "You're free to speak."

"A beach," came a voice from a man seated three down from Williams. He was younger, with an educated face hidden behind an unkempt beard and wild hair. His dark, piercing eyes were focused on his lap.

"Davey? Is that right?" Williams asked, eyeing the man intently.

He nodded.

"You said a beach?"

He nodded again.

"Why's that?"

Davey sat in silence, eyes darting across the floor as if struggling under the question.

"It's okay if you don't have an answer..."

"Plenty of beaches here in Wilmington..." Ronnie murmured.

Williams opened his mouth once more.

"Not those beaches," Davey interjected, still looking at the floor. "Not beaches here, or north."

Williams turned. "Why not?"

"Too rocky," Davey replied. "Surf is too strong."

There was more silence.

"I can see that," Elliot finally said. "I always thought the Gulf beaches were much calmer."

Davey looked up and met his gaze.

"It's true," Elliot continued. "My family used to go down to Key West every summer, and every day we had calm, warm water. It was Paradise."

"That does sound nice." Williams nodded, keeping an eye on Davey.

"Yeah, I want that too," Ronnie replied. "I'll take his answer. I'm looking for a beach."

Again, the group laughed. Williams allowed it to die down before addressing them once more. "So," he began, looking at each of them, "you know why you're here, and you know where you want to go, so only one question remains..." He paused, and his gaze specifically met Davey's. "How do you get there?"

The session ended about an hour later. As everyone left the room, Williams called out for one to remain.

"Davey," he said aloud, "would you mind sticking around?"

The man stopped in his tracks and hesitated for a moment before returning and resuming his seat in the circle. The room finally emptied out.

"Thanks for coming tonight," Williams said after a moment, to which Davey nodded.

"Can I ask you a question? Maybe two?"

Davey continued looking at the floor. He gave a brief nod.

"This is your fourth week coming to this meeting, correct?"

Davey nodded.

"Do you know what this meeting is for?"

Davey nodded.

Williams smiled. "Forgive my inquiry, but I have to say, you don't look like someone who needs this meeting."

"What do I look like?" Davey finally asked.

"I don't know," Williams said. "But not an addict."

"I like the class," Davey replied. "I like hearing them talk."

"Why?" Williams countered. "If I may ask…"

Davey shuffled his feet, which could be seen through the tops of his worn shoes. "I like their honesty."

"Honesty?"

He nodded. "They're honest about themselves. They aren't afraid."

Williams turned his head. "Most of the men here have lost a lot. Some have lost everything. It's easier to be honest when you have nothing to lose."

"I like hearing it," Davey concluded.

Williams continued looking at the man, even though his gaze was not met.

"Where are you staying tonight?" he finally asked, assessing the man's situation clearly.

Davey did not answer.

"You can stay here if you like," Williams finally said. "It's a modest place, and I can't guarantee a timeframe, but fresh sheets and a mattress are always a plus."

He said nothing.

Williams stood up. "Is that okay?"

Davey met his gaze briefly and nodded.

"Settled, then." Williams smiled, beckoning for the man to follow him. "Let's get you to the dorm."

He followed Williams out the main entrance and down a sidewalk, taking great care to hold onto the bag that swayed at his side. They walked quickly, and Williams shivered in the brisk night air.

They walked up a set of stairs and into a large brick building. "Davey will be staying here," Williams announced as he entered near what appeared to be a large kitchen.

"Davey?" A woman entered the foyer from the kitchen.

"He'll need linens and clothing," Williams said.

"Our beds are full…" the woman replied softly, as if telling a secret.

"I think we can fit one more," Williams replied, his eyes telling the woman of his sincerity.

She pulled him aside, but Davey heard her words plainly, even as he tried to ignore them.

"We are down in food and clothing, and I do not know this man."

"He's fine," Williams assured. "We can endure one night."

"Was he on the street?"

"Yes," Williams responded. "For weeks, maybe months, I assume."

She shook her head, clearly hesitant but powerless.

"One," she whispered, even more softly.

Williams nodded. The woman turned to Davey and motioned for him to follow her down a hallway to the right.

"Bathroom is to the left," she said before leading him to a large room full of double cots. Her voice lowered to a whisper as she led him past row after row of beds, and he noticed an empty one for every four that were full.

"I'll bring you a fresh set of clothes and linens in a moment," she whispered as she stopped at a bed near the end of the room. "You'll sleep here."

He nodded and looked at the empty mattress.

"I anticipate you'll be out come morning. If you need anything, I can usually be found in the kitchen."

She did not wait for a response before turning and walking out of the room, leaving him alone with the bottom bunk.

She returned a minute later carrying a stack of bedsheets, a pair of shoes, and a set of clothes.

"I could only find two shirts in your size," she whispered. "I didn't think you'd mind if they were the same ..." Her voice trailed off as she saw him in the fetal position on the bed, sound asleep.

She sighed and carefully set the sheets on the side of the bed, taking care not to disturb him. She then hung the shirts on the support beam and tucked the rest of the clothes under the bunk. As she stood, she saw that his hand loosely held the strap of a bag. She quietly pulled the bag from his grasp and placed it under the bed next to his clothes.

She turned from the bed and walked back out of the room.

It was morning when he woke.

Blinking wildly, he jolted upright, unsure where he was.

The room around him was empty for the most part, though a few souls slumbered on cots nearby. He looked to his left and saw that the door to the dormitory was closed. Curtains hung from the windows, making the room darker than he'd anticipated.

He swung his legs off the bed and shook his head as his feet hit the floor. He turned and looked back to his bed.

Eyes wide, he moved the stack of unused linen and then the pillow that sat with them.

His bag was nowhere in sight.

His eyes darted around as he stood up. He looked at the top bunk and on the floor around the bed, but it was not there.

Panic gripped him, and before he knew what was happening, he was wrenching open the dormitory door and letting it slam against the back wall. Taking a quick right, his eyes continuously darted as he went from gallop to full sprint down the long hallway, all the while looking for anyone who could help.

He rounded the corner into the entry and saw a maid with her back to him.

"My bag!"

The maid turned and saw him approaching.

"My bag!"

Fear took hold and she took a step back.

"What's wrong, Davey?"

He turned to his right and saw Williams exit the kitchen.

"My bag!" he exclaimed as if it would make sense.

"I'm sorry?" Williams rushed toward him.

"My bag!"

He grabbed hold of Williams' shoulders and looked him squarely in the eyes.

"I don't—" Williams explained.

"My bag! Where is it?"

The force of his grasp had forced Williams back a step. The grasp grew harder as Williams stumbled further.

"Let go of him!" a voice behind him said roughly.

"Where's my bag?!" he yelled.

"Help!" It was the woman from the night before.

The next sequence went by in a blur.

He was blinded by rage. Before he knew it, Williams was falling backward onto the floor and he was on top. He felt Williams' head hit the floor, but he kept his grip tight. As he continued to roar in his face, he felt several sets of hands grab him from behind, pulling at him like a pack of wild animals.

"WHERE'S MY BAG!" he raged.

Before long, six hands had hauled him, still shouting, off the man on the floor.

"WHERE'S MY BAG! MY BAG!"

He tried to stand, but a punch hit him squarely in the stomach. Instead of crumpling him, however, it only enraged him further, and before long, a volley of kicks and punches rained down as the hands worked to subdue and then restrain him.

It took only minutes, but it felt much longer. Dripping in blood and sweat, he felt himself lifted, this time by the arms of men whose badges he saw gleaming in the morning light.

"My bag—" he whispered with the only force he had left.

"Outta here," he heard the woman say furiously. Tears streamed down her cheeks as she shielded Williams' unconscious body.

As he was thrown into the car and driven away, he looked back to no avail. Before long, the dormitory and bed, the hospitality, and the warmth, were long gone. All the while, he kept repeating to himself words he barely heard.

"My bag…my bag…"

Four days passed.

Propped against the wall of his cell, he kept his eyes focused on the ceiling, as he had done for the previous days. He had eaten little and slept even less. The first day had been laborious, but by the end of the second day, he had calmed and had regained a clear head. He could do little else.

"Lucky day." He heard the jailer's voice and the clink of his keys before he saw the man. The jailer paused at the cell door and opened it. "Charges were all dropped."

He cocked his head, unsure if it was a prank.

"Let's go," the jailer finally said, motioning for him to move.

He rose from the bed and walked out the door without a word.

"We have something in common," a familiar voice said as he walked out into the jail's parking lot.

He squinted in the afternoon sun as he recognized the man in front of him. He did not know how to react.

"Your name," Williams continued. "It isn't Davey." His face was friendly, as it had been in their previous encounters.

He felt sympathy for the man he had harmed, but he knew there was little he could say.

"And my name," Williams added, "isn't Williams." He stood from the hood of his Buick and took a step closer. "Scott Lashon," Williams said after a moment. "That's your name."

His eyes flickered upon hearing the words spoken, yet he held tight to his resolve. He nodded slightly.

"Thirty-six years old, from New York City, specifically the Upper West Side."

He stood silent but nodded again.

"How long has it been since you left?"

He took a deep breath, eyes focused on his counterpart. "A couple years…"

"Five for me," Williams said. "I was a broker. Graduated second in my class. Worked for a few years and left it all behind."

He listened, knowing that Williams was speaking those words for perhaps the first time.

"Who's Davey?" Williams asked after a moment.

He looked up and met Williams' eye. "He was nobody."

Williams nodded, somehow understanding. After a moment, he turned to his Buick and grabbed something from the backseat.

"This belongs to you," he said as he handed over his bag. "I apologize for not bringing it sooner."

He took the bag hastily, a wave of emotion washing over him as he held it once more.

They stood in silence for a moment, both sensing the unresolved words between them.

"Thank—" he began, looking up at Williams. "Thank you…"

Williams nodded. "I hope you find that beach." He turned toward the Buick. "And I hope it's what you're looking for."

He stood in silence as Williams pulled open the driver's door. He hesitated in the doorway, clearly wanting to say more.

"I—" Williams took a deep breath. "I just…" He paused, looking for the words. "Whose—"

"My wife," he replied, feeling deep sorrow at the words. "She's my wife. She was my—"

Williams smiled. "Is," he corrected, smiling again warmly. "That never stops."

He returned a faint smile as Williams stepped inside the car.

"I owe you…an apology," he finally said, speaking the words he had desperately wanted to say.

Williams looked down into his car and then back up to him. "And one day," he replied, "you can come back here and give it to me."

With that, he got in the car and started it up. He shifted into gear and moved out onto the road.

He stood alone in the morning sun and looked out across the city landscape. It was almost an affirmation to be standing outside the prison holding everything he needed. He was dirty and grizzled. He was worn and wavering. If life had been difficult before, finding meaning now would be even more challenging.

He set the bag down carefully and opened it, finding the Ziploc directly on top as if placed there deliberately. Underneath, he noticed something new.

The shirt was bold and gaudy, but to his eyes, it was something clean and dry. Even the vibrant orange color was appealing to him. Pulling it out, he noticed its twin underneath, almost as though it were a backup.

Smiling faintly, he folded the shirt and placed it in the bag.

It was true that he was dirty. It was true that he was grizzled. It was true that he was worn, and it was true that his mind was not as sound as it once was. Nevertheless, at that moment, more than at any other in the last four years, he was not without hope. His bag had returned. He was still on his path. He was a solitary person on his journey, but he was not alone.

He was never alone.

***

76 Miles to Spokane

The road sign several miles back had filled him with dread. Spokane was drawing closer and closer.

He had wondered what he would feel at this moment, knowing he was about to face the demons he had spent years suffocating, but through the dread and the panic, he kept coming back to the young man in the backseat who was holding on despite it all. He was no longer driving to face his fate; he was driving to save another's.

Back in South Dakota, he had decided to protect his friend. Even then, he'd known what protecting meant. He had thought it all through and known that the only place he never wanted to see was the only place he could go. He'd known it all, but in that moment between stopping the Jeep and ramming it into the squad car, he had come to peace with the decision. It had done nothing to calm him, however. Even now, he found his foot tapping the floorboards.

"This story probably doesn't make much sense," he said aloud, thinking about his life, "but I guess there's a lot of things that way…"

He took another deep breath and checked the rearview.

Up ahead, another sign read seventy-three miles.

He sighed once more. Seventy-three miles to Spokane…

***

3,702 Miles and Three Years, 347 Days to Spokane

He stood in the doorway with his bag in hand.

The briefcase was bulky, yet its weight did not concern him today. He shut the door to the flat and proceeded down the steps and into the waiting taxi.

It was a Tuesday at approximately 7:30 a.m. It was a workday in New York City.

Scribbs Investments sat a few blocks from the Bull on Broad Street, but the attitude inside was no different from those further up the island.

He entered the building and stepped onto the elevator. Before long, he had reached the fifty-sixth floor. As he emerged, the receptionist gave him a look of surprise.

"Scott," she said, "it's good to see you."

"Thank you, Marsha," he replied, sidestepping the desk, and proceeding down the hall to the left.

He barely noticed the stares from coworkers as he strode past them. Before long, he was in his office, staring at the envelopes and flowers adorning his desk. He ignored them all, set his briefcase on his desk, turned on his computer, and opened his email.

"Scott," a voice at his door said. "It's good to see you."

"Thanks, Marty," he said. The man lingered for a moment before moving on wordlessly.

Two hours later, the phone near his computer trilled. Allowing it to disrupt his focus, he picked it up.

"Scott here," he said without emotion.

"Welcome back," came a solemn voice.

"Thanks, Bill."

"You mind coming down here?" Bill asked in the same tone.

Scott hung up the phone and proceeded down the hallway. Again, there were more stares, but again, he barely noticed.

"Hey Bill," he said as he entered his boss's ornate office.

"Scott, so good to see you, man," Bill said, standing abruptly and embracing him with a hug. "Come in." He closed the door and took a seat behind his desk. "First, we are all so sorry. Emily was a treasure…"

"Thank you." He nodded, expressionless.

"When did you get back in?" Bill asked after a second.

He looked at his watch and sat back, thinking. "Sunday night…late."

Bill looked astonished. "And it's Tuesday."

He nodded. "Yeah, the plane was a red-eye. I would have been in yesterday, but I—"

Bill raised a hand to silence him. "I don't care that you missed a day. I'm wondering why you're here now. The company is fine if you need more time."

"I'd rather be here."

Bill leaned over the desk. "I understand that, but five days…"

"I can assure you, I'm fine," he replied.

"But I think—"

"I'm fine."

Bill sighed. "Your morning report." He pulled a piece of paper from his desk. "It was off by six thousand."

Scott sat for a moment, unmoved.

"The Jackson account. The Bolwich account. All off," Bill elaborated, still holding the paper.

Scott finally reached for the paper and scanned it. "You had Marty check my work?"

"I had him go over it," Bill replied. "I'd do that with anyone…"

"Anyone whose wife died?"

Bill leaned back. "Now, you know I didn't mean that."

Scott did not answer.

"I think," Bill continued, "you need some more time off, Scott." He paused, contemplating his words. "I promise we are here for you. Anything you need, you know Rita and I are here. Take the week and come back next week. If you need more time, that's fine, too."

Scott rubbed his tongue against his bottom teeth, but he said nothing. In the silence that followed, he simply stared out the window behind Bill.

"Alright," he finally said.

"Alright?" Bill asked after a moment.

He nodded. "Alright."

Bill smiled faintly before standing. "I'll call the cab, don't worry."

As he stood, Bill came around the desk and patted him gingerly on the back. "Don't worry," he repeated. "If you need anything, you just call."

He said nothing in return. In minutes, he was downstairs with his briefcase in hand, waiting on the cab he had not called to go to a place he did not want to be.

The taxi dropped Scott directly in front of his apartment, but he seemed lost as he peered up at the façade. He clutched his briefcase and looked both ways down the sidewalk, paying no heed to the spring chill that blew past.

There was no one waiting for him.

Sighing, he took several steps toward the large doorway that loomed over him like a sentry. He pulled a key from his pocket and unlocked the door. It swung open to a clean and dark room.

He took a step inside and set his briefcase down. Again, he looked left and right as though expecting someone to meet him. There was no one, however. He was alone in a large and silent flat.

He looked back toward the street as a car passed by, and again he felt the chilled wind. It was cold outside. It was colder in.

He stood in the entry for a few moments. As though in a trance, he ascended the stairs to his bedroom and opened the large suitcase that lay on the bed. He pulled out a small metal box. Tucking it under his arm like a delicate egg, he reached back into the suitcase and pulled out the gun. He closed the luggage, left the room, and walked back down the stairs.

On the ground floor, he knelt beside his briefcase and removed the loose papers and files. Taking the metal box from under his arm, he carefully set it inside, next to the Hemingway book he was halfway through. He set the gun on top of the book. Snapping the briefcase shut, he grabbed it with his right hand and stood up. He took a final look around the apartment and walked back outside, taking care to shut the door gently behind him.

"What can I help you with?" the woman at the counter asked. It had been almost twenty-four hours since he'd left the apartment, and for most of that time, he'd sat motionless at a nearby coffee shop until they had decided he had been there too long. He walked out without incident, even though his mind kept going to the contents of his briefcase.

"Car, please," he replied, ignoring the need to scratch the stubble on his face.

"How many days?"

He stared at her. "Three."

"SUV, truck?"

"Anything."

"I can do an intermediate for three days, returning here, at $110 a day."

He nodded.

"Credit card and driver's license, please," she requested, sensing that he was in no mood for extra talk.

He pulled out his wallet and handed both over, sighing as he realized what his attitude was conveying. "There's enough on that card to cover whatever."

She looked up as though not understanding. "We only hold $400 to start. It'll go back once you return the car."

He nodded. "I know. I'm just saying that the card can handle the car." He leaned over the counter. "Remember that."

She handed over his card and license, still clearly confused. "Your car is just outside, over in the second row. An attendant will be there to assist."

"Thank you," he said without expression.

"If I may ask," she finally said as he walked away, "where are you going?"

He never turned around, yet he said the words loud enough for her to hear.

"Away from here."

The gas gauge read "zero miles to empty."

He rolled up the windows as he moved to the shoulder, allowing the car to run its last miles before finally coming to a stop.

Exhaling deeply, he opened the driver's door and stepped out onto the cool pavement. He did not flinch as the semis and cars flew by. In fact, he barely noticed them.

He walked to the trunk, opened it, and pulled out his briefcase. He returned to the driver's door. As he had done in his mind for the past four hundred miles, he reached into his back pocket and pulled out his wallet before throwing it, along with the keys, onto the front seat.

He had no idea what his goal was. He only reasoned that whatever he needed; it was not in the city. He had achieved his first step: liberation. What was next, he did not know.

As he shut the door, a black huddled mass caught his attention in the ditch. He stared at it for a moment, wondering if it was a mirage. Finally, he saw it move.

"Hey," he said aloud as he slowly moved towards the pile of fur in the ditch.

Immediately, the dog's head perked up. He approached carefully and knelt, allowing the animal to smell his hand cautiously. Soon after, he leaned forward and rubbed the dog's tangled fur, taking care to acknowledge the collar it wore.

"Davey," he said aloud, looking around for signs of an owner.

After several minutes, he stood and picked up his briefcase.

As he took off down the side of the highway, he glanced over his shoulder before turning back to the dog.

"You coming?"

There was apprehension at first, and he stood for a moment longer. Finally, the dog stood from its seated position and took a step forward. He turned around and continued to walk, and soon he heard the clanging of the collar as the dog followed behind.

Perhaps it was the dog, or perhaps it was the warm sun on his face. Perhaps, even more, it was the thought that he was no longer tied to anything. Regardless of what it was, he thought he felt a smile stray across his face. It was fleeting, to say the least, but it gave him warmth and comfort that he was heading somewhere that made sense.

The remaining shreds of evidence of a life left behind and of a man no longer living lay in the car. There were no more office desks and no more managers who understood. There were no more apartments in the city or taxi rides to and from. There was no more life there. There was no more life anywhere.

Scott was no more.

***

0.5 Miles to Spokane

He had only been on this road a handful of times, but it was as fixed in his mind as any other route. Slowly, he drove past the rows of homes until he finally found the one he had been searching for. Swallowing the lump in his throat, he parked the Jeep in front of the two-story brick Tudor. He turned off the ignition and stared at the house for a long minute, allowing the sounds of midday to register. Finally, he sighed.

They had made it to Spokane.

He turned and looked into the backseat before reaching for Ryan's hand. The pulse felt weak, and the blood-soaked clothing and cloth of the seat did not give a good impression.

He closed his eyes, knowing what was next. Turning from the backseat, he reached over into his bag; the same one he had carried through several states and for thousands of miles. Carefully, he removed the Hemingway book and opened it to reveal the revolver. He pulled the gun from the pages and closed the cover. He opened the door and stepped into the snow-covered street.

He made no attempt to hide the firearm, and the midday sun glinted off the black casing. Quietly closing the Jeep door, he paused to catch his breath in the cold. He walked around the front of the car, stepped onto the sidewalk, and made his way up the walk to the front door.

He leaned in the doorway of the home he knew well. Gun in his left hand, tears in his eyes, he looked back to the Jeep. Then, without hesitation, he pounded on the door.

Someone stirred inside. A few moments passed, and then he heard the lock unlatch. His breath caught in his lungs.

A second later, the door finally opened.

Chapter 22
Fifteen Years to Spokane

"Hey," she said, smiling as she stood in the doorway.

"Hi." He smiled awkwardly as he made eye contact before breaking it. He shuffled his feet and took a step back from the door.

"Right on time," she continued, still smiling. "And you even found the place."

He nodded as he ran his fingers through his hair. "It wasn't too difficult."

"Let me grab my purse." She stepped inside. He thought about following her, given the cool December air, but he stood planted in his spot.

His eyes followed her. She was the image of perfection, clad in a yellow sundress with her light blond hair pulled into a ponytail. The dress itself was modest, but it clung to her as though tailor made. There was truly nothing more ravishing.

He almost considered turning around right there, as his nerves and her looks had meshed to create a feeling he could not handle. Somehow, though, he kept his feet planted in the doorway.

He heard her speak in another room before she reappeared with her purse in hand.

"Ready now." She smiled sweetly.

As she passed him, he noticed the small palm trees that adorned her dress. Unsurprisingly, the color of the trees matched the clip she wore in her hair. It was one of her many charms.

"Is it weird not meeting in the hotel lobby?" she asked as she reached the Tacoma.

He walked over to the passenger side and helped her step up. "A little…"

"Same here." She smiled as she sat down.

He walked around to the driver's side and climbed in.

"Are you nervous?" she finally asked, sensing his quiet disposition.

He laughed. "Not nervous," he replied. "Okay, maybe a bit…"

She reached out and put her hand on his as he shifted into drive and began moving down the road.

"Do you think I should have introduced myself back there?" he finally said.

She laughed. "To who? My dad?"

"Yeah…"

"It wouldn't do any good," she replied. "He wouldn't remember your name. It's Friday after four…he's long gone."

"Really?"

"Yeah. He was already asleep on the couch, half-murmuring about something."

He nodded, still not feeling at ease.

"It's cute that you thought of that, though…" She smiled again and squeezed his hand.

He smiled back, realizing how much he enjoyed her touch.

"What would you have said?" she asked after a moment.

"To your dad?"

"Yeah…"

He muffled a laugh as he exhaled. "I don't know, honestly…"

"Hi, sir," she said, mimicking his voice before returning to her own. "You'd call him sir, right?"

"Of course."

"Good," she replied. "Doctor would be too formal."

"Sir works."

"Hi, sir," she repeated in his voice. "I'm the rogue who's been seeing your daughter for two months…"

"Rogue?"

"It sounds…debonair," she replied.

"It sounds like a comic book villain…"

"Fine. Hi, sir, I'm the guy who's screwing your daughter…"

He considered it. "Maybe a bit too revealing."

"Well, then." She put her leg up on the dash. "You tell me what you would say."

He kept his eyes on the road, but his mind was focused solely on her. "What would I say…" he trailed off. "How about, 'Hello, sir.'" He put his finger to his lips. "'My name is Scott Lashon, and it's a pleasure to finally meet you…'"

"Pleasure?" she scoffed.

"Sure," he replied. "It sounds wholesome."

"Maybe you can bring him a twelve-pack." She laughed. "It'll set you on a good path. He'd have it gone before you finished your introduction."

"He can't possibly drink that much."

"You'd be surprised."

"At least not on the weekdays."

"Doesn't matter," she replied, now more serious.

"That's crazy."

"No one can tell," she countered. "No one but me. Mom could, too."

He could tell she was growing somber.

"Plus, when you are as 'gifted' a surgeon as he is, the faults get overlooked."

He considered this, knowing she had thought about it much more than he had.

"But continue," she said, turning back to him as the wave of sadness passed. "What else would you say?"

He turned down another road.

"Ignore my buzz kill," she added with a smile.

He laughed. "Let's see," he began. "I'd say that I live in New York…"

"That's far away," she mimicked in her gruff, fatherly voice.

"It is." He nodded.

"Why the hell are you here, then?"

"Well," he said delicately, "my company is expanding offices, and we've opened a new branch here in Phoenix…" He turned to her, whispering, "And I'd hope your daughter already told you this…"

"She never tells me anything," she continued gruffly.

"Oh, she doesn't?"

"Not a damn thing."

"She hasn't said that she's infatuated with me?"

She rolled her eyes.

"Or that she has dreams of going to college and writing about traveling the world?"

"You wouldn't dare tell him that," she said in her normal voice.

He laughed. "You really don't tell him anything?"

She sighed. "He wants me to be a doctor or something like him. He would never understand his only child wanting a different life."

"I guess a travel writer doesn't really fit that mold."

She shook her head as if distracted by the sudden change in topic. "Continue," she said in her mock-father voice. "How long have you been in Phoenix?"

"Well, I've been traveling between here and New York for the last two months." He turned down another road. "And I will continue to travel here for the next two as well."

"Sounds expensive."

"It is. But, to be honest, I actually finished my work a month ago." He paused. "I keep coming back because I'm in love..."

There was silence.

He looked over to find her staring at him. Tears welled in her eyes.

"What?" he asked, looking between her and the road.

"You're...in love?" The father voice was gone.

He looked back at her. "Of course."

She lunged over the seat and flung her arms around him in a wave of emotion.

"I didn't say with you," he said, laughing as he held her.

She ignored the joke as her tears fell on his shoulder.

"I'm kidding." He smiled as he continued to drive. "Of course, it's you."

She looked up, her face red. "I love you, too."

Later that night, the rental car sat parked in the lot about eight rows back from the drive-in screen. The movie had just finished, and cars were starting up and heading out of the large gravel lot one by one. The Tacoma stayed put.

"I don't know if I got it..." she said after a moment.

"The movie?"

"Yeah."

He turned to see her head cocked sideways and resting on her hand. "What do you mean?"

"I mean...he was an asshole."

He nodded, even though she could not see.

"Are we supposed to feel good for them?"

"I think so..."

"But they were on completely separate pages," she continued. "She had her shit together, and he did not. There's no way that works."

"I mean," he tried to reason with her, "he gave a good speech. Maybe that was him changing."

She rolled her eyes.

"Maybe not."

"Regardless, in no way is that love..."

"What do you mean?"

"I mean,"—she sat up— "That's Hollywood's version of love: popular jock guy falling for single mother he would never notice in the real world. That's not real. It never would have been that easy. That isn't love."

"All right." He smiled as he turned and sat to face her. "What's love, then?"

"To me?" she asked as though buying time to think.

"Yeah," he replied. "You're the screenwriter...tell me your love story." He paused.

"Since you think that one is fake."

"A real love story?"

"Yep."

"Let's see," she said. "Real love would be if they never got back together..."

"Clearly," he mocked.

"Listen!" she exclaimed. "If they never got together, then flash forward forty years later, and he's sitting on his money like Scrooge McDuck, but he's miserable. No family. No one to love. Just random girls in and out of his life. Then, through a random series of events, he happens to see her again."

"And the plot thickens..."

"Yeah," she continued. "And they have a passionate night remembering their brief fling, and they briefly consider a permanent rekindling...but at the last second, they fall apart again."

"Why?"

"Because...because she is in love with her husband, whom she met after he left her."

"Drama..."

"Exactly."

"One question?"

"Yeah?"

"How is that love?"

She laughed. "Because!" She thought about it, and he sensed that she knew it made little sense. "It's love because they know how they feel, but they never end up together."

"That's depressing."

"Love *is* depressing!" she said. "That's the point! All good love stories are depressing! Romeo and Juliet, Cleopatra and Marc Antony, Jay Gatsby and whatever that girl's name is..."

He laughed.

"Love ends," she said passionately. "Love dies. Even if it does survive, eventually, people die. That's the way it is, and that's depressing."

He listened intently, enthralled more by her vigor than by her words.

"But it's the truth. We need more depressing love stories. Especially in Hollywood. Those are the true ones."

"What about that *English Patient* movie?"

"Oh God...that was depressing."

"Did you appreciate that one?"

"I mean...I guess that one works. Maybe too much, though. He let her die in a freakin' cave."

He smiled at her turn of phrase. "That wasn't his plan..."

"Still...thanks for reminding me of that one."

"Anytime." He laughed.

"Eventually, someone's going to write a good depressing love story, and Hollywood won't screw it up," she concluded after a pause. "And maybe the girl will let the guy die this time."

He laughed. "There's always next year..."

She looked silently out the window at the stars. He watched her, knowing she could never understand exactly how he felt about her. Every word she spoke, every smile or tear—they all made her perfect in his eyes. He loved her fire, her passion. He wanted to drown in her presence.

She reached over and turned on the radio, as though seeking something to fill the silence. He watched her turn the dial.

"You know you're on AM…" he said with a laugh as she struggled to find reception.

"I know," she said, though he could tell she did not. "I'm finding something."

"Like?"

She scrunched up her face before a song finally came on. "This."

"This?"

"Yep. I love this song."

"You do?"

"Yep."

He listened for a moment. She attempted to mimic the words, to no avail.

"You clearly know it so well."

She laughed. "I do. Here, watch this…" She paused letting the next line start before she repeated the words, albeit a bit behind.

"I hear you calling me. You called me when the moon had veiled her light."

"Not bad," he replied.

"It's a really deep song," she replied. "About a guy who can…you know…hear his woman…."

"Calling him?"

She finally broke her ruse and started laughing as well. "Yep, you got it."

He joined her in laughing as the song played on. After a moment, the laughter died down.

"You know I don't believe most of that," she finally said, looking back at him. "The stuff about love."

"Of course." He chuckled. "I know you by now, Emily."

"Good," she replied, still thinking. "I mean, I do think love is depressing sometimes." She looked back out the window. "But that's because it's hard, not because it ends."

He nodded.

"Besides," she whispered, "love isn't defined by how it ends. It's about how it thrives. How it makes you feel. That's real love—how you feel when it's happening." She looked up at the stars again. "It can last five minutes or five million years. It can end in fire or just falling apart, but when you're in it…that's the real stuff. That's all that matters."

He sat back in his seat, considering every word. "I don't know about you," he finally said. "But I prefer the five million years kind."

"Me, too." She turned to face him with a smile. "Me, too."

The song played on in the background as they gazed at each other. There were no concerns for the world around them. This was their perfection.

***

The months came and went in a flurry, and before long, winter changed to spring. In New York, it was a welcome sight, given the typically cold and snowy months that never seemed to end.

The weather was of little concern in the Scribbs building. It was a typical Monday morning marked by hustle and commotion. All around the building, people moved like ants, each on their own path with no regard for the outside world.

On the twenty-sixth floor, he sat among an oasis of cubicles surrounded by offices with sliding glass doors and abundant potted plants. He sighed as he moved between the computer screen and the files that crowded his desk.

"Scott," a voice said behind him. "Good to see you back."

He rose from his chair and shook the man's hand. "Thanks, Bill."

"You mind coming down to my office to chat?"

"Sure," he said as he pushed in his chair.

As he followed Bill, he could sense the eyes and ears of his colleagues homing in on his movements, but he tried to ignore the attention.

"How was Phoenix?" Bill asked as they entered his office.

"Hot," he replied. "Especially for winter. Had one or two cool days, but mostly hot."

"Always is." Bill sat in his oversized chair behind his oversized desk. "I was there in July when we first considered the acquisition, and it hit 110. Try walking around in a monkey suit when the sweat beads on your back are sweating."

"I can't imagine," he mused.

"They say it's a dry heat, but my ass wasn't dry," Bill laughed.

He laughed as well, though more forced than usual.

"Listen," Bill finally replied, "I wanted to talk a bit about the numbers from Phoenix."

He felt his heart skip a beat. "All right," he heard himself say cautiously.

"For Q1," Bill began, grabbing a document he had laid to the side, "we are looking at sales of 45 percent."

He swallowed the lump in his throat. "Forty-five percent of the goal?"

Bill smiled. "Above."

His eyes went wide. "Above?"

"Yes. The team exceeded its goal by almost 50 percent."

"That's awesome!" The wave of nausea passed.

"That's better than awesome," Bill replied. "They're doing better than all three other acquisitions, and better than the Seattle and San Antonio markets combined."

"Wow." He smiled, still relieved. "I can't believe they did that."

"They? No, Scott, you did it," Bill replied. "You went out there and kicked ass."

He sat there, silent.

"Don't be modest, Scott. I know your work ethic. I know how much you put in. Hell, you were there almost every week through the weekend. I almost thought you had moved entirely!"

He laughed.

"That work shows. It shows to me, and it definitely shows to my boss."

"Well," Scott said, "I appreciate that."

"You keep this up, and you'll be out of that cubicle and into this side of the building."

He nodded, knowing what type of honor that would be—to have his own office, to have the mahogany desk and the Rolex watch. It was more than he had ever thought he would achieve.

"I don't know when you sleep, Scott." Bill laughed and removed a flask and two glasses from a desk drawer. "I don't know how you have time outside of this job, but I'm damn sure glad you're here."

"Thank you, sir."

"It's only going to get steeper from here," he continued, pouring a trace. "The climb, I mean."

"Indeed, sir."

"But you'll make it. I have faith in you."

"Thank you, sir."

He offered a glass, and they both drank the strong bourbon.

"So." Bill sat back, savoring the burn. "You really liked Phoenix, huh?"

Scott leaned back in his chair and examined his glass. The question hung on the air as he rolled his fingers over the smooth edge. In truth, the city was the furthest thing from his mind. "Parts of it," he finally replied with a smile.

"Parts of it?" Bill considered the statement. "Must be some good parts."

Scott poured another drink and took a sip, this time savoring the flavor and all its associated memories. As much as he tried to repress them, they always came back. "Yeah," he replied as he downed the drink. "Some of the best."

Later that day, he sat in a cab on the way back to his apartment on the Upper West Side. As the driver passed row after row of hustle and bustle, he found himself gazing at the people out and about, from the tourists to the students to the families. The weather was pleasant, and there were plenty of pedestrians on the sidewalks.

For a moment, he envied them. They seemed so happy and relaxed after a winter indoors. They did not have to worry about promotions, travel, life, or love. For this moment, it was just them and spring parlaying for the first time in months.

He would have no such peace. He needed to get home and get dinner going. Then it was off to prepare for bed because the morning alarm would come calling soon enough. Then another cab ride, or maybe even the subway, before a ten-hour day of work and another ride home. It was simplistic. It was monotonous. It paid the bills. It allowed him to live. Success was never easy, especially in this city.

When the cab pulled up in front of his apartment, he gave the driver a twenty and a ten before grabbing his briefcase and opening the door. Stepping out, he stopped short.

"Hey," she said, sitting on the third step of the entry stoop.

He blinked, not knowing what to say.

"Emily?"

"I—" she stood rigidly, as if scared. "I hope you didn't forget about me."

"How—" His briefcase dropped from his hand to the concrete, but he did not care. "What...are you doing here?"

She took a step down, and he could see that she was clad in the same yellow dress that burned in his memories each night.

"I missed you," she breathed.

He stared at her incredulously. "You're in Phoenix, though..."

"Not anymore," she replied with a laugh.

"Why?"

She smiled again. "Daddy moved north to his sister's place. He's finally getting help."

He heard the words but did not quite understand them. "That's wonderful," he heard himself say.

"And," she whispered, "there's nothing else for me there."

"So…you came here?"

"Here is where you are," she replied.

His heart dropped, and once again, he no longer owned any part of it.

He moved to close the gap between them.

"How did you get here?"

She laughed. "Does it matter?"

Tears in his eyes, he finally reached her. "No," he said, embracing her with his entire being. "No, it doesn't."

He could feel her breath on his chest and love in her embrace.

"Did you miss me, too?"

A tear rolled down his cheek. It was more than he could ever say, but he knew she did not see. For the first time in a long time, he felt peace and happiness. He felt warmth and passion—a love that blazed in fury. He felt all those things but knew his words would never match. He continued embracing her because it was all he wanted to do.

"Yes," he said. "I have always missed you."

***

Eleven Years to Spokane

"Are you nervous?" she asked as he stared at his phone.

He continued scrolling.

"You've never officially met," she added, clearly awaiting a response.

He finally looked up to her as though pondering the question. "I wouldn't say I'm nervous." He picked the phone back up.

"What would you say you are?"

"I don't know," he replied.

"Well, you have to feel something…"

He set the phone back down. "I don't know." He thought for a moment. "What is the absence of feeling called?"

"Man?"

"Ha…"

"I'd be nervous if I met your family," she continued as he picked the phone back up.

"Well, good thing you don't have to," he replied.

The gate attendant said something over the loudspeaker. He strained to hear as he focused on the device in front of him, but he heard the keynotes: Flight 5578, Spokane International, boarding in ten minutes.

"He's excited to meet you," she said after some minutes. "It's been over three years of just hearing about you."

Her inflection let him know that they were not through discussing the topic. He set his phone off to the side as throngs of people continued moving around them.

"I didn't realize it'd been that long," he replied.

"Yeah, three years. He's been in Washington for over two and a half. Aunt Janey's been taking good care of him."

He nodded, knowing there was not much else to add.

"What are you going to say to him?" she asked after a moment.

"What?"

"What are you going to say to him?" she repeated. "When you first meet?"

"I'm not following."

"Are you going to call him sir? Introduce yourself as my husband?"

"I feel like we've had this discussion before…"

"Humor me."

He turned and positioned himself closer. "I'll say…hi, sir. I'm Scott, and I'm…"

"It's hard, right?"

"You've thought about this?"

"Of course!"

"You've thought about what I'm going to say to your father?"

"Of course!"

"What did you come up with?"

She sat back in her seat, oblivious to the discomfort she was causing. "I would say," she finally began, teasing him. "I'd say 'Hello, sir. It's good to finally meet you after so long.'" She nodded in approval.

"That's it?"

"What?"

"That's it?" he asked with a smile. "That's all you'd say?"

"Yep. That and then let him talk."

He considered it for a moment. "I like it."

She took his arm and leaned toward him.

"Are you nervous?" he asked after letting the silence settle a bit.

She considered her answer. "Yeah, I am."

"Understandable," he replied, masking his own growing unease.

"Last time I saw him was in the passenger seat of my aunt's car," she recalled, "and he could barely look at me without crying."

He said nothing as she talked.

"That was tough," she finished.

"I bet."

"It'll be nice to have a memory of him sober," she added, "even if this visit goes down in flames."

"Why would it go down in flames?"

She laughed. "Because it's my family!"

He shook his head and tried to stifle laughter of his own.

The gate agent began calling rows over the speaker.

"Remember when you first picked me up in Phoenix?" she asked as he slid his phone into his pocket.

"Of course."

"You ever think we'd end up here?"

"Here, like the airport?"

She rolled her eyes. "You know what I mean."

He laughed. "I don't know," he finally said. "I guess I always hoped we would."

"It's funny how time flies, isn't it?" She smiled as she rose and collected her bags.

He considered it for a moment before standing as well.

"You coming?" she asked, suddenly steps ahead of him.

For the first time, he felt the faint flutter of butterflies in his stomach. It was a unique feeling, and one he was unaccustomed to. For just a second, he let it take hold, complete with a quickening heartbeat and a heavy chest. Then, just like that, it was gone. He sat for a moment longer, knowing it would be the first of many such encounters.

"Yeah," he replied. "I'm coming."

He could tell that she had seen his bout of nerves, but she said nothing. Perhaps she felt it too and did not want to give it away, or perhaps she just wanted to hold onto the thought a few moments more. Whatever the case, he did not know her reasoning.

He knew that the time had indeed flown by, but he also knew that he had much more to discover about her. He proceeded down the jetway after her. As he walked, he found himself completely enthralled by her magic and mystique as though seeing them for the first time.

He had never been so eager to learn.

***

Four Years to Spokane

He sat in the living room and stared at the computer perched on his lap. The autumn wind howled outside the building, making the deafening silence inside the apartment even more obvious. He continued gazing at the screen, though he could not make out the images properly.

"You're not even going to look at me?" she asked, almost as brisk as the air outside.

He remained silent and stared blankly at the computer. He had nothing to say. His leg shuddered as the cold seeped in. There was no warmth to be found.

The years and the seasons had changed.

"Look at me," she demanded again in a dangerous voice.

He stared at the computer a moment longer before raising his head to meet her gaze.

"Better?" he asked.

She gritted her teeth. The landscape was ever changing. She spoke dangerously. "Did you hear me?"

He stared at her. "I did."

"What did I say?"

"I don't want to go through this." He turned away, back to the laptop.

"What did I say?" she repeated, raising her voice slightly.

He continued looking at his computer.

"Scott," she snapped, "look at me."

He did not.

"Look at me, goddamn it."

He turned his face up and back to her.

"What the hell is happening here?" It was her first line from the conversation, and it still was not addressed.

"What do you want me to say?"

She exhaled. "I want you to tell me the truth."

"What's the truth?"

"You tell me."

He laughed mockingly, but words would not come.

She ignored it. "You sit there and act like I don't exist. Like I'm a ghost." He continued to look past her as she spoke. "You barely speak. You can't carry on a conversation. You never sleep. Hell, you're not even here most of the time."

His jaw tightened, but he gave no response.

"I can't do this, Scott."

Finally, he sighed. "I work."

"What?"

"I…work," he repeated. "That's what I do." He finally turned to her. "That's why I'm tired. That's why I'm never here. That's why I'm too busy to have conversations. Because I work." His voice grew louder. "That's why we have a three-bedroom apartment in the most expensive city in the world. That's why we aren't living in the street. That's why we have the things we have. Because," he snapped, glaring daggers, "I work."

She glared back. "And no one is making you."

"You don't get it," he replied. "You have no concept of how life works."

"Educate me, then."

"This house? This life? The fancy shoes and five-star meals? None of that exists if I don't work. Everything you love doesn't exist if we don't have money."

"I love you," she countered. "I don't love anything else."

"That's such bullshit." He shook his head. "You have no idea what it takes to live."

"Why?" Her voice grew louder. "Because I don't work? Is that it?"

"No," he sparred. "It's because you have no ambition to work. Ever."

"Work is not life."

"It is when you live here!"

"I never asked for any of this."

"And you never turned it down."

"I came here for you."

"And this is my life," he maintained. "This is my life. My life is my job. It's what pays the bills. It hasn't changed since the day I met you. You know that."

"No," she countered. "It wasn't always this way. It wasn't always this bad."

"Is this what you do? You sit at home and stammer out an argument to bitch about when I get back?" His tone was lethal. "No," he continued, "I know. You go to school. That's what you do. You attend classes. Two. From this couch."

"You are so bitter."

"I am surviving," he countered. "I am doing what I have to do to get us through life."

"Your life," she corrected.

He stared at her.

"Do you know how I got here to you?"

"I don't care," he replied, turning back to his computer.

"I used my last dollar to buy a Greyhound ticket to wherever I could."

"I don't care."

"I got as far as Dallas, and over the next nine days I hitched rides, I sneaked onto trains. Hell, I almost got arrested in Pittsburgh. But I did it. It took a lot of time and patience, and I did it."

He never looked up.

"I did it with no money. I did it with nothing, except the drive to get to you."

"You did it because you had nowhere else to go." His words cut like glass.

"Don't you say that."

"It's true. What, were you going to move to Spokane? Live with your drunk dad in your aunt's house and watch as he tried to get his shit together?"

"Don't say that…" A tear rolled down her cheek.

He could tell he had gone too far, but he could not take it back.

"I can't believe…" she whispered.

"What do you want me to say? Congratulations on making it here? Is that somehow supposed to prove me wrong? To say that I'm ridiculous for working?"

"Money doesn't matter…" She was openly tearing up now. "Not if you have—"

"Love doesn't pay bills," he corrected. "Work does."

He did not even know if he agreed with his statement, but he said it anyway. He was tired of arguing. He was tired of defending himself. He was tired of it all.

"How can you treat someone you love this way?" she sobbed.

He turned back to her. "How can you?"

She stood up, clearly defeated. He did not move. He returned his gaze to the computer on his lap, but his focus was on anything but.

She moved past him and he listened as she walked briskly up the stairs to the bedroom. He continued to sit.

Moments later, she was back with her purse in hand. Her crying had stopped, but her pain lingered. She walked right past him again. He could feel the wind in her movement, and he closed his eyes as it rolled past him. He could have stopped her there. She was close enough for him to reach out, but his hands would not move. He could have said something, anything, but he did not.

He continued to sit.

In seconds, she was at the door. He continued to sit. He heard the door open, and he could feel her pause as though debating everything that had happened. It seemed like an eternity, but it lasted only a moment. Before his eyes opened, she was out the door and down the steps. The door closed behind her.

He continued to sit. Tears rolled down his cheek as he sat in silence. He had done nothing. He had continued to sit, and just like that, she was gone.

Late that night, he lay asleep on the same couch. He did not remember closing his eyes, but a mixture of rage and tears had fueled his slumber. He had tried her phone several times, all to no avail.

His own phone's ringtone woke him. Dazed, he reached for it and pressed it to his ear.

"Emily?"

The voice on the other end was soft. "Sir? Is this Mr. Lashon? Mr. Lashon?"

"Huh?"

"Mr. Lashon, this is Sergeant Coleman with the Spokane PD. Mr. Lashon, there's been an accident…"

***

He had never been inside a prison before.

If he had paid it any attention, he would have noticed how rigid everything was—from the floors and ceilings to the walls and doors; he would have noticed the dank color scheme, a mix of pale greens and off whites; and he probably would have noticed just how much it looked like a film scene. It was rare to find something that looked just as it did on a movie set, yet somehow prison seemed to fit. If he had paid it any attention on a normal day, these thoughts may have come to him. Today, however, was anything but a normal day.

He entered a small room and pulled his license from his back pocket for the officer at the next door. The officer scanned it and wrote down the information before handing it back.

"Here to see?" the officer asked.

"Mr. Claire."

The officer wrote down the information before buzzing open the door.

"He'll be there in a bit," the officer said.

He walked through the open door to a long line of seats and windows. Benches sat along the far wall.

He sat for several minutes, face expressionless, and ignored the conversations from the three groups at the windows. Finally, he heard another door buzz open, and he heard movement from beyond the windows. He stood as he saw the person he had come to see. Their eyes met.

The man was older, though the prison garb and handcuffs made him look older still. He had a receding hairline and grizzled skin. Better days were clearly far behind him. Standing about five and a half feet tall but slouching slightly forward, he looked more like a wounded dog than a fearless canine.

"Ten minutes," the officer called as he seated the man in a window unit. Without expression, his visitor took the seat opposite the window.

They sat facing each other for a few seconds before he picked up the phone on his side. Seconds later, the older man did the same.

"I'm surprised you didn't turn around," he said flatly into the phone. "I didn't expect you to sit here." He eyed the man in the jumpsuit intently, as if looking for cracks. "Did you read the paper today?" he asked, pulling a clipping from his pocket. "I'd assume not, given your…incarceration. But I figured I'd ask."

He unfolded the article and held it in front of the glass.

"I'll let you read it," he continued. "Or I can summarize." He set it down, but the man on the other side seemed less than amused. He moved the phone to his other ear. "It says, 'Beloved Spokane Doctor Loses Loved One in Vehicle Wreck.'" He turned the paper around as if to read it word for word. "Listen to this. 'Dr. C., as he is called by most of his patients, only ran a practice in Spokane for a little over two years, yet in that time, he was known for both humanitarian and community contributions across the area.'" He paused as he looked up to the man. "It goes on and on to talk about your accolades and praises." He sat back and continued staring at the man. "The ending is a bit depressing. Something about an icy road and driving too fast, causing a wreck that resulted in the death of one person…I forget how the story goes, though; the article really glosses over it. I don't even think they mention her name." He leaned over the ledge in front of him and whispered mockingly, "Or that the 'loved one' was your own daughter…"

The man in the jumpsuit was perfectly still. He stared intently through the glass.

"Five days in, and they've already forgotten her name." He leaned back in his seat.

"But you, you're the tragic soul. The one that everyone feels sorry for."

"What do you want?" the man finally asked, still unmoved.

He smiled sardonically. "What do I want?" He looked to his right as if sensing the answer would come from there. "I," he said carefully. "I want the truth." He leaned forward, his face inches from the glass. "I want you to look me in the eyes and tell me the truth."

The man met his gaze the entire way. The air was toxic.

He gritted his teeth. "Did you even try to stop?"

Silence settled over the chairs as the men stared at each other.

"That's what the paper doesn't say," he continued. "They don't say whether you even tried to stop drinking. Did you? That's why you moved here, right? To get better? To quit? Did you even care about hiding it from her?" He glared at the man. "Did she know your sister left you, too? Did she know that absolutely nothing had changed?"

Tears welled in the man's eyes.

"You're pathetic," he continued, already knowing the answers. "You had this entire community fooled into thinking you were a god. I went through the police report, and you know what I found?" He paused, knowing no answer was coming. "They didn't even breathalyze you until four hours after you were arrested." He continued whispering in a voice so sharp it could have cut glass. "You were barely over the limit." He sat back in his seat. "I bet that's the most sober you've ever been."

"That's enough," the man finally said.

"You fucking murdered my wife," he growled.

"I said enough."

"She was my wife!" he continued.

"She was my daughter!" the prisoner finally gasped, breaking his gaze in a rage of tears.

"And you murdered her," he replied, twisting the knife deeper.

For a moment, the man in the jumpsuit said nothing. Instead, he blinked wildly through his tears. "Is this what you came here for?" he sobbed. "To see an old man rage?"

"I don't give a damn about you," he hissed. "You're a murderer, even if you and I are the only ones who know it."

"What do you want me to say?" he moaned.

"Nothing." He paused, staring at the wretched man. "I want you to say nothing. I want you to do nothing." He leaned forward to the glass. "I want you to serve your pathetic time here and go home, and I want you to spend every day for the rest of your sorry life knowing exactly who and what you are."

He watched the tears stream down the man's face.

"You took everything from me."

He finally looked up. "She was my everything, too…"

He reeled back, sickened. "Don't you dare!"

The old man whispered incoherently.

"What'd you say?"

He spoke louder now. "I'm sorry."

"Sorry?" He seethed. "You're sorry?" He exhaled deeply. "No, you're not." The words hung on the air. "But you will be." He stood up as the man's gaze met his once more. "She's coming with me," he finally said as he looked down through the glass. "She's not staying in this hellhole. I've signed all the papers. You'll never see her again."

The man looked down once more, again openly crying.

"I also stopped by your house and picked up her things. You don't deserve a shrine." His voice was deadly calm. "I also took one more thing, at the request of your sister." The man looked up once more, face red in ire and sorrow.

"You don't get to end it yourself," he finally said. "Your gun comes with me. I decide when you get to die." He leaned forward once more to be sure only the prisoner could hear him. "Pray you never lay eyes on me again...because if you do, me and that gun will be the last things you see."

He leaned back to a rigid standing position. "Look at you, the great and noble Bowman Claire." He shook his head in disgust. "You're fucking pitiful. Enjoy your cell, you pathetic bastard."

He turned and strode away from the glass. He did not look back, and he did not want to.

There was nothing left for him in that prison. There was nothing left for him in that town. He had lost it all already.

***

Late that night, the taxi dropped him off at the apartment. He wearily pulled his suitcase up the steps and entered through the front door.

Silence.

The apartment was cold, hollow. Even in the busiest city in the country, he could hear nothing beyond the walls. It was sterile. It was voiceless.

He walked into the kitchen and opened the refrigerator. The light illuminated the room around him. Looking on the shelves, he found a tinfoil-covered plate and pulled it out. Unwrapping it, he found a half-eaten pie. He walked to the counter, pulled out a fork, and took a bite of two-week-old pastry.

Spitting it out, he angrily threw it onto the floor in disgust. Closing his eyes, he took a deep breath before returning into the living room and grabbing his suitcase. As he turned, he saw a pillow on the floor in front of the couch. Instinctively, he recalled the phone call that had caused the pillow to fall.

Taking another deep breath, he carried the suitcase up the stairs and into his bedroom. He carefully set it on the bed and unzipped it.

He hung there for a moment, staring at contents of his suitcase before finally sitting on the bed. Once again, he heard nothing but silence. He reached for the remote and powered on the TV as he lay on the bed. He removed his shoes and watch and emptied his pants pockets onto his nightstand, just as he had every night for years. In the same fluid motion, he found his alarm clock and flipped it on.

Turning back to the TV, he found himself pressing the channel button up once, then twice. Then again. Then again. Then again. Eyes blankly staring, he continued pressing the button as if it were the only thing he could do. Again. Again. Again. Up. Up. Up. He continued staring at the screen without seeing it. He simply kept pushing the button as if it were all that mattered.

Thirty hours later, his alarm would go off. An hour more and he would be in a cab on his way to work. It was the end of one path and the beginning of another. It was the end of one life and the beginning of something new…

…and it all happened then, in the apartment in New York City—four years, two months, and 4,212 miles from Spokane.

***

In Spokane

The door opened.

The man on the inside went rigid upon seeing Bo in the doorway. His eyes moved from the visitor to the gun clutched limply in his left hand. He swallowed the lump in his throat and took a deep breath.

"Mr. Claire…" Bo spoke softly as the tears continued to roll.

Bowman Claire closed his eyes. "Scott…" he breathed. Somehow, he did not seem surprised. "I guess this is it," he finally said. With bated breath, he stood rigid; waiting for the fate he knew awaited him.

There was a thud.

Bowman jumped slightly and then slowly opened his eyes. He looked at Bo, then to his empty hand. He looked down and saw the gun lying at his feet.

"I don't understand…" Bowman whispered.

Bo straightened up, though his face was the picture of agony. He looked over his shoulder to the Jeep at the curb and then back to the man in front of him.

His voice was hurt. His sound was weary. The exhaustion in his voice was overwhelming, and yet his urgency was as strong as ever. Bowman felt his eyes go wide as Bo finally spoke.

"I need your help."

Sunlight cascaded through the window and onto the bed, giving it a warm and soothing appearance. In the individual rays of light, stray dust particles floated to and from, uninhibited by any additional airflows or drafts. It was peaceful and serene. It was quiet and calm. It was almost like home.

Ryan felt the warmth on his eyelids before he opened them. For a moment, he lay there in bliss, allowing the feeling to cover him like a blanket. It was everything he needed to feel in that bit of time. He opened his eyes.

He instantly felt the pain in his arm. It was dull, almost more of an ache than severe throbbing, but it radiated down his right side. He tried to move it and found it bound to a piece of board. It seemed both proper and professional.

Blinking his eyes, he lifted his left hand and saw that it was bandaged. Lifting his head slightly, he saw his legs in a similar state. He moved each one slightly as if fearful that functioning would be gone. To his relief, however, everything responded just as he requested.

He was beaten up, but alive.

Slowly, he sat up in bed and took stock of his surroundings. The room was old, with dark wood paneling and a low ceiling. If he had not seen another room across the hall, he would have assumed he was in an attic. The room was dusty but nicely adorned. Clearly, he was the first inhabitant in a while.

He swung his feet off the bed and onto the floor, wincing as his body woke. He took great care to keep his arm level and even, knowing the pain there would be greater than anywhere else.

Using his left hand as a brace, he stood, shaking under the weight of his own body. Finally, he steadied himself and made it to the door.

There was a door to his left and one across the hall. Both were shut. To the right, a staircase led to the main floor. He descended slowly, wincing with nearly every step. When he finally reached the bottom, he took a moment to look around.

The house was older and on the small side, and the downstairs had the same wood paneling and low ceiling as the bedroom. The staircase, brass and polished, seemed almost out of place. Surprisingly, he found the living room empty, save for a littering of furniture and a television that mutely displayed a local newscast.

To his right was a doorway to a small kitchen with a table in the middle. A man sat with his back to Ryan, reading a newspaper held at eye level. The man, however, was not Bo.

He knew he had a choice: address the man or run past him to front door. He considered both. He did not get an uneasy feeling about the house, and this, coupled with the obvious care that had gone into treating his arm, helped him reason that the man at the table was not a threat. Besides, he figured, answers were more important than running at this point.

He stepped into the room and cleared his throat.

"Oh!" the man exclaimed in the softest surprise possible. "Ryan, you're awake." He set down the paper and stood up. "Good to meet you. I've heard good things."

Ryan nodded. "I, uh…" He looked from the paper to the man. "I haven't heard anything about you."

"Forgive me," the man said quietly. "I'm sure you're a bit confused. Please have a seat. Have some cereal."

The man was much shorter than Ryan and almost mousy in appearance. His skin was darker and rather rough, though given his age this was not much of a surprise. Though he seemed much older, Ryan pegged him to be in his late 60s.

"Where's Bo?" Ryan asked cautiously as he sat down.

"Bo?"

"Yeah, Bo…" Ryan looked back, sizing the man up. "Taller, homeless-looking guy…"

The man nodded. "Oh. He's here. Upstairs, actually. He'll be down in a bit." He pointed to the cereal. "Please. You need some food."

Ryan looked at the cereal and then to the milk next to it. Gingerly, he poured himself a bowl with his left hand, taking care not to disturb his bandages.

"How's your arm?" the man asked softly.

"It hurts," Ryan responded, eyeing the man before spooning a bite into his mouth.

"It was a pretty severe fracture." the man responded.

"You did this?" Ryan asked, nodding at his bandages.

"I did."

He took another bite of his cereal and look at his arm as though admiring the work. He turned back to the man. "You're a doctor?"

"I was."

"Was?"

"Yes."

They sat in companionable silence for a bit.

"You don't have any other questions?" the man finally said.

Ryan swallowed and darted a glance at the man, who continued to watch him. "No," he began, spooning another bite. "I've got a ton of questions. I'm just pretty hungry." He felt like a deer at a watering hole.

The man smiled, obviously understanding the point of view.

"So…" Ryan finally said. "Who are you?"

The man sat back and crossed his legs. "My name is Bowman Claire, and I am—" He paused. "Bo's father-in-law. Or…I was."

Ryan took another bite, instantly recalling the news article he had read an eternity ago.

"And you live here?" Ryan asked, indicating the house.

"I do."

Ryan nodded. "Where is here?"

Bowman chuckled slightly. "Spokane. Washington."

"Spokane?"

"Yep."

Ryan took another bite. The answer almost surprised him.

"What day is it?"

"It's Thursday."

He acknowledged the comment with another nod and took another bite. "It's past Christmas?"

Bowman nodded. "It's the day after."

Ryan took another bite but remained silent. It was difficult to hear, but somehow, he had expected it.

His counterpart struggled to change topics. "You're from Florida, correct?"

"Yeah," he replied with a full mouth. "Clearwater."

"I've never been."

"It's all right. Nice this time of year." His voice was even, which surprised him.

"I can imagine," Bowman replied. "Although winter here has been mild so far."

Ryan looked up from the bowl and set the spoon down, knowing the small talk was more of a courtesy than anything else.

"Best to eat slowly," the man replied. "You haven't had anything in a while."

"So, I was out for...what, two days?" Ryan asked, trying to gauge time in his mind.

Bowman considered the question. "You got in Monday night, so since then, I think." He paused as he thought. "Bo...he kept me out of the loop as to how long you were out prior to that."

Ryan picked his spoon back up, took another bite, and looked back up with a full mouth. "So, Bo isn't Bo."

The man sat back. "Excuse me?"

"Bo," Ryan said. "His name isn't Bo."

Bowman stood up and went to the coffee pot. "I'd rather let him explain..."

Ryan took another bite and was about to acknowledge the comment.

"My name is Scott," a voice said from his left.

He turned to see Bo standing in the doorway, clearly having just come from upstairs. Ryan's jaw dropped. The man's mat of facial hair was now clean-shaven skin. The shoulder-length hair had been cut so now it barely touched his ears. It was still wet with product, and Ryan could tell it was a recent change.

"You look...young."

"Young?" Bo asked as he moved to the coffee pot and poured a cup.

"Yeah. And kempt."

Ryan could tell the back of his hair was a more difficult reach, yet he admired the effort. He was truly a changed man.

"Kempt?"

Ryan tried not to stare as he took another bite. "Yeah." He swallowed. "Like Robin Williams after he got out of Jumanji."

A smile crept across Bo's face. He sipped his coffee. Ryan could tell the smile was the first in a while.

"I'll be on the porch," Bowman said quietly.

Bo nodded and leaned against the counter with a mug in hand. Ryan kept his eyes on his bowl but occasionally glanced to his right to read Bo's gaze.

"He buys a lot of stuff online," Bo said as he motioned to the old man. "Spends most of his time on the porch..." He sipped his coffee and neither spoke for a moment.

"So," Ryan finally said. "Scott, huh?"

"Yeah."

"You don't look like a Scott."

"Did I look like a Bo?"

"Kind of."

Bo smiled. "You can call me Bo if you prefer."

"I do."

"All right."

Ryan pushed his bowl away. He stared at the table, not knowing what to say. Finally, he turned. "You backed my car into that squad car."

"I did," Bo replied. He sipped his coffee again.

"Yeah," Ryan said. "That was pretty awesome."

"Not really," Bo countered. "I think it broke your arm."

"Probably. But it saved my life."

Bo considered it but said nothing.

"I mean you could have tried something before he kicked the crap out of me."

Bo smiled weakly. "Hard to throw rocks at guys with guns."

"True," Ryan considered it. "Seriously though, who knows what would've happened if you'd driven away..." Ryan's voice trailed off. There was a long silence as the weight of his words filled the room. "Why'd you do it?"

"Why'd I do what?"

"Wreck the cars. Bail me out." Ryan thought for a second. "Save my life."

Bo rinsed the cup and set it in the sink. "You did the same for me."

"I did a lot of stupid stuff, but I didn't wreck a cop car..."

"No," Bo replied in all seriousness. "But you saved my life."

"Come again?"

Ryan watched as Bo chose his words. "The day you picked me up. I was on my way to the ocean, and I wasn't coming back. You saved my life."

Ryan thought for a moment. "But your sign—"

"It wasn't my sign," Bo replied. "I was holding it for another guy while he went to get a sandwich."

"It wasn't your sign?"

"Nope."

"Then why'd you get in?"

Bo sighed. "I don't know."

Ryan stared at him. "I'm confused."

"Can I ask you something?" Bo replied, ignoring the comment.

"Shoot," Ryan replied.

"Where'd you get the money?"

"What?"

"Where'd you get that money?"

Ryan's eyes went wide.

Bo added. "This house doesn't have much, but it does have crap internet..."

Ryan sat back in his chair.

"Where did you find an ATM in Shannon?" Bo clarified.

"Shannon?"

"Yeah."

"I didn't find an ATM in Shannon..."

"Then where'd you get the money?"

"I got it in Tennessee. Some random truck stop we parked at."

"I don't understand..."

"What?"

Bo sat in the chair opposite Ryan. "We made it to Shannon, you met that girl, and you wanted to stay…"

"Okay."

"Then you stole that money so you could—"

Ryan shook his head. "No."

"What?"

"I stole the money long before I ever met her…"

Bo sat back. "Then that means…" Understanding dawned in his face. "That means…you stole the money…" He looked up. "For me?"

Ryan swallowed. "I made a promise."

Bo gazed at the young man across from him. "Why would you do that?" he finally asked.

Ryan thought about it. "It just seemed like the right thing to do."

"You had to know…"

"That it was illegal?" Ryan chuckled. "Of course."

"And stupid."

"Yep."

"But you did it anyway."

Ryan nodded.

Bo leaned back. He motioned to the porch. "Do you know who that man was?" He finally asked.

"Your father-in-law," Ryan replied. "I got that much."

"That's correct. He's also the only family I have." He paused. "The gun you found," he said through gritted teeth, "it was his. I took it from him because I felt he was responsible for my wife's death."

"He was driving…" Ryan recalled the article.

Bo exhaled. "No…he wasn't." His face showed pain as he spoke. "Two weeks earlier, he was stopped for drunk driving. It was his third offense. He was ordered to serve ninety days. She had no idea. No one did." He paused and looked down at the table. "She got off the plane and realized he wasn't coming, so she did what anyone would do—she rented a car. She wrecked it either on the way here or on the way back; the cops couldn't tell."

"Where were you?"

Bo looked up. "Asleep on our couch in New York City. We'd had a fight. I said some terrible things. She left. I could have gone after her, but I didn't."

"What was the fight about?"

"Money." He shrugged. "It was always about money or careers or some bullshit. It wasn't our first fight." He looked down at the table. "I could have said something— anything to make her stay. But I didn't. When I landed here in Spokane and found out why her dad never picked her up, that's when I really lost it." He shook his head. "I blamed him. If he weren't in jail…if he weren't drunk…if he'd had his shit even somewhat together…maybe she'd be alive."

He looked up. "Truth is, we both let her down. I couldn't see what was important. I never listened to her. I was always so focused on 'making life better' that I didn't see what made it so good to begin with. It wasn't just his fault. It wasn't just mine. It was both of us. At the time, I didn't understand that." He paused again. "We were the two most important people in her life, and we both let her down."

Ryan leaned forward. "But you didn't do it," he insisted. "It was an accident."

"You're right." Bo sighed and returned his gaze. "It was an accident, one that either of us could have stopped, but we didn't."

"I left here on a Sunday," he recalled. "I went back to New York, but nothing was the same. I guess it was to be expected, but I didn't know what to do. I felt like dying. I felt like my life was no longer my own, so I decided to leave it. I rented a car and drove as far as it would take me, and then I got out and became someone new."

"Bo."

"There were others first...but yeah, finally Bo."

"Where were you going?"

"A peaceful place where I could be with her. I found it, too—a nice stretch of beach that she would have loved...I guess I just wasn't meant to join her yet."

Ryan could feel Bo's emotion and knew the story was painfully true.

"What was she like?" he finally asked.

"Emily?" Bo asked. "Wonderful." He smiled. "She was vibrant and full of vigor. She was the only person who made me feel that way you're supposed to feel. You know what I mean?"

Ryan nodded with a smile.

"She loved the outdoors." Bo closed his eyes. "And she loved to love. Her heart was as big as the ocean." He exhaled hard and opened his eyes. "She was dealt a tough life, and she persevered through it all."

"She sounds perfect," Ryan replied.

"She was. She most certainly was."

They sat in silence as Ryan processed the conversation.

"I'm sorry about Mel," Bo finally said.

The name cut like a knife, and he was unprepared to hear it. It took a moment for him to gather his thoughts.

"It's...it's all right."

"No, it's not," Bo replied. "I know you cared about her."

Ryan nodded. "At the end of the day, it's my fault. I made us leave."

The words hung on the air.

"Can I ask you something?" Ryan asked.

Bo looked up.

"Why did you want to come here?"

"What?"

"Why did you want to come here? Of all places? There's obviously so much pain here..."

Bo took a deep breath. "Well, not knowing why we were felons, I didn't have many options." He smiled a bit.

Ryan returned the smile. "In my defense, you weren't a felon until you wrecked that car..."

Bo managed a small chuckle. "The pain that's here," he began, looking out the porch through the window. "The pain that's here is here because of me. Directly or indirectly. It was time to come back. I needed to. I never thought I would, but I did. I needed to right my wrongs."

"And did you?"

Bo looked up. "I think so. I feel more at peace, as weird as that sounds."

Ryan turned away. "One day, I'd like to think I could right some of mine…"

"It's never too late," Bo replied. "You'll do it soon enough." He stood up and walked around the table, patting Ryan's shoulder as he walked. "Soon enough," he said softly.

Ryan closed his eyes as Bo moved up the stairs behind him. He then opened them once more, still processing the words Bo had spoken.

It was past noon when Ryan moved to the living room. The small space was adorned with photos and keepsakes, all preserved as though in a museum. His eyes were drawn to a wall hung with family photos from decades ago. It may have not been the family home growing up, but it was a shrine to one now.

Ryan recognized none of the people in the pictures, but that was to be expected. A baby in a bathtub, surrounded by suds and toys. A prom photo of a young couple in complete bliss. A family of five at Mt. Rushmore. Another at the Space Needle. And another of two parents and a young daughter in front of a house with cacti in the front yard. A young woman standing in front of an expanse of sea and sand. An old couple in front of a cake with a big "97" and many flaming candles.

As he looked at the photos, he realized he had the same ones at his own home. Not the people, of course, but the same situations: his family at Cape Canaveral, him and his parents in front of their house. The prom photo that he hated but which continued to grace the wall. They were pictures of life. They were pictures of family.

He paused at another photo and this time; he knew the subjects. A younger Bo was sitting in a pickup truck with his hands on the wheel; a goofy grin on his face conveyed a sense of relief. Emily sat in the passenger seat, hand on Bo's knee and smiling sweetly as she looked at the camera through the driver's window. It was as though she was prepared for the photo and he had no idea.

Ryan smiled as he picked up the picture. In the silence, he heard a chair rocking back and forth. Ryan followed the sound and walked out onto the porch.

He scanned the horizon and then the street in front of him. The mailbox stood out, and he squinted to read the number 58, and under it read Peters Way. He refocused his eyes and spied the neighbor's house, which read 55.

"I wonder where 56 and 57 went," he said, attempting to spark a conversation.

Bowman did not move.

Ryan stood awkwardly in the doorway. "Your address," he tried to clarify, "is just kind of weird. Maybe someone hated the number 57…"

Again, Bowman did not reply. Ryan was thinking about going back inside when the old man finally spoke.

"It's never this warm in December," Bowman said softly as Ryan stepped forward on the old wood. "Crazy year we've been having."

He nodded as he took a seat next to the man. There were only two chairs, but Ryan doubted if they'd ever been used simultaneously.

"I love that picture," Bowman said, eyeing the Polaroid in Ryan's hand.

"It looks more recent than some of the others."

Bowman nodded. "It is. They came and visited me soon after they got married. I took that on the day they left, which is probably why Scott looks so thankful."

Ryan smiled at the joke.

"She really was heavenly," Bowman whispered as he rocked back and forth.

"She looks like it," Ryan replied.

"I assume you've been filled in..." Bowman said after a moment.

Ryan looked over to see the man staring straight ahead.

"There's a cross," he began, "on the road where she...where the accident was. Some kind folks put it up to honor her, I guess." He looked over at Ryan. "I've torn it down four times." He looked out at the street. "They just keep putting it back up. It's funny to me that they want to memorialize a stretch of road as if that had any bearing on her life." He took a deep breath. "Why do we care about where someone died?"

Ryan knew the man had not shared this thought before, but he had no reply.

"Sorry," Bowman finally added. "I can be a rambling old man sometimes."

"It's fine," Ryan replied. "I agree with you, though."

Bowman looked over. "Thank you."

Ryan set the photo on his leg. He and Bowman continued rocking.

"I spent four years wondering where Scott was," Bowman continued after a moment. "He really is a son to me, despite it all. Do you know what he said the first time he met me?"

Ryan shook his head.

Bowman began to laugh. "He stuck out his hand and, I don't know, I guess he was trying to decide between Doctor and Sir, and he said, 'Hello, Socter, I'm Scott.' Socter!"

Ryan smiled as the man laughed.

"I was taken aback," Bowman said, shaking his head. "I said, 'What did you call me?' and then his eyes got real wide. Then I just started laughing! Poor guy had never been so nervous!" His laughter died down. "We had such a good time. It was the happiest I had ever been."

"That's the thing about drinking," he said, slowing his rocking. His voice was deep, yet soft. "When you do it enough, you begin to forget about the good times. You think that this drunken moment is the best you've ever felt, and you forget about the real best moments."

"I apologize," he said after a moment. "I'm sure you don't care to hear about this stuff."

"It's all right," Ryan finally whispered.

The old man sighed deeply. "I've made a lot of mistakes in my life."

Ryan stared straight ahead, letting the words wash over him. Bowman may have spoken the words, but somehow, they hit his core. "So have I..." he finally said.

Bowman looked at him. For a moment, no one spoke. Ryan continued to gaze at the horizon.

"One thing I learned," Bowman finally said, "is that when it's all over, some mistakes live longer than others." He turned to Ryan. "If you plan on fixing any, fix those first."

Ryan looked back.

"And if you can't fix them," Bowman said, eyes widening, "own them." He turned back and lit a cigarette. "I never smoked." He inhaled. "I never smoked until I quit drinking." He blew out the smoke and ashed the cigarette. "You always have your vices, I guess." He turned back to Ryan. "Least this one kills me, too..."

Ryan could not tell if it was a joke. The man was difficult to read. Finally, he leaned forward. "Can I ask you something?"

Bowman took another drag and nodded.

"How do you keep going?"

Bowman turned to him.

Ryan sighed. "I mean no disrespect, but how do you do it?"

"Keep going?"

"Yeah. After the mistakes. It's like the world is against you ..."

Bowman turned back, as if finally understanding the question. Ryan wondered if it had registered correctly.

"The world isn't against me," Bowman said slowly. "I made this world. The decisions and results, it's all things I've done. Keeping going is as simple as learning to live with those things, which isn't simple at all..."

Ryan turned to look at him, though he had no reply.

Bowman ashed the cigarette. "I don't know the right answer, Mr. Ryan. I don't know how to do it. You just do."

They sat quietly for a few moments more.

"That's a good picture," Ryan heard Bo say behind him. He half-turned, wondering how long he had been standing there.

"Remember when I took it?" Bowman asked, staring at the street.

"I do," Bo replied, looking over Ryan's shoulder. "That was a good trip."

Ryan felt awkward sitting in the middle of their exchange, but he did not move. The silence that followed hung on the air, and he could tell there was something on Bo's mind.

"What's wrong?" Ryan finally heard himself ask.

Bo did not reply immediately. Instead, he stood there, contemplating the floor in silence.

"What is it?"

Bo and Bowman exchanged a brief glance. Suddenly, Ryan knew he was the only one in the dark. He felt his pulse quicken.

"There's no delicate way to bring this up," Bo finally said. "But do you have any idea what to do next?"

Ryan shook his head, unsure.

"I mean," Bo continued, "we should probably get a plan together for our next move now that you're doing better physically."

"Next move?"

"Given our current situation," Bo replied. "I think we should figure out where we go from here. Have you given it any thought?"

Ryan looked over to Bowman. "Considering I just woke up a bit ago..."

"I know but think about it. Time is not our friend."

"He needs a doctor," Bowman said.

Ryan looked from Bo to Bowman and then back to Bo.

"He isn't lying." Bo shrugged. "That arm needs more attention than you can get from us."

"Well..." Ryan looked at his arm and tried to lift it. "I guess I need a doctor. I'll probably need a lawyer after that because I won't last ten minutes before the cops come and arrest me..."

"I agree," Bo replied.

"I assume you've already thought this out," Ryan countered, sensing the mood of the porch.

"We have," Bo said as he looked to his father-in-law.

"We?"

Bo sighed. "Ryan, the way I see it, we have two options. Option one: hospital and prison."

"Doesn't seem like a good one."

"Option two, you drive back to Florida and make it home with the money you've got…"

Ryan shrugged. "Seems like a worse one."

"Not necessarily."

"No? And how do you expect me to make it back there? If I don't die along the way, I'd surely get arrested." He looked between the men. "My car doesn't necessarily blend in."

"You make it back by not driving that Jeep."

"Excuse me?"

"Bowman's car has been sitting in the garage, practically untouched. It's red. It's a Toyota. It's as different as could be."

Ryan's confusion showed on his face.

"It'll get you back to Florida unmarked. You will make it back on your own terms. You will make it to a hospital, and you will make it to your family…"

"And then get arrested."

"Likely," Bo replied with a sigh. "But you won't be alone. You can be with your family."

"And my Jeep?"

"Stays here. We'll hide it until you get home."

Ryan sighed.

"It may not seem ideal, Ry, but it's what we have. It's the only way to get you medical help and get you home."

Ryan shook his head. He did not like the conversation, but he could do nothing to control it. It was overwhelming and frustrating.

"Home is the best option," Bo finally said.

"I don't want to go to prison," Ryan replied. He felt tears welling in his eyes.

"I don't want you to, either," Bo replied. "But as much as I don't want that, I can't even remotely think about the alternatives." He looked at Ryan's arm.

Ryan sighed. "There was probably no point in saving me back in South Dakota then."

Bo stared at him. "Jail is better than death."

Ryan took a deep breath and tried to compose himself. "What about you?" he asked Bo over his shoulder.

"What do you mean?"

"I leave here. I make it back, presuming one-armed driving doesn't kill me first. What about you?"

Bo looked over to Bowman, who remained silent.

"I'll lie low for a few days," he finally said. "Then I guess I'll start something new."

"As Scott?"

Bo sighed. "As Scott…as me."

"How long will you lie low?"

"However long it takes for you to get secure. Once you make it, we'll find a way to get the Jeep taken care of, and then we'll move on."

Ryan finally looked up. "Can I think about it?"

"Of course," Bo replied. "Take the night. Decide tomorrow, but we need to act."

Ryan nodded. "Understood."

Bo turned away from the young man and looked across the front yard. Storm clouds were gathering in the distance. They were still far away, but there was no mistaking their intensity. It would not be long before the cold and snow returned.

After a moment, he looked down to Ryan and saw him staring at the floor, deep in thought. He closed his eyes, knowing the weight he had just put on his friend. He hated himself for doing it, but he knew no other option. It was time to make decisions. It was time to act. It was time for resolution.

Bo opened his eyes and checked the clouds once more. He took a deep breath.

There was more than one storm rolling in.

Chapter 24
In Spokane

Ryan woke late the next morning.

The night before, he had wondered how he would ever be able to sleep. Between the pain medicine and the strain of the day's discussion, though, he'd found the ability.

Blinking, he ran his left hand through his long, unkempt hair. Unlike the day before, there was no sunlight shining in the window, hinting to a cold and cloudy day outside.

A thud at the door drew his attention. Bowman stood in the doorway, clearly not expecting Ryan to still be in bed.

"Apologies," Bowman said as he pulled the door shut.

"It's fine." Ryan said through the closed door.

Bowman hesitated before opening the door back up. He then stepped inside. "I...uh..." He paused and extended a towel and a washcloth. "I'm not used to guests."

"It's all right."

"I should have let you sleep."

"I was awake," Ryan countered. "It's fine, I promise."

Bowman nodded as he set the towel down. "Keep the arm dry," he finally said. "But you need a shower."

Ryan sat up slightly.

"I...I," Bowman stammered, "I've got soap and shampoo in the shower."

Ryan nodded.

"May I check your wrappings?"

"Sure," Ryan replied. He pulled off the covers and set his feet on the floor.

Bowman moved to a nearby nightstand and pulled out additional dressings and wraps before softly sitting next to Ryan. Carefully he helped Ryan undo the sling before removing the layers of gauze and dressings. Ryan tried to avoid looking down.

"A lot of swelling," Bowman breathed. "Stiches are holding well for now." He moved another part of the wrappings. "Maybe some minor infections, but nothing egregious for now."

Ryan nodded.

"For now," he repeated, "being the key phrase." He began wrapping the arm with fresh bandages and gauze. "You need proper medicines. Things I don't have. If this gets infected further, it could turn ugly."

Ryan nodded again. Bowman continued to wrap. There was silence for a moment.

"I didn't kill my daughter," Bowman finally said, still looking down at his work. "I didn't kill her."

Ryan swallowed the growing lump in his throat but said nothing.

Bowman closed his eyes before he opened them once more. "The road was wet. She was tired and emotional. She had never driven it before." He paused, as though saying the words as they entered his mind. "I didn't kill my daughter. Her death was the result of a thousand things that went wrong. I know that." He finally finished the wrappings and looked at Ryan. "But I'm not innocent. I made a mistake that could have prevented it. I'm as much to blame."

Ryan met his gaze.

"You asked how I keep going," Bowman said. "I lied when I said, 'You just do.'" He paused once more, welling with emotion. "You don't keep going. You don't move on. You die, just like they do."

The weight of his words hit Ryan hard.

"The world is against you. It was against her. And it killed her. It killed me, too. You can't move on from that." He paused. "The truth is that you learn to live with not going on. You learn to live with the fact that you won't be okay. You learn to live with a piece of you dying every time you see her picture or hear her name. You do it because there is nothing else to do. You don't get a choice." Tears streamed from his eyes as he spoke. He turned slightly from Ryan.

Ryan's pity for the man was profound. Try as he might, words would not come, but he was struck by Bowman's strength.

Bowman wiped his eyes and looked down at the floor. "This world is as cruel as it is beautiful," he said. "But so is everything else." He turned to face the young man. "Nothing lasts," he added. "Nothing goes on forever. So, learn to love the beauty, and learn how to live with not being okay."

He stood up with a weak smile. Seconds later, he walked out of the bedroom and down the hall, leaving a young man struggling to make sense of the words.

***

He stepped out of the shower sometime later that morning. He struggled to wrap the towel around himself one handed, but after he achieved the minor goal, he brushed his hand across the mirror.

His face was concealed beneath a mat of stubble and patches of facial hair. This helped to hide the numerous cuts and bruises across his face that would have normally stood out. His normally piercing eyes were sullen and reserved, as if they were coals in a fireplace. His lips were cracked, and his skin was dry. The more he looked, the more he barely recognized himself.

Before long, he walked gingerly down the stairs and found himself alone. Stepping into the kitchen, he found a pitcher of orange juice and a plate of toast on the table. Taking care to be quiet, he grabbed a piece of toast and poured a glass of juice. He polished them off quickly and picked up the pitcher.

A knock from behind the door caused him to jump, but he finished pouring before investigating the noise. Opening the door, he found himself in a small two-car garage with a red Toyota in one bay and his black Jeep in the second.

He blinked, unsure of how to feel.

"Still got some bloodstains," he heard Bo say from behind the Toyota, "but I was able to get a few cleaned out." He stepped out and stared toward the Jeep.

"I'm sure it was tough." Ryan replied.

"You'll also be sad to know that I also had to throw away your USF jacket. I don't think their school colors are red, although people around here probably wouldn't know."

"It's fine," Ryan said with a sigh. "I probably shouldn't have spent that money anyway, given our situation." He sipped the juice and examined the Jeep's scratched body and crumpled rear bumper. "She looks like hell."

"She looked like hell before I ever saw her," Bo said with a wily smile.

Ryan returned the smirk.

"Still runs," Bo continued as he walked around the red car. "Somehow."

"That pretty much sums up her life," Ryan replied.

Bo chuckled. For a moment, neither spoke.

"I never asked," Bo finally said. "Was she your first car?" He paused. "I was going to make that one of my questions on the trip, but some other question was always more pressing."

"Missed your chance, then," Ryan replied as he took another sip.

"Damn."

"I know—tough break."

"In my defense, I answered all your questions. You were just playing dead in the backseat."

"Oh, that's it?"

"Exactly."

"Well, given that you were the reason I was there, I'd say that's half your fault."

Bo smiled. "There's my thanks for saving your life."

"I already thanked you," Ryan joked. "I can't help it if you got screwed out of the game."

Bo did not have an immediate response. Instead, he flashed a sarcastic smile and returned to the back of the Toyota. He crouched down to check one of the tires.

"You know, I hated that game," Ryan finally said. He joined Bo behind the car.

"Oh, really? I couldn't tell." Bo looked at the tire gauge in his hand. "Except, you know, always."

Ryan grinned. "Was it that evident?"

"Only when you were awake," Bo chided. "For the record, I wasn't a big fan, either."

"You created it!"

"I did," he said as he screwed on the valve cap. "But once we made it past the first day, I regretted creating it."

"Why's that?"

"Same reason you hated it," Bo replied. "I didn't want to answer those questions." He stood and wiped his hands on a rag. "I knew you'd eventually ask something I couldn't lie about."

"Then why'd you continue to play?"

Bo shrugged. "You could ask why about a lot of things, I guess."

Ryan stood in silence for a moment.

"You going to answer the car question?" Bo finally asked, bringing him back to reality.

"Yes, it was my first car. It has been my only one."

Bo moved on to another tire. "It seems like a good car."

Ryan turned his attention back to the Jeep. "It has been." He returned his gaze back toward Bo and the red Toyota. "I assume this will be my new ride?"

Bo stood up and wiped his hands. "I want to ask one more question."

Ryan felt the air catch once more, and he could tell this question would be more serious.

"Why did you pick me up?"

Ryan cocked his head, not understanding the question.

"Back in Florida," Bo replied. "Why did you pick me up?"

"Why did I pick you up?"

"Ry, you're a smart kid," Bo began, leaning on the car as he made his point. "You had every opportunity to back out, and you didn't. Why? Why did you pick me up?"

"Why does it matter?" Ryan finally replied.

"I don't know. But it does. It matters to me. It's been on my mind since we left."

Bo watched Ryan stare off into space as he pondered the question. The moment seemed to tick by into eternity.

"Why?" Bo repeated after a moment.

Ryan sighed. "I don't know," he began, trying to find something deeper than what he was thinking. "I don't know…" He paused again. "Why'd you get in?"

Bo turned his head as though not hearing the question.

"What?"

"Why'd you get in?" Ryan repeated.

Bo stared at him, still puzzled. "I don't know," he finally said.

Ryan looked up to meet his gaze, "I think that's all right."

A smile crept across Bo's face.

Ryan returned the smile.

"I think you're right," Bo finally said. He returned to the car to screw on the final valve cap.

Ryan turned and made for the door, but before he reached it, Bo called out.

"You'll need this."

Ryan half-turned to see Bo rise and toss something his way. Holding his glass, the object bounced off Ryan's immobile arm and fell to the ground.

"Shit," Bo sighed, "I forgot about your arm."

Ryan managed a smile as he set his glass down before bending to pick up the object. As he stood back up, he saw the object was a passport, complete with a card inside. Looking at the card, he saw that it was a driver's license from more than six years ago belonging to a much younger Scott Lashon.

"What's this?" He asked as he turned to Bo.

"Option three."

"Option three?"

Bo nodded. "No one has seen Scott Lashon in five years. He could look like anyone— even you."

"And?" Ryan began.

"Option three is to go north."

"North?"

"Canada," Bo replied. "You'll take this car. You cross the border as Scott Lashon." He paused. "As me. You'll cross it and leave here behind. You'll find a doctor. You'll find a job. You'll have a clean slate."

Ryan felt a lump rise in his throat. He was sure he was not hearing properly.

"You'll avoid prison for now," Bo continued. "But you'll lose everything else. Family, friends, everything."

Ryan shook his head. The entire notion was ridiculous.

"It's by far the most drastic," Bo replied. "Which is why we—" He looked down at the car. "Which is why I didn't say it the first time."

Ryan stared at the passport and driver's license. "What changed?" he asked finally.

Bo leaned on the car again. He chose his words carefully. "Five years ago, I had the same choices that you do. I tried returning home. I tried making it work. In the end, I chose leaving it all. I can't deny you that choice."

"I don't understand…"

Bo took a step toward Ryan. "It's a second chance," he whispered. "It's your freedom."

"And then what?" Ryan replied, still reeling at the notion.

"That part is up to you." Bo moved back to the car and continued examining it, though Ryan could not tell exactly what he was doing. "The choice is yours, but now you have options."

Ryan was rooted where he stood. His mind was racing with thoughts and feelings, yet he said nothing. After a minute, he walked out of the garage, back through the kitchen, and into the living room. He did not know what had brought him to this room, but he knew he could not be in the garage any longer.

It was a crazy notion—no doubt. It was crazy to run away, let alone flee the only country he had ever known. But what part of this entire journey hadn't been crazy? It was all senseless. It was all irrational. It was all…

Mel.

He exhaled deeply, shaking the memory from his head. He could not think of her at a time like this. He needed sense and reason.

He closed his eyes, and his mind immediately went to the last night with her. He pictured her standing in front of his car, illuminated only by the headlights. He pictured her standing there, hesitating between him in the driver's seat and the passenger seat. He pictured that soft country song on the radio. It was all he could do not to break down.

He opened his eyes. He swallowed and took a deep breath, tamping down her memory. Looking up, he saw the television in the corner of the living room. On top of it was the picture from the day before, one of a much younger Bo and an even younger Emily.

Ryan stared at the photo for what seemed an eternity. They were so content. They were so in love. There was no pain, no fear. It was as if the world had stopped for that moment, and they were the only things that mattered. It was a beautiful picture, and its image captivated him for reasons he did not understand.

Tears welled in his eyes as he gazed at the image, but his internal conflict began to wane. He had made his decision the moment Bo mentioned it.

He knew what he wanted to do.

Bo finished up with the Toyota and softly closed the hood. Wiping his hands, he turned and lifted the garage door to reveal a cold and cloudy December day. He turned back toward the house. His eyes grew wide as he saw Ryan standing in the doorway.

"Option three," Ryan said.

Bo nodded. "I thought you would."

***

The next few hours flew by. In a matter of minutes, he went from standing in that doorway to packing a bag with clothes and toiletries he had been missing for over a week. Both Bo and Bowman were there intermittently, offering support and lending hands to help with the packing. It was all unexpectedly lighthearted, but somehow, among the socks and old-man shirts that found their way into his bag, Ryan kept coming back to a thought that he couldn't quite articulate: how does one pack for eternity?

He followed Bowman into the kitchen, where a collection of foods and goods was packed into a trash bag. It was enough food to last one man a month, and as Ryan entered the garage, he knew he had more possessions now than he'd ever had before.

The last item, however, was the most surprising. As he struggled to fill the car with his one arm, Bo approached with an item wrapped in cloth. Ryan almost jumped upon seeing the .38 special gun he had spied days earlier in the hotel parking lot.

"I was never trying to worry you," Bo whispered as he handed it over. "But at one point in time, this gun felt like the only thing left."

"Why are you giving it to me?" Ryan asked worriedly.

"I don't need it," Bo replied. "Not anymore. You, however, will be on your own and miles away."

"I've never fired a gun…"

"And hopefully you never will. But you have it if you need it."

Ryan stared at it intently.

"Just hide it at the border," Bo said with a smile.

In all, there was no structure to the events of that day, and no rhyme or reason to the timing of his leaving. It was simply determined by what was logical once his decision was made. Ryan knew the roller coaster of packing and leaving would have followed whatever choice he'd made, but it did not stop it from feeling awkward and difficult.

"Once you cross," Bowman reminded him, "you need to head directly to Creston. It's only a few miles past the border. There's a hospital there that will get your arm addressed."

Ryan nodded. He had heard the plan once before.

"I hope that jacket is enough for you," Bowman said. "I'm sorry we had to throw away your other clothes." He tugged on the jacket as it lay draped over Ryan's right shoulder.

"This is more than enough," Ryan said appreciatively. "You've done more than enough."

Bowman brushed aside the words. "It was a pleasure," he said as he stuck out his hand and shook Ryan's. At that moment, he seemed even older and frailer, as if the past days had made him wearier than anyone else.

"Thank you," Ryan said, knowing there was no way he could ever thank the man.

"Thank you," Bowman replied. He glanced at Bo, who leaned against the garage door frame. He let go of Ryan's hand and stepped back into the house, leaving them alone.

"Take care of her," Ryan said, nodding to his Jeep in the darkened and closed bay of the garage.

"Of course," Bo replied with a smile. There was no joking. There was no wit. He was as serious as Ryan had ever seen him.

Ryan opened the driver's door of the Toyota carefully. He slid off his new jacket and set it in the passenger seat.

"You sure you don't want this one, too?" Bo asked, pointing into the Jeep's backseat. Ryan peered in and saw the sweatshirt he had carried since Florida. The one that was his but wasn't anymore. The one with all the memories.

"No. I'm good leaving that one."

Bo nodded and turned away from the Jeep. "You'll call once you're settled?"

"You'll be the first," Ryan replied. "Then you get to be you again."

Bo sighed. "I won't know what to do…so many jobs to choose from."

Ryan leaned against the open door. "McDonald's, perhaps?"

"Always a good start," Bo said with a smile.

"I wouldn't work at Gibson's," Ryan said. "I hear they have employee issues."

"Really? I heard they got rid of all those issues…"

Ryan smiled, knowing he had set himself up for the joke. He was glad for the humor.

"You think you'll stay here?" Ryan finally asked.

"Here?"

"Spokane…"

As Bo considered the question, Ryan realized that he had not begun to process the thought of returning to the world. He seemed timid and leery, and Ryan regretted his asking.

"You'll keep me posted," he finally replied.

Bo smiled as he returned to the present. "I'll miss you, Ry."

"You aren't going to hug me, are you?" he asked dubiously.

"Of course," Bo replied, doing just that.

For a second, Ryan pretended to cringe. Then he returned the hug. "I'm glad you don't smell anymore," he finally said.

Bo chuckled. "I never smelled."

"Yes, you did."

"All right, fine. But I didn't smell that bad."

"Whatever," Ryan countered.

"You're making this goodbye so much easier."

"Not even going to cry?" Ryan retorted, finally letting go with his one good arm.

"Not anymore." Bo stepped away.

"I think I see a tear," Ryan teased, leaning on the Toyota's door.

"Get out of here."

"Need a tissue?"

"I hope a bear eats you."

"That's not funny," Ryan replied. "There are more bears than people up there."

"Fine," Bo replied. "I hope a person eats you. Better?"

The men looked at each other in silence. The time had finally come.

Ryan opened the door, knowing he could delay no longer. He reached inside and started the engine, albeit rather slowly.

"Good luck out there," Bo finally said, just loud enough to be heard.

"Same to you."

Bo smiled as Ryan got into the vehicle. He waved and then quickly brushed his eye. Ryan shut the door and shifted the car into reverse. It took only seconds, but it was the longest part of the day.

Bo stood in the garage doorway as Ryan carefully backed the car into the street. He waved again.

Ryan returned the wave. He blinked away tears and reached over to shift the car into drive. Seconds later, he was gone, back onto the road and headed away from Spokane.

He never looked back, though he wanted to more than once. There was no point to it, he knew. What was done was done. He was already gone.

There was no going back now.

Chapter 25
130 Miles from Spokane

The snow was beginning to intensify.

Ryan dared not look away from the road. Occasionally, he spied headlights behind him in the distance. Each time, he held his breath, waiting for the flash of red and blue, or the flicker of high beams, as they grew closer. Each time, the vehicle passed him.

He was not sure where the road ultimately led, but the occasional sign indicating the Canadian border ahead led him to believe he was traveling on the correct path. In the end, it did not really matter which path he chose—north was north, and that was where he needed to go.

His arm was beginning to hurt once more. Every so often, he would attempt to move it, and every time he did the pain intensified. Driving with one arm was proving more difficult than he had envisioned.

The light had faded in the west long ago, and now it was but a distant memory. He continued driving with the radio low, wiper blades screeching as they brushed away the snow. The drive had been quick but deep down, he'd hoped it would take longer.

Canada—Five Miles.

The sign was a beacon. Eyes blinking in the darkness, he looked down at the car's clock, which read a quarter past nine. It had been a long day.

It had been a long week.

It was crazy to do what he was doing, he thought. Canada. It seemed like a distant planet, not a country he was about to enter. It was so close and yet so foreign. It was remote and isolated. It held his freedom, but it was not the thing he wanted most of all. It was not home.

Home. He'd once thought that home was a house in Florida. Home was also a feeling of love and understanding. Now? He had no home. He had no place he felt that feeling…

Yet with her…

He shook his head. Not again. Not now. He would not think of her again.

He felt his heart rate increase. The passport sat face up on the passenger seat. It was his future; one he could not run from.

His palms grew sweaty. His mind began to race. What if he was caught? What if he made it? What if he broke down somewhere over the border? What if he couldn't find a life? What if he could? There was no way this was going to work.

His chest began to heave under the weight of his worries. A yellow light flashed ahead, undoubtedly letting him know that it was time to slow. It was time to leave the States.

He closed his eyes briefly, but the anguish did not leave. His heart was galloping. The music on the radio was muted by the sounds of his pulse in his ears. Sweat dampened his back and brow, even in the cold December air. He swallowed hard, over and over. His hands shook with anxiety.

Border Ahead.

His breathing became audible. His body shook with fear. He was terrified. He was a wreck. He was all these things, but deep down, he knew he was going to do it. He was going to make it across. The weight of his worries would not keep him from what he knew he needed to do. He was going to make it. He had to make it.

The border came into sight.

He pulled off the road before he knew what he was doing. Before he could even grasp the decision, the Toyota came to a stop amid a cloud of gravel dust in the vacant lot of a long-abandoned store.

He sat for a moment, hands still shaking as the panic attack began to subside. Gasping for air, he opened the car door and stepped out. Without a coat, he shivered in the cold air, but he barely noticed. Leaving the door open, he stood with a hand on his knees, breathing deeply and trying to calm himself.

He closed his eyes and felt his heartrate begin to slow. He stopped sweating. His legs and arms became steadier. Before long, he regained focus.

As he stood, a light to his right caught his eye.

Blinking the panic from his eyes, he glimpsed the Canadian border a quarter mile ahead. It looked calm and desolate in the snow that fell. This was not what caught his attention, though. At the edge of the gravel lot, only twenty feet from his current position, Ryan saw something he had not seen in several days—a payphone.

He approached it cautiously, nervously looking around the perimeter as though it were a trap. His nervousness returned, but this was different in nature. It was not fear. It was not panic.

He fumbled in his pocket for some change, half-surprised that he found two quarters in his jeans. He lifted the receiver as though in a trance and pressed it to his ear. He dialed ten digits, knowing the order by heart. It was a familiar number—one he was long overdue in calling. Perhaps this was divine intervention. Perhaps he was meant to see this phone.

If he was going to go away, he thought, then it made perfect sense to make one last call.

"Hello?"

"Mom?" Ryan whispered.

There was a pause. Ryan stared at the phone, wondering if it was going to melt away in his hand.

"Ryan?" The voice broke him into a million pieces.

Ryan exhaled. She remembered him.

"Hi, Mom…" His voice trailed off, and for the first time, he did not know what to say. He paused, knowing he was hearing her tears through the phone. He stumbled as he tried to think of what to say. It would not come.

"I'm sorry…"

"Are…" she said her between sniffles, "are you okay?"

Tears trickled down his face. He had no idea what his mother's voice would do to him. "Yeah."

"You're…safe?"

He hung his head. "Yeah."

There was another pause. He could hear her crying softly.

"Where…" she trailed off.

He gritted his teeth. "I'm…fine. I'm…safe."

She tried to speak once more. "I'm…sorry…"

His heart broke. "No, Mom. You have nothing to be sorry for."

"I'm…sorry…"

"I'm sorry," he sobbed. "I'm sorry." There was no use in holding his feelings in. His tears had broken the dam. Together they cried openly.

He felt his body shake in remorse. No words would come. He could do nothing to control the feeling.

"I tried…" she finally said. "I tried…understanding…"

"I…know…" he replied.

"I couldn't…"

"I know."

He could feel her trying to reel in her emotions. He could feel her trying to understand once more.

"Help me, Ryan…"

He wiped his face. He kept his gaze on the snow-covered ground, knowing the answers were not easy.

"Where did you go?" she asked finally.

Ryan closed his eyes. "I had to leave…"

The voice could not conceal the hurt. "Why?"

"I don't know…"

"You do," she whispered. "You have to."

In the pause that followed, he heard her regain her composure.

"I know about Gibson's. I know about Rebecca."

He kept his eyes closed, growing tense at her words.

"What I don't know…" she continued softly, "is you…"

Tears fell once more.

"I don't know you…" Intentional or not, the words cut like a blade.

He sighed. "I don't know, either."

"Why did you leave? Why are you still gone?"

He shook his head. "I don't know."

"I don't know how to help."

He opened his eyes and allowed the cold to sting them. "I don't know if you can."

"I want to," she replied. "I want you home."

The statement hit him straight in the gut. It was all he wanted to hear. It was simple and so easy. The pause that followed extended longer than he expected. He allowed the pain to wash over him, and he dared not speak until he had dried his tears.

"I…" he finally exhaled. "I need to ask you something."

"What is it?"

He blinked back more tears. "Why?" he asked. "Why did you change your job wish?"

"What?"

He spoke slowly once more. "Your report cards back in school…your job wish…you changed it."

"I don't understand."

"For eleven grades," he replied softly, "you…you wanted to be a model. You wanted it. You changed your last one to teacher."

"That was in high school…many years ago."

"Why did you want to become a teacher?"

"I don't understand…"

"Why did you change it?"

He waited, not speaking. He needed the answer.

"I didn't write 'teacher.'"

"I saw it…"

"I didn't write it. My teacher did."

"Why?"

"Because I left it blank."

Ryan did not speak.

"I left it blank," she repeated.

"You didn't want to be a model," Ryan whispered, somehow sensing the answer he sought.

"Everyone said I'd be a perfect model. I believed them, so I picked it."

"You didn't want it."

"I didn't want anything," she replied. "I never answered the question on my own."

"Why?"

"Because that wasn't my calling," she answered softly. "I wasn't meant for those things."

"What were you…?" His voice trailed off. His eyes closed.

"You."

The word was heavier than the earth itself. Tears streamed down his face.

"You are the most important thing in this world," she continued. "You, your father, our family. It is all I was meant for." He could hear her exhale. "I didn't know what I wanted until I met your father—until I saw you." She paused once more. "Being your mother was never on that list of jobs."

He continued weeping openly.

"Help me understand, Ryan," she whispered. "Help me."

"I don't know… I feel…" He gasped as he looked up. "like I'm just a disappointment. I feel like I'm failing." He took a deep breath. "I'm not who you wanted."

He heard her sniff, and he knew she was crying again.

"Ryan…"

"I'm so lost." He blinked and turned his gaze back toward the phone.

His mother sat silent; he could feel her listening to him.

"I'm sorry," he said. "I've messed it all up."

She took a deep breath. "Never…"

"What?"

"You…you are always what I wanted." Her voice cracked. "You are my son." She broke once more. "You are my love."

Ryan loosened his grip on the phone.

"There…" He heard her choke back tears. "You are never a disappointment. There is nothing you can do to fail me." She breathed once more. "I'm so sorry that you think differently…"

He took a deep breath. His words caused more pain than he ever had planned.

"I'm sorry—" he repeated once more.

"No," she replied. "I'm sorry."

Ryan did not reply.

"I'm sorry," she repeated. Her words were deep and purposeful. He knew that she meant every syllable. "I understand now…"

"What?"

"I…understand."

He closed his eyes. It was all he had ever hoped to hear.

"I understand," she repeated, this time in whispers. "I understand…"

Ryan looked up. Although the snow was falling harder, he saw the border clearly. It was like a beacon now, calling him onward.

"I don't know what to do…" he finally said, saying what he felt inside.

There was silence, and he knew she was steeling herself.

"Yes, you do."

He said nothing.

"You do." She exhaled. "You always do."

Ryan shook his head. "Not this time."

"You'll figure it out," she said. "You'll make it right. You'll understand."

"How do you know?"

After a long pause, she spoke. "You're safe. And you made it this far."

He hung there for a moment, letting her words sink in. Perhaps he would understand. Perhaps he would make it right. Yet right now, he knew nothing of it. He was as lost as before.

Then, he heard it.

It was soft at first, almost dreamlike. In the silence of the phone, he heard the faint murmurings. He continued listening as it build, turning from a faint whisper to a low hum before he finally turned away from the payphone.

The car door to the Toyota sat fully ajar while the engine was still running and the lights still shining.

He dropped the phone and walked toward the car. The sound grew louder. He could hear it clearly. He walked slowly, allowing the melody and words to fill his brain. It was something he now knew he had heard before. It was a recollection from a long-ago era.

He moved closer and closer, and the radio's music grew louder and louder.

He closed his eyes, allowing it to consume him. Suddenly, he was no longer in a gravel lot. He was no longer at the Canadian border.

He was in his car. He was in the passenger seat. He was looking at her as she kept her eyes on the road ahead. He was admiring her beauty. He was idolizing her aura. She was everything he'd ever needed. She was next to him. She was in front of him. She was standing in the headlights of the Jeep as the snow fell around her. He never wanted her to move. She was all around. She had never left. That moment was everything he'd ever wanted. It all came back to him though it had never left. The song played on and on.

He took a deep breath and hurried back to the phone that dangled from the hook.

"I love you, Mom," he said.

"I love you, too," she replied, confusion in her voice. "You're okay?"

Ryan closed his eyes and opened them once more. There were headlights on the horizon coming from the north.

"Yeah," he replied with urgency. "I'll be okay." He considered his words carefully. "I promise."

Ryan hung up the phone and hastened back to the Toyota. He slammed the door and buckled his safety belt, no longer wincing under the pain of his arm. Shifting the car into drive, he did a U-turn in the gravel lot before turning back onto the road.

He was no longer heading north.

In Florida, Ryan's mother hung up the phone and looked at the wall clock. It was well past midnight. On the table next to the house phone, her cell phone lit up. She wiped her face and picked it up.

"Mrs. Collins? Officer Meadows here. Payphone in Idaho. Near the Canadian border. I have an officer en route."

"He's already gone," she whispered. "He already left."

"The officer will be arriving shortly…"

"It's no use," she replied. "He's long gone now."

"Do you know where?" the officer inquired.

She considered the question for a moment and then, for the first time, smiled faintly. "No," she replied, "but he'll be all right."

Ryan felt sweat on his brow as his heartbeat increased. He kept his foot on the gas and continued south on a path he had never traveled before. Emotions clouded his mind, but somehow, he saw more clearly than ever before.

The song played over and over in his head. He knew his destination. He knew his purpose. He knew exactly what he had to do.

Chapter 26
1,081 Miles from Spokane

It was another cold winter day in Shannon.

Despite the weather, the atmosphere in the diner was hectic and chaotic. It seemed that most of the town was inside. It may have been the holiday season, but business was always frenetic, especially on the weekends.

Behind the counter, the phone rang. A young waitress hurried to answer it, taking care to avoid a busboy in her way.

"Hello?"

"Melanie, please."

"Okay." She put the phone to her shoulder and peered out among the patrons at the counter and in the booths. She finally spotted Melanie in the corner of the restaurant.

"Mel!" she yelled. "Phone."

Melanie nodded and made her way around the tables and behind the counter. She set her tray down as she accepted the phone.

"Hello?"

"Hi…" Ryan whispered on the other end.

"Hi?"

He took a deep breath. "It's me."

Silence.

"I—" Ryan began, struggling for words he had rehearsed all night. "I need to apologize."

Click.

Mel hung up the phone and stepped away. The phone rang again. Agitated, she sighed before returning to it and answering.

"Hello?" she asked, annoyed.

"Please don't do that," Ryan replied softly.

"What do you want?" she asked dangerously.

"I want—" He took another breath. "I want to apologize."

"For what?"

"Come on, Mel. You know…"

"I know," she replied. "I know. But do you?"

There was silence.

"That's what I thought."

"I lied to you," he replied. "I lied to you, and I broke a promise." He paused. "I told you that I wouldn't leave. I told you that I'd stay…and I didn't."

She did not answer.

"I never wanted to hurt you…"

She turned from the counter and toward the wall in an effort to remain as private as possible. "You have no idea," she finally said. "You didn't just lie. You didn't just break a promise. You lied. And you kept lying. And you knew you were lying. You made promises you knew you could never keep." She sighed. "You knew it, and you did it anyway."

His voice became small. "I did."

"I know you did."

"I had no idea how to tell you."

"You didn't even try…"

He was whispering again. "I know…"

"I appreciate this attempt at an apology," she said mockingly. "But I'm going to hang up now."

"No," he replied louder.

"Excuse me?"

"Don't hang up again."

"Why?"

"Because…if you don't talk to me on the phone, I'm going to have to come in there."

Mel's breath caught in her throat. She turned and looked through the windows facing the parking lot.

"Southwest corner. Randall's truck…"

She turned to the left and saw the pickup partly hidden from view. Squinting, she made out Randall in the driver's seat and a passenger wearing a ball cap sitting beside him.

The passenger raised his hand slightly.

"Hi," Ryan said through the phone.

"Son of a bi—" she whispered.

"It's nice to see you, too."

"You wouldn't come in here," she said. "You know who's in here." Her eyes darted from the truck to a booth where a bandaged Sheriff Ransom and two other city cops dined on breakfast halfway between the far wall and the main door. Truly, the entire town seemed to be in the diner.

"I do." Ryan sighed. "Which is why I'd rather have this talk over the phone…"

"Well, that's too bad."

"Please, Mel," he replied. "You hang up, and I'll have no other choice."

"Sure, you do," she countered. "You can just lie."

Ryan ignored the comment. "I will."

She laughed mockingly, drowning out the rest of his words. "Not even you are that stupid."

He took a deep breath. "I think you underestimate my level of stupidity…"

"Goodbye," she replied.

Click.

It was cold in the truck. Ryan exhaled as he lowered the phone from his ear. He handed it over to Randall, who looked at him, perplexed.

"Well." Ryan shrugged. "I guess we figured it was going to go like that…."

Randall stared at the young man. "I'm sorry it didn't work out," he drawled, looking at the young man gathering his courage beside him.

"Yeah," Ryan replied. "Me, too."

He opened the passenger door.

"Where are you going?"

Ryan stepped out and turned back toward the driver. He seemed confused by the question. "I'm going in there."

"What?"

"Yeah," Ryan replied. "I told her I would."

"And?" Randall countered. "So what?"

"She has to hear what I need to say."

"No, she doesn't," Randall argued. "She clearly doesn't want to."

"Maybe not, but I need her to hear."

"I think she's pretty set."

"So am I." He adjusted his ball cap with his left hand, keeping his right arm steady near his chest. He no longer wore his sling, knowing the attention it would bring.

"Ryan," Randall began, "I can't watch you go in there."

"I know," Ryan replied. "That's why you're going to drive out of here, just like we talked…"

"That cop," Randall pleaded. "He'll kill you."

Ryan ignored the comment. "You'll mail that letter?"

"He'll see you, and he'll kill you."

"You'll mail the letter?"

"Ryan—"

"Randall!" Ryan yelled, silencing the old man. For a moment, neither spoke. "You agreed to help."

Randall nodded sheepishly.

"You knew what this was," Ryan continued. "You knew how this could end. Now I need to know, will you mail that letter?"

Randall stared at his steering wheel. He nodded.

"Good. Right away?"

He nodded.

"And the car?"

"Right away…" Randall replied.

"Thank you," Ryan said softly, looking at the man with affection. "I appreciate all you've done…"

He shut the door to the truck.

"It doesn't have to be like this," Randall said through the open window.

Ryan stopped in his tracks and stepped back to the window. "What?"

"It doesn't have to be like this…"

Ryan stuck his head in. "No," he replied, "It doesn't."

"There are a million other options," Randall continued. "There are a million other choices."

Ryan looked down at the seat of the truck, then back to the driver. "I'm sure there are…"

"You're sure it's the right one?"

Ryan exhaled with a smile. "Not at all," he replied. "But it's my choice." He paused as he looked back at the diner. "And I can live with that."

The pickup vanished in a cloud of dust as Ryan lowered the ball cap as far down as it would go on his forehead. Taking a deep breath, he looked to the left and then the right as he crossed the cold parking lot. He shivered in the brutal wind, and his arm throbbed under the cold. Keeping it tucked against his chest, he attempted to ignore it as he had for the past hours.

As he approached the door, a young family stumbled out, and he held the door for them. As they passed, he peered inside the restaurant. Thus far, no one had paid him any attention, save for the girl behind the counter who stared at him with horrid anticipation.

Ryan did not meet her gaze as he stepped inside, suddenly consumed by the din of the full restaurant. He swallowed the lump in his throat as he finally looked up. He turned away once more and casually walked to the counter, taking a seat among three open stools directly in front of her.

"You are so fucking stupid," she muttered under her breath. He could feel the nervousness in her voice.

"If this is where it has to happen," he replied, staring up toward her, "then this is where it has to happen."

Her hands shook as she grabbed a coffee mug and filled it in front of him, taking care to mask his appearance. He could sense her eyes darting toward the left corner, where the officers sat.

"You need to leave," she whispered.

"I'm not leaving."

"Why the hell not?"

"Because I'm here to talk to you."

"We already talked."

"No," Ryan replied, ignoring the coffee. "We didn't."

She stared at him in contempt. "Fine," she said, darting another look at Ransom. "Talk."

Ryan moved forward on his seat and adjusted his hat again. All the while, he continued looking at her, once again feeling completely overwhelmed.

"Talk," she urged once more.

"You're right," he began, meeting her gaze. "I lied to you, and I broke my promise. And you're right; I knew what I was doing when I was doing it."

"We've been through this…"

"I wanted to make it happen," he ignored her comment.

"What?"

"I made the promise, and I said what I said." He sighed. "I wanted it to happen. I thought it could happen. I was stupid, I know, but it changes nothing. Everything else I ever said to you about how I felt was true. Everything."

She leaned back against the wall. She said nothing.

"You are amazing—"

"Stop it."

"No." He was not backing down. "You need to know."

Her jaw tightened, but she remained quiet.

"I told you that I've only known you for three days, and I said that those three days were the best three days I've had in a long time. That's all true. Every word of it." He looked down at his mug as he collected his thoughts. "You talked about us 'finding something to make us stop walking,'" he continued, "but I found something better; I found something that made me turn around and head back. And that something is you. You astound me in ways I have never known, and I find myself completely in awe of you." He looked up and saw her eyes wide before he looked back down. "I said what I said, and I did what I did, and I ruined it all. I don't deserve forgiveness, and I don't deserve you. I know that, and I understand that." He met her eyes once more. "The main thing, though…the main thing I want you to know is that you have changed my life. I mean that. I mean every word. And when I told you that I would stay, that I'd never leave, I wanted that more than anything else."

"Stop," she finally said. "Stop talking." Her tone had changed.

He exhaled deeply.

They sat in silence and her eyes darted to the space behind him.

"Turn around," said a deep voice.

Ryan sat in his chair, unmoving.

"I said, 'turn around.'"

Ryan looked up to Mel and knew who was behind him. He gave her a faint smile and nodded slightly.

Slowly, he stood and turned around. As he did, he saw Ransom's broken and bruised face some fifteen feet away. His hand was at his side.

"Stupid son of a bitch," Ransom muttered. Behind him, the other two officers got up from their seats.

Ryan said nothing. Ransom took a step forward. As he did, Ryan's mobile hand fell to his sides, near his pockets.

Instantly, Ransom pulled his gun. "*Hands in the air!*" he yelled.

All commotion stopped. The restaurant was silent. Ryan closed his eyes but did not move his hands.

"*Hands in the air!*" Ransom yelled. The other two officers were at his side, though neither unholstered their guns.

Ryan did not move.

The second officer muttered something to Ransom, though Ryan did not hear the words.

"Shut up, Krager," Ransom muttered out of the side of his mouth. Ryan could see his gun hand shaking with rage.

"There are civilians…" Krager repeated, louder.

"I said shut up," Ransom replied.

"*Put the gun down!*" came a roar from the kitchen. From the corner of his eye, Ryan saw Mel's father emerge with a shotgun in hand. It was aimed directly at Ransom.

"Willis!" Krager yelled. "What the hell?"

Mel's father held the gun steady. "He's aiming at my daughter."

"I'm aiming at the boy, you stupid ass!"

"And my daughter's behind him!"

"What a coincidence," Ransom snarled.

The third officer pulled his gun and aimed it at Mr. Willis.

"Jesus Christ, Reeves!" Krager exclaimed.

"*Put your goddamn gun down!*" Ransom roared.

"You first, asshole."

Ryan stood in silence. Despite the standoff around him and his throbbing arm, he felt surprisingly at peace. He closed his eyes but did not move his hands from near his waistband. In his mind, he played through the options.

"*You want to go to jail, Willis?*" Ransom shouted at Mel's father, though his eyes stayed on Ryan.

"*Shut up and drop your gun!*" Mr. Willis roared back.

Krager stepped forward slightly. "*Everyone calm down!* Willis, put the damn gun down."

"Not until that asshole does!"

"For God's sake, Ransom," Krager pleaded.

"Fuck you!" Ransom yelled. "I'm here for that prick." He motioned toward Ryan.

Krager turned to Reeves but knew it would do no good. Shaking his head, he approached Ryan.

"Ryan? Is it Ryan?" Krager asked.

Ryan did not move.

"Ryan, I need you to turn around," Krager said, stepping in front of Ransom's gun.

"*What the hell are you doing?*" Ransom screamed.

"*Ending this fucking mess!*" Krager focused on Ryan once more and became calm. "Ryan, turn around, please. Sit on the barstool."

Ryan stared into the officer's eyes. His hand remained firm at his waist.

"Ryan," Krager said, "there's a lot of ways this can end, but only one that's good. Turn around. Sit. Please."

He saw the officer look down to his hand. Ryan took a deep breath. He knew the man was speaking truthfully. There was a kindness in his voice, and he appreciated the compassion. It was simple, and it was peaceful. *Turn around. Sit.* He had already done enough. Of all the choices he had, this was the easiest to do. He nodded to the officer.

"Okay," he finally said. He turned around and sat down. Blinking his eyes, he finally looked up and met Mel's gaze. Instantly, he felt her anguish, and he knew how scared she was. He immediately felt ashamed.

"I'm sorry," he mouthed.

Behind him, Krager and Ransom continued arguing, this time about approaching him. Ryan ignored the noise, instead focusing on the fear-stricken girl in front of him.

"If you've got anything left to say, I'd say it now," Mr. Willis said to Ryan. He kept the shotgun trained on Ransom.

"I'm so sorry," Ryan repeated, this time barely audible. She stared at him with her mouth agape but said nothing.

"The things you've heard about me," he finally said as he felt Krager approach from behind. "The things you will hear about me…"

Mr. Willis finally lowered his shotgun, and Ryan knew that Ransom and Reeves had done the same. The standoff was over.

"That's not me." Ryan continued, louder still.

Mel continued staring at him.

"Stand up, Ryan," Krager said. Ryan did so slowly, and he felt as Krager ran his hands over his pants and coat. He reached towards the waistband where Ryan's hand previously rested but found nothing. Ryan winced in pain when the officer got to his broken arm.

Ryan stared at Mel. "None of it is me," he continued. "Not anymore."

"Hands behind you," Krager said sternly.

Ryan gingerly moved his right arm behind him, and he flinched in pain. All the while, he stared at Mel. "It isn't me," he insisted. "It isn't me."

The handcuffs snapped into place, and Krager pushed Ryan against the counter as he continued the pat down.

Ryan could feel the heat of his arm behind him, but he continued talking to Mel, telling her anything he could.

"You know me," he said as he turned to meet her gaze. "You know me."

As he was jostled, he felt the pain intensify. The room began to spin.

"You're under arrest..." Krager began, though Ryan tuned him out.

"You know me!" Ryan yelled over the officer's words. Tears welled in his eyes. "You do."

"Let's go," Krager said, grabbing Ryan by the cuffs.

Ryan struggled under the pressure of the restraints, and the room continued to whirl. Sweat poured from his brow as the pain magnified. His eyelids began to flutter, yet he continued calling out over his shoulder as he was led out.

"You know me, Mel! I'm sorry!"

Before long, he was out in the parking lot with Krager alone.

"You know me, Mel!"

"It's over," Krager finally said as they approached the squad car. "It's all over."

Ryan attempted to yell, but his words caught in his throat. The cold air whipped across his face, drying the tears of his eyes. He tried to maintain walking, but it was no use. He no longer felt in control. The pain was too much to bear.

"It's all done," Krager said again.

Ryan stood as rigid as possible as Krager opened the door.

"Hopefully, it was worth it," Krager added as he slid Ryan into the car. "Hope you said what you needed to."

Ryan barely heard him. His eyes continued to fall in and out of focus. In between black voids, he found himself looking back into the restaurant and he saw her father consoling her.

He realized the pain he had caused her. He had never wanted any of it. He wanted her happy. He wanted her free. He wanted her to know how much she meant to him. He wanted all those things. He had never wanted pain.

His wants, however, were of little concern now. His journey was ending in the one place he had spent so long hoping to avoid: a squad car.

This was his burden. This was his punishment. This was his only path forward.

He slid down in his seat as he finally allowed his pain and anguish to overcome him. He heard Krager call his name into the radio as he shut his eyes.

It was done. It was over. There were no words left to say.

***

In Spokane
Nine Days Later

Bowman sat on the front porch, sipping coffee from an ancient mug. It was just past midday, but the sun struggled to be seen among the winter clouds. It was much colder than it had been in the past few days, but he did not mind. He rocked back and forth as the wind blew around him.

He struggled to keep his eyes open as he continued his motion. The calmness in the day put him at ease. He allowed them to close, and in a few moments, he was in a light and dreamless sleep.

A slamming door woke him from his slumber, and he quickly opened his eyes. Next door, he spotted the mail carrier standing outside his truck. Bowman watched him look at his neighbors' mailbox and then his own with an expression of consternation.

"You need some help?" Bowman asked in an uncharacteristically loud voice.

The carrier jumped at the voice, clearly not having seen the old man on the porch. He looked at Bowman before returning to the manila envelope in his hand.

"No," he called out, "just a wrong address."

"Wrong address?"

"57 Peters Way," the carrier called back.

Bowman looked over to his neighbor's house at 55 and his own at 58.

"Must be a typo," the carrier said.

"What's the name?"

"No name. Just an address." The carrier made for the door.

"Return name?"

The driver shrugged.

Bowman considered this as the carrier climbed into his truck. "I'll take it," he finally said, waving his hands.

The carrier stepped out of the vehicle again. "What?"

"It's mine," Bowman said, standing up from his porch and making his way down the steps to the lawn.

"It's yours?"

"Yeah," he lied.

"You sure?"

"Yeah," he said as he reached the truck. "I've been out here waiting for it."

The carrier hesitated, looking around in suspicion.

"It's fine," Bowman reassured him.

The carrier looked up once more before finally handing over the envelope.

Bowman nodded before stepping out of the way of the truck. He waited for the carrier to drive off before finally sighing in relief. He looked down at the package, returned to the porch, and looked around to ensure no one had seen the transaction. Then, from his rocking chair, he opened the envelope.

Peering inside, he saw the unmistakable cover of a small blue book.

Bo heard Bowman yelling. Sensing the worst, he ran down the stairs and through the living room. Throwing open the front door, he stopped once he stepped foot on the porch. Turning to his right, he was surprised to see Bowman sitting perfectly normal, save for the opened envelope on his lap. The passport was in plain view.

"It came in this," Bowman explained, turning over the envelope.

Bo stared at the address before looking at the top right corner to see the postage stamp.

Sioux Falls, SD.

He reached for the passport. As he opened it, he caught his driver's license in his right hand. A small scrap of paper fell with it. Taking a deep breath, he unfolded it slowly before reading the scribble that had clearly been written in haste:

You be you. I'll be me. It's better this way.

"What's it say?" Bowman asked.

Bo looked up, a half-smile on his face. "It says he chose a different option."

Bowman nodded. "A better one?"

Bo shrugged. "I'm not sure, but he took it."

Bowman turned back toward the street. "I'm sure it made sense to him."

Bo sighed as he leaned against the porch post with the contents of the envelope in hand.

"He clearly wanted to get these back to you," Bowman said after a moment. "It's like he's telling you what to do this time."

"Maybe."

"No maybe about it," the old man continued. "He sent them the way he did for a reason. He's a smart kid."

"Someone will track this," Bo replied. "Eventually, some officer will show up here."

"Let them," Bowman replied coldly. "He wrote the wrong address so they couldn't track it here." He took a deep breath. "Plus, you'll be long gone by then, and I'll be an old man with nothing to hide." He turned to Bo with a smile.

Bo returned the smile before peering out into the yard once more. He took a deep breath, unsure of how to feel.

"I hope he'll be all right." Bo sighed.

The old man lit a cigarette. "He will be," he replied softly. "And so will you."

Bo continued to peer into the vast landscape in front of him. "I don't know," he countered. "The world is a much different place than it was years ago…"

Bowman blew out the smoke as he pondered the statement. "The world hasn't changed. The people have, but the game is still the same."

Bo looked to the old man and leaned his head onto his arm.

"I can sense the same thing in you that I saw in her when she headed to New York," he said softly. "It's courage. It's determination. It's the ability to keep moving forward." He ashed his cigarette. "You're already a thousand miles from Spokane; you just don't know it yet." He paused. "You'll find peace. Both you and Ryan will."

"How do you know?"

Bowman took another drag and exhaled, smoke curling out of his nose. Taking a deep breath, he gazed out ahead of him.

"Because now," he said softly, "you're looking for it."

"Let's go down to the Sunshine State once again to find another crazy story! Seems like it's never in short supply. It's everyone's favorite segment... 'What's up, Florida?!' Today's story is one we've been following for years. It even has a connection right here in Siouxland."

"Don't tell me..."

"Yep, Jimmy, Clearwater Boy is back in the news. For a good reason, this time!"

"He get arrested again?"

"No! His sentence is up!"

"My God..."

"For those who haven't been listening to the show for the past two years, Clearwater Boy is Ryan Collins, a twenty-four-year-old native of Clearwater, Florida—"

"Now twenty-six!"

"Thanks, Jim. Well, Ryan stole his daddy's identity and money and went on a cross-country joyride, spending those fat stacks—"

"Kid of the year right there..."

"No doubt. It was all good and clean until he made a stop in Shannon, South Dakota, about two hours west of the Falls, where a local officer attempted to make an arrest based on a tip from the locals. Clearwater Boy managed to get away by assaulting the officer and leaving him for dead."

"You just upped your jail time!"

"Now, here's the best part—the really Florida part—of the story..."

"Get ready..."

"Clearwater Boy is clear! He made it out! He escaped after the assault and went on the run. No leads. No nothing. Then, this dumb you-know-what, he comes back to the town and goes to a local diner where—surprise, surprise—the officers make a full arrest."

"Crazy!"

"He got away! He made it out! And he came back!"

"Absolutely stupid."

"Well, he's back in the news today because his sentence is finally over. He served a total of forty-five days before being released on good behavior, and he was under house arrest for an additional eleven months before a final fifteen months of parole."

"I need his lawyer!"

"I know, right? Assaulting an officer and you get a two-year slap on the wrist?"

"He won't make any police benefit dinners..."

"No doubt. Well, Clearwater Boy, congrats on your freedom. Hope the joyride was worth it."

"And on behalf of the Derek and Jim Morning show, remember—if you're on the run, don't run back to the town where you committed your crime—"

"Ha-ha, ain't that the truth!"

"It's Derek and Jim in the Morning, and here are some crisp Caribbean sounds to hopefully calm us down after all that stupidity...it's Bob Marley on 104.3 FM..."

Ryan barely heard "Jammin'" on the speakers as he walked inside the pawnshop on the west side of Sioux City. The store was empty, save the shopkeeper, who sat at the counter reading a newspaper. He adjusted his ball cap and scratched his scalp. Exhaling, he approached the counter.

"'Morning, sir," the clerk said, setting his paper off to the side.

"Hey," Ryan replied, ignoring the man's appraisal of his unshaven face and worn clothes. "Wondering if you buy firearms." His eyes rested on the shopkeeper's name tag: Tom.

"What kind of gun are we talking about?"

Ryan reached into his back pocket and pulled out a cloth-wrapped bundle. He laid it on the counter and watched as Tom used a nearby pen to unwrap the bundle to reveal a worn Smith and Wesson Model 36.

"Thirty-eight special," Tom said.

"Yeah," Ryan replied uneasily.

"How much do you want for it?"

"I don't know," Ryan replied. More than anything, he wanted to be rid of it. "Fifty?"

"Dollars?"

Ryan nodded as Tom picked up the gun and noticed the soot around the muzzle. "Was it used in any crimes?"

"I can take it somewhere else…"

"No," the clerk replied. "I'm sorry. None of my business. It's just…the cylinder's empty."

Ryan took a deep breath. He wondered how much his discomfort was showing.

Tom moved to the register. "I'll give you fifty dollars." He counted out the bills. "You don't know much about guns, do you?"

Ryan shrugged.

"The gun's worth a lot more than fifty," Tom replied, counting out more bills. "I'd say $150 is a bit fairer."

Ryan sized up the money before scooping it into his hands and proceeding to the door.

"Did you get 'em, at least?" he heard the clerk ask behind him. He half-turned.

"The bad guys," Tom clarified. "Did you get them?"

Ryan considered it. It was such a layered question, yet one he knew the clerk would never understand. How could he? The journey. The pain. He closed his eyes as he recollected it all. Maybe he was the villain. Maybe he was destined for this path. Or maybe he was just a young man trying to figure it out once more.

He sighed as he tried to piece his words together. "No," he finally said. "Some bad guys need more than that." As he spoke the words, his eyes moved to a display stand near the front window.

"Everything okay?" Tom asked.

Slowly, Ryan made for the bookstand. He carefully reached out and plucked a book from one of the shelves.

"New this month," he heard Tom said. "Some new travel company out of Arizona. Really great travel books if you ask me."

Ryan gazed at the book in his hand.

"You interested in traveling?" Tom asked. "Or just the islands in general?"

Ryan examined the image on the front and turned to the owner, book still in hand. "A little of both, I guess."

Tom nodded. "Well, those will work with either goal, I suppose."

Ryan turned back to the book and then back to the display, which showed the writer in an adventurous jungle setting next to the title words.

Emily Travel Co.—Books by Scott Lashon.

Ryan smiled.

"You should go to Hawaii," he heard the shopkeeper say.

He turned, realizing the topic of the book in his hand. He ran his fingers over the peaceful beach setting on the cover, already knowing why he had chosen this specific locale.

"Maybe someday."

"Always a good reason to go to Hawaii." Tom laughed.

"Yeah." Ryan smiled. "I've got one or two…"

"Take it," the shopkeeper finally said, referring to the book.

"I can't…"

"Sure, you can," the man replied. "Then I won't feel so bad for the deal I pulled on the gun."

Ryan stood frozen in the aisle.

"You all right?" the shopkeeper finally asked.

Ryan continued staring at the display, then back to the book. It had been so long. There was so much…

"Yeah," he replied, turning to the man with a smile. He stepped toward the door and opened it slightly.

"Are you sure?" the man asked.

"No," Ryan replied as he walked out, "but I will be."

He shielded his eyes from the May sun as he crossed the street to the old Chevy pickup parked at the curb. Opening the door, he threw the book into the passenger seat next to his duffel and drawstring bag.

Turning the key, he found himself smiling once more.

He was as far from sure as possible, but he was still here, despite his best efforts. He was still breathing, and he was still alive, even with everything that had happened. He had no idea what future lay before him, but somehow, he would be okay. He would make it. He would survive.

Again, he glanced at the travel book. Exhaling, he found himself smiling once more. *One day*, he thought. *Maybe one day.*

He shifted the truck into drive and set off toward the east, into the unknown.

He was not sure where he was headed or what was ahead, but somehow, that was perfectly fine with him.

1,640 Miles from Clearwater and 1,204 Miles from Spokane